Robert Henry Eddy, Francis Greenleaf Pratt

The Eddy Family

reunion at Providence to celebrate the two hundred and fiftieth anniversary of the

landing of John and Samuel Eddy at Plymouth, Oct. 29, 1630

Robert Henry Eddy, Francis Greenleaf Pratt

The Eddy Family
reunion at Providence to celebrate the two hundred and fiftieth anniversary of the landing of John and Samuel Eddy at Plymouth, Oct. 29, 1630

ISBN/EAN: 9783337733933

Printed in Europe, USA, Canada, Australia, Japan

Cover: Foto ©Raphael Reischuk / pixelio.de

More available books at **www.hansebooks.com**

CONTENTS.

———◦•◦———

ILLUSTRATIONS.

6 ILLUSTRATIONS.

PRELIMINARY MEETING.

PROVIDENCE, R.I., Jan. 6, 1880.

A MEETING of the descendants of the Pilgrims John and Samuel Eddy was held this day in the Bell-Street Chapel in Providence. It assembled in response to a call signed by James and John Eddy of Providence, R. H. Eddy of Boston, Joshua M. Eddy of Middleboro', and Charles E. Eddy of Westboro', Mass. Printed notices of the object of the gathering had been sent to all persons of the name of Eddy whose addresses were known.

James Eddy was chosen Chairman, and John Eddy Secretary.

The unanimous desire of all present was expressed that the anniversary of the landing of our Pilgrim Fathers should be appropriately observed.

On motion of R. H. Eddy it was voted, That John Eddy and James Eddy of Providence, and Thomas F. Eddy of Fall River, be appointed a committee to make the necessary arrangements for the celebration. It was decided to hold the meeting on the twenty-ninth of October, 1880, the two hundred and fiftieth anniversary of the landing of our Eddy ancestors at Plymouth.

JAMES EDDY, *President*.   JOHN EDDY, *Secretary*.

THE INVITATIONS.

THE committee having in charge the duty of making arrangements for the Eddy Festival extended an invitation, immediately after their appointment, to the Rev. Zachary Eddy, D.D., of Detroit, Mich., to deliver the address, which he cheerfully accepted.

Miss Alice Maud Eddy of Detroit was invited to contribute a poem, to which she assented.

Plymouth was at first selected as the most appropriate place of meeting. The First Unitarian Society, by William H. Whitman, Esq., and the Church of the Pilgrims, by their pastor, Rev. George A. Tewkesbury, tendered their houses of worship for the purpose, and the people of the town offered a most hospitable welcome. But it soon became evident that Plymouth was so inaccessible as to prevent many from attending, and after much earnest consideration the place of meeting was changed to Providence.

James Eddy, Esq., offered the use of his elegant chapel on Bell Street, which was of convenient size for the meeting, and he cordially welcomed the guests to the hospitality of his house and grounds.

EDDY FESTIVAL AT PROVIDENCE.

THE various families began to assemble several hours before the time appointed, and the interim was most agreeably spent in social greetings and in tracing relationships. It was easy to discover in the faces of the throng the intense interest which animated every heart.

About three hundred and twenty-five persons having Eddy blood in their veins were in attendance, a greater part of whom recorded their names and residences in a register placed in the vestibule for the purpose.

On a table at the right of the platform were displayed many pictures of our English cousins, who had with thoughtful consideration contributed the same, together with several views of places of interest ; namely :

Photograph of Rev. Charles Eddy, M.A., eldest son of Rev. John Eddy, late Rector of Elworthy, Somerset, by whom, on behalf of our English namesakes, an address was presented to this festival.

Pictures of John Eddy, youngest son, and Katharine Sophia Eddy, and Francis Anne Eddy, daughters of said Rector.

Photograph of Jane Elizabeth Tompkins, daughter of Rev. Charles Eddy, Rector of Bemerton, and wife of the Rev. Henry George Tompkins, late Vicar of Branscomb, Devon.

Photographs of Katharine H. Tompkins, daughter of the last named, and Miss Evelyn Frances Eddy, daughter of Dr. Charles Walter Eddy hereafter mentioned, with whom the name becomes extinct in this branch of the family.

Photograph of Charles James Lilly of the Royal Irish Constabulary, son of Rev. Peter Lilly and Maria S. Lilly, *née* Eddy.

Besides the above-named, there were also five engravings and views of St. Dunstan's Church in Cranbrook, in which our progenitor, William Eddye, officiated as Vicar from 1591 to the time of his death, Nov. 23, 1616.

From the same source a tracing *fac-simile* of the handwriting of Rev. William Eddye.

A "lay-out" of the town of Cranbrook, taken from a government survey.

Two photographic pictures of the town, — one looking from the church down Stone Street, and the other down High Street, including the White Lion and the St. George Inns. It is said these streets have changed little in the last two hundred and fifty years.

Coat-of-Arms and Crest of the Eddy family, the latter having been taken from an old silver seal remaining in the possession of the family.

A large and excellent photograph of Dr. Charles Walter Eddy of London stood upon the table. It will be remembered by many of the family that he visited the United States in the years 1858–9, during which time he held the Ratcliffe Travelling Professorship of Oxford University, and became very favorably known to all those who had the good fortune to make his acquaintance. He was a most agreeable gentleman, and took a lively interest in the immense expansion of the family-tree on this side of the water. He made a pilgrimage to Eddyville, the Jerusalem of the tribes, where he was the guest of the late Hon. Zachariah Eddy. He also spent a week or two with John Eddy, Esq., of Providence. He took great delight in having the boundaries of the original purchase — made by Samuel Eddy and others of the Sagamore Wampatuck — pointed out to him with the locations of the original houses, and the Indian paths and names with which Mr. Zachariah Eddy was familiar. He died in 1874, at which time he was Honorary Secretary of the Royal Colonial Institute. His widow, Mrs. Frances Rose Eddy, has kindly furnished us with his picture and a memoir of his life.

ORDER OF EXERCISES.

———◦◦◦———

THE following is the Order of Exercises, prepared by
the Committee, and distributed at the meeting:—

ADDRESS OF WELCOME by the PRESIDENT.

———

MUSIC: Under the direction of Mr. A. B. EDDY.

Mrs. D. S. EDDY, Accompanist.

———

QUARTETTE . . . . *"Green be your fame forever."*

Mrs. S. S. CHAFFIN,   Mr. E. EDDY,
Mrs. A. B. EDDY,   Mr. A. B. EDDY.

———

INVOCATION and SELECTIONS FROM THE SCRIPTURES.

By HIRAM EDDY, D.D., of Jersey City, N.J.

———

SOLO: *"The breaking waves dashed high."*— Mr. ELIJAH EDDY.

———

ORATION.

REV. ZACHARY EDDY, D.D., of Detroit, Mich.

———

HYMN: *"York."*

O God, our help in ages past,   Time, like an ever-rolling stream,
Our hope for years to come,   Bears all its sons away;
Our shelter from the stormy blast,   They fly, forgotten, as a dream
And our eternal home.   Dies at the opening day.

O God, our help in ages past,
Our hope for years to come,
Be thou our guard while troubles last,
And our eternal home!

RECESS.

SONG: "*The Better Land.*"—MRS. S. S. CHAFFIN.

POEM.—By Miss ALICE MAUD EDDY.

CONTRIBUTIONS IN VERSE.

ADDRESSES.

SONG.—Mr. A. B. EDDY.

COMMUNICATIONS FROM MEMBERS OF THE EDDY FAMILY ABROAD.

"*Auld Lang Syne.*"

Should auld acquaintance be forgot,
  And never brought to mind;
Should auld acquaintance be forgot,
  And songs of auld lang syne.
For auld lang syne we meet to-day,
  For auld lang syne;
To sing the songs our fathers sang
  In days of auld lang syne.

We've passed through many varied scenes
  Since youth's unclouded day;
And friends, and hopes, and happy dreams
  Time's hand hath swept away.
And voices that once joined with ours,
  In days of auld lang syne,
Are silent now, and blend no more
  In songs of auld lang syne.

Here we have met, here we may part,
  To meet on earth no more;
And we may never sing again
  The cherished songs of yore:
The sacred songs our fathers sang,
  In days of auld lang syne;
We may not meet to sing again
  The songs of auld lang syne.

But when we've crossed the sea of life
  And reached the heavenly shore,
We'll sing the songs our fathers sing,
  Transcending those of yore.
We'll meet to sing diviner strains
  Than those of auld lang syne:
Immortal songs of praise, unknown
  In days of auld lang syne.

OPENING EXERCISES.

At eleven o'clock the meeting was called to order by James Eddy, Esq., who said, —

"The time has now arrived for choosing the president of the day; and while you are considering whom to nominate, permit me to say I am happy to meet so many relatives of this numerous family, to which I have the honor to belong. And I am especially gratified to meet them here on my own ground, and in the vestry of this chapel, erected by an humble member of your family for religious purposes. May you enjoy and ever hold in pleasant remembrance this reunion to celebrate the two hundred and fiftieth anniversary of the landing of our progenitors at Plymouth."

John Eddy, Esq., of Providence, was unanimously elected President. On taking the chair he said, —

"FRIENDS AND RELATIVES:

"I am very grateful that I am called to preside over such a select, distinguished, and goodly company, and I shall ever esteem it as one of my most agreeable honors. When I was nominated to this office I felt, as I have sometimes in political matters, like voting for myself.

"What was said by a celebrated play-actor of my younger days is expressive of my own feelings. When he was called before the foot-lights on the evening of his benefit in Boston, he declared, as nearly as I can remember:

"'Like a grate full of coals I glow,
     A great full house to see;
And if I am not grateful too,
     A great fool I should be.'

John Eddy

" In behalf of the family of Eddy residing in this city, and especially in behalf of our namesake, by whose generosity and hospitality we are so admirably accommodated and pleasantly surrounded, I bid you a most cordial welcome, and extend to you our heartfelt congratulations.

" It was originally intended to hold this family party in Plymouth, which would seem to be the more appropriate place. But we remembered how inhospitable it was to our forefathers, and finding it very inaccessible, we reluctantly concluded to adjourn to the place where the first white man was saluted with ' What cheer?' and we thrice welcome you to what cheer the city of Roger Williams and Providence Plantations are capable of affording, with most fraternal greetings. I congratulate you that within this edifice—this private chapel of a namesake—there are so many fine Eddy faces. Here at least each one, by speaking truthfully of his neighbor, will say a good word for himself.

" In my youthful days, when the agreeable passions predominated, I delighted in social companies. On one such occasion a bright young lady, who was always equal to the opportunity, addressed me as I entered the parlor, ' You are looking splendid this evening; how do I look?' Do you take the hint?

" I have been exceedingly anxious for the coming of this festal day so auspiciously ushered in. Besides the sentiments which come flying like clouds, and which I will not try to express, I have, as something of a physiognomist, been very curious to see if I could imagine the lineaments and physical forms of John and Samuel Eddy reproduced in their children, and discern their souls, as they ' go marching on,' shining through the faces of their posterity. Taking a survey from the vantage ground of this platform, I assure you that this day is ' a consummation devoutly to be wished.' What a text for an article on heredity is here presented! That essay must be written, and if I am here when you celebrate the three hundredth anniversary, it shall be presented for your approval.

" It is recorded in the Talmud that ' ten measures of talkativeness were sent down from heaven, and woman took nine of them.' Now the Talmud is not *my* Bible, but an opportunity will be given to 'our sisters, our cousins, and our aunts' to exemplify and illustrate the truthfulness of the Jewish Scriptures, and to Edify us to the limit of their ambition. Failing with them, we shall call upon such gentlemen of the family as have inherited from their mothers.

"Youth boasts of its ancestry. The hopes and joys of age centre in their children. There is no sentiment of the human heart that would deprive age of such happiness; but to the young it hath been well said, 'Boast not of your ancestors, brave youths, lest it shall appear that the race has degenerated.' I am so old in years that I take pleasure in the latter, and so young in heart that as to the former, for once in a lifetime, and in the family circle, I shall boldly and quietly assume the privilege for myself, and I doubt not it will be freely accorded to others.

"A distinguished living divine said on one occasion that a text was the gateway by which an audience was conducted into a garden of fruits and flowers, but that some preachers spent most of their time in swinging on the gate. Lest we should be subject to the same criticism, we will throw open the gate, and introduce you to the garden of many generations, full of fruit and fragrance.

"The name *Eady* signifies 'prosperity.' You will therefore unite with me in the prayer of the sweet singer of Israel, 'O Lord send now prosperity,' which, for aught I know, may have been the origin of the name."

On motion it was voted, That Dr. William Pratt (whose wife is the daughter of the late Nathaniel Eddy, and who resides on the estate purchased by Samuel Eddy and others of Sachem Wampatuck) be elected Clerk.

The musical performances were under the direction of Mr. Andrew B. Eddy, assisted by Mrs. D. S. Eddy, accom-

panist, and Mrs. S. S. Chaffin of Providence, and Mr.
Elijah Eddy of Westboro', Mass.

The opening song by the quartette was most artistically
executed, and was received with hearty applause. It was
as follows : —

> "Green be your fame forever,
> Sires, who our nation planted,
> By storm and death undaunted,
> Firmly on Freedom's rock.
>
> "When danger rose around you,
> Loudly glad hymns ye chanted,
> While every bosom panted
> Wildly with freedom's glow.
>
> "Dark grew the clouds above you,
> Loud howled the midnight tempest,
> While through the pathless forest
> Rang out the savage yell.
>
> "Still rose your song triumphant,
> Danger and death despising,
> Still to Jehovah rising,
> Proudly your anthems swell."

Selections from the Scriptures, beginning with "Lord
thou hast been our dwelling-place in all Generations,"
were read by the Rev. Hiram Eddy, D.D., of Jersey City,
N.J., after which he conducted the devotional exercises
of the day.

Mr. Elijah Eddy sang, as a solo, with fine effect : —

> "The breaking waves dashed high
> On a stern and rock-bound coast,
> And the woods against a stormy sky
> Their giant branches tossed;

And the heavy night hung dark
  The hills and waters o'er,
When a band of exiles moored their bark
  On the wild New England shore.

  .   .   .   .

" What sought they thus afar?
  Bright jewels of the mine,
The wealth of seas, the spoils of war?
  They sought a faith's pure shrine.
Aye, call it holy ground,
  The spot where first they trod;
They have left unstained what there they found —
  Freedom to worship God."

The Chairman stated that on a former occasion he had been delegated, by the Central Congregational Church of this city, to present to Dr. Eddy the call of that church for him to become their pastor; which he had seen fit to decline. On a subsequent occasion he had presented to the same gentleman the call of the Eddy Family, in which better fortune had prevailed, and he now had the pleasure of introducing the orator of the day, the Rev. Zachary Eddy, D.D., of Detroit, Mich.

ORATION.

BY THE REV. ZACHARY EDDY, D.D.

LADIES AND GENTLEMEN, MY GOOD COUSINS:

There is a tree in the east, popularly called the Banyan, — technically, *Ficus Indica* — remarkable for its mode of propagation. Its horizontal boughs send down to the ground aerial roots which penetrate the soil, and themselves become stems, sometimes almost as large as the parent trunk. In this manner, it is said, a single tree spreads over a large extent of ground, often having some four hundred trunks, and offering a bivouac for an army. It produces a kind of fig, and its bark is highly esteemed as a tonic. It is tenacious of life, and keeps on growing for many centuries.

Our Eddy family is a sort of Banyan tree. I would call it, but for an obvious joke, *Ficus Eddyca;* but a fig for the joke! This tree sprang from a sturdy trunk in England, which, two hundred and fifty years ago, stretched across the Atlantic two boughs that dropped their roots at Plymouth and at Watertown, Mass. These took fast hold of the soil, and sent forth roots which, in like manner, became trunks. Middleboro', Swansea, Taunton, Providence, are in no long time overshadowed with the luxuriant growth, to which may be fitly applied our national motto, "*E pluribus unum.*" In the course of generations the same goodly tree makes its appearance in Maine, in Vermont, in Connecticut, in New York, in New Jersey, in Pennsylvania, in Ohio, in Michigan, in Illinois, in Wisconsin, in Minnesota, in Missouri, in Iowa, in California, indeed, in almost every State of the Republic. Our tree is spread over the continent; it bears abundant fruit; and it has proved a good national tonic.

Is this boasting? Why should we not value ourselves a little upon our blood, provided it is good blood? Science itself warrants it; besides, it runs in our blood to do so.

Who was it that thanked God, every day, that he was not born a Frenchman? Really, I have forgotten; but you could safely swear that the devout Christian whose piety ran in this peculiar vein lived in Great Britain south of the Tweed. There is something sublime in the genuine Englishman's pride of blood. We laugh at it; we are not seldom angry at it; but in our hearts we rather like it. The consciousness of being well-born, of belonging to a brave, hardy, cultivated race, is sometimes manifested in absurd and offensive ways, but it is so closely intertwined with the roots of many private and public virtues, that it commands our respect. Besides, we may well take heed lest the shafts of ridicule which we aim at our English cousins rebound upon ourselves; for it is doubtful whether our own pride of blood is less exorbitant than theirs. This assembly witnesses that even in America, where the "glittering generality that all men are born equal" is accepted as the foundation of civil society, many practically hold that blood is not only thicker than water, but that *good* blood is very precious, and the possession of it a reason for jubilant festivities.

We are, after all, thoroughly English even in our pride of ancestry; and if that is incompatible with democracy, it is the worse for democracy. It is not true that men are born equal, except in a limited sense. That they are by nature entitled to equal rights under the law, is willingly conceded; and that the humanity common to all is infinitely more than the variation of that humanity in races and families, we do not deny. Nevertheless, speaking here *in the family*, I may be permitted to assert that it is better to be an Aryan than an African, or even a Mongolian;

that it is better to be of the Teutonic than of the Keltic blood; and finally that to be an ENGLISHMAN is — when ridicule is exhausted — something to thank God for. And we, I repeat, are English. The name belonged to our race ages before an Englishman set foot on the soil of Britain; and it is justly claimed by all who are of the same blood, and who speak the same language, the world over. The name designates race rather than country; and this our pilgrim ancestors recognized when they called the country of their adoption *New* England. Now we American Englishmen do not attach less dignity and value to the race of which we come, than the Englishmen of Great Britain.

This matter of ancestry is a strangely interesting subject of speculation. A little reflection suggests some odd doubts and misgivings touching the purity of our blood, even though we belong to the best descended and best regulated families. We commonly think of our ancestry as a straight line from some one forefather; but the fact is quite otherwise. I find myself at the point where innumerable lines meet. I am a poor arithmetician, but I can scarcely be mistaken in the following calculation. I am descended from four grand-parents, from eight great-grand-parents, from sixteen great-great-grand-parents, from thirty-two in the fifth remove, sixty-four in the sixth, one hundred and twenty-eight in the seventh, two hundred and fifty-six in the eighth, five hundred and twelve in the ninth, one thousand and twenty-four in the tenth. By this method of computation it would appear that, at the time of the battle of Hastings, some 33,000,000 were living whose blood now flows in my veins! Of course this calculation, making no allowance for intermarriage between persons of the same blood, is misleading; but it renders it highly probable that, in the flow of countless generations, families and peoples have become strangely commixed. If any man could present a complete genealogical record for forty generations, it would be the most interesting book in the world.

It would almost certainly appear that some of our ancestors were princes, others slaves; some, painted savages, dwelling among the bogs of Ireland, the Highlands of Scotland, the swamps of the Netherlands, the forests of Germany, the plains of Asia; others were civilized Greeks and Romans, possibly Phœnicians, Egyptians, and Chaldeans; for, in the migrations of nations, blood has been pretty thoroughly mixed, and it has doubtless become richer and stronger by the intermixture. The best wines of Burgundy, they say, are those which are skilfully compounded of the grape-blood of many vineyards.

Of what race do we come? Who can tell? We sometimes call ourselves Anglo-Saxons; but that, as the historians Freeman and Greene have taught us, is a misnomer. The Angles and the Saxons were only two of the many tribes that contributed to the formation of the race to which we belong. Even before the Saxon conquest, Britain was inhabited by many heterogeneous races, the most of whom were of Keltic, but not a few of Teutonic origin. We know that the Romans preceded the Saxons by several centuries, and we cannot doubt that they largely infused their blood into the aboriginal population. The Anglo-Saxons were followed by the Danes, and hardly had the two nations become thoroughly amalgamated when the island was conquered by the Normans. These last, though of Scandinavian origin, had become blended with the French, having lost even their ancient tongue; and the French, themselves a mongrel race, were descended from Gauls, Italians, Franks, and many other tribes. The Normans therefore carried over to England a mixed blood and a new language. Out of this chaos of nationalities emerged a new race, neither Keltic, Anglo-Saxon, Danish, Norman. nor French, but ENGLISH. Doubtless the rather coarse, but strong and manly substratum of this new ethnological formation is Teutonic; but it is vain for us to deny that we are a mixed people, composed, as Ralph Waldo Emerson has said, of the mud of all races. For my own part, I do not account this a misfortune ; for, when I look over the world, I find that the so-called pure-blooded races have the thinnest, poorest blood of any. Mixed blood, if well mixed, is the only good blood.

What first strikes us, in the English race to which we belong, is its physical strength and toughness ; its large, overflowing vitality. Many nations are constitutionally feeble, predisposed to disease, and incapable of energetic, persevering labor. The genuine Anglo-Saxon — I find that I cannot avoid the use of this inaccurate name — is hardy, full of health, with bones of granite, and muscles of iron. He eats well, sleeps well, works well, and, if need be, — under Wellington, Nelson, Grant, Sherman, Sheridan, Farragut, Garfield, and Hancock — fights well. He transmits a sound constitution to his descendants ; and they are like the stars of heaven for multitude.

Anglo-Saxon energy, however, is not a mere quality of stomach and muscle ; it is energy of brain ; it is executive force ; it is the spring of enterprise, irrepressible, unresting, inventive, aggressive, enduring, victorious. The race has always been a productive one ; and the world is to-day filled with the monuments of its commercial, manufacturing, military, and missionary achievements. Its intellectual ability is of a high order. In philosophy, in science, in literature, our race ranks with the first. Liberty runs with its blood. The lines in which Tennyson glorifies his own country are at least as applicable to ours ; indeed they are true of the now wide-spread English people the world over :

A land of settled government,
 A land of just and old renown,
 Where freedom slowly broadens down
From precedent to precedent :

Where faction slowly gathers head,
 But by degrees to fulness wrought,
 The strength of some diffusive thought
Hath time and space to work and spread.

On the whole, we cannot hesitate to apply to the whole Anglo-Saxon race what Milton says of the race in Great Britain: "If we look at the Englishman in the rough-cast, without breeding, some nature or other may haply be better composed to a natural civility and right judgment than he; but, if he once get the benefit of a wise and well-ratified nurture, I suppose that wherever mention is made of countries, manners, or men, the English people, among the first that shall be praised, may deserve to be accounted a right-pious, right-honest, and right-hardy nation."

Now and then, in genealogical researches, we light upon a particular family which, for many generations, seems to represent the distinctive characteristics of the race from which they sprung. In some families indeed there is a wide divergence from the national type. We sometimes meet an Anglo-American who, in temperament and character, is thoroughly un-English, belonging rather to the hot-blooded tribes of tropical lands than to the sober, prudent, yet bold and independent race of Alfred and Washington. To trace the history of a family which has, for centuries, been marked by the same traits, cannot but be instructive and interesting.

Such a family is represented in this assembly. Two hundred and fifty years ago JOHN EDDY and SAMUEL EDDY landed on Plymouth Rock. Their descendants are now numbered by the thousand. They are scattered all over the continent. They are engaged in every calling and pursuit. Many are clergymen. There are not a few lawyers and physicians. There are many merchants, bankers, and manufacturers. The majority are, probably, farmers and artisans. After a pretty wide acquaintance with the family, I incline to think that certain hereditary qualities, even a certain physique, mark them out as a distinct *tribe* of the English race. They have of course largely intermarried with other families, but the Eddy blood has predominated in the transmission of hereditary characteristics. This, I think, will appear highly probable to all, after we shall have finished our review of the history of the family. In tracing that history I cannot of course exhibit to you a genealogical tree embracing the numerous branches. That, if possible, would be wearisome. I can only in this discourse touch upon such facts as are likely to be of interest to all branches of the family, — such, especially, as appear to manifest common characteristics.

I regret that in tracing up the stream of Eddy blood I am unable to get beyond the sixteenth century. As far as we are concerned, three hundred years carry us back to "prehistoric times." It would be interesting to trace our blood to earlier generations. Our ancestors were living during the wars of the Roses: did they follow the White or the Red? They were numerous in the time of William and Harold: did they bend the bow, or lift the spear, or level the lance, for the great Saxon or the mighty Bastard? Where did our ancestors live, and what were they doing in the time of Alfred, of Hengist and Horsa? Are we Saxons or Normans? We are neither; we are both; we are NORTHMEN. We once roamed the sea as pirates. We once drank our beer out of skulls, not objecting to wine when we could get it. We once were worshippers of Thor and Wodin. We were a rough-hewn people then, but no cowards, thank God!

You tell me that our Northmen blood is Teutonic. Whence came that Teutonic blood? Tell me, scientist! "The Teutonic blood," says the scientist, "flowed down through the veins of the Aryan race." Well, that Aryan race — who shall tell its genesis? Did it slowly emerge in the lapse of dateless ages from savagery? And did the savagery still more slowly emerge through myriads of ages from bestiality? Were we once gorillas? Are the apes our cousins? Then we ought to be very modest, very "umble," ever so much "umbler" than Uriah Heep! Understand me: I do not on this, or on any occasion, impugn any rational doctrine of evolution. Believe it, if you will, — it is rather a matter of will, than of scientific proof, — that our physical nature was somehow evolved from the brute creation. There was nevertheless a first MAN; and that which made him man came from God. "Adam was the son of God." Thus have I reached the beginning of the Eddy genealogy. It runs up, like all genealogies, whether of man, or beast, or vegetable, into the Unseen. We Eddys belong, not only to a very ancient, but to a noble family : WE CAME FROM GOD.

Our historical genealogy, however, we can only trace back some three centuries. Our historical Adam is WILLIAM EDDYE.

The name Eddy is evidently Anglo-Saxon. According to Ferguson's "English Surnames," it comes from *Ead*, which signifies *prosperity*. Æde. Eada, Eadig. Eddi, Eday, Eadie, Eady, Eddy, are variations of the same name. The name, though Saxon, signifies nothing in respect to race. It belongs to a class of names like Edwin, Edgar, Edwy, Edward, which the Normans adopted. There was a celebrated Saxon monk who bore the name of Ede. I hope, for the sake of his vow, we are not descended from him! But it was not then a surname. Such names came in long after the conquest. The name Eddy, therefore, cannot help us in tracing our medieval genealogy.

WILLIAM EDDYE was a native of Bristol. This we have in his own handwriting. The name cannot now be found in the Parish Records of Bristol; but an English correspondent informs me that many Eddys are still living in the West of England. They are, probably, of the same blood. If we ever get a clue to an ancestry earlier than William Eddye, it will, probably, be found among the Eddys of the counties of Somerset, Gloucester, and Cornwall.

Putting several facts together, I am led to believe that William Eddye was born between 1560 and 1565. The date is, of course, conjectural.

He evidently belonged to a highly respectable, though not distinguished family. The fact that he was liberally educated, and not as a pensioner, is sufficient evidence that his parents were neither illiterate nor very poor. His father was probably a well-to-do citizen of the middle class.*

It is entered in the Records of Cranbrook Parish, in William Eddye's own handwriting, that he was Master of Arts of Cambridge University. He was educated at Trinity Hall, and was graduated B.A. in 1583. He afterward migrated to the illustrious Trinity College, and was made Master of Arts in 1586.

It is a glorious age for England and Europe. Elizabeth is on the throne. The Cecils and Walsinghams, the Drakes and Frobishers, the Sidneys and Raleighs, shed a stellar lustre on her reign. Spenser, Shakespeare, Ben Jonson, Chapman, Thomas Hooker, and Launcelot Andrews are already famous, or are struggling into fame. Cambridge University is all alive with the enthusiasm of the Renaissance, and also with new-born Puritanism. Robert Browne, the founder of Independency. had left the university some eight or ten years before William Eddye was matriculated. John Robinson was matriculated six years after William Eddye was graduated Master of Arts. The great Separatists, Cartwright, Perkins, Ames, Jacob, Ainsworth, Penry, Barrow. and Greenwood, are already suffering persecution.

In a university thus permeated with the New Learning, and instinct with nascent Puritanism, William Eddye was trained for the Christian ministry. The Puritanism. as there is good reason to believe, he imbibed, though in moderation. That he attained any marked distinction as a scholar we have no evidence. In-

---

* Extract from a letter by John Eddy, Esq., Providence: "Charles Walter Eddy told me that William Eddy's family was a very good one, and had done most excellent service in the cause of letters; and he mentioned one of his (William's) ancestors who had endowed a professorship, and that he, the said Charles Walter, was then the travelling professor on the foundation (whatever that may mean), so provided for by a remote ancestor. This is recollection of twenty-two years' standing, and may be inaccurate."

deed, I may as well say at once that he was not a man of mark in his generation. He was no genius. He attained no eminence in literature. He was not a famous preacher. He was, however, a good man and a useful clergyman, an average English parson of that age, but not famous for his gifts. He was intellectually inferior to his predecessors in St. Dunstan's Church, Fletcher and Stroud, and to his successors, Abbott and Johnson; but he was a better administrator, a better pastor, than any of them.

This brings us to the appointment of William Eddye as vicar of Cranbrook, Kent, in 1691. He commenced his labors there in 1687, probably as curate of Richard Roades, who seems to have been non-resident.

Cranbrook, during the Middle Ages, was a place of considerable commercial importance as a local centre of the wool trade. It is now reduced to a population of some 4,000. In the time of William Eddye it had already lost some of its medieval prosperity, but was still a place, relatively, of considerable importance.

Should you wish to visit this cradle of our family, take an early train from London on the Dover Railway. If you are wise you will stop for a few hours at Tunbridge Wells, and see one of the most lovely watering places in England. In the afternoon take a train to Staplehurst, six miles from Cranbrook, or you may stop at Marden, which will give you a drive of eight miles. You are in the midst of the great hop-region of England. Your way lies over the gently undulating Kentish downs; you will pass through green lanes winding between hedges of box, holly, and hawthorn; you will drive through broad stretches of moorland covered with golden heather; you will see on either hand groves of pines, with inviting aisles beneath their dark branches, picturesque limestone rocks, lawn-like fields dotted with cattle, "forty grazing like one": here and there a stately manor-house, yet with a homelike look, surrounded with the

WHITE LION INN & POST HORSES   LOOKING W

STONE STREET SHOP, HOTEL, LOOKING S   WEST

STREET VIEWS IN CRANBROOK

trim cottages of the peasantry. As you approach Cranbrook in the evening twilight, the air will be filled with dream-like sounds, and with the fragrance of the hawthorn mingled with the rich odors of the fields. So at least one traveller recently found it.* As you drive into the little village you will find it small indeed, but interesting because so intensely English. You must alight at the "George," an ancient inn, which generations ago saw merry days, but is now fallen into the sere and yellow leaf. Like all the old houses of Cranbrook, it is built in the old Dutch style; that is to say, a stuccoed exterior with inlaid timbers; a steep tiled roof, with eye-like windows, and many gables; the lower windows, with small diamond-shaped panes of glass, admitting but little light; an interior dark and uncomfortable, with small, low, irregular rooms, and stairs springing up in the most unexpected places; odd corners and passages where you must walk with special circumspection. Do not be surprised if your arrival causes a sensation. You will find the inn thronged with villagers, looking somewhat rough, and gazing with even more than Yankee curiosity. Here they nightly congregate to smoke and drink and gossip, as did their fathers before them.

After a night's rest and a good English breakfast, stroll along the principal street till you come to the church. Before entering it, however, call on the Rev. Mr. Carr, the courteous vicar, and send for Mr. William Tarbutt, the antiquary and historian of St. Dunstan's Church. Meanwhile take a look at the church from the outside. It is what we should call ancient; and even in England it has a respectable though not a venerable antiquity. It was built some six hundred years ago, and is remarkably well preserved. It is in the perpendicular Gothic style, with groined roof, mullioned windows, and well-proportioned nave and aisles. The tower is square and heavy, and scarcely high enough to be either graceful or majestic. A

---

* Miss Clara Avery of Detroit, a descendant of Captain Jonathan Eddy of Maine: her journal has been largely drawn upon in this description.

projecting turret is attached to one of the angles and carried
above the tower. Within this turret is a stone stairway leading
up to the battlements. The tower, which is said to be older
than the church, is supported by heavy buttresses on three of its
angles, while the turret strengthens it on the fourth. Those
Englishmen of the thirteenth century built well.

Now enter the church with the vicar and Mr. Tarbutt. The
interior is tastefully modernized. Look around you and you
will see little that is three hundred years old; but over this floor
William Eddye went in and out before his people twenty-six
years. Within these walls he preached his last sermon; and
in the churchyard without his dust reposes, though the precise
spot is forgotten. One memorial of him however survives, the
old Parish Record of Births, Baptisms, and Burials, eighty pages
of which are engrossed in William Eddye's handwriting, three
title-pages being richly illuminated. I hope that those pages,
with the prefaces to the several books, will be photographed and
distributed among his descendants.

The life of William Eddye at Cranbrook was not eventful. I
retract: there was one event extremely interesting to him and
to us. This is recorded by his own hand: "1587, November
20. William Eddye, vicar, to Mary Fosten, virgin. She was the
daughter-in-law to Mr. Andrew Ruck." Mary was the daughter
of John Fosten and Ellen Munn, who were married January 19,
1561–2. John Fosten died a few years after, leaving to the care
of his widow his only child Mary. She was married again to
Mr. Andrew Ruck, evidently a notable of the place, in 1573.
Mary, our ancestress, was therefore well brought up. What
a shadowy old world it is! All these are mere names, yet
how much is implied in the simple record that William Eddye
was married to Mary Fosten! They had human hearts, after
all, in that far-off age. The Puritan clergyman from Cambridge
was a lover. There was a courtship, perhaps a grave one, —
and yet, I have known Eddys, even Eddys calling themselves

Puritans, and Puritan ministers besides, who could relish a joke, and even crack one on occasion. I have an idea that William Eddye though a Puritan was full of jolly vitality. That courtship may after all have been a lively one; but at any rate William Eddye was married, and I am glad he was married to Mary Fosten. I like the name and I profess myself her admirer.

From this union sprang ten children,—about our normal number except in the degenerate and feeble branches of the family,—namely: Mary, Phineas, John, Ella (who died young), Abigail, Anna, Elizabeth, Samuel, Zecharias, and Nathaniel, an infant, who followed his mother to the grave in 1611. These names you observe are all scriptural, a sure sign that William Eddye was of Puritan proclivities. The most of these names may still be found in all branches of the family. You will rarely find an Eddy as old as I am who does not bear a Hebrew name. It is a marvel that the surname was not also changed to Levi, Israel, or Isaac. Let us be thankful that the passion for scriptural names has not bequeathed to us the names of Maher-shalal-hash-baz, Belshazzar, Belial, and Beelzebub! One of William Eddye's Puritan predecessors,—a famous preacher in his day—while suffering persecution from Archbishop Whitgift, named his son '·Faint-not Fenner." There was piety in the name at least.

In the later generations the name of *Phineas* does not appear. I incline to believe that Phineas was a sort of Ishmael, or Esau, in the family. Though he was married and settled in Cranbrook, and though he held a parish office, he was tried—and fined I hope—for fighting with his step-brother in the churchyard. I am glad that Phineas did not come to this country. He had children however, and his descendants may be living in England. Zecharias also remained in England. He was twenty years old in 1630, and he seems to have been remembered with affection by his brothers who emigrated, for they preserved his name, and it has come down in several lines till the present time. I con-

jecture however that the name Zechariah (I changed mine in
my youth to Zachary) will die out after some half dozen of us
shall have passed away.

William Eddye remained vicar of Cranbrook till his death in
1616. He was methodical, judicious, and thorough in admin-
istering the affairs of the parish, whose finances he established
on a sound basis. He kept the church in repair. He was a
faithful pastor, sympathizing and diligent. When the plague
broke out in the town he summoned the people to humiliation
and repentance ; he was a faithful reprover of immorality, and
his own life seems to have been above reproach. He was on
the whole a successful minister.

There is no portrait extant of our ancestor, nor any written
description of his person ; but he doubtless transmitted to his
descendants his own physical characteristics. He must have
had a sound physique. I judge that he was not less than six
feet tall, some forty-three inches in girth, and that he weighed
not less than two hundred pounds avoirdupois. He was probably of immense muscular strength. Does this strike you as
fanciful? Consider the case a moment: where did we get
our physique? We are a family of giants. I trace my own
descent to the pilgrim through six men, every one of whom was
a Samson. When my father still lived he and his six sons
measured forty-two feet. My grandfather was of the same
stature ; my great-great-grandfather, as I shall show, was famous for his muscular strength ; and the son of the pilgrim,
Obadiah, was also a mighty man. Many other branches of the
family have preserved the same robust and manly build. These
having been the characteristics of the family since the landing
of the pilgrim fathers, we are warranted by a true scientific
induction in attributing them to the hale old vicar of Cranbrook.
There are many variations from this family type but it reappears
in every successive generation.

William Eddye died in 1616. John was then only twenty

years old and Samuel only eight. The family was not rich, but they lived on, and prospered in a small way. John and Samuel were both married as early as the year 1630.

Before the death of the vicar a general interest had been created in England touching the planting of colonies in the New World. Sir Walter Raleigh and Captain Smith had brought back wondrous reports concerning the fertility and beauty of Virginia, a name then given to the whole Atlantic coast. Jamestown had been already founded. John Robinson and the Pilgrims at Leyden were preparing to emigrate to the New World. Their commissioners were in England trying to secure royal permission and protection. The subject, it seems, excited deep interest at Cranbrook, as we infer from the Church Warden's Record for 1617: "Paid 2s 4d that was spent in charges riding to Canterbury for to carry the first money gathered here for Virginia." Was this collection for Jamestown, or was it intended to assist the Leyden Pilgrims to carry out their scheme, now almost ripe for execution. I incline to the latter opinion; but however it was, John and Samuel Eddy were in sympathy with the Pilgrims, for they determined to cross the ocean, — not to Jamestown but to Plymouth. Accordingly they took passage in the ship *Handmaid*, Captain Grant, and landed at Plymouth Rock two hundred and fifty years ago this very day.

JOHN EDDY AND HIS DESCENDANTS.

JOHN EDDY was thirty-four years old when he came to Plymouth. He and his wife Amy settled at Watertown. He soon became a member of the church and was elected a "freeman" of the town in 1634. He was repeatedly chosen what would now be called — perhaps it was so-called then — a Selectman; and he was evidently held in high esteem. He became in the course of years an extensive land-holder, and he left a good estate to his numerous family.

An interesting notice of him may be read in Governor Winthrop's book: "John Eddy," says the Governor, " a godly man of the Watertown congregation fell distracted, and getting out one evening, could not be found; but eight days after he came again to himself. He had kept his strength and color, yet had eaten nothing, as must needs be conceived, all that time. He recovered his understanding again in good measures, and lived very orderly, but would now and then be a little distempered." This is the only instance of even temporary insanity which I have ever heard of in any branch of the family; and this probably occurred in John Eddy's old age, and was a failure of mental power rather than the result of mental disease.

I have made diligent inquiry touching the history of John Eddy's posterity; but besides bare names I find no material for the present discourse.

SAMUEL EDDY AND HIS DESCENDANTS.

SAMUEL EDDY was in his twenty-third year when, with his wife Elizabeth, he stepped on Plymouth Rock. He first settled in Plymouth. A lot was set off to him on which he built a house where he lived several years. He soon joined the Pilgrim Church and was made a "freeman" in 1633. His wife was evidently a woman of marked character. She was probably of Kentish blood, and was doubtless educated in the lax notions of the Church of England concerning the Lord's Day, and her conduct gave much vexation to the Governor and Council. Once she anticipated the going down of the sun and "wrung and hung out" her clothes during holy time. For this she was fined, but the fine was remitted. Again she shocked the colony by walking to Boston on the Sabbath. Again she was brought before the magistrates; but when they understood that she went to Boston to see a sick lady whom she had known in England, they chose to regard it as a work of mercy, but admonished her

to do so no more. This version of the story I had many years ago from Z. Eddy, Esq., of Middleboro'. It must be confessed that our ancestress was an independent and energetic woman. Her Sabbath-breaking cannot be held up to her daughters as exemplary, but her physical vigor and endurance they may well covet. That Sabbath walk to Boston is memorable. It is our good fortune to have sprung from a Kentish woman of perfect physique.

In the year 1640 Samuel Eddy with several of his neighbors bought a large tract of land of the Indians and founded the town of Middleboro'. His portion included several hundred acres in the north-east portion of the town of Middleboro' and a part of the town of Halifax; and there, as his descendants multiplied, grew up the little village of EDDYVILLE, which we all — of his line — regard as our Jerusalem. On the very spot where the Pilgrim built his house his children's children now live, the old homestead having never been alienated.

A visit to Middleboro' will richly repay you for the trouble of going there. Though the scenery is not grand or striking the town is very lovely. You will there see *old* New England at its best. Be sure and visit the old graveyard and spend an hour among the tombstones of the saints who sleep. Almost every other one has inscribed upon it our name.

> " Beneath those rugged elms, that yew-tree's shade,
> Where heaves the turf in many a mouldering heap,
> Each in his narrow cell forever laid,
> The rude forefathers of the hamlet sleep."

"*Rude?*" Not so. They were plain men but not unlettered. They had the best elements of culture, — intelligence, humanity, courtesy, and reverence. *Requiescat in pace!*

Samuel Eddy had five children: John, Zechariah, Caleb, Obadiah, and Hannah.

JOHN EDDY, born at Plymouth in 1637, settled in Taunton. He was a man of substance, being a large land-owner, and blessed with fifteen children, — somewhat *above* the normal number.

One of his distinguished descendants, through John his eldest son, was Colonel JONATHAN EDDY, born in Mansfield, Mass., in 1726. He was a brave and active officer in the old French war, holding a commission as Captain from Governor Pownall. After the war he settled in Nova Scotia; but at the breaking out of the War of Independence he was compelled to flee to the United States. He was commissioned as Colonel and did good service. He was a man of capacity and resolution. He was the progenitor of the numerous and highly respectable Maine branch of the family. Many of the great lumber-merchants of Maine and the Northwest are of his blood. The late Newell Avery, Esq., of Detroit, the model business man of Michigan, married his great-granddaughter. Edwin Eddy, Esq., of East Saginaw is his great-grandson. Probably not less than sixty of his descendants reside in my own State of Michigan.

CALEB EDDY, the second son of the Pilgrim, lived in Swansea, Mass., and was a deacon of the church there. There is a tradition that the Pilgrim died at his house in 1688. The date at least is questionable. Caleb Eddy, the son of Caleb, was a shipwright and merchant in Boston. The late Caleb Eddy, Esq., so universally respected, was his descendant. To his careful researches, and to those of his son R. H. Eddy. Esq., we are indebted for the most of our knowledge touching the Eddy genealogy. Permit me to say in passing that as an accurate genealogist Mr. R. H. Eddy has no equal in our family and probably no superior in the country. Should he ever print his book it will take rank at once as the first of its class.

The two eminent Presbyterian ministers — the Rev. Dr. CHAUNCEY EDDY, and his brother, the Rev. ANSEL D. EDDY, D.D. — were also descended through John from Samuel the Pilgrim.

The former was well known throughout the country as an eloquent advocate of Foreign Missions, and the latter as pastor of the First Church in Newark, N.J. In 1842 he was Moderator of the General Assembly of the Presbyterian Church. I had the honor of being a member that year as Commissioner from Buffalo Presbytery. I never knew a presiding officer who carried himself with more dignity, courtesy, and wisdom than did Dr. Eddy at that time.

Both those excellent brothers are gone to their rest. Chauncey was struck down by apoplexy at Beloit, Wis., several years ago; and Ansel died, not long since, at Seneca Falls, N.Y. A son of Chauncey, the Rev. W. W. Eddy, is now a missionary of the Presbyterian Board in Syria.

ZECHARIAH, the third son of the Pilgrim, lived first at Swansea and afterwards here in Providence. I presume that the most of the Rhode Island Eddys are his descendants. The late Samuel Eddy, LL.D. (born 1769; died 1839), must have been of his line. He was for several terms a Member of Congress and afterwards Chief Justice of this State. He was the author of several valuable historical papers and of a volume on "Antiquities."

OBADIAH, my own ancestor, was the fourth son of the Pilgrim. In 1845 I received a letter from the late Zechariah Eddy, Esq., of Middleboro' containing this remarkable statement: "I saw an old man of ninety-three when I was young who knew Obadiah when he lived and described his person and habits. He spoke of him as a very strong, muscular man, and said he lived to extreme old age. He was much respected." Mr. Eddy also wrote that he had often visited the place where Obadiah's house stood. The cellar and two trees planted probably by his hand remain to show that human beings once dwelt there.

The eldest son of Obadiah was BENJAMIN, who, after several years in Middleboro', removed to New Jersey. Touching that branch I have no information.

The second son, SAMUEL, was my great-great-grandfather. While he was greatly respected for his piety, he was even more distinguished for his bodily strength. Mr. Z. Eddy describes him as huge in build and very muscular. He was a maker of the old-fashioned truck-wheels. One morning before breakfast he went into the woods, felled a white-oak tree, sawed off the butt with a handsaw for hubs, and carried it home on his shoulder. At another time, having ordered a load of cedar logs, he was disappointed in the size of the load, and said somewhat testily to the man who brought it: " Why, I can carry that load on my back!" " Carry it," was the reply, " and you shall have it for nothing." Mr. Eddy bound the logs into a bundle, took them on his back, and carried them away. " There were giants in those days;" and we are the sons of the giants.

SAMUEL, the Samson of our family, had several sons, among them Zechariah, a godly man and greatly respected. He was the father of Captain JOSHUA EDDY, an officer in the army during the Revolutionary War. He was a noble man and his memory is blessed. Says Mr. Zechariah Eddy, his distinguished son, in the " New-England Historical and Genealogical Register," for July, 1854: " He was of a firm, well-knit physical constitution, of about six feet stature, usually enjoyed good health, and was never known to be depressed in spirits. He was enterprising and persevering in every kind of labor and calling which he undertook. His descent, on the part of his mother, was from Governor Bradford, George Morton, and other Pilgrims of the *Mayflower;* and he truly inherited the Pilgrim spirit as well as the Pilgrim blood. The religious and ecclesiastical principles of John Robinson were household words with him. He was true to his principles and his code of morals was severe. His reverence for the Bible was profound and he would tolerate no deviation from its teachings. He had a large heart and an ingenuous mind, which was always open to consider and receive any new truth; he was world-wide from big-

otry of every kind." This noble man left behind him a noble family.

In the year 1845 I was a pioneer missionary in Western Wisconsin. There, through a distant relative of the family, I first heard of Zechariah Eddy, Esq., of Middleboro', Mass., and opened a correspondence with him. From that time he treated me more like a son than a third cousin. On his invitation a few years afterwards I visited Middleboro'. Four brothers were then living in the town, Joshua, Nathaniel, Zechariah, and William. They were all true Christian gentlemen, noble in presence, genial in manners, spotless in character. Zechariah was an eminent lawyer. Judge Shaw told me at a later day that there was no better chancery lawyer in the State. He probably understood the Congregational polity better than any layman in the United States. He was an able writer, and contributed largely to various newspapers and periodicals. Above all, he was a man of spotless honor, and sincere though not demonstrative piety. He was a tender father, and was much afflicted in the loss of two promising sons in their early manhood. One brother of that estimable family still survives in an honored and vigorous old age, — Deacon Morton Eddy of Fall River, now present with us.

I cannot refrain from here interjecting an anecdote, less complimentary to myself than to the family at large, and especially to the Middleboro' branch. In 1867 I was called to the pastorate of the First Church at Northampton, Mass. When I preached there as a candidate, the late Hon. C. A. Dewey, Justice of the Supreme Court of Massachusetts, a member of the church, happened to be absent. On being consulted he said, "*Eddy?* Call him; he comes of good blood." He was an old friend of Zechariah Eddy of Middleboro', and I am happy to say he became a true and dear friend to me.

So much concerning the descendants of Zechariah, the son of Samuel, who was the grandson of Samuel the Pilgrim. Zechariah

had a younger brother, SAMUEL, whom I have the honor to call
my great-grandfather. He was a man of mark in the Old
Colony. Zechariah Eddy, from whose letters I have so often
quoted, wrote me thirty-five years ago: " Samuel Eddy, your
great-grandfather, my great-uncle, was distinguished for his
sobriety, gravity, sound sense, and piety. When I was a boy,
my grandmother said to me : ' I never laid aside my spinning-
wheel for any body but that man ; but when I saw him coming
down the road, I put aside the wheel, and prepared to sit down
with him to get improvement from his conversation.' " Samuel
Eddy seems to have been an oracle in his own parish and with
neighboring churches. He also rendered valuable service to
the General Court. His wife, who lived to extreme age, was
Lydia Alden, a great-granddaughter of John Alden, the Mayflower Pilgrim, and of that Priscilla Mullins who said to him,
" John, why do you not speak for yourself?" Through that
blood we are allied not only to the Alden family — no slight
honor — but to Longfellow and Bryant, and to President John
Adams and his descendants.

Samuel Eddy's son NATHAN, my grandfather, lived several
years after his marriage to Hannah Sampson, in Middleboro',
and then removed to Vermont, settling ultimately in Pittsfield,
Winsor county. EPHRAIM, his eldest son, while they were yet
in Middleboro', went into the army as his father's substitute,
became after a little time one of Washington's life-guards and
a member of his camp family. He came out of the army a
Captain, died young, but left a daughter of rare loveliness and
excellence, whose sons — Robert Hale, Judge and Member of
Congress, of national reputation ; Matthew Hale, Esq., an emi-
ment jurist ; W. C. Hale, well known as a banker ; and Dr.
Hale, a successful physician — rise up and call her blessed.

Nathan's second son, NATHAN, lived in Western Pennsylvania,
Kentucky, and St. Louis. He had two distinguished sons,
Judge Harry Eddy of Shawneetown, Ill., and the Rev. Ira

Eddy, a devoted and successful minister of the Methodist Episcopal Church, who died several years since, at Painesville, O.

Nathan's younger brother, Isaac, lived first at Pittsfield, Vt. He was at first a merchant, and afterwards a minister, and the founder of a Congregational church in Jamestown, Chautauqua county, N.Y. He was a winning preacher, a wise pastor, a good father, a saintly man. At a public celebration, two years ago, the chairman declared that Isaac Eddy was the best man who ever lived in Jamestown : and this was more than forty-five years after his death. He died in 1833, leaving me — a youth of seventeen — fatherless. My brother, the Rev. Hiram Eddy, D.D., present to-day, and myself both feel that blessed with such a father we ought to have been better men and better ministers.

Zechariah Eddy, youngest son of Nathan, died some four years ago, at the age of ninety-three, in Warren, Pa., leaving numerous descendants, intelligent, well-to-do, and highly respected. Some of them are here to speak for themselves.

To go back a moment. Nathan Eddy's brother Samuel emigrated early in the century to Western New York. He had a large family of the highest respectability. His son, the late Judge Eddy, is represented by several sons and grandsons, distinguished lawyers, physicians, and clergymen. The Rev. Alfred Eddy, D.D., of Niles, Mich., is his son, whose niece was the beautiful and accomplished wife of the present excellent governor of Michigan ; so we have the honor of claiming the governor's lovely daughters as our cousins. Through another son of Samuel several distinguished Baptist ministers have been given to the church, — among them, the Rev. Seth Eddy and the Rev. R. J. Eddy, D.D., both, I believe, still living. The eminent Baptist minister of Boston, Rev. D. C. Eddy, D.D., belongs, I think, to another branch of the family. Though I once heard him say that, for certain reasons, he felt no interest in his Eddy genealogy, could not help thinking that from head to foot he was a remarkably fine specimen of the Eddy physique. We certainly claim him as a cousin.

No member of our family has done more to illustrate our name than the late Rev. Thomas Mears Eddy, D.D., of the Methodist Episcopal Church. I am told by his son, in a recent letter, that his father belonged to the Samuel branch of the family. This is rather vague; but some of the genealogists present can probably trace his descent from the Pilgrim. Augustus Eddy, the father of Thomas, was born in Berkshire county, Mass. He was also a Methodist preacher, and had great fame in Ohio and Indiana. When I was a youthful itinerant missionary I happened to meet Augustus Eddy, who was then in the prime of life and an Eddy all over. I still remember my conversation with him. "What was your father's name?" he asked. "Isaac." "*Isaac! Isaac!* I had an uncle [perhaps it was a more distant relative] whose name was Isaac; but of course you are not his son; HE WAS VERY RICH." I suspect that I was a seedy-looking evangelist at that time.

Thomas M. Eddy was born in 1823 near Cincinnati. With scanty advantages he entered early on the work of preaching the gospel. He soon attained great popularity as a preacher and as a writer. He was sought for in Chicago, in Baltimore, in Washington; and was, at length, elected by the General Conference one of the three corresponding secretaries of the Missionary Society of the Methodist Church. He proved himself in every position a man of signal ability; an eloquent preacher, an able editor, a wise manager of a great institution. More than all, he was a saint. His life was spotless. Had he lived a few years he would undoubtedly have been raised to the episcopate. But he was struck down by sudden disease, at the age of fifty-one. It was unexpected to him; but he was ready. He calmly arranged his worldly affairs and waited for the change. Among his last words were, "I am now in a most sweet state of mind, nearing the gates. Eternity dawns! Hallelujah!"

This imperfect genealogical history of our family is all that I can now offer you. Many of the details are unknown to me; and many that are known would be out of place in a discourse of this kind. Some mistakes I have doubtless made, and some of you will notice many omissions. Should the address be printed, it will be submitted to the careful criticism of the best genealogist among us, and the errors, at least, corrected.

This review suggests several rather fruitful remarks on our family history.

1. The family has been marked, for three hundred years, for what Dr. Bushnell calls "the power of population." The rule in these branches of the family has been large households, especially many *sons*, so that *the name* is now very widely spread. It is estimated that the number of the descendants of William Eddye in the United States is now not less than six or seven thousand. This, considering how many families in New England have become extinct, and that others are now only represented by a few, is noteworthy. The Irishman said it was hereditary in his family not to have any children. We certainly cannot say that of ours.

This extraordinary multiplication accounts for the fact that, while the Eddys as a family are not poor, not many of them are very rich. Few great estates have passed from father to son. Estates that were in a fair way to become large have been divided among many heirs. I do not regard this as a misfortune.

2. This power of population implies large hereditary vitality. Few families have such a "physical basis" for family immortality as ours. We are a large-limbed, muscular, vigorous race; and we have been since our "pre-historic times." I can find few traces of *hereditary* diseases, like scrofula, consumption, gout, insanity. We still have a sound physique, and many branches are remarkable for longevity. There are of course many instances of physical debility and disease, just as in a field of

western corn there are many feeble stalks; but such instances are usually the result of intermarriage and, more frequently, of the violation of hygienic laws.

3. We are a large-brained family; but hitherto there have been but few manifestations of remarkable intellectual power. When I first undertook to prepare this discourse, I said to a friend: "It is a hard case; we have been a dead level of respectability for three hundred years." Since then my estimate has been somewhat raised. We have, it is true, during these three centuries been living on a plain, but it has been rather a high plain, with here and there a respectable hill, and in a few instances a Mount Holyoke, or even a Greylock, or a Mount Equinox, but never a Mont Blanc or a Jungfrau. Our family has produced no great statesman, or philosopher, or orator, or poet, or historian, or man of science: a few distinguished lawyers, physicians, and clergymen, there have been; one or two of national reputation. That is a respectable showing, but nothing to boast of. And yet, considering that the Eddy gens has made a victorious struggle for existence, and considering their present vigorous vitality, we may reasonably look hereafter for more splendid intellectual developments. I quite concur in the sagacious remark of Mr. R. H. Eddy, in a recent letter, "Though as yet the Eddys have not a *brilliant* record, I think there are in the race latent qualities which will in future bring about such a record." All depends upon the training of our children. EDUCATE! EDUCATE! and the result is certain.

4. The moral average of our family has been high from the first. Few have been convicted of crimes. Few of the name have been shut up in prison: one such I have heard of, but I ascertained that the prisoner was a colored woman; how she came by our name I know not; she probably thought it a good name to steal! Drunkards and libertines have doubtless been in the family; but they are exceptional in its history. The old Puritan

sobriety and conjugal faithfulness are still characteristic family traits. The name does not figure in trials for divorces, or for embezzlement of trust funds, or for any kind of fraud. The late Judge Eddy of Western New York once remarked to Dr. Ansel D. Eddy, that there "was never a *mean* Eddy." Mr. Z. Eddy of Middleboro', hearing of the remark, wrote to me with some emphasis: " *That* is not true!" He was a man so sensitive touching every point of honor, that he detected meanness where ordinary mortals saw nothing that was not high-minded and generous.

5. The religious character of the family is strongly pronounced. We must, I think, recognize an hereditary religious tendency in our blood. To be sure such a tendency clings to human nature, but it is more strongly marked in some families than in others. Since the days of our pious ancestor, the Vicar of Cranbrook, there has been no break in the transmission of Christian faith and devotion. And the tendency has been to earnest forms of piety. In the time of Whitfield, the Eddys — certainly at Middleboro' — were New Lights, and built a meeting-house for themselves. And here comes in one of Mr. Z. Eddy's anecdotes: "One of our grandmothers used to ride to church, and she had to pass the old church in order to reach her own. Now at the old church was the stake at which she formerly tied her horse. Going to meeting one Lord's Day, as she was musing, her horse turned up to the old stake. She saw some of the Old Lights standing near smile; so she suddenly caught up the loose rein and said: 'Get away! It seems to me that every irrational creature in the parish will go to this old meeting-house!'" The Eddys have generally affiliated with what are popularly (perhaps invidiously) called "evangelical" churches. Many are still, as were the Pilgrims, Congregationalists; many have passed naturally into the Presbyterian Church; not a few are Baptists (who are, they say, but wet Congregationalists), and a large number are Methodists. The name however is somewhat cele-

brated among the Friends; and a highly-respectable section of the family is identified either with the Unitarians or the Universalists. A few are going back to the church of their ancestor, William Eddye. But the inherited tendency of the race to religion in some form seems irresistible. However it may be with other families, the Eddys must have a religion. This is not a superstitious or unreasoning tendency. It comes, not merely from the natural instinct of humanity yearning after God, but it has been developed and nurtured by ages of enlightened culture. It is the highest glory of our blood. Personally I believe that it is a signal fulfilment of a divine promise: "I will be a God to thee, and thy seed after thee."

It is religion more than blood which unites the scattered members of the Eddy brotherhood; it is religion that unites the living and the dead in one fellowship. It is my belief that on this occasion the fathers, who toiled and prayed for us while they were on earth, still survive; and I cannot but think they are really though invisibly with us to-day.

Ye sainted ones, now resting from your labors, in the name of my kindred and with filial reverence I salute you! We remember your names, your virtues, your prayers; and we promise that this memory shall be our inspiration to consecrated lives and noble deeds. We will tread in your footsteps till we also are called over to the majority.

Hark! Is it fancy; or do I hear a manifold benediction sounding out still and clear from the Unseen, the venerable pastor of Cranbrook leading the voices of his glorified descendants?

"The Lord bless you and keep you:

"The Lord make His face to shine upon you, and be gracious unto you:

"The Lord lift up His countenance upon you, and give you peace!"

AND LET ALL THE FAMILY SAY, AMEN!

The oration was listened to with great attention and was frequently applauded. R. H. Eddy, Esq., of Boston, said that he might not be able to attend the afternoon exercises, and asked permission to remark that several persons present probably little knew how near they came to never having had existence, and related an anecdote in regard to their ancestor John Eddy (the son of Samuel the Pilgrim), who, when at work in his field one day during King Philip's War, was discovered by several Indians who determined to kill him; but as he was a favorite with them, they drew lots to determine who should be the executioner. John having his gun with him, and suspecting the enemy to be near, kept strict watch; and discovering signs of an Indian crouching beneath a bank, fired at him as he rose, the savage firing at John at the same time, and receiving and being killed by the ball from the firearm of John. On John attempting to reload his gun, he found that the ball from that of the Indian had struck and carried away the hammer of the lock of the piece, leaving John unharmed.

The exercises of the morning were concluded by the audience joining in the singing, to the tune of "*York*," —

> " O God, our help in ages past,
>   Our hope for years to come,
>   Our shelter from the stormy blast,
>   And our eternal home!"

The President announced that a telegram had just been received from James H. Eddy, Esq., stating that, owing to an accident on the railroad the New Britain and Connecticut Eddys would be delayed three hours.

The President, on behalf of James Eddy, Esq., extended an invitation to all to repair to his dwelling in close proximity to the chapel, and partake of a collation there in readiness, for which there would be a recess of an hour. Nearly all accepted the hospitable invitation. While some were occupied with the viands and good cheer so sumptuously provided, others were critically observing the works of art which adorned the mansion in great profusion. Still others were walking the grounds and taking note of the picturesqueness and beauty of the situation; while many others remained in the chapel in order to become better acquainted with some new-found relative, or to clear up some doubtful genealogy.

AFTERNOON.

At two o'clock the meeting was called to order, and the exercises were opened with the singing of a song by Mrs. S. S. Chaffin, beginning, —

> "I hear thee speak of the better land.
> Thou call'st its children a happy band."

It was admirably executed and highly appreciated.

The poem of the day, written by Miss Alice Maud Eddy, daughter of Dr. Zachary Eddy, was read by her sister, Mrs. Leonard A. Treat of Boston.

POEM.

BY MISS ALICE MAUD EDDY.

THE wild October gale sweeps in across the sunlit sea;
Beneath his tread the flashing waves are stirred to restless glee;
And far and wide his voice is heard in conquering jubilee.

That voice has travelled o'er the land, abroad from East to West;
The last fleet swallow at the sound forsakes his chilly nest;
And frightened gentians bow their heads high on the hilltop's
    crest.

A message to the poplar leaves to take their golden flight;
A message to the keen blue skies to glow more keen and bright;
A word he brings to every heart to beat more full and light.

Meet is it that on such a day we come from all the land,
To greet each other kindred here with eager heart and hand,
And gaze upon that far-off height whereon our fathers stand.

So here we meet, a joyous band, among the floating leaves;
While, through the maple boughs, the sun his shining network
    weaves,
And o'er the beds of dying flowers all Nature softly grieves.

For 'twas on such an autumn morn, that, up the rippling bay,
The ship that bore our fathers passed, and at the pierhead lay,
While men ran out to welcome them through all the town that
    day.

Full pleasantly the Plymouth shores lay spread before their sight;
For then, as now, along the land the woods were fair and bright
With all the beauty Autumn weaves each year for our delight.

And there the settlers' children played, as joyous children do,
Held up the scarlet maple leaves to see the sun shine through,
Or scoured the woods for glossy nuts, with many a glad halloo.

And there their mother, at her toil, went swiftly to and fro,
With snatches of some quaint old psalm sung fervently and low,
As steadily from the humming wheel passed off the soft brown
    tow.

Perhaps, at times, the secret tears might dim that mother's eyes,
When through the dappled clouds at night she watched the white
    moon rise,
With just the same fair face that blessed the far-off English skies.

Or when the maidens of the town came in on cold Spring days,
With sprigs of pink arbutus flowers plucked from the woodland
    ways,
The matron's heart might mourn the bloom of verdant English
    Mays.

Perhaps on sunny Sabbath morns, when all folks churchward
    went,
E'en as the young wife passed the door, and o'er her psalm-book
    bent,
Her heart might wander far away to the old gray church in Kent—

The bare, unpainted meeting-house, forgotten for a while,—
Her dreamy eyes might glow at thought of Dunstan's buttressed
    pile,
With forms of many an early friend along the echoing aisle.

And yet, when at the sound of prayer her swift thoughts home-
     ward sped,
Where, o'er the silent worshippers, rose Brewster's hallowed head,
No wish was hers that she might kneel in Cranbrook church in-
     stead.

For pilgrim souls were stout and brave, and woman's faith was
     strong,
And no true wife in Plymouth town with coward heart would long
For flowery field or stately church dimmed with a mist of wrong.

Ah, glorious was that place of prayer, with bare unvaulted roof,
And sentinel watching by the door for Indian forms aloof,
Where flickering woodland shadows wove their mystic warp and
     woof.

For there, 'mid many a noble form, grave and intent of mien,
With firm-set lips and prayerful eyes, stern Bradford's head was
     seen,
With Alden's fair and gentle face, and Winslow's brow serene.

And burly Standish, restless eyed, and turning o'er and o'er
Toward where the loaded guns stood stacked beside the open
     door;
And Cushman's thoughtful countenance, and many an elder more.

And o'er the forms of men and maids, and rosy children fair,
The light of one great purpose shone, ennobling all things there,
As hill and dale transfigured lie, 'neath Autumn's amber air.

And in that light our fathers lived and labored, year by year;
With steadfast courage took their way through paths of doubt
     and fear:
The winds of earth might strive with them, but faith's blue sky
     was clear.

But little thought was theirs, I ween — as from the upland field
They harvested the scanty crop that iron soil would yield —
Of all the power the Pilgrim name in future days would wield.

Not power or fame they coveted; they sought, through good
    and ill,
Freedom to serve the Lord they loved — freedom to learn his
    will !
And through long lives of honest toil they kept his blessing still.

What more can we their children do than follow where they led !
Like them, in manly toil below, our heavenward pathway tread,
Till lulling notes of angel-songs float o'er our dying bed.

And then through death's calm midnight lie, silent, with peace-
    ful breast,
Until the dewy winds of dawn shall blow from East to West,
And golden light of endless day break through our honored rest.

After the applause had subsided with which the poem had been received, the President stated that an effort had been made to secure a delegation of the Eddy Family from England. Although at first it had been hoped for, he was sorry to say that the anticipations of the committee had not been realized. We have, however, a communication from them which will be read.

The Clerk read the following : —

"To John Eddy, Esq., *as representative of the American Eddys:*

"We, your English namesakes and cousins, offer you, the Eddys all and sundry, our hearty congratulations upon the peaceful and prosperous celebration of your anniversary. We hope you will accept this cordial expression of our sympathy, and allow us, though absent, to be associated with you in your family reunion. We only wish we could join you upon this interesting occasion, and that thus united with you by the tie of kindred, we could thus represent, in our one family, the common blood, the common language, and the common associations of history and country, which we trust may always knit together in friendship England and America.

"I, Charles Eddy, who am writing this as spokesman of our family, am a clergyman of the Church of England, as were my father and grandfather before me, and the common ancestor of our race. We do not know of any relations outside the small circle of my grandfather's descendants ; and this will be signed by as many of these as we can communicate with. I have myself attached my brother's signature, as he sympathizes warmly with your meeting, and would have very much liked to come to you. But, alas, on this side of the Atlantic the Eddys have not managed to accumulate any great store of wealth, and the journey from Rome (where my brother is established, in the Bank of Messrs. Plowden & Co.) is long and expensive.

" I have sent in a former letter our genealogical tree, so far as we can trace it back, with such particulars as seemed likely to be interesting to you; and now enclose a photograph of myself, taken six or seven years ago. My relations, to whom I am sending this for signature, will, I hope, send theirs also.

"In conclusion, let me express the pleasure with which we received your friendly invitation and greetings, and repeat our hearty congratulations and good wishes. Should you or other Eddys visit England, I shall be glad to welcome you at my quiet country parsonage.

"Please send us any account which may be published of your meeting, and of Dr. Zachary Eddy's address.

> "CHARLES EDDY, M.A.,
> > "*Vicar of Bramley, Hants, Late Fellow and Tutor of Queen's College, Oxford.*
> "JOHN EDDY,
> "FRANCES ANN EDDY,
> "CATHARINE SOPHIA EDDY,
> "MARIA SUSANNA LILLY,
> > "*Collaton Vicarage, Paignton, Devonshire.*"

The President said that if it be the pleasure of the meeting, a few minutes would be occupied in reading extracts from other communications from our English cousins. Assent being given, the Clerk read a portion of a letter from Mrs. Sarah Beeman, *née* Eddy, wife of the Rev. Thomas Beeman of London, a native of Cranbrook: —

"MY DEAR SIR:

" . . . My husband and myself feel greatly interested in the proposed celebration, and hope the 29th of October may witness a happy and successful gathering; and that the noble spirit that animated the Pilgrim Fathers may be largely shared by their descendants. Their memory is dear to every Englishman."

In another letter, from the same lady, she writes: —

"I have in my possession a handsome set of very old China which once belonged to the Brewster family."

Extract from the letter of Mrs. Maria S. Lilly, *née* Eddy, wife of the Rev. Peter Lilly.

" COLLATON VICARAGE, PAIGNTON, S. DEVON.

" DEAR MR. EDDY:

" As one of your unknown English relations, I write to assure you of the lively interest we take in the approaching Eddy jubilee.

" We have not yet heard whether any English representative can be present, but we shall very much rejoice if this is found possible.

" We beg that you will present our best regards, and most sincere good wishes, to those who are united with you in promoting this reunion.

" Very truly yours,

" MARIA SUSANNA LILLY."

Extract from the letter of Mrs. Jane Elizabeth Tompkins, *née* Eddy, wife of the Rev. Henry George Tompkins of Park Lodge, Weston *Supra Mare :* —

" . . . With cordial wishes for a happy gathering, and for many blessings on the many branches of the family for the future, — as by God's mercy in time past, — in which good wishes my husband and daughter beg to join, believe me,

" Dear sir, sincerely yours,

" JANE ELIZABETH TOMPKINS."

Under the date of August 4, 1880, Mrs. Tompkins writes : —

" My grandfather John Eddy's second wife was the daughter of Rev. Hollier Allen, and Mary his wife, daughter of Peter Bathurst, Esq., of Clarendon Park, Wilts. Peter Bathurst married Lady Selena Shirley, daughter of Earl Ferrers. They had fifteen children ; one of these married Lord Tracey, and was one of the ladies of the bed-chamber to Queen Charlotte, wife of George III.

" This lady adopted her niece, who was the second wife of my grandfather, John Eddy, Rector of Toddington."

" QUEEN'S GATE TERRACE, S.W. LONDON,
" August 5, 1880.

" Mrs. Eddy regrets very much that it is not possible for her or her daughter to be present at the Eddy Festival in October. In addition to the interest of seeing so many of such a large and prosperous family, Mrs. Eddy would have been very pleased to make the acquaintance of the Mr. Eddy who welcomed and so hospitably entertained her late dear husband, Dr. Charles Walter Eddy, some two and twenty years ago ; and she begs that gentleman's acceptance of the accompanying photographs, and little pamphlet, in remembrance of her husband. Mrs. Eddy wishes she could send any information relative to the family ancestors which would be interesting, but it is not in her power to do so. She begs, however, on behalf of her daughter and herself, to give her most cordial good wishes to their American cousins."

This concluded the arrangements which had been made by the Committee ; and the President requested the various branches of the family to occupy the remaining time.

Miss Sula S. Eddy, — a graduate of Cornell University, whose home is in Elmira, N.Y., but who at present is connected with the Classical Institute of Schenectady, N.Y., — was then introduced. She read a poem of considerable length, portions of which are as follows : —

Charles Walter Eddy

POEM.

BY MISS SULA S. EDDY.

From North, from South, from East and West
   We bring our hearty greeting,
To those who come with one accord,
   In friendly concourse meeting.

We see before us faces strange,
   Whose kindred blood is flowing,
And as we trace the subtle tie,
   A kindred love is glowing.

Two hundred years and more have passed,
   Since in this country landed
The honored men who bore our name,
   With other pilgrims banded.

To God who gave the favoring gale
   Their hearts and voices lifting,
Forth from that band, o'er sea and land,
   A song of praise went drifting.

Prophetic eyes were none to see
   This land with millions teeming;
That day on Plymouth rock this band
   Had little time for dreaming.

Before them, as they cast their eyes,
   No life of ease was laying, —
They knew the hand must grasp the plow
   Without the least delaying.

Their faith and trust helped smooth the way,
   And heavy clouds were rifted,
When up to him who brought them safe
   The eye of faith was lifted.

With pruning-hook and sword they fought,
   A road to freedom clearing ;
A temple, where they made a home,
   To God and freedom rearing.

   *   *   *   *   *   *

One little hour we linger here,
   The past, so precious, viewing ;
Now let us clasp each other's hands,
   Their pledge of faith renewing.

My friends, and more, my kinsmen, all,
   Accept this little song, —
May blessings brighten all your days,
   And life be sweet and long ;

And when your years are numbered full,
   And all of life is past,
May you with blessed ones above
   Find heavenly rest at last.

The president remarked that the Eddys of New Jersey had distinguished themselves in the learned professions, and as patriots in the late civil war, and called upon the Rev. Hiram Eddy, D.D., of Jersey City, who had some experience in Libby prison.

He responded by saying that he knew nothing of genealogy, but was greatly interested in what others had said. He was delighted to believe that while but few Eddys had made for themselves a national reputation, yet, as a family, they had attained a high rank in the learned professions and as men of business; and that in almost every branch of the family they had exhibited those noble qualities of mind and heart which go to make the greatness of any people. He was also exceedingly pleased with the Eddy physiognomy, and the perfection of physique, — that there was in us so much of the angular, for he had never known any great people who had no points. He felt that he was in the company of congenial spirits and greeted the audience heartily, and declared that being one of this family was a privilege more to be rejoiced in than to sway the proudest sceptre.

John Eddy, Esq., of Caribou, Me., spoke as follows : —

" Mr. President :

" The gentleman who has preceded me has been extending his greetings and words of welcome to the members of the Eddy family present, from the States of Rhode Island, Massachusetts, Vermont, Ohio, &c.

" He has not mentioned Maine, probably supposing there is no one here from that State; but I wish to inform the audience that there is one representative of the family here to-day from Maine, — your humble servant. I am probably the most eastern representative of the family in the United States. You have all heard of Bangor, and that is regarded as *away* down east. But my home is one hundred and seventy miles beyond Bangor, where it is sometimes said we have to pry the sun up with a crowbar; but this is not so. The sun rises in the natural way, and shines as brightly upon our pleasant farms and cheerful homes, our grand old forests and babbling brooks, as anywhere in the Union. (The President inquires the name of the speaker.) My name is John; my great-grandfather's name was John, and he having emigrated from Middleboro', Mass., was probably descended from the original John who landed at Plymouth. About one hundred years ago my great-grandfather, with his family, including my grandfather Seth, then a boy ten years of age, left his Middleboro' home to start anew in the then unsettled region of Western Worcester County, Mass. The location selected was on Ragged Hill, in the west parish of Brookfield, so called from its exceedingly rough and rocky soil. An incident of the journey may be interesting. While climbing the Leicester hills the old cow that was tied behind the load of goods became so tired as to be unable to proceed. They were at their wit's end to know what to do. They couldn't get along in the new home without the cow. Finally, the old gentleman, who had no doubt often refreshed his drooping spirits with the 'O be joyful,' concluded to try its effects upon the cow. Taking an ear of corn he cut a deep cavity in the butt with his knife, and filling it with rum, gave it to the cow to eat. She soon revived, and was able to prosecute the journey successfully.

"When my grandfather became a man he took a part of the original farm, which was large, and settled near by. Here my father, Titus Eddy, was born. When he was of age he became possessed of the original homestead, where he raised a family of six boys and two girls. Mr. Elijah Eddy, who sang ' The breaking waves dashed high' so finely this morning, and myself, counted two of the number.

"The enterprise and ambition of the great-grandfather John was inherited to some extent by his namesake the great-grandson, who stands before you; and when my health failed me, as a mechanic in Massachusetts, and a change of business became necessary, I picked up my little all, and with my family started for the wilds of Aroostook. This was nineteen years ago. Aroostook is the most northern County of Maine, and comprises an area of territory about the size of the State of Massachusetts, and at that time was covered with a dense forest growth. I went away into the wild woods, four miles from any travelled road, and reared my log-house. A few other settlers were in the vicinity.

"But to me, coming from busy Massachusetts, an oppressive stillness seemed to pervade all. No hum of machinery ever greeted our ears; no steam whistle; no pleasant church-going bell; no rattle of wheels ever passed our dwelling for years. The work of felling the trees and clearing the land, to one unused to wielding the axe, was laborious and slow. And where a man of some other name would have been discouraged, as many were, the grit of an Eddy said: '*Live or die, I have come to stay.*' And I have succeeded beyond my fondest dreams. Our little openings have broadened into well-tilled fields. Sleek herds of cattle graze upon our hillsides. Comfortable farm buildings have been erected, and the conveniences of life surround us.

"And to-day the little river-steamer lies at her wharf in Caribou. The thundering train comes whistling across the plains and meadows of the Aroostook valley; and the puffing engine, with its sinews of iron and nerves of steel, driven by the hissing steam, is grinding our home-raised wheat into flour for an industrious and happy people. I am so glad that I am able to be with you to-day. And the extreme *East* would here extend hearty congratulations to the extreme *West*, and all between, for the felicitous circumstances of this occasion. God bless the Eddy family. May we be honest and true. Ever cherish an earnest devotion to the best interests of our country and a common humanity."

Morton Eddy, Esq., of Fall River, Mass., being called upon by the President, responded as follows: —

" Mr. President :

" This first gathering of the different branches of the Eddy family is an occasion of peculiar interest to us, who are the descendants of those renowned men who laid the foundation of this great nation upon religion, education, and republican principles. Surely we have a right to rejoice in our ancestry and to express our gratitude for our birthright.

" With great satisfaction I see this large gathering of the Eddy relatives, coming from all parts of New England and the Middle and Western States, presenting cheerful and intelligent countenances, bright with Eddy blood, — a happy company, glad to congratulate their cousins with affectionate grasp.

" I feel highly favored that at my advanced age, eighty-fourth year, I am able to be present. I am the son of Captain Joshua Eddy of Middleboro', and am the last living of ten children. Nine of them had families and numerous descendants, many of whom to the fourth generation I see before me. My father was born in Middleboro', May 4, 1748. He was the son of Zechariah, who was the son of Samuel, who was the son of Obadiah, who was the son of Samuel the Pilgrim.

" On the side of his mother, Mary Morton, his genealogy is traced to George Morton, one of the most distinguished of the Pilgrims. So my father had a double line in the Pilgrim blood. His wife, Lydia, daughter of Zechariah Paddock, born in 1756, was a descendant of John Faunce, one of the Pilgrims. His son, Thomas, an Elder much beloved and respected, died Feb. 27, 1745, aged ninety-nine years. He had four children. His two daughters lived to be about ninety-nine. The last of the family died about the year 1804. My brother Zechariah, then residing in Plymouth, purchased the Elder's great chair, and sent it to my mother. At my mother's death, on Feb. 13, 1838, this famous chair fell to my lot, and I have kept it as a precious relic. It

has the original cane-wrought back, and is still sound and good, although more than two hundred years old, as believed.

"My father was a Captain in the Revolutionary war, and was engaged in the battle of Saratoga, and witnessed the surrender of Burgoyne. He gave me a thrilling account of the battle. He was in several other battles. At the close of the battle of Monmouth he was present at the meeting of Washington and Lee, and heard General Washington profanely accuse Lee of disobedience of orders. He said to General Lee, in much excitement, ' had you taken the position with your command, as I directed, we should have captured the whole British army.' He was surprised at Washington's use of such language, as it was so unlike his well-known habits and chaste conversation.

"At the close of the war my father engaged in mercantile business, and largely in the manufacture of iron wares. Few men in Plymouth County were more enterprising or more largely engaged in like operations, — none of better reputation for fair and honorable dealing. He was greatly respected as a gentleman, and honored the religion of the Pilgrim Fathers.

"In my childhood I remember he ranked among the most honorable men of his time. He had a span of horses and carriage for his family, unusual in the country in those days. On public occasions of the last century he dressed in the style of a gentleman, with cocked hat, short breeches, silver knee-buckles, and large silver buckles on his shoes, and his hair clubbed and powdered. I am happy to say that his descendants, more of whom are here present than of any other branch of the Eddy family, are loyal to the traditions of the Pilgrim Fathers."

Lewis Eddy, Esq., of Plymouth, Mass., responded as follows: —

"Mr. President:

"I am the only Eddy here present representing Plymouth. There are now living in the place where John and Samuel landed, two hundred and fifty years ago to-day, but two other Eddys beside myself; and my brother, John Eddy, resides on the spot where our great ancestor Samuel had his dwelling-place in the new world. The old house has gone to decay, but it has been replaced by another on the same site.

"We are descended from Samuel. My grandfather was Seth, a brother of Captain Joshua, of the Revolution. They were companions in arms during that war, and my grandfather heard the conversation between Generals Washington and Lee, at the battle of Monmouth, which has been spoken of. On our maternal side we trace our descent from Dr. Samuel Fuller of the 'Mayflower'; so that we can boast of pure Pilgrim blood in more than one direction. What is far better, I am able to say that the family have honored the faith of their fathers, and have that strong attachment for their kith and kin which has been referred to by the orator of the day.

"The striking peculiarity which I have observed in all Eddys is their great dread of being in debt; and I have never known a race that has more rigidly adhered to the maxim: 'Owe no man anything, but to love one another.'

"We, as well as the good people of Plymouth, were greatly disappointed that this festival was not holden there; and I would express the hope that when another occasion like the present shall arise, the way may be opened for us to show you how hospitable are the citizens of that famous old town."

The president said that among the lawyers and legislators of the State of Vermont none had acquired a more honorable position, or a better fame, than some of our namesakes; and called upon Charles B. Eddy, Esq., of Bellows Falls, who spoke as follows:—

"MR. PRESIDENT:

"Ladies and gentlemen,—I anticipated much pleasure in this gathering of the descendants of John and Samuel Eddy, but have had my anticipations more than realized. All that I have seen and heard has transcended even the bright and happy fore-

cast I had made. I had underestimated the number of people belonging to the Eddy tribe, and therefore did not expect to meet so many. Before entering this audience-room I thought of the great pleasure I should have in taking all the Eddys at this festival by the hand, and exchanging greetings with them. I supposed I should become intimately acquainted with each and every Eddy present. But as I entered this Chapel, and looked at this large assembly, the shadow of a disappointment for a moment rested upon me, as I saw I should be compelled to abandon my plan for a general hand-shaking and word-greeting. But only for a moment, for this shadow was quickly dispelled by the multitude of happy-looking Eddys I saw before me. I was made content to look at this multitude of faces and to exchange cordial heart-greetings. I read them in your countenances and knew you saw them in mine. We all knew that these greetings and recognitions were none the less cordial and fraternal because of the necessity that they should be given and returned in the silent language of the heart. May the Eddys who suggested and arranged for the celebration of this anniversary, and whose labors have brought together so many, and given us such a splendid service and entertainment, be most richly blessed and prospered. For this they shall have our lasting gratitude. Every passing moment of this festival-gathering has yielded to me the richest enjoyment; and as long as my reason shall remain, and memory shall wait upon me, I shall often in imagination revisit this city, this chapel, and recall these faces now before me. I shall often recall the exercises of this anniversary; the cordial words of welcome from you, Mr. President, in behalf of the Eddys resident in this city; the words of prayer and thanksgiving to the God of our fathers; the songs that have been sung; and the address of the orator of this occasion. The day is spent, and the hour of separation is at hand. I must not occupy more of your time.

" As I could not do what I had planned, — take each of you by the hand and converse with you, — I am grateful for this opportunity afforded me by the President to thus briefly address you,

and for the few moments of your time and the attention which
you have given me."

Mr. A. B. Eddy sang a fine tenor solo, "*Behold the Lilies
of the Valley*," which was admirably rendered, and loudly
applauded.

The president stated that he had received by the same
mail two letters, one from Samuel Eddy of Auburn, N.Y.,
and another from Samuel Eddy of Auburn, Mass.   The
last-named was aged eighty-four, and he hoped to be able
to be present to-day.   Not finding this patriarch among the
audience, I will request the secretary to read a few verses
forwarded to us by his daughter, Mrs. Ellen A. Eddy Pond
of New York City : —

> " To my good Irish girl I said,
>   Of those old Pilgrims who are dead,
>   ' Just five times fifty years ago
>   They landed here 'mid ice and snow.'
>   She looked at me with quizzical air —
>   ' An' sure,' said she, ' Will they be there?'
>
>   And then *I* fell to wondering too
>   If they would here appear to view,
>   And felt assured that we should see
>   Them, reproduced, in you and me.
>   Their virtues here you'll surely find,
>   Their strength of body and of mind ;
>   And if their vices too have come,
>   On that grave subject we are dumb.
>   Their eyes and noses, lips and chins,
>   Their stature tall, their ruddy skins,
>   They all are here without a doubt. —
>   You only have to find them out.

Then rightly join them all in one,
And you shall see the pilgrim John ;
Or else — I'm sure I cannot tell —
Perhaps it may be Samuel,
Or Benjamin, we greet them all,
And every Eddy, great and small.
Dangerous Eddys too they are,
The men so brave, the maids so fair,
To those who hate, and those who love,
And those who would their valor prove.
The time is short, we must away,
But hope to meet another day,
With Samuel, and Ben, and John,
In that 'sweet home,' where they have gone.
Then for a blest reunion there,
Let every Eddy's son prepare."

The Connecticut Eddys, who had been delayed by an accident on the railroad, entered the hall, and were received with a round of applause.

Subsequently James H. Eddy, Esq., of New Britain, made a brief reference to the genealogy of his branch of the family which he had never been able to trace back to either John or Samuel, and hoped to obtain the information.

Semun Eddy of Lenox, N.Y., said : —

" My interest in this festival may be inferred from the fact that when I heard incidentally, for the first time, that a meeting of the Eddys was this day to be holden in this city, I immediately dropped all engagements, and without any delay have travelled night and day ever since, and did not arrive till a considerable portion of the exercises were over.

" I cannot trace my ancestry beyond my grandfather, and I shall be very grateful for further information. My grandfather, Reuben Eddy, came from the west side of the Green Mountains in Vermont. By occupation he was a farmer. He married the widow Aelsworth, and had three children, William, Lydia, and Rhoda. While my grandfather was living in Vermont he had his only cow driven off to pay the Priest Tax. In 1795 he moved to Whitestown, near Utica, N.Y., and from thence to Casenovia, where he died. My family are now living in Lenox, Madison County, N.Y., in the village of Wanesville. If any one here present can trace my genealogy further back, I shall be glad of the information."

This announcement created a general interest, as this seemed to be a lost tribe, while nearly all others could trace their genealogy accurately.

Isaac S. Battey of Providence announced himself as the descendant of William Eddy of this city, who was of the fifth generation from William Eddye, Vicar of St. Dunstan's in England. He said: —

" By the record which I have made, I find that my grandfather, who was born July 26, 1751, had eleven children, sixty-one grandchildren, one hundred and thirty-two great-grandchildren, one hundred and twenty of the fourth generation, and two of the fifth, making three hundred and twenty-six.

" It is a fact worth recording on this occasion, that Margaret S. Eddy, the youngest daughter of William, in the year 1817, at their homestead still standing on Eddy Street, gathered the first Sunday-school in this vicinity, and perhaps in the United States. It was subsequently transferred to the Beneficent Congregational Church."

Dr. William Pratt of Eddyville, the Secretary, read a poem descriptive of an imaginary conversation supposed to have occurred between John and Samuel Eddy and other members of the family, concerning their proposed emigration, which was well received and applauded. The doctor, however, for some reasons best known to himself, declines to furnish a copy.

On motion it was voted, That the thanks of this assemblage be presented to the Rev. Dr. Zachary Eddy for his instructive and entertaining address, and to Miss Alice Maud Eddy for her graceful poem, and that they be requested to furnish copies for publication.

On motion it was further voted, That the thanks of this assemblage be tendered to the committee who made the necessary arrangements for this festival, and that they continue in charge of the publication of the record of the proceedings of this meeting.

On motion it was voted, That the Rev. Edwin B. Eddy of Providence be requested to put into words the thanks of the family to James Eddy, Esq., for his hospitality; and that gentleman responded felicitously, but declines to furnish to this committee the remarks which he made.

Loud calls for Mr. James Eddy elicited the following response : —

"The last speaker has kindly alluded to this as being an appropriate locality for this gathering of the Eddy descendants of our Pilgrim fathers, as also to the simple collation which it has been my privilege to furnish on this pleasant occasion, and I feel honored and gratified for the unanimous vote of thanks which you have just kindly paid me.

"Allow me to make a few remarks personal to myself and my immediate family. My father, Benjamin, singularly enough descended directly through four Zachariahs of four families, beginning with Zachariah the son of Samuel the Pilgrim ; there was also a child named Zachariah among my father's brothers, through whom no doubt I ought to have descended, but unfortunately he died young, so the Zachariah in my own immediate line was wanting, but to compensate I had two brothers named Zachariah, both dying young.

"Being the eleventh child out of twelve children, a natural modesty with which I have always been afflicted would prevent my taking precedence of them in speaking on this occasion. But my parents have both passed away, and I am now the only remaining child left out of the twelve children my mother bore.

"There is one trait of character in the Eddy family which seems to have been ingrained in their mental constitutions, and that is a profound devotional feeling. Through all the descendants from our venerated ancestor William Eddye down to the present assemblage, this religious trait of character has been conspicuous, and I believe it has always been united with a kindly charitable feeling towards those who honestly differed from them in religious views and creeds. Who ever heard of a member of the Eddy family assisting in the hanging of the so-called witches, or proving the truth of any special creed by cutting off the ears of the poor Quakers? We should all feel proud that whilst our family have dignified themselves by the exercise of a sincere religious sentiment, our ancestors, no matter to what religious sect they may have joined themselves, have never been debased and disgraced by a superstition and bigotry leading to cruelty towards those honestly differing from themselves.

"May all bearing the name of Eddy in the future preserve the high moral and religious standing of our family."

On motion it was voted, That R. H. Eddy, Esq., of Boston, Mass., be elected permanent secretary and genealogist of the family; and that all additional information that may be hereafter acquired be communicated to him for preservation.

On account of the approach of evening some communications intended to have been read were necessarily omitted.

The exercises were therefore brought to a close by the company uniting in singing "*Auld Lang Syne.*"

Should auld acquaintance be forgot,
   And never brought to mind ;
Should auld acquaintance be forgot,
   And songs of auld lang syne.
For auld lang syne we meet to-day,
   For auld lang syne ;
To sing the songs our fathers sang
   In days of auld lang syne.

We've passed through many varied scenes,
   Since youth's unclouded day ;
And friends, and hopes, and happy dreams,
   Time's hand hath swept away.
And voices that once joined with ours,
   In days of auld lang syne,
Are silent now, and blend no more
   In songs of auld lang syne.

Here we have met, here we may part,
   To meet on earth no more ;
And we may never sing again
   The cherished songs of yore :
The sacred songs our fathers sang,
   In days of auld lang syne ;
We may not meet to sing again
   The songs of auld lang syne.

But when we've crossed the sea of life,
   And reached the heav'nly shore,
We'll sing the songs our fathers sing,
   Transcending those of yore.
We'll meet to sing diviner strains
   Than those of auld lang syne ;
Immortal songs of praise, unknown
   In days of auld lang syne.

There were social gatherings in the evening at the houses of James Eddy, John Eddy, John H. Eddy, and others.

The committee would here express the obligations they are under to their English cousins for the interest they have taken in this celebration, and for the kindly sentiments expressed in our behalf in their letters; viz.: —

To Rev. Charles Eddy, Rector of Elworthy; John Eddy, Esq., of Rome, Italy; Rev. and Mrs. George Tompkins of Branscomb, Devonshire; Rev. and Mrs. Peter Lilly of Collaton, South Devonshire; Rev. and Mrs. Thomas Beeman of South Kensington, London; and to Mrs. Dr. Charles Walter Eddy of London.

JOHN EDDY,
JAMES EDDY, } *Committee.*
THOMAS F. EDDY,

WILLIAM PRATT, *Secretary.*   JOHN EDDY, *President.*

GENEALOGICAL MEMOIR

OF

Rev. William Eddye, A.M.

[*Vicar of the Parish of Cranbrook, England,
from 1589 to 1616*]

AND HIS

AMERICAN. DESCENDANTS,

BY

ROBERT HENRY EDDY

OF BOSTON, MASS.

1881.

"Our fathers, Lord, to seek a spot
  Where they might kneel to thee,
Their own fair heritage forgot,
  And braved an unknown sea;
Here found their pilgrim souls repose,
  Where long the heathen roved;
And here their humble anthems rose
  To bless the Power they loved.
They sleep in dust! — but where they trod,
  A feeble, fainting band,
Glad millions catch the strain, O God!
  And sound it through the land."

INTRODUCTION.

[According to Ferguson's work on English Surnames, that of *Eddy* is derived from the Anglo-Saxon, *Edda* and *Eadig*, or *Eddi*, formed from *ead — prosperity*.]

In the preparation of this work the author deems it necessary to state that it has been compiled principally from a manuscript volume written by his late father, Caleb Eddy, Esq., who for the most of his life was a resident of the City of Boston; and for several years prior to his death devoted much time in obtaining data relating to the genealogy of the Eddys of this country.

Soon after the decease of Mr. Eddy, his son visited Cranbrook, England, and made efforts to obtain information as to the ancestry of the Vicar, William Eddye. He has since pursued his inquiries, but thus far has been unsuccessful in discovering even the names of the parents of the Vicar. He hopes yet to get some trace of them, and, at a future period, to present such, with other matters of interest, in a supplement hereto. It is believed that this genealogy, so far as it goes, is generally correct; although owing to the great difficulty of obtaining genealogical information, and the occasional inaccuracy of public and private records, there will, undoubtedly, be errors discovered in it, as in most works of the kind. Though incomplete in accounts of some of the recent generations, it will serve as a key to enable almost any person bearing the name of Eddy to ascertain his ancestry. A late writer states : —

"A desire to trace a lineage, and to perpetuate its remembrance, seems to have been so prevalent among enlightened and civilized people and even among barbarians, of all ages, that it may be regarded as an instinct of human nature. When persons affect an utter indifference to their lineage, or a history of the past generations of their families, and deride any attention to them as a foolish weakness and vanity, they are contravening an innate principle ; and it may be generally suspected that they have some knowledge of a lineage which they would consign to oblivion because it is untitled and without a good renown."

The Eddys of this country, descendants of the Rev. William Eddye of Cranbrook, England, may justly feel proud of their "Genealogical Tree," whose trunk had piety, virtue, and intelligence for its roots, and whose branches have generally been fruitful in all that leads to worth and respectability, if not to great wealth and very exalted station.

The author has made considerable effort to obtain the "Armorial Bearings" of Eddy ; having sent therefor to the Herald's College of London. He has been informed that the arms are not to be found therein ; but, from the best authorities, the shield had upon it three old men's heads couped at the shoulders. One branch had three cross-croslets in the shield, with a cross-croslet and dagger salticrwise for the crest; the motto being "*Crux mihi grata quies.*"

As those only who were in the holy wars were entitled to have the cross in their armorial bearings, it is fair to presume that, as the Eddy family is a very ancient one (*Eady* being a surname found in "Domesday Book"), some, if not many of the race, like their descendants. manfully combatted against irreligion and infidelity ; and, having devoted the sword to the cross, found in the latter the grateful rest, as indicated by the above admirable motto.

R. H. E.

CRUX MIHI GRATA QUIES

Eddy

GENEALOGY.

EXPLANATION.

———◆———

IN the accompanying Genealogy paternal names are printed in ROMAN CAPITALS; the prefix to each, in parenthesis, denoting the number of the generation of the party. Two columns of numbers are placed in the left margin of each page, the right-hand column commencing with 1, opposite the first name of the genealogy. A number of the left column, opposite any number of the right column, refers the reader to that number, where other information may be found. If it be less than the number in the right column against which it stands, it will refer back to the parentage of the individual; if it be greater, it will refer forward to his marriage and distinct family.

In England and the Colonies the *Julian Calendar* was retained until 1752, when the *Gregorian Calendar*, or *New Style*, was adopted. In order therefore to make the dates previous to 1752 correspond in the solar year to the *New Style*, it is necessary to add 11 to dates of days between 1600 and 1700, and 12 to dates between 1700 and 1752. Thus the ship *Handmaid* arrived at Plymouth, Mass., on Oct. 29, 1630 (O. S.), to which, adding 11, would be Nov. 9, 1630 (N. S.)

ABBREVIATIONS. — b., *born;* d., *died;* m., *married;* dau., *daughter;* adm. f. c., *admitted to full communion.*

PARTICULAR NOTICE. — Any person who may discover any error in the accompanying Genealogy, or be possessed of any unpublished information relating to the ancestors or descendants of any individual mentioned therein, will confer a great favor on the author of this work by notifying him thereof.

GENEALOGY.

1. WILLIAM EDDYE, A.M., Vicar of the Church of St. Dunstan, of the town of Cranbrook, of the County of Kent, England. A native of Bristol, educated at Trinity College, Cambridge, England, and Vicar of Cranbrook from 1589 to 1616; m. Nov. 20, 1587, Mary Fosten (daughter of John Fosten, d. Sept., 1573), who d. July, 1611, leaving an infant, Nathaniel, who survived his mother 9 days. In 1614, Mr. Eddye m. Elizabeth Taylor (widow), and in the same year she had a daughter, Priscilla. On Nov. 23, 1616, he died, and was buried in Cranbrook Churchyard, but where therein is not known. He was a gentleman of much merit and order; a faithful clergyman to his parishioners.

LIKE GOLDSMITH'S "*Village Preacher.*"

"Unskilful he to fawn, or seek for power,
By doctrines fashioned to the varying hour;
Far other aims his heart had learn'd to prize,
More bent to *raise* the wretched, than to *rise.*
Thus to relieve the suffering was his pride,
And ev'n his failings lean'd to virtue's side:
But, in his duty, prompt at every call,
He watch'd and wept, he prayed, and felt for all;
And, as a bird, each fond endearment tries
To tempt its new-fledg'd offspring to the skies;
He try'd each art, reproved each dull delay,
Allured to brighter worlds, and *led* the way."

The financial affairs of the parish were, through his instrumentality, placed on a better footing than before, and all its loose Registers, dating back from 1588, were collected, arranged, and by him properly entered in a new parchment book. He beautifully engrossed about eighty of its pages, and illuminated three title-pages, — one for the Births, another for the Marriages, and a third for the Deaths. This book is now (1881) to be seen at the Vicarage.

The following is a fac-simile of his signature:

The church (dedicated to St. Dunstan) is a substantial, uniform building, and the most spacious within the Weald of Kent. It comprises a nave, side aisles, and chancel, with a square embattled tower at the west end containing a ring of eight bells and a set of musical chimes which play every third hour. The range of slender piers between the nave and the side aisles, and the width of the arches, give to the interior of the building a light and airy appearance, which is much improved by the windows in the louvre above the nave amounting to six on either side. From the corbel heads, immediately above the impost of the piers, rise small cluster shafts, finishing with other corbels; no doubt intended originally to carry the main ribs of the roof. In the church is a large baptismal font.

The town of Cranbrook was once the centre of the clothing trade which existed there for several centuries prior to 1774. The town was famous for its "strong, durable *broad-cloths*, of very good mixtures and colors." The trade was originally introduced through the policy of King Edward III., who, having witnessed while in Flanders the advantages of the manufacture, engaged a body of Flemings, by promises of great rewards and immunities, to teach the English the art of making "broad-cloths." So extensive did the business become that many persons or families acquired great riches by it, and several were ennobled. This trade has long since disappeared, and traffic in hops has become the chief business. The town (originally termed *Cranebrook*) probably derived its name from a small rivulet, called the "*Crane*," which flowed through the lower part of it.

Children:

		1	MARY, b. Sept., 1591.
5	2	2	PHINEAS, b. Sept., 1593.
6	3	3	JOHN, b. March, 1597.
		4	ELLEN, b. Aug., 1599.

5   ABIGAIL, b. Oct., 1601; d. May 20, 1687, in Charlestown, Mass., she m. John Benjamin, who arrived at Boston, Mass., Sept. 16, 1632, in the ship *Lion*, of Bristol, England, and settled in Watertown, Mass. He d. June 14, 1645. He appointed, in his will, dated two days before his death, "*my brother John Eddie of Watertown* and Thomas Marrett of Cambridge," executors. His widow, Abigail, went with her son-in-law to Charlestown about 1654. For the descendants of John Benjamin and Abigail Eddy his wife, see *Bond's History of Watertown*, 1855.

		6	ANNA, b. May, 1603.
120	4	7	SAMUEL, b. May, 1608.
		8	ELIZABETH, b. Dec., 1606.
		9	ZACHARIAS, b. March, 1610.

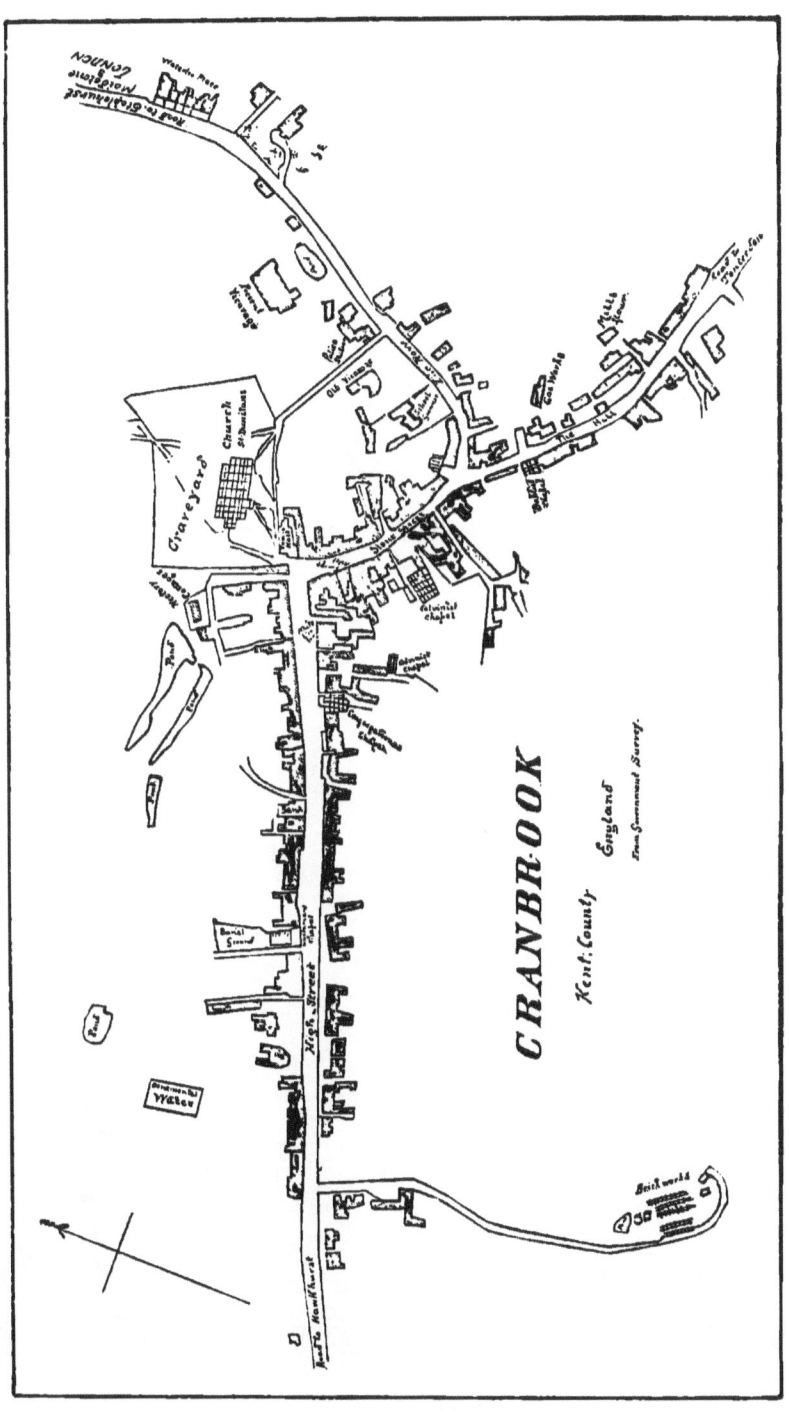

CRANBROOK

Kent County England

From Government Survey.

10   NATHANIEL, b. July, 1611.
11   PRISCILLA, b. ——, 1614.

2   5 (II.) PHINEAS EDDYE. Probably resident in Cranbrook. At
Easter, 1618, he was appointed one of four sidesmen;
1618, July 26, d. an unbaptized child of Phineas Eddye;
1619, Nov. 8, d. Peter Eddye, a youth.

3   6 (II.) JOHN EDDY, b. March, 1597; d. Oct. 12, 1684. He, with
his brother Samuel, left London for America, Aug. 10,
1630, in the ship *Handmaid*, John Grant, Master. Arrived at Plymouth, Mass., on Oct. 29, 1630. The ship was
twelve weeks at sea, spent all her masts, and of twenty-
eight cows lost ten. She had about sixty passengers.
John Eddy is believed to have previously resided in one
of the towns of Boxted, there being one in Suffolk and
another in Essex County, England. Also, that he and
his brother, soon after their arrival in Plymouth, viz., on
Nov. 11, 1630, went to Boston with Captain Grant and
Captain Standish, and visited Governor Winthrop, who
termed them "two gentlemen passengers." Prior to Feb. 6,
1631-2, John Eddy settled in Watertown, Mass.; was admitted freeman Sept. 3, 1634. Selectman, 1635, 1636, and
1637. d. Oct. 12, 1684. He applied to Court, Dec. 15, 1673
(then seventy-six years old), to be excused from training!
He had a temporary attack of insanity in March, 1633.
He had two wives: (1st) Amy, the mother of his children,
and (2d) Joanna, who d. Aug. 25, 1683, aged eighty.
Some of his children b. before he came to Watertown.
His will, dated Jan. 11, 1677-8, proved Dec. 16, 1684, mentions two sons, Samuel and John: and four daughters, Mary
Orton, Sarah Marion, Pilgrim Steadman, and Ruth Gardi-
ner. Inventory, Dec. 9, 1684, £216.

Children:
1   PILGRIM, b. Aug. 25, 1634; d. young.
7   2   PILGRIM, b. in Watertown, Mass., m. Baker, April 22,
1656. She had one son, Nathaniel, a baker, 1694, in Boston. Second husband, Steadman.
10   8   3   JOHN, b. Feb. 16, 1636; d. 1694.
11   9   4   SAMUEL, b. Sept. 30, 1640; d. Nov. 22, 1711.
5   ABIGAL, b. Oct. 11, 1643.
6   MARY, m. Thos. Orton of Charlestown; her dau. Mary
was wife of Samuel Pierce of Boston prior to 1703.
7   SARAH, m. John Marion, a shoemaker in Watertown,
Mass.; admitted freeman 1652; removed to Boston, and
became a selectman in 1693. He d. Jan. 7, 1785, aged 76.

Children:
1 *Mary*, b. 1640; d. Jan. 24, 1642.
2 *John*, "member Artillery Co., 1691"; b. May 12, 1643; resided in Cambridge. Afterwards removed to Boston, Mass., and m. Ann Harrison. He was deacon of the church, and selectman in 1698. His children were:

1 *John*, b. May 30, 1683; d. young.
2 *John*, b. Aug. 17, 1684; d. young.
3 *Joseph*, b. Aug. 10, 1686.
4 *John*, b. Aug. 29, 1687; d. young.
5 *John*, b. June 28, 1689.

3 *Isaac*, b. Jan. 20, 1653.
4 *Samuel*, b. 1655; "member Artillery Co., 1690." His first wife, named Hannah, d. 1688; his second, Mary. He resided in Boston, and had children:

1 *John*, b. Dec. 25, 1681; d. young.
2 *Hannah*, b. June 23, 1685.
3 *Mary*, b. June 18, 1687.
4 *Samuel*, b. June 8, 1689.
5 *Catharine*, b. Sept. 15, 1690.
6 *Edward*, b. Dec. 2, 1692.
7 *Isaac*, b. March 8, 1694.
8 *Elizabeth*, b. Nov. 21, 1695.
9 *Joseph*, b. Dec. 18, 1698; d. young.
10 *Joanna*, b. May 10, 1701.
11 *John*, b. April 5, 1703.
12 *Joseph*, b. July 22, 1705.

8 RUTH, m. Ezekiel Gardiner of Boston.
9 BENJAMIN, buried 1639.

---

8 10 (III.) JOHN EDDY, m. Sarah Woodward July 6, 1693. He died 1694. Selectman, 1671.

---

9 11 (III.) SAMUEL EDDY of Watertown, Mass., b. Sept. 30, 1640; d. Nov. 22, 1711; m., Nov., 1664, to Sarah Meade. Admitted freeman March 22, 1689–90; tithingman, 1693; sealer of leather, 1702–11. Will dated Aug. 6, 1702; proved Dec. 30, 1711. Inventory, £212.

Children:
14 12 1 SAMUEL, b. June 4, 1668; adm. f. c. Dec. 12, 1697; m., Dec. 13, 1693, Elizabeth Woodward.
2 SARAH, b. Oct. 31, 1670; adm. f. c. Aug. 3, 1690; m., Nov. 15, 1699, Thomas Coolidge.
26 13 3 BENJAMIN, b. Sept. 16, 1673.

4   DELIVERANCE, b. July 15, 1676; adm. f. c. Aug. 17, 1701; m., 1719, William Webb.

5   ELIZABETH, b. Feb. 2, 1578-9; m., April 2, 1700, Ebenezer Allen.

6   RUTH, b. Nov. 3, 1681; m., Nov. 15, 1699, Jonathan Stone. She died Oct. 13, 1702, leaving son, Jonathan, b. 1702.

7   JOANNA, b. April 24, 1685; m., Dec. 14, 1720, Thomas Fillebrown.

---

12 14 (IV.) SAMUEL EDDY of Watertown, b. June 14, 1668; m., Dec. 13, 1693, Elizabeth Woodward; adm. f. c. Dec. 12, 1697; 1718, sealer of leather to 1722.

Children:

19 15   1   JOHN, b. May 6, 1696.

        2   ELIZABETH, b. July 28, 1697.

        3   SARAH, b. May 9, 1700; m., June 11, 1730, Peter Hurd.

61 16   4   SAMUEL, b. Aug. 14, 1701.

        5   ELIZABETH, b. July 29, 1703.

90 17   6   EBENEZER, b. June 9, 1704-5 (?), of Oxford; m. Ruth Ward.

107 18   7   BENJAMIN, b. Nov. 30, 1707. Settled in Newton, Mass., and by his wife, Elizabeth (?) Ward, had four sons and four daughters between 1734 and 1748.

---

15 19 (IV.) JOHN EDDY, b. May 6, 1696, baptized in Old Cambridge, and was one of the earliest settlers in Oxford; d. in Oxford. Will dated Jan. 21, 1762; approved April 20, 1762.

Children:

21 20   1   JOHN, b. Feb. 28, 1726, in Oxford.

        2   JOSIAH, b. Nov. 13, 1728.

        3   BENJAMIN, b. Feb. 11, 1731.

        4   HESEKIAH, b. Aug. 17, 1735.

        5   MARY, b. May 28, 1738.

        6   ESTHER, b. Jan. 15, 1742.

        7   MARY, b. April, 1746.

---

20 21 (V.) JOHN EDDY of Oxford, Mass.

Children:

24 22   1   JOSIAH, b. Feb. 25, 1747, Deerfield, Mass.

        2   EDMUND, b. April 16, 1749, Charlton.

        3   JOHN, b. June 23, 1751.

25 23   4   EDMUND, b. in Charlton, 1753; was a soldier in the Revolution, in the company of Captain Nathaniel Healy; enlisted April 29, 1775; served eight months.

22 24 (VI.) JOSIAH EDDY lived in Southbridge, Mass.; d. previous to April 6, 1824. He served in the Revolutionary War, in Captain Josiah Stebbin's Company, Colonel Brewer's Regiment.

---

23 25 (VI.) EDMUND EDDY of Charlton, Mass. (Dexter Blood administered will of Edmund Eddy, Dec. 3, 1839.)

Child:
SAMUEL.

---

13 26 (IV.) BENJAMIN EDDY of Oxford, Mass., b. Sept. 16, 1678; d. previous to 1728. First wife, Abigal Holden, m. Dec. 7, 1707; she d. Nov. 9, 1714. Second wife, Grace Holden. Third wife, Elizabeth Phillips.

Children:
28 27   1   WILLIAM, b. Feb. 5, 1725; d. March 16, 1805.
        2   ELIZABETH, b. Nov. 13, 1719.
        3   GRACE, b. Oct. 24, 1714; m. Isaac Stockwell.
        4   JONATHAN, b. Aug. 6, 1717; d. before 1729.
        5   JONAS, b. March 20, 1721.

---

27 28 (V.) WILLIAM EDDY, b. Feb. 5, 1725; d. March 16, 1805: was a private in Captain Benson's Company, Colonel Putnam's Regiment.

Children:
33 29   1   JAMES, b. Nov. 10, 1749.
42 30   2   SILAS, b. Sept. 1, 1749.
49 31   3   REUBEN, b. May 20, 1751.
        4   PERSIS, b. Sept. 18, 1753.
        5   BENJAMIN, b. July 28, 1756.
        6   LYDIA, b. Oct. 7, 1758.
        7   WILLIAM, b. Feb. 15, 1761.
56 32   8   PARLEY, b. Aug. 14, 1763.
        9   SARAH, b. May 20, 1766.
        10 RACHAEL, b. Nov. 7, 1769.

---

29 33 (VI.) JONAS EDDY, b. Nov. 10, 1747; d. Dec. 10, 1825. Lived at Oxford, Worcester County, Mass.

Children:
        1   SARAH.
37 34   2   WILLIAM, b. July 30, 1773.
40 35   3   ALPHEUS, b. Oct. 2, 1775.
41 36   4   JONAS, b. June 19, 1778.

5 REUBEN.
6 RUFUS, b. Oct. 20, 1781.
7 LUCY.

---

34 37 (VII.) WILLIAM EDDY, b. July 30, 1773; m. Hannah Burnap, Dec. 18, 1797. He died June 9, 1817; lived in Orange, Cuyahoga County, Ohio.

Child:
39 38 1 CYRUS EDDY, b. June 18, 1809.

---

38 39 (VIII.) CYRUS EDDY, b. June 18, 1804; m. Louisa Rawley, April 4, 1829. Lived at Orange, Ohio, in 1846, having moved there from Illinois, where he resided in 1842.

Children:
1 WILLIAM MARCELLUS, b. Sept. 3, 1838.
2 CYRUS ORSON, b. Dec. 8, 1840.

---

35 40 (VII.) ALPHEUS EDDY, b., Oxford, Mass., Oct. 2, 1775.

Children:
1 JOHN FISK, b. Oct. 19, 1819.
2 FRANCIS FAIRBANKS, b. May 3, 1817.
3 DAVID FISK, b. June, 1821.

---

36 41 (VII.) JONAS EDDY, b. June 19, 1778. Betsey Eddy of Oxford, Mass., administratrix of Jonas Eddy, late of Worcester, Nov. 10, 1832. Worcester Probate Records.

---

30 42 (VI.) SILAS EDDY, Oxford, Mass., b. Sept. 1, 1749; d. Aug. 31, 1807. His son, Benjamin, his executor, Oct. 6, 1807

Children:
1 STANTON, b. Feb. 29, 1776.
46 43 2 BENJAMIN, b. April 13, 1782; d. Oct. 31, 1826.
3 WILLIAM, b. July 23, 1784.
47 44 4 SILAS, b. May 3, 1792.
48 45 5 JOTHAM, b. Jan. 5, 1795.

---

43 46 (VII.) BENJAMIN EDDY, b. April 13, 1782; d. Oct. 31, 1826.

Child:
LUCINDA (of Southbridge, Mass.), married.

---

44 47 (VII.) SILAS EDDY, Oxford, Mass., b. May 3, 1792.

Children:
1 HARVIN TOWNE, b. Oct. 24, 1815.

    2　DELANO PIERCE, b. July 22. 1818.
    3　NATHANIEL LAW, b. July 20, 1821.

---

45 48 (VII.) JOTHAM EDDY, b. Jan. 5, 1795; resided in Webster, Mass.

    Children:
    1　LORING, b. Dec. 28, 1824.
    2　RUFUS BENJAMIN, b. Dec. 30, 1827.

---

31 49 (VI.) REUBEN EDDY, b. May 20, 1751; d. Oct. 3, 1813.

    Children:
    1　LUCRETIA.　　2　LAVINIA.　　3　BETSEY.
53 50　　 4　JOEL, b. Oct. 12, 1786.
54 51　　 5　DANIEL P., b. Aug. 17, 1788.
55 52　　 6　LEONARD, b. Oct. 30, 1793; d. Oct 24, 1825, at Oxford.
    7　POLLY.　　8　RACHAEL.

---

50 53 (VII.) JOEL EDDY, Oxford, Mass., b. Oct. 12, 1786.

    Children:
    1　REUBEN, b. Dec. 7, 1811.
    2　EMERSON, b. June 2, 1815.
    3　NATHANIEL, b. Oct. 27, 1818.

---

51 54 (VII.) DANIEL P. EDDY, b. Aug. 17, 1788; lived in Worcester, Mass.

    Children:
    1　CHARLES, b. Nov. 4, 1823.
    2　HORACE, b. May 19, 1825.
    3　JAMES, b. June 24, 1830.
    4　JOHN.
    5　ALDEN.

---

52 55 (VII.) LEONARD EDDY, b. Oct. 30, 1793; d. Oct. 24, 1825, at Oxford, Mass. Joel Eddy, administrator, Nov. 1, 1825.

---

32 56 (VI.) PARLEY EDDY, b. Aug. 14, 1763; d. Dec. 13, 1813.

    Children:
59 57　　 1　PARLEY, b. March 29, 1790.
60 58　　 2　RUFUS, b. Oct. 29, 1797.
    Several daughters.

---

57 59 (VII.) PARLEY EDDY, b. March 29, 1790; d. April, 1841.

    Child:
    RUFUS MERRIAM, b. Nov. 8, 1820.

58 60 (VII.) RUFUS EDDY, b. Oct 29, 1770; living in Oxford, 1840.

Children:
1 HENRY, b. Feb. 2, 1833.
2 ADDISON. b. Feb. 26, 1840.

16 61 (V.) SAMUEL EDDY, b. in Watertown, Aug. 14, 1701; m. Ruth Ward; went in 1726 to and d. in Oxford, Mass., in 1762.

Children:
64 62   1 SAMUEL, b. 1732; d. 1798.
78 63   2 LEVI, b. 1745.
      3 JOHN, d. in Army. French and Indian War.

> NOTE. — Samuel Eddy went to Oxford about 1720. He lived in a cabin. One evening he found a rattlesnake had taken possession of his bed during his absence, and had to be ejected before Mr. Eddy could retire.

62 64 (VI.) SAMUEL EDDY, b. 1732; d. 1798. He lived on the farm of his father, in Oxford, and kept a public house during the war of the Revolution. He represented the town of Auburn (then Ward) in the General Court about 1787.

Children:
68 65   1 SAMUEL, d. May 11, 1813, aged 48.
88 66   2 JOHN.
89 67   3 RUFUS.

65 68 (VII.) SAMUEL EDDY, d. May 11, 1813; aged 48. He lived upon land cleared by his great grandfather of rattlesnake memory.

Children:
73 69   1 JAMES, living at Auburn in 1840.
75 70   2 SAMUEL, living at Auburn in 1840; 43 years old in 1840.
76 71   3 LEWIS, living at Auburn in 1840.
77 72   4 LEONARD, living at Leicester, Mass., 1840.
      5 LYDIA, b. in Oxford, Mass.; m. Daniel P. Eddy, Oct., 1815. (He was son of Reuben and Mary Eddy of Oxford.) They resided in Providence, R.I.

      Children:
      1 *Sarah*, b. Sept., 1818.
      2 *Harriet*, b. Oct., 1816.
      3 *Charles*, b. Nov., 1825.
      4 *James*, b. Aug., 1822; d. 1827.
      5 *Horace*, b. May, 1828; d. Dec., 1847.
      6 *James*, b. June, 1830.

    7 *John F.*, b. Aug., 1833.

    8 *Alden II.*, b. Oct., 1837.

6 SARAH, m. Thomas Baird in Auburn, Mass.; m., second, Swan Knowlton.

    Children by Baird, first husband:

    1 *Samuel.*

    2 *Jane.*

    3 *Thomas.*

    Children by Knowlton, second husband:

    4 *Sarah.*

    5 *Nathan.*

    6 *Maria.*

    7 SUSAN.

    8 MARY, m. W. T. Warren; lives in Holden, Mass.

        Children:

        1 *Ann Eliza*, m. Rev. Lester Williams; lives in Springfield, Mass.

            Child:

            1 *Waterman.*

        2 *Susan Ellis.*

        3 *Samuel.*

        4 *Bertha.*

        5 *Henry W.*

---

69 73 (VIII.) JAMES EDDY, living at Auburn, Mass., 1840; administrator of Daniel Eddy, late of Ward, April 17, 1826.

    Children:

    1 MARTHA.

    2 GEORGE.

    3 JAMES.

---

70 75 (VIII.) SAMUEL EDDY, resides 1881, on the homestead of his father. He was b. July 19, 1796.

    Children:

    1 SARAH CAROLINE, m., Sept. 10, 1845, John Warren of Auburn.

        Children:

        1 *John F.*

        2 *Jonah Goulding.*

        3 *Richard Henry*, m. Ella Taft; live in Auburn.

            Child:

            1 *Robert.*

4 *Rhoda C.*
5 *Waterman.*
6 *Anna M.*
7 *Frank E.*

2 RHODA MARIA, m. Rev. Isaac N. Hobart in Chicago, Ill.

Children:
1 *Charles Henry.*
2 *Eddy Harris.*
3 *Martha M.*
4 *Caroline.*
5 *Nellie M.*

3 SAMUEL, m. Hannah A. Barrett of Barre, Mass.; m., second, Clara H. Walker.

Children by first wife:
1 *Sarah Brown*, m. Harry A. Milliken of Boston, Mass.

Children:
1 *Harry Eugene.*
2 *Edith.*

2 *Nellie M.*, m. Samuel F. Brewer of West Newton, Mass.
3 *Samuel B.*, b. July 4, 1858; m., Feb. 16, 1881, Emma J. Newton of West Boylston, Mass. Resides at the old homestead in Auburn, Mass.

Children by second wife:
4 *Anna.*
5 *May Huxley.*
6 *George W.*
7 *Everett S.*
8 *Edith.*

4 MARY STONE.
5 ELLEN AUGUSTA.
6 LAURA SOPHIA, m. George Warren; lives in Newton Centre, Mass.

Children:
1 *Fanny.*
2 *Grace Augusta.*
3 *George Eddy.*
4 *Alice.*

---

71 76 (VIII.) LEWIS EDDY, Auburn, Mass., 1840, m. Almira Smith of Auburn, Mass.

Children:

1 HENRY WILLIAM, b. Oct. 17, 1826; lives in Worcester, Mass.

    Children:
    1 *Frank.*
    2 *Charles.*

2 SAMUEL SMITH, b. April 27, 1838; lives in Rochester, N. Y.
    Child:
    1 *Flora.*

3 LEWIS MITLON, b. June 9, 1834.
4 LUCIAN ALPHONSO, b. May 5, 1841.
5 ELIZA.   6 AMELIA.   7 EMILY.
8 MARY.   9 ALBERT.   10 THEODORE.

---

72 77 (VIII.) LEONARD EDDY, Leicester, Mass., 1840; m. Lucretia Stone; m., second, Isabella Newton.

Children:
1 LUCY, b. 1837, only child by first wife.
2 WILLIAM.   3 ELIZA.   4 FRANK. ⅄
5 LUCRETIA.   6 AUSTIN.

---

63 78 (VI.) LEVI EDDY, b. 1745; d. at Oxford (near Auburn), Mass., May 6, 1821, aged 76; m. Sarah Smith; second, Mary Pratt.

    Children by first wife:
83 79   1 DAVID.
86 80   2 LEVI.
        3 LIPPITT.
        4 ABAGAIL.
        5 BETSEY.

    Children by second wife:
        6 AMOS, m. Annie Stone of Oxford, Mass.

        Children:
        1 *Emerson.*
        2 *Sarah.*
        3 *Mary.*
        4 *Emery*, m. ——
            Child:
            1 *Annie.*

        7 ARTEMUS.
87 81   8 JESSE.
   82   9 AMASA, m. Damaris Newton.

10 ISAAC.
11 POLLY.
12 HARVEY PRATT, d. 1867; m. Margaret Cole of Sutton, Mass.

Children:
1 *Harriet Ann*, m. Andrew J. Copp of Oxford, Mass.; lived in Grafton, Mass.

Children:
1 *William*, graduated at Yale College, 1869; is a lawyer in New York City (1880); m. Emily Maltby of New Haven, Ct.

Children:
1 *William Maltby.*
2 *Ethel.*

2 *Andrew J.*, graduated at Yale College, 1869; lives in Millerton, N.Y.; m. Carrie Bostwick of Salisbury, Ct.

Child:
1 *Eddy B.*

3 *Anna*, d. young.

2 *Adeline*, m. —— Gardner.

Children:
1 *Charles.* 2 *Harriet.* 3 *Asby.*

---

79 83 (VII.) DAVID EDDY, m. Lydia Hawkins, and had seven sons and two daughters, most of whom d. young.

Children:
1 MARCIA, b. about 1792
2 ADALINE, m. Hubbell; living in 1848.
3 LEANDER, d.
4 STEPHEN, d.
85 84   5 GEORGE R., b. 1803.

---

84 85 (VIII.) GEORGE RODNEY EDDY, b. Nov. 19, 1800, in Peterboro', N.H.; m., 1834, Mary Sawtelle; b. 1796 in Jaffrey, N.H. They lived in Charlestown, Mass., 1878. He held the office of Deputy Warden of State Prison.

Children:
1 MERCY.
2 CAROLINE.
3 REBECCA M., b. Dec. 19, 1836.
4 GEORGE W., b. May 13, 1839.

80 86 (VII.) LEVI EDDY was a physician, and a highly respected gentleman.

Child:
1 EMELINE, b. Aug. 6, 1812; m., April 18, 1833, Daniel M. Salisbury; b. March 25, 1808.

Children:
1 *Ellen L.*, b. April 16, 1836; m., Aug. 26, 1851, —— Fitz.

Children:
1 *William E.*, b. June 19, 1858.
2 *Arthur S.*, b. March 24, 1860.
3 *Eddy E.*, b. Aug. 23, 1862.
4 *Howard W.*, b. March 6, 1866.
5 *Emeline E.*, b. Aug. 2, 1876.

2 *Levi E.*, b. Dec. 25, 1841; m. ——

Children:
1 *Louisa E.*, b. April 5, 1871.
2 *Alice Frances*, b. Oct. 26, 1875.

---

81 87 (VII.) JESSE EDDY, Auburn, 1840, m. —— Pitts of Auburn, Mass.

Children:
1 HIRAM, b. Sept. 25, 1808; d. Sept. 9, 1819; fell into a coal pit and was nearly consumed.
2 ELIPHALET, b. Oct 12, 1810.
3 HORACE, b. March 14, 1812.
4 LEVI, b. Oct. 11, 1817; m. Eliza Eddy, dau. of Lewis Eddy.

Children:
1 *Albert*, d. at Yale College; was in class of 1871.
2 *Arthur*.
3 *A daughter*, d. young.

5 ELIZA, m. Wright Merriam of North Oxford, Mass.

Children:
1 *Irving*.
2 *Frank*.

---

66 88 (VII.) JOHN EDDY, d. in Rutland, N.Y., in 1839, aged 72.

Children:
1 JOHN, living in 1840 in Rutland, N.Y.
2 REUBEN, living in 1840 in Champion, N.Y.

67 89 (VII.) RUFUS EDDY, aged 71 in 1840, and was then living in New Salem or Petersham, Mass.

Child:

1 RUFUS, who, in 1840, lived in New Salem or Petersham, Mass.

---

17 90 (V.) EBENEZER EDDY, b. in Watertown, Mass., Jan. 9, 1704; d. at Oxford (now Auburn), Mass., 1767; m. Ruth Ward.

Children:

93 91 1 THOMAS, b. March 15, 1738; lived in Warwick.
94 92 2 ABEL, b. April 19, 1741; lived in Belchertown.
      3 ENOCH, b. Nov. 5, 1748.
      4 RUTH.
      5 EUNICE.

---

91 93 (VI.) THOMAS EDDY, b. March 15, 1738; removed to Warwick.

Children:

1 JOHN, b. May 4, 1764.
2 EBENEZER, b. March 24. 1770.
Five daughters.

---

92 94 (VI.) ABEL EDDY, b. April 19, 1741; went from Oxford to Warwick about 1770.

Children:

99 95 1 EBENEZER, went to Eaton, N.Y.
100 96 2 ABIJAH.
      3 BENJAMIN, d. in Eaton; was a drum-major in the war of 1812.
105 97 4 ASA.
106 98 5 PHINEAS WARD.
      6 WARNER.   7 EZRA.   8 LUCY.   9 JOHN.

---

95 99 (VII.) EBENEZER EDDY. Belchertown, Mass.

Children:

1 WASHINGTON.
2 WARNER, farmer in 1840 in Eaton, N.Y.
3 EBENEZER, farmer in 1840 in Eaton, N.Y.
4 JESSE.
5 ABEL, boatman on Erie Canal.
6 GEORGE.
7 JOHN.

96 100 (VII.) ABIJAH EDDY, b. in Belchertown, June 1, 1776; m. Beulah Cheney, in Orange, Mass., June 2, 1801. She was b. in Orange, Jan. 26, 1784, and d. April 3, 1853. He d. in Warwick, Mass., March 23, 1836.

Children:

103 101 1 ERASTUS, b. June 16, 1802, in Warwick.
104 102 2 ABIJAH, b. Aug. 6, 1807; d. Nov. 25, 1880, at Somerville, Mass.
       3 BEULAH, b. Dec. 11, 1803; d. Feb. 13, 1872; m. Otis Brooks, Feb. 16, 1830. Lived in Warwick, Mass. He d. June 5, 1872.

    Children:
    1 *Caroline S.*, b. Jan. 16, 1831; d. June 9, 1831.
    2 *Gratia Elmira*, b. June 14, 1832, in Orange, Mass.; m., Oct. 14, 1851, Elias Skinner, in Petersham, Mass. He b. in North Dana, Aug. 2, 1828. Reside in Grand Rapids, Mich.

      Children:
      1 *Clarence W.*, b. 1853; d. Oct. 11, 1864.
      2 *Mary Lillien*, b. Dec. 21, 1857.
      3 *Martha A.*, b. Jan. 22, 1860.
      4 *Charles Otis*, b. Dec. 11, 1862.
      5 *Merick Eddy*, b. March 14, 1865; d. Nov. 6, 1870.
      6 *Wilfred Henry*, b. Feb. 29, 1868.

    3 *Frances Maria*, b. July 6, 1834; m. Henry G. Mallard in Orange, Mass., March 15, 1854. He is dead, 1881. She resides in Grand Rapids, Mich.

      Children:
      1 *Sarah Yetta*, b. June 6, 1856.
      2 *Henrietta L.*, b. March 28, 1859.

    4 *Henry Coleman*, b. April 12, 1836; m. Irene C. Putnam in Orange, Mass., June 8, 1857. Resides, 1880, in Denver, Col.

      Children:
      1 *Stella I.*, b. Aug. 23, 1862.
      2 *Henry Coleman*, b. Jan 29, 1871.
      3 *Nathaniel Cheney*, b. April 10, 1873.

    5 *Abijah Eddy*, b. Aug. 16, 1842; m., June 2, 1869, in Orange, Mass., Julia E. Ward. Resides in Grand Rapids, Mich., 1880.

      Children:
      1 *Sarah H.*, b. May 11, 1870.
      2 *Marcus Dearborn*, b. June 10, 1873.

4 EBENEZER CHENEY, b. Nov. 9, 1809, in Warwick, Mass.;
   m. Margaret Ann Gale of Shoreham, Vt., Sept. 4, 1842.
   They removed to Washington County, Iowa, thence to
   Grand Rapids, Mich., where he d. Jan. 14, 1878.

   Children:
   1 *George S.*, b. June 16, 1844, in Brighton, Iowa; m.
      Hattie L. Rigdon of Chicago, Ill., Oct. 5, 1869. Re-
      sides (1880) in Independence, Iowa.

      Child:
      1 *Henry Cheney,* b. Aug. 2, 1870.

   2 *Clara J.*, b. Jan 27, 1858, in Brighton, Iowa; d. Jan.
      29, 1858.

5 HANNAH CHENEY, b. Sept. 28, 1812, in Warwick, Mass.;
   m. Harvey Conant, Jan. 19, 1836. He d. May 15, 1872.
   She lives in Keene, N.H., 1880.

   Children:
   1 *Henry Coleman,* b. Oct. 22, 1836; d. July 20, 1861.
   2 *Susan E.*, b. Nov. 16, 1844; d. Feb. 28, 1867; m.
      George Proctor.
   3 *Horace M.*, b. Jan. 13, 1850; m. Abagail (?) Pratt.

6 ABAGAIL, b. Dec. 23, 1814 ; m. John S. Emery. He d.
   May 16, 1878. She resides in Warwick (1880).

   Children:
   1 *Abby S.*, b. Sept. 8, 1840; d. Dec. 13, 1845.
   2 *William Stanley,* b. July 8, 1845. Resides (1881) in
      Grand Rapids, Mich.
   3 *Mary S.*, b. April 27, 1846; m. William Barrows.
      Resides in Warwick.
   4 *James E.*, b. May 18, 1853, in Orange, Mass.; d.
      Aug. 25, 1853.
   5 *John W.*, d. April 30, 1878.
   6 *Hattie J. B.*, b. April 8, 1858, in Orange, Mass.

7 SUSANNAH ELLIS, b. June 8, 1817, in Warwick, Mass.:
   m. R. E. Carpenter, March, 1837, of Orange, Mass. She
   d. March 8, 1846.

   Children:
   1 *Susan M.*, b. Aug. 18, 1843 ; d. Aug. 30, 1843.
   2 *Susan E.*, b. Nov., 1845 ; d. April 1, 1846.

8 CHESTER WALES, b. Dec. 22, 1818, in Warwick, Mass.;
   m., Nov. 22, 1845, Sarah Jane Bowman; b. in Warwick
   in 1820, and d. in Orange, Mass., Oct. 14, 1875. He resides (1880) in Orange.

Children:

1 *Wales Bowman*, b. April 19, 1848 ; m. Kate Willard ; lives in Amherst, Mass.

2 *John Winthrop*, b. Sept. 26, 1849 ; m. Wealthy Heartson ; lives in Morris, Minn. (1880).

3 *Eugene Leslie*, b. Feb. 7, 1851 ; resides in Orange.

4 *Robert Carpenter*, b. Jan. 14, 1853 ; m. Ella M. Harding.

5 *Mabel Alice*, b. Oct. 10, 1854 ; m. Henry B. Allen ; resides in Amherst, Mass.

9 MARTHA EMILY, b. Sept. 20, 1820, in Warwick, Mass. ; d. in Troy, N.Y., Jan. 23, 1848 ; m. Houghton Hall.

Child:

1 *Martin E.*, b. Dec., 1847 ; d. July, 1868.

MARY ANGELINE, m. Nathaniel Cheney. Resides in Brooklyn, L.I. (1880).

Children:

1 *Rose.*

2 *Charles E.*, m. Lillian Walker. Resides in Brooklyn, L.I. (1880).

3 *Clara*, m. Arthur Newhall. Resides in Orange, Mass.

4 *Lizzie.*

11 BENJAMIN, b. in Warwick, Mass. ; d. young.

12 GRATIA, b. Sept. 26, 1805 ; m., Nov. 11, 1835, Henry Brooks of Petersham, Mass., who d. Aug. 25, 1857. She lives (1881) in Athol, Mass.

Children:

1 *Maria*, b. Oct. 3, 1837 ; d. March 20, 1876.

2 *Lucius*, b. March 11, 1840.

3 *Mary*, b. Oct. 24, 1842 ; m. Levi Cheney of Athol.

4 *Martha*, b. Dec. 27, 1844 ; m. Leander B. Morse.

5 *Josephine*, b. Feb. 22, 1849.

---

101 103 (VIII.) ERASTUS EDDY, Athol, Mass., 1840 ; b. Jan. 6, 1802, in Warwick, Mass. ; m. Abigail Allen. She b. in Roxbury, Mass. Both are dead.

Children:

1 ERASTUS WEBSTER, b. June 3, 1835, in Warwick, Mass. ; m. Martha J. Shelley, b. Dec. 9, 1839, in Cornish, N.H. Resides (1880) in Sterling, Mass.

Children:

1 *Calvin W.*, b. Nov. 12, 1850.

2 *Walter E.*, b. July 20, 1862.

3 *S. Lizzie*, b. March 7, 1870.

4 *Burt W.*, b. Aug. 11, 1874.

102 104 (VIII.) ABIJAH EDDY, b. in Warwick, Aug. 6, 1807 ; d. Nov. 25, 1880, at Somerville, Mass.

Children:
1 ANGELIA MARIA, b. July 5, 1834 ; m. Emerson A. Sabcn. Resides (1881) in Somerville, Mass.
2 GEORGE WELLS, b. July 24, 1837.
3 THOMAS WILSON DORR, b. May 11, 1844 ; d. Oct. 7, 1848.
4 MAVERETT ELLEN, b. May 12, 1840.
5 FREDERICK ABIJAH, b. May 15, 1847. Resides in Somerville, Mass.
6 THEODORE CLAPP, b. Aug. 19, 1850; d. Sept. 15, 1873.
7 ARTHUR STEACEY, b. March 4, 1855.

---

97 105 (VII.) ASA EDDY, farmer in Loudonderry, N.H., 1840.

Children:
1 CLARK.	2 COLLINS.	3 GEORGE GILBERT.
4 CHARLOTTE.	5 HARRIET.	6 JARVIS C.
7 WASHINGTON.		

---

98 106 (VII.) PHINEAS WARD EDDY, a farmer in Stratton, Vt., in 1840; b. May 13, 1790; d. in Loudonderry, Vt., Aug. 2, 1878. He was b. in Orange or Warwick, Mass.; m. Lois Goddard in Orange. She b. April 4, 1790 ; d. in Stratton, Vt., March 20, 1836. He m., second, Amanda Goddard, b. April 28, 1807.

Children:
1 SOPHRONIA, b. Sept. 28, 1813; d. Dec. 12, 1813, in Orange.
2 JUSTUS, b. April 7, 1814, at Orange ; m. Lucy M. Smith in Grafton, Mass., June 8, 1842.

   Children:
   1 *William J.*, b. Jan. 14, 1845, in Milbury, Mass.; m. Martha A. Prescott, Dec. 31, 1868; she b. Sept. 9, 1844.

      Children:
      1 *Harrison P.*, b. April 30, 1870, in Worcester, Mass.
      2 *William Clifton*, b. Sept. 20, 1875, in Worcester, Mass.
      3 *Ernest J.*, b. Nov. 13, 1878.

   2 *Ella M.*, b. Aug. 28, 1849; m. A. T. Briggs, Oct. 17, 1872, at Milbury, Mass.

Children:
1 *Florence E.*, b. April 23, 1875.
2 *Russell E.*, b. May 30, 1877.

3 ORRIN, b. May 22, 1816, in Orange, Mass.; m. Mary J. Moran, b. July 13, 1830. They now reside in Stratton, Vt.

Children:
1 *Phineas O.*, b. July 30, 1854.
2 *Edgar J.*, b. Aug. 24, 1856.
3 *Newton W.*, b. Oct. 23, 1864.

4 DAVID G., b. Nov. 15, 1817, in Stratton, Vt.; d. Nov. 26, 1878.
5 LUCY E., b. Jan. 22, 1820, in Stratton, Vt.; d. March 28, 1851.
6 FRANCIS W.. b. March 30, 1822, in Stratton; m. Susan Bartlett June 6, 1849. Resides in Townsend, Vt., 1881.

Children:
1 *Edwin F.*, b. July 27, 1852; m. Dec. 7, 1875.

Children:
1 *Francis E.*, b. Aug. 2, 1877. } Twins.
2 *Fannie E.*, b. Aug. 2, 1877. }
2 *Walter A.*, b. Nov. 16, 1858.
3 *Gertrude S.*, b. Jan. 27, 1862.

7 ASA, b. Aug. 14, 1824; m. Mary Barrett. Resides in Wardsboro', Vt., 1880.

Children:
1 *Frank.*   2 *Fred.*   3 *Maria.*   4 *Herbert.*
5 *Edgar B.*, b. June 6, 1860; d. Aug. 2, 1867.

8 ALBERT, b. Dec. 9, 1826, in Stratton, Vt.; m. Chloe M. Rice. Resides in Stratton, 1881.

Children:
1 *Elmer.*   2 *Albert.*   3 *Laura.*
4 *Herbert.*   5 *Emery.*

9 WILLIAM HENRY, b. Feb. 4, 1829, in Stratton, Vt.; m. Sarah Ann Hartwell.

Children:
1 *Herbert.*   2 *Florence.*   3 *William.*

10 PHINEAS E., alias EMERY P., b. May 15, 1830; d. Feb. 29, 1880; m. Frances Haynes. Resided in Townsend, Vt.

Children:
1 *Flora.*   2 *Jennie.*

11 ERASTUS A., b. June 12, 1832, in Stratton, Vt.; m. Henrietta W. ——, b. Oct. 12, 1850, in St. Louis, Mo. Resides (1880) in Hollywood, Minn.

Children:
1 *Ella Louise*, b. March 22, 1868.
2 *William Henry*, b. June 26, 1869.
3 *Phineas Emery*, b. Nov. 24, 1876.

---

18 107 (V.) BENJAMIN EDDY, b. Nov. 30, 1707. Settled in Newton, Mass; d. in Royalston, aged 91; m. Elizabeth Ward (or Truesdale); she d. 1751. He m., second, Hannah Day, April, 1753.

Children:
110 108   1 BENJAMIN, b. 1737; d. in Royalston, aged 95.
       2 SAMUEL, b. April 29, 1744; moved to Detroit, Sept., 1764.
117 109   3 JOHN, b. Sept. 25, 1745; d. Aug. 31, 1787.
       4 WARD, b. Feb. 5, 1748; a physician; d. 1831; lived in Dublin and Stoddard, N.H. Served eight months in Revolutionary War.
       5 TABITHA, b. July 19, 1738; m. Blackington of Needham.
       6 HANNAH, b. July 3, 1741.
       7 ELIZABETH, b. March 6, 1736; d. 1737.
       8 TABITHA, b. Aug. 27, 1734; d. 1738.

---

103 110 (VI.) BENJAMIN EDDY, b. Oct. 21. 1739; m. Sarah Holland; d. in Royalston, June, 1832, aged 95. Was in Revolutionary War.

Children:
114 111   1 BENJAMIN, b. Sept., 1764.
       2 ELIZABETH, b. April 9, 1761; d. 1790; m. Elisha Cheney, Jan., 1781. He m., second, Sarah Stone.

         Children:
         1 *Mary*, b. Dec. 26, 1781.
         2 *Sarah*, b. June 29, 1783.
         3 *Joseph*, b. Oct. 19, 1784.

       3 HANNAH, b. Dec. 23, 1760.
       4 MEHITABLE, b. April 9, 1767; m. William Foster of Boston, Feb. 2, 1792.
119 112   5 ABRAHAM, b. Sept. 28, 1768; d. June, 1832.
       6 ABIGAIL, b. Dec. 4, 1770; d. July, 1820; m. George Brimmer, Oct. 20, 1791.

    7   SARAH, b. Sept. 25, 1772; d. June, 1838.
    8   SAMUEL, b. Aug. 14, 1774; d. June, 1775.
    9   ANN, b. July 28, 1776; d. Oct., 1838.
   10   LUCRETIA, b. Feb. 3, 1779; d. May, 1809.
   11   SUSAN, b. Feb. 27, 1781.
118 113   12   SAMUEL, b. March 4, 1784; d. March, 1827.

---

111 114 (VII.) BENJAMIN EDDY, b. Sept. 13, 1764; d. 1852; resided in Newton, Mass., 1840; m. Zelida Pierce, Dec.
29, 1785. She d. at Fitzwilliam, N.H., Oct. 10, 1820.
In 1821 he removed to Rindge, N.H., and Oct. 16 of
that year m., for his second wife, Mrs. Mary Stone of
Rindge. She d. Sept. 17, 1826. Two years later he
removed to Newton, Mass., where he d. in 1852. He
was chosen deacon of the Congregational Church in
Rindge, Aug. 4, 1823, and continued in the office during
his residence in that town. Third wife, Martha Jackson of Newton, Sept. 27, 1827; d. Nov. 1, 1852.

Children:
    1   POLLY, b. May 25, 1876, in Newton; d. Aug., 1808.
116 115   2   BENJAMIN, b. July 1, 1787, in Newton.
    3   ZELIDA, b. May 7, 1791, in Fitzwilliam, N.H.; d. Aug.
8, 1835; m. Luke Hayward at Fitzwilliam, April 8,
1821.
    4   JOHN, b. Feb. 11, 1793, in Fitzwilliam; d. May 7,
1817; m. Mary Wadsworth.
    5   ALEXANDER SHEPHERD, b. June 29, 1797; d. July 16,
1820.
    6   MARY ANN, b. June 20, 1805; m. George Hayward of
Rindge, N.H., May 28, 1820.

---

115 116 (VIII.) BENJAMIN EDDY, b. in Newton, Mass., July 1, 1787;
m. Esther Capron of Royalston, Mass., Aug. 7, 1808.

Children:
    1   BENJAMIN F., resided in Winchendon, Mass., 1840; m.
Mary Goodridge, daughter of David and Susan Goodridge. After his decease, she m. (second) William
A. Sherwin of Rindge, and her two children became
residents of this town.

Children:
    1   *Benjamin Webster*, b. July 4, 1842; m. June, 1868,
Lizzie Wilson. He is a dealer in books and sta-
tionery in Fitchburg.
    2   *Mary A.*, b. July 3, 1844; m. Frederick Spaulding
of Jaffrey.

2 OTIS A., lives in Dixon, Ill., b. with one arm only; d. April, 1848.

3 NELSON, lives in Milbury, Mass.

4 GEORGE, lives in Winchendon, Mass.

5 JOHN, lives in Winchendon, Mass.

Six daughters.

---

109 117 (VI.) JOHN EDDY, d. Aug. 31, 1787, aged 42; m. Ann Jeffries, Sept. 25, 1782.

Children:

1 GIBBS WADSWORTH, d. June 11, 1805.

2 JOHN, drowned in Boston Harbor, May, 1805.

3 SARAH JEFFRIES, m. Dr. John Dix in 1810; her son, Dr. J. H. Dix, now living in Boston, 1880, recent owner of the Hotel Pelham.

> NOTE. — John Eddy, student Divinity, was a scholar; preached a short time, but, owing to ill health, was obliged to accept the offer of Mrs. Gibbs, widow of Henry Gibbs of Newton, Mass., to attend to her secular affairs, etc. She, at her decease, left him her large estate. He m. Ann Jeffries, dau. of David Jeffries, Esq., of Boston. His wife d. March 21, 1793.

---

113 118 (VII.) SAMUEL EDDY, b. March 4, 1784; d. March, 1827.

Child:

1 VALENTINE.

---

112 119 (VII.) ABRAHAM EDDY, b. Sept. 28, 1768; d. June, 1832; Feb. 10, 1832, m. Sarah ——, b. about 1768; d. Nov. 16, 1835.

Children:

1 WILLIAM, b. Jan. 20, 1796, in Royalston, Mass.; d. March 3, 1868; m., April, 1824, Hannah H. Knight, who was b. March 5, 1804; d. Sept. 24, 1861.

Children:

1 *Hannah M.*, b. July 2, 1825, in Royalston, Mass.; m. Daniel Mason, April 5, 1846. He d., 1859, at Haverhill, Mass., aged 37. She m., second, Rodney A. Phippen, April 15, 1866, at Gardner, Mass.

Children:

1 *Warren E.* 2 *Lizzie A.*

2 *Mehitable A.*, b. Oct. 28, 1827; d. July 11, 1861; m. Rodney A. Phippen.

3 *Willaim H.*, b. Feb. 15, 1830; d. July 20, 1859.

Child :

1 *Charles H.*, resided in 1859 in Mountain City, Texas.

4 *Augustus Franklin*, b. Feb. 9, 1832.
5 *John H.*, b. April 15, 1834.
6 *Francis P.*, b. Nov. 3, 1837.
7 *John M.*, b. July 19, 1835.

2 GIBBS WADSWORTH, b. July 7, 1807, in Royalston, Mass.; d. Sept. 18, 1867, in Boston, Mass.; m. Hannah A. Chase, b. Jan. 2, 1809.

Children :

1 *George W.*, b. Sept. 16, 1832, at Royalston, Mass.; m. Elizabeth H. (dau. of William H. McCurdy of St. Georges, Bermuda). Resides, 1880, in Phila., Pa.

Children :

1 *Elizabeth H.*, b. April 16, 1856, in Phila., Pa.
2 *George Henry*, b. Dec. 14, 1859, in Baltimore, Md.
3 *Manton Wadsworth*, b. Sept 25, 1865, in Phila., Pa., and d. Aug. 5, 1866.

2 *Thomas Henry Halland*, b. Oct. 10, 1834; d. Jan. 24, 1849.

3 MEHITABLE, m. Elias Emerson of Royalston, Mass.

Child :

1 *William ;* his widow lives in Royalston, 1880.

4 HENRY, d. 1830 in Royalston, Mass., unmarried.

4 120 (II.) SAMUEL EDDY of Plymouth, Mass., b. May, 1608. His wife's name was Elizabeth. He d. 1685, she in 1689. He, with his brother John, left London, Aug. 10, 1630, in the ship *Handmaid*, Captain John Grant. Arrived at Plymouth, Mass., Oct. 29, 1630, O. S., or by N. S., Nov. 9, 1630. On Jan. 1, 1632, admitted to the freedom of the Society, and received the oath. Nov. 7, 1637, had three acres of land in Plymouth set off to him; 1641, had six acres of land and thirty acres of meadow set off to him ; April 3, 1645, he sent his son John to dwell with Francis Gould until he shall accomplish the age of 21; Oct. 7, 1651, Elizabeth, wife of Samuel Eddy, was fined for wringing out clothes on the Lord's day. The fine, ten shillings, was afterwards remitted. May 1, 1660, Elizabeth was summoned to Court to make answer for travelling on Sunday to Boston from Plymouth. She affirmed that she was

necessitated to go on account of the illness of Mistress Saffin. The Court excused her, but admonished her. Samuel Eddy bought a house and lot of Experience Mitchell, May 9, 1631, at Spring Hill at the end of Main Street, Plymouth. This house he sold in 1645. He was one of the original purchasers of Middleboro', Mass. He was a large landowner at other places, and in 1631 his assessment was half that of Captain Standish. In 1633 it was the same.

Children:

125	121	1	JOHN, b. Dec. 25, 1637; d. May 27, 1715.
185	122	2	ZACHARIAH, b. 1639; d. Sept. 4, 1718.
339	123	3	CALEB, b. 1643; d. March 23, 1713.
354	124	4	OBEDIAH, b. 1645; d. 1722.
		5	HANNA, b. June 23, 1647; d. young.

121 125 (III.) JOHN EDDY, b. Dec. 25, 1637; d. May 27, 1715. He m. Susannah Padduck of Dartmouth, Mass., Nov. 30, 1665. She d. March 14, 1670. For his second wife he m. Deliverance Owen, May 1, 1672. His third wife, Hepzebah, d. at Tisbury, May 3, 1726, aged 83. He, in 1660, was a blacksmith in Plymouth. Was one of the one hundred and five proprietors of Taunton, Mass., 1689. Lived in Taunton, 1669. In Sept., 1711, he resided in Tisbury, and in 1687 he was chosen into office there, and at various other times.

The following anecdote is related of him: "On the breaking out of King Philip's War, 1676, a party of Indians who were acquainted with him discovered him at work in his field. Their respect for him was such that neither of them was willing to shoot him; and, in order to determine who of them should do it, they drew lots. As the Indian on whom the choice fell was creeping under the bank of the river near by to get within proper distance, John, who was on the watch, discovered the savage's rump above the bank, and conjecturing where he would rise, fired at him as he rose and the Indian fell. On attempting to reload his gun, John to his surprise found the hammer of the lock gone, carried away by the ball from the gun of the Indian, discharged at the same time John fired his. John at once made his escape to his home.

Children: *1666-7*

1 MARY, b. March 14, ~~1666-7.~~ in Taunton; m. Mr. Coffin.

130 126   2   JOHN, b. Jan. 19, 1670.

            3   MERCY, b. July 1, 1673; m. Mr. Lambert or Fisher.

            4   HANNAH, b. Dec. 6, 1676; m. John Manton of Tisbury.

151 127   5   EBENEZER, b. May 16, 1679; d. 1757.

309 128   6   ELEAZER, b. Oct. 16, 1681; d. in Norton, 1739.

            8   SUSANNAH, b. Sept. 18, 1692.

            9   PATIENCE, b. June 27, 1696; m. William White, b. Oct. 28, 1692. Resided in Taunton and Newton, Mass.

> Child :
>
> 1 *Susannah*, b. 1732; d. Aug. 14, 1811; m., 1755, Jonathan Whitaker, b. Oct. 1731; d. Jan. 11, 1812. Resided at Stafford, Ct.
>
> > Child :
> >
> > 1 *Ede*, b. Sept. 8, 1772; d. Dec. 18, 1846; m., Sept. 29, 1798, Hannah Bugbee, b. June 18, 1779; d. Sept. 11, 1823. Lived in Stafford and Monson.
> >
> > > Child :
> > >
> > > 1 *William*, b. March 14, 1815; d. Jan. 3, 1879; m., Nov. 26, 1840, Emma Louise Barker, b. March 20, 1815.
> > >
> > > > Child :
> > > >
> > > > 1 *Helen Augusta*, b. July 9, 1853; m., June 24, 1878, John Osborne Austin, b. Dec. 28, 1849. Resides (1881) Providence, R.I.

         10   JONATHAN, b. Dec. 15, 1689; probably m. Deborah Farley in Stoughton, Mass., March 7, 1727.

162 129   11   JOSEPH, b. Jan. 4, 1683; d. 1758.

         12   ABIGAIL.

         13   BENJAMIN, b. 1685; d. May 19, 1709, at Tisbury.

---

126 130 (IV.) JOHN EDDY, b. Jan. 19, 1670, of Norton, Mass.; m. Hepsibah, d. in Tisbury, May 3, 1726, aged 83. He d. at Tisbury, May 27, 1715.

Children :

136 131   1   JOHN, b. in Norton previous to 1700.

            2   BENJAMIN.

            3   EBENEZER.

            4   JOSHUA.

284 132   5   ZACHARIAH, b. about 1700.

303 133 6 CALEB.

         7 JOSEPH.

         8 OBEDIAH,

         8 JONATHAN.

308 135 9 ELEAZER. ?

       10 EZRA.

---

131 136 (V.) JOHN EDDY, b. in Norton previous to 1700.

          Children:

139 137 1 JOHN, of Preston, Ct.; b. 1736.

148 138 2 ZEPHENIAH, of Preston, Ct.; lived and d. at Stillwater, N.Y.

---

137 139 (VI.) JOHN EDDY, b. in Preston, Ct., 1736.

          Children:

         1 JOHN EDDY, b., 1756, in Chatham, Ct.

             Children:

             1 *Charity.*   2 *Festus*, d. without issue.

141 140 2 LEVEUS, b. Dec. 12, 1758, at Chatham, Ct.

         3 ELIZABETH.   4 CHARITY.

---

140 141 (VII.) LEVEUS EDDY, b. Dec. 12, 1758, in Chatham, Ct., now Middle Haddam, Ct.; d. in Newark, N.J., Jan. 19, 1846, aged 87 years.

          Children:

         1 JUSTIN, b. Aug. 17, 1786; d. at Worcester, March 31, 1852; no issue.

145 142 2 ALANSON, b. Oct., 1788.

         3 DEBORAH, b. March, 1790.

         4 BETSEY, b. 1792.

146 143 5 CHAUNCEY, b. June 2, 1794.

         6 POLLY, b. May. 1796, in Worcester.

147 144 7 ANSEL DOANE, b. Oct., 1798.

          NOTE. — *Justin Eddy* in 1840 was living in Edinburg, Ohio; was a Justice of the Peace and a farmer.

          Deborah Eddy m. Rev. Harvey Coe. In 1840 was living in Hudson, Ohio, and had six daughters.

          Betsey Eddy m. Ira Loomis; lived in 1840 at Cayahuga Falls, Ohio; had one daughter.

          Polly Eddy m. Levi Smedley in Williamstown; had one son and two daughters.

          Leveus Eddy in his youth was distinguished for his enterprise, fortitude, and endurance in conflicts of the Revolutionary War. He was a man of strict integrity, was greatly respected and beloved. His wife was Deborah Doane.

142 145 (VIII.) ALANSON EDDY, b. Oct., 1788, in Chatham, Ct. In 1840 he was living in Euclid, Ohio, a farmer.

Children :

1 ELIZETTE, b. in Williamstown about 1800 ; m. Bostwick of Cleveland, Ohio.
2 EDWIN ANSEL, b. April 5, 1812. Lived in 1840 in Palmyra, Ohio.
3 GEORGE ALANSON, b. in Edinburg, Ohio, May 20, 1829. Two daughters.

---

143 146 (VIII.) CHAUNCEY EDDY, b. in Chatham, Ct., June 2, 1794. In 1840 he was a clergyman, residing at Saratoga, N. Y., and General Agent for the A. B. C. F. M.; d. 1861.

Children :

1 JULIA MARIA, b. Morgantown, N.C., Dec. 30, 1823.
2 WILLIAM WOODBRIDGE, b. Penyan, N.Y., Dec., 1825. He graduated at Williams College in 1845, and at the Union Theological Seminary in New York in 1850. He m. Hannah Maria Condit. In 1859 he was a missionary in Syria.

Children :

1 *William King*, b. in Syria, March 13, 1854.
2 *Harriet Mollison*, b. in Syria, Dec. 7, 1855.
3 *Robert Condit*, b. in Syria, April 17, 1858.

3 EMILY, b. Penyan, N.Y., 1828.
4 ELIZABETH, b. Penyan, N.Y., 1830,
5 LEVEUS, b. Cazenovia, N.Y., June, 1834. In 1859 a teacher in the Deaf and Dumb Institution at Delevan, Wis.
6 MARY SMEDLEY, b. Saratoga, Oct., 1837.
7 MARIA WALWORTH, b. Saratoga, Feb. 14, 1841.

---

144 147 (VIII.) ANSEL DOANE EDDY, b. Oct., 1798; d. Feb. 7, 1875, at Lansingburg, N.Y. He was born in Williamstown, and in 1840 was pastor of the First Presbyterian Church in Newark, N.J.

Children :

1 BEULAH A., b. 1825.
2 MARY V., b. 1827.
3 WILLIAM C., b. 1830; d. 1830.
4 ELIZA M., b. 1834.
5 GEORGE H., b. 1838.
6 THOMAS A., b. 1843.

138 148 (VI.) ZEPHENIAH EDDY, b. Preston, Ct. Lived and d. in Stillwater, N.Y.

Child :

150 149   1 NATHAN, b. at Stillwater, N.Y.

149 150 (VII.) NATHAN EDDY. b. at Stillwater, N.Y.; m. Miss Higgens; went to Watertown, N.Y.

Children :

  1 NATHAN.   2 RUSSELL.   3 CLEMENT.

127 151 (IV.) EBENEZER EDDY, b. May 16, 1679, in Taunton, Mass.; d., 1757, in Norton, Mass.; m. Sarah Leonard, b. May 21, 1680.

Children :

  1 ICHABED, m., Feb. 9, 1727, Joanna Herndon. Lived in Norton, Mass.

    Child :

    1 *John*, b. Feb. 8, 1728. '

  2 SAMUEL, b. Aug. 24, 1712.

  3 WAITSTILL, b. April 4, 1715; m., Nov. 3, 1735, Cornelia Tucker.

— 4 JEREMIAH, b. Feb. 28, 1709.

  5 EBENEZER, b. April 16, 1707; m. Martha Leonard of Bridgewater, Mass., 1734.

    Children :

    1 *Mary*, b. April, 1737.

    2 *Martha*, b. June 16, 1739.

    3 *Ebenezer*, b. May 3, 1743.

    4 *Ephraim*, b. April 1, 1745.

    5 *Moses*, b. April 4, 1747.

    6 *Deborah*, b. May 14, 1750.

  6 ELEAZER, b. Feb. 2, 1703.

  7 MARY, b. Nov. 22, 1704.

  8 SARAH, b. May 9, 1705; d. June 14, 1705.

  9 OBEDIAH, b. March 16, 1711; d. young.

152 154 (V.) SAMUEL EDDY, Norton, Mass., b. Aug. 24, 1712; d. previous to 1761. He m., April 10, 1733, Sarah Page of Rehobeth.

Children :

  1 SARAH, b. Dec. 29, 1735.

  2 HANNAH, b. June 4, 1739. } Twins.

  3 CHARITY, b. June 4, 1739. }

4   SAMUEL, b. Jan. 31, 1741.
5   SIMEON, b. Dec. 30, 1742.
6   FREELOVE, b. Sept. 10, 1744.
7   ANNA, b. May 25, 1746.
8   COMFORT, b. June 25, 1748; m. Mary Drown of Providence, R.I.

Children:
1   *Comfort.*
2   *George W.,* b. in Providence, R.I.; m. May, 1821, Fidelia Freeman of Springfield, R.I.

Children:
1   *Alexander,* b. Jan. 21, 1821, in Providence, R.I.; d. 1876, in San Francisco, Cal.
2   *Phœbe A.,* m. McLean of Toledo, Ohio.
3   *John S.,* b. Oct. 21, 1823, in Providence, R.I.; m. Jane D. Sewall. Resides in Boston, Mass., 1880.

NOTE.— *Comfort Eddy* was a soldier in the Revolutionary War in Captain Josiah King's Company, Colonel David Bremer's Regiment; was in service eight months in such, and afterwards from April, 1778, to Aug., 1779. Resided at time of enlistment in Norton.

153 155   (V.)   JEREMIAH EDDY, m. Elizabeth Pierce, July 30, 1724.

Children:
1   MERCY, b. April 1, 1725.
2   PELEG, b. Dec. 7, 1726.
158 156   3   BARNARD, b. Oct. 11, 1729.
161 157   4   ESEK, b. Dec. 14, 1731; d. Aug. 23, 1820.
         5   RHODA, b. June 3, 1734; m. Peleg Marston, April 5, 1752.
         6   RUTH, b. April 3, 1737.
         7   ELIZABETH.
         8   PHEBE.

156 158   (VI.)   BARNARD EDDY, b. Oct. 11, 1729; m. Patience, dau. of Zachariah Eddy.

Children:
1   JEREMIAH, b. 1759; d. Aug. 25, 1820, at Providence, R.I.
160 159   2   BARNARD, b. 1762.
         3   BETSEY.   4   RHODA.   5   RUTH.
         6   PATIENCE.   7   NABBY.   8   EUNICE.

159 160   (VII.)   BARNARD EDDY, b. 1762; lived in Providence, R.I., in 1840; was a ship-builder; d. July 3, 1847; m., first, ——; m., second, Westcott. His widow m. John S. Eddy, 1852; she d. 1865.

Children:

1 STEPHEN W.
2 EDWARD BARNARD.
3 JAMES A., b. Dec. 15, 1819; m. Sarah Hathaway, 1839. Resides in Providence, R.I.

    Children:

    1 *Sarah*, m. T. A. Bateman; had three children.
    2 *Emma.*
    3 *James*, m. Mary D. Potter, 1865.

        Child:
        1 *Frederic P.*

    4 *Julia.*
    5 *Edwin.*
    6 *Imogene.*
    7 *Elinora.*

4 JEREMIAH.
5 JEREMIAH.
6 STEPHEN G.
7 RUTH, b. Aug. 8, 1735; m. Benjamin W. Gardiner; had three sons and five daughters.
8 PATIENCE, b. 1791; m. Benjamin W. Gardiner.
9 BETSEY, b. 1798; m. Deacon Williams of Springfield, Ct.
10 MARIA, b. 1808; m. Daniel H. Clarke of Pawtucket, R.I.; had two sons and one daughter.
11 JULIA FRANCES, b. Jan. 11, 1828; m. John L. Colden, 1847.

    Children:

1 *John.*	2 *Edwin.*	3 *Lewis.*
4 *Charles.*	5 *William.*	6 *Herman.*

157 161 (VI.) ESEK EDDY, b. Dec. 14, 1731; d. Aug. 23, 1820; m. Mary Perry, Sept. 12, 1758, b. July 7, 1738, and d. April 12, 1826.

    Children:

    1 MARY, b. Oct. 12, 1759; m. —— Greenman; she d. March 14, 1839.
    2 PELEG, b. March 1, 1762.
    3 LYDIA, b. Feb. 28, 1764.
    4 ESEK, b. Feb. 25, 1766.
    5 ABAGAIL, b. Dec. 28, 1767. } Twins.
    6 THOMAS, b. Dec. 28, 1767. }
    7 SARAH, b. Jan. 14, 1770.
    8 MARTHA, b. June 12, 1772.

9   AMEY, b. April 2, 1774.
10   CYRUS, b. April 2, 1774. } Twins.

11   CYRUS, second, b. Sept. 21, 1775; removed to Marietta, Ohio, about 1800; d. Dec. 22, 1812.

     Children:

1   *Abby*, m. —— Brown ; had four children.
2   *Mary Ann.*
3   *Marcy.*
4   *Cyrus*, had children.
5   *Amy*, m. Eli Brown ; had four children.
6   *Sarah*, m. —— Vincent; had eight children.
7   *Lydia*, m. —— Harrington ; had ten children.
8   *Henry*, m. ——; had seven children.
9   *Thomas*, m. ——; had seven children.
10   *Martha*, m. —— Rathburn ; had eight children.
11   *Ruth*, unmarried.

PELEG (son of Esek), b. March 1, 1762 ; d. Dec. 26, 1827 ; m. Elizabeth Waterman, Sept. 26, 1783, who was b. Aug. 13, 1762 ; d. Aug. 24, 1827.

Children:
1   THOMAS, b. April 11, 1784.
2   MARY, b. Nov. 16, 1786 ; m. Zachariah Chaffee of Providence, R.I. They have children and grandchildren.
3   ANNA, b. June 3, 1791 ; d. Feb. 27, 1793.
4   PELEG, Jr., b. Sept. 30, 1796 ; d. Oct. 20, 1827 ; unmarried.
5   BETSEY, b. June 15, 1801 ; m. Caleb Godfrey of Providence, R.I. Had children and grandchildren.

THOMAS (son of Peleg, son of Esek), b. April 11, 1784 ; d. Feb. 25, 1871; m. Selene Edwards, Sept. 13, 1809 ; she was b. in Trumbull, Ct., Oct. 29, 1786 ; d. Aug. 2, 1816. m., second wife, Eliza L. Hoppin, June 14. 1818 ; she was b. in Providence, R.I., March 21, 1789; d. Jan. 21, 1827. m., third wife, Roby Proctor Phillips, Nov. 24. 1828 ; she was b. in Warren, R.I., Oct. 30, 1796, her father being Nathaniel Phillips, who was born in Boston.

Children:
1   SELENE EDWARDS, b. Dec. 5, 1818; d. Jan. 29, 1819.
2   FRANCES ELIZA, b. March 11, 1820; m. John Pool Hardenburg of New York City.
3   WILLIAM PHILLIPS, b. Aug. 21, 1829 ; d. same day.

4 PELEG ESEK, b. Sept. 15, 1830. Resides in Providence, R.I., 1880.
5 THOMAS WATERMAN, b. April 15, 1832.
6 WILLIAM JOSEPH, b. March 23, 1836.

PELEG ESEK (son of Thomas, son of Peleg, son of Esek), b. Sept. 15, 1830 ; m., Feb. 1, 1859, to Caroline S. Howe, dau. of George Howe of Boston. They reside in Boston, Mass. He is an insurance agent of eminence, and greatly respected.

Children :
1 GEORGE HOWE, b. July 3, 1861.
2 JAMES WILLIAMSON, b. March 6, 1865. } Twins.
3 JOHN HARDENBERGH, b. March 6, 1865. }

WILLIAM JOSEPH (son of Thomas, son of Peleg, son of Esek), b. March 23, 1836 ; m. Mary Elizabeth Barton, Sept. 22, 1858. She was dau. of Henry Barton, and b. in Providence, July 17, 1838 ; resides in Providence, 1881.

Children :
1 HENRY BARTON, b. Feb. 4, 1860.
2 MINNIE GREENE, b. July 3, 1866.

---

129 162 (IV.) JOSEPH EDDY, b. Jan. 4, 1683 ; d. 1758.

Children :
166 163   1 ODED.
171 164   2 PAUL, d. March, 1843, aged 94.
174 165   3 PELATIAH.
           4 JOSEPH, b. probably in Taunton, Mass., about 1706.

Child :
1 *Elikim*, b. about 1740; m. Eunice Ferrand; was a soldier in the Revolutionary War; and afterwards removed to Canada.

Children :
1 *Augustus*, b. Oct. 5, 1798, in Adams, Mass.; m. Martha Thomas, May 25, 1820. She was b. Oct. 26, 1800, at Mason City, Ky. He was a Methodist minister.

Children :
1 *Zara*.

2 *Mary Eliza.*
3 *Thomas Meares*, b. Sept. 23, 1823; d. Oct. 7,
   1874; m. Anna White. He was a D.D., and
   a Methodist minister of distinction.

   Children:
   1 *Augustus Newland*, b. June 3, 1846, in
      Rising Sun, Ind.; m., June 27, 1872, Abby
      Louise Spencer of Chicago, Ill., where they
      reside 1880.

      Child:
      1 *Spencer Fayette*, b. June 18, 1873.

   2 *Olive Meta*, m. Otto M. Hasselman. Re-
      sides in Indianapolis, Ind., 1880.
   3 *Mary Elizabeth*, b. Feb. 13, 1851, in Madi-
      son, Ind.; m. Lewis C. Tallmage of Wash-
      ington, D.C. Resides in Chicago.

      Children:
      1 *Thomas Eddy*, b. April 24, 1876.
      2 *Abby Louise*, b. Nov. 18, 1877.

      Thomas Raymond Ames, resides in Chicago,
      Ill., 1880.

4 *Alice.*
5 *John Reynolds*, b. Oct. 10, 1829; d. June 14,
   1862; m. Sarah J. Nichols. He was a chaplain
   in the war of the Rebellion, and was killed in
   service.

   Children:
   1 *Mabel*, b., 1856, in Rushville, Ind.
   2 *Albert J.*, b., 1859, in New Carlisle, Ind.
   3 *Horace J.*, b., 1860, in Delphi, Ind.
   4 *Florence*, b., 1861, in Attica.

6 *Elizabeth J.*, b. Nov. 5, 1837; m. James W.
   Somers, Jan. 1, 1863. Resides in Washington,
   D.C. (1880).
7 *Morris R.*, b. Feb. 25, 1842, in Richland, Ind.;
   m. Clara Hall, Feb. 2, 1871. (She b. in Newark, Ohio, Jan. 3, 1848.) Resides in Indianapolis, Ind.

   Child:
   1 *Oliver Hall*, b. July 21, 1879.

2 *Lovina*, m. —— Allen.
3 *Saloma*, m. Willmarth Smith.

4 *Cynthia.*
5 *Eli.*
6 *Mary Ann*, m. —— Randolph.
7 *Emma Rilla*, m. —— Harris.

5 ABAGAIL.
6 EXPERIENCE.
7 MARY.

NOTE. — *Joseph Eddy* had a large estate near Taunton-Green, which by will he gave to his children.

---

163 166 (V.) ODED EDDY was Lieutenant, Second Company, First Regiment, Revolutionary War, June 17, 1778; Second Lieutenant in Caleb Hill's Company, 1776.

Child:
168 167   1 ODED, went to the West.

---

167 168 (VI.) ODED EDDY.

Child:
170 169   1 ODED of Deerfield, N.Y.

---

169 170 (VII.) ODED EDDY of Deerfield, N.Y.

Child:
  1 WELCOME A., of Buffalo, N.Y.; in 1841 was going to Wisconsin.

---

164 171 (V.) PAUL EDDY, b. 1749; d. March, 1843. In the Revolutionary War as a soldier.

Children:
173 172   1 PAUL, m. Mehitable Dean.
  2 BARNEY, m. Stacy.

    Children:
    1 *Barney.*
    2 *James.*
    3 *Tisdale.*
    4 *Alonzo.*
    5 *Levi.*
    6 *William H.*, resided in Cleveland, Ohio, Jan. 1, 1857.

      Children:
      1 *William Origen*, d. 1856, aged 7 years.
      Two daughters.

   7 *Martin.*
   8 *Hannah.*
    Eight others, probably all daughters; one of them
    had "six children at two births."

   3 RUFUS, m. Smith.
   4 JAMES, dead.
   5 HANNAH, m. Carpenter.
   6 RANEY, dead.
   7 ADELIA, dead.
   8 NANCY, m. Field.

---

172 173 (VI.) PAUL EDDY.

    Children:
   1 DEAN. 2 LABAN. 3 HORACE.
   4 LEANDER. 5 ELIZABETH. 6 MARY.

---

165 174 (V.) PELATIAH EDDY was in Revolutionary War; a
    captain in Colonel Abiel Mitchell's Regiment, Third
    Brigade, Lieutenant-Colonel J. Williams. Marched
    from Taunton to Tivaton, R.I., Aug. 1, 1780; served
    eight days.

    Children:
178 175 1 ABISHA, b. 1762; d. Feb. 25, 1855.
181 176 2 ASEL.
   3 JOSEPH, went East; never had issue.
184 177 4 TIMOTHY.

---

175 178 (VI.) ABISHA EDDY, b. 1762; d. Feb. 25, 1855.

    Children:
182 179 1 ABISHA of Taunton; b. Jan. 11, 1784.
   2 DANIEL, d. at sea; all his children dead in 1840 except
    Polly and Eliza.
   3 WELLS, d. without issue.
   4 POLLY, m. Stephen L. White.
   5 MERCY, m. Jedediah Wilbur.
   6 SARAH, m. Gideon Lincoln.
   7 ZEBULON.
   8 ABAGAIL, m. Charles Wilber.

---

179 180 (VII.) ABISHA EDDY, b. Jan. 11, 1784.

    Children:

   1 SUSAN B., m. Abiather Leonard, also David Bossett;
    had one daughter, Susan M. Leonard.

2   CHANDLOR, m.; had no children, 1840.

3   JOHN, m.; has two children, John and Charles.

4   SAMUEL, lived in Boston.

5   JULIA F.

6   ALFRED L., b. Sept., 1823.

7   ANDREW J., b. Dec. 2, 1825.

---

176 181 (VI.) ASEL EDDY.

    Children:

183 182   1 ASEL.

       2 SILENCE, m. Amos Lincoln.

       3 LYDIA, m. Leonard Field.

       4 LUCY, m. Abijah Eddy.

---

182 183 (VII.) ASEL EDDY.

    Children:

       1 PELTATIAH.

       2 STIMPSON.

       3 GEORGE.

       4 WILLARD.

---

177 184 (VI.) TIMOTHY EDDY, m. Mary Leonard.

    Children:

       1 CLARISSA, m. Lewis Whitney.

       2 ABIGAIL, never m.

---

122 185 (III) ZACHARIAH EDDY, b. 1639; d. Sept. 4, 1718; m. Alice Padduck, May 7, 1663. She was b. March 7, 1640, and died Sept. 24, 1692. His second wife was widow Abigail Smith, whose daughter Bethiah m. Caleb Eddy, son of Zachariah.

> NOTE. — *Zachariah Eddy* was a farmer. At the age of seven years, in 1646 and 1647, he was bound by his parents to Mr. John Brown, a shipwright of Rehoboth, until he was twenty-one years of age. At the session of Court, June 16, 1681, he, with many others, was propounded for admission as a freeman, but it does not appear that he was ever admitted; June 7, 1665, the Court granted him twelve acres of land between his land and the Whetstone Vineyard Brook. He then resided in Plymouth; July 10, 1667, he bought of Thomas Savery thirty acres adjoining the land in which Zachariah then lived; he also bought other lands. His house stood on the twelve acres granted him by the Court, near what, in 1840, was the "Eddy Furnace." The house afterwards fell into the possession of the Palmer family. From Middleboro' he removed to Swansea.

Children:

192 186   1 ZACHARIAH, b. April 10, 1664; d. 1737.
214 187   2 JOHN, b. Oct. 10, 1666.
          3 ELIZABETH, b. Aug. 3, 1670; m. Samuel Whipple of
             Prov., R.I., Feb. 26, 1690 (he b. in Prov., 1669, and d.
             at Groton, Ct., April 17, 1728). They removed to Gro-
             ton, Ct., prior to 1712.

             Children:
             1 *Alice*, b. April 10, 1693.
             2 *Samuel*, b. April 10, 1693; d. young.
             3 *Samuel*, b. Nov. 8, 1695.
             4 *Daniel*, b. Oct. 27, 1698.
             5 *Hope*, b. Aug. 12, 1701.
             6 *Nathan*, b. April 5, 1704.
             7 *Zachariah*, b. Feb. 2, 1707.

          4 SAMUEL, b. June 4, 1673.
215 188   5 EBENEZER, b. Feb. 5, 1675.
216 189   6 CALEB, b. Sept. 21, 1678.
227 190   7 JOSHUA, b. Feb. 21, 1680.
328 191   8 OBEDIAH, b. Sept. 2, 1683.
          9 ALICE, b. Nov. 28, 1684.

186 192 (IV.) ZACHARIAH EDDY, b. April 10, 1664; m. in Middle-
             boro', Mass., Mercy Baker, Feb. 13, 1683. She was of
             Swansea. He moved to Providence, R.I. (Nestacon-
             henett), 1707. His second wife was Ann Phillis. Her
             children were Anna, b. Dec. 27, 1708. Elisha, b. Nov.
             14, 1710. Joseph, b. Feb. 14, 1713. Samuel, b. Dec.
             21, 1715. Zachariah Eddy had a son Eliphalet; was
             m. to Phebe King, Nov. 10, 1737. Second, Tabitha
             Inman. Zachariah Eddy's will is on record at Glocces-
             ter, R.I. In it he mentions some of his children by both
             wives.

             Children by his first wife:
          1 ALICE, b. Nov. 28, 1684; d. Sept. 24, 1692.
          2 ELENOR, b. May 16, 1684.
          3 JEMIMA, b. Aug. 5, 1688; m. Stephen Hardin, April 21,
             1707.
194 193   4 ZACHARIAH, b. Sept. 13, 1691.
          5 ALICE, b. Jan. 5, 1694; m. Obediah Jenks, May 21, 1713.
          6 JOSEPH (son by second wife), b. Feb. 14, 1713; m.,
             Nov. 23, 1735, Barsheba Smith and lived in Glocester,
             R.I.

             Children:
             1 *Joseph*, m. Mary ——.

2 *Gideon*, m. Rachael Bowdich, April 4, 1769.
3 *Franklin.*
4 *Elisha.*
5 *Jacob*, m. Susanna Sprague, Oct. 28, 1770.

Children:

1 *Hosea.* 2 *Aaron.*
3 *John.* 4 *David*, m. ——.

Children:

1 *Seth Arnold*, deceased (1857).
2 *David Arnold.* Resided in Cleveland, Ohio,
1857.

7 ELISHA (son by second wife), b. Nov. 14, 1710; m.
Sarah Phataplace, Dec. 2, 1734; resided in Glocester,
R.I. He d. Jan. 27, 1764. She d. Nov. 9, 1795.

Children:

1 *Enos*, m. Aug. 30, 1761, Sarah Brown; d. June 25,
1782.
2 *Jesse*, m. Lydia ——.
3 *Amasa*, b. March 19, 1754; d. Sept. 10, 1843; m.
Abagail Harrington about 1775. She b. April 15,
1755; d. Oct. 4, 1806. They resided in Glocester,
R.I.

Children:

1 *Mary*, b. Jan. 13, 1776; m. her cousin Eli Eddy.
2 *Elisha*, b. Aug. 14, 1777; d. ——
3 *Stephen*, b. March 2, 1779; d. Jan. 14, 1784; m.
Lucy Cady.

Children:

1 *Betsey*, b. Aug. 3, 1800.
2 *Hiram J.*, b. June 2, 1811; m. Emeline Brown.

Children:

1 *Hannah S.*, b. Sept. 30, 1844; m. William
Fenno, and has one son, Hiram, b. Dec. 22,
1868.
2 *Hiram*, b. March 16, 1847; m. Nellie Newman and had one son, Augustus H., b. Feb.
11, 1860.
3 *Lucy E.*, b. Dec. 9, 1859.

3 *Clovis H.*, b. Dec. 22, 1814; m. Lydia A.
Arnold.

Children:

1 *Stephen A.*, b. March 10, 1838.
2 *Elisha*, b. July 2, 1839; m. Angie Arnold.

Children:
1 *Carrie M.*, b. March 26, 1867.
2 *Louis II.*, b. June 23, 1876.

3 *Mary E.*, b. April 22, 1841; m. Gilbert
Rounds.

Children:
1 *Lydia A.*, b. May 31, 1864; d. June 4,
1868.
2 *Cloris E.*, b. Nov. 20, 1868.

4 *Emily C.*, b. April 28, 1843; d. Feb. 27,
1847.
5 *Harriet A.*, b. Nov. 14, 1844; d. Oct. 15,
1865.
6 *Emma E.*, b. Dec. 26, 1847; m. Orland
Saunders.
7 *Julia A.*, b. Dec. 21, 1848.
8 *Cloris II.*, b. Nov. 2, 1850; d. July 2, 1851.
9 *Cloris II.*, b. April 25, 1852; d. Dec. 16,
1852.
10 *Henry E.*, b. Oct. 9, 1853.
11 *Frederick A.*, b. June 27, 1855; d. Aug. 27,
1855.
12 *Arthur A.*, b. Sept. 7, 1857.
13 *Eveline*, b. April 17, 1859; d. July 11, 1859.

4 *Stephen*, b. Feb. 15, 1827; m. Prussia Randall;
d. May 29, 1869.

Children:
1 *Susan C.*, b. March 31, 1847; d. Feb. 7,
1849.
2 *Clara E.*, b. March 22, 1849; m. William
J. Holders.
3
4 } Infant Twins, b. and d. March 7, 1851.
5 *Clovis R.*, b. Aug. 21, 1853.
6 *Eugene F.*, b. Feb. 25, 1856.

5 *Lucy A.*, b. Nov. 18, 1829.

4 *Amasa*, b. Jan. 30, 1783; d. Oct. 12, 1784; m.
Mary Owen, b. Jan. 17, 1788, and d. Sept. 24,
1852.

Children:
1 *Albert*, b. March 27, 1807; d. Oct. 31, 1876;
m. Olive Arnold, May, 18—; who d. same
year; m., second, Sarah A. Peckham; m.,
third, widow Eunice Brotherton. He resided
in Providence and Glocester, R.I.

Children:

1 *James F.*, b. Dec. 12, 1826; d. Aug. 23, 1873; m. Mary Brownell.

    Children:

    1 *Martha M.*, m., 1870, Julius Williams.
    2 *Walter J.*   3 *Frank A.*

2 *Augustus F.*, b. Aug. 17, 1833, in Glocester, R.I.; m. Sophia Harkins.

    Children:

    1 *Georgiana*, b. June 10, 1870.
    2 *Emily*, b. June 9, 1871.

3 *Joseph G.*, b. Dec. 23, 1834; d.
4 *Albert O.*, b. Mar. 10, 1836; d.
5 *Miranda B.*, b. April 13, 1837; m. Samuel Crossman.
6 *Solomon A.*, b. Nov. 8, 1838; d. June 13, 1850.
7 *Jedediah S.*, b. July 14, 1840; d. Aug. 8, 1853.
8 *Jesse P.*, b. June 22, 1842, in Glocester, R.I.; m., Sept. 5, 1865, Josephine A. Wilbur, b. Dec. 25, 1845. He resides in Providence, R.I. (1880).

    Children:

    1 *Infant daughter*, b. Feb. 25, 1869; d. Feb. 26, 1869.
    2 *Albert*, b. June 29, 1871; d. Aug. 20, 1871.
    3 *Calvin E.*, b. May 27, 1872; d. June 15, 1872.
    4 *Jesse P.*, b. July 12, 1873.
    5 *Reta Florence*, b. Jan. 15, 1878.

9 *Helen Josephene*, b. July 9, 1847; d. Dec. 7, 1848.

2 *George*, b. Oct. 14, 1809; m. Nancy Ann Mowry.

    Children:

    1 *Sarah*, m. Albert Reynolds.

        Children:

        1 *Amanda*, m. Stephen Irons; have two children.
        2 *George.*   3 *Nettie.*
        4 *Lafayette.*   5 *Walter Scott.*

2 *Ellen B.*, m. James Woodwarth.

    Child:
    1 *Nellie*, living in Providence, R.I. (1880).

3 *Amanda*, m. John Webster.

    Children:
    1 *John.*   2 *Lillian.*   3 *Mary.*

4 *George S.*, m. Mary Vic Steere.

    Child:
    1 *Ednah.*

3 *Adfur*, b. Feb. 24, 1812; d. Feb. 18, 1875; m. Ruth, b. Dec. 8, 1816, dau. of Jesse Tourtellot of Glocester, R.I.

    Children:
    1 *Alexander Duncan*, b. June 10, 1839; m. Mary P. Thorp. Resides in Chepachet, R.I., and has one child, *Walter Albert*, b. Sept., 1864.
    2 *Adfur Owen*, b. July 24, 1840; d. Dec. 30, 1877.
    3 *Amasa Fiske*, b. May 25, 1842; m. Mary F. Horton of New Rochelle, N.Y. Resides in Providence, R.I.

        Children:
        1 *Florence Mary*, b. May 17, 1877; d. July 27, 1877.
        2 *Everett Horton*, b. June 6, 1878.

    4 *Abby Frances*, b. Dec. 22, 1843; m. Leman F. Warden; she d. June 14, 1877, in Providence, R.I.

        Children:
        1 *Frank Foster*, b. Oct. 2, 1872.
        2 *Louisa Eddy*, b. June 13, 1874.

    5 *Mary Alice*, b. Jan. 2, 1847.
    6 *Elizabeth*, b. July 20, 1849; d. Dec. 24, 1856.
    7 *Ruth*, b. May 31, 1851; d. Sept. 5, 1851.
    8 *Franklin Pierce*, b. July 11, 1852; m. Addie Francelia Greene. Resides in East Providence, R.I., and has one daughter, Gertrude Ruth, b. April 3, 1873.

4 *Alexander,* b. Oct. 29, 1814, in Glocester, R. I.; m., May 5, 1840, Caroline E. Burlingame, b. 1822.

Children:
1 *Richard A.*   2 *Mary E.*

5 *Gilbert,* b. March 28, 1817; m. —— Harris.
6 *Owen,* b. April 19, 1819; m. Lillie Sayles, and had one child, *Owen Sayles,* b. June 8, 1857; d. 1878.
7 *Abigail Ann,* b. Nov. 16, 1821; m. John T. Fiske.

Children:
1 *Eliza Taylor,* b. Jan. 14, 1844; m. Charles Paine.

Children:
1 *Louisa,* b. June 14, 1869.
2 *John Fiske,* b. Feb. 12, 1876.

2 *Caleb,* b. April 13, 1846; d. April 15, 1846.
3 *John T.,* b. May 21, 1847; m. Kate Arnold, and have one child, Abby Eddy, b. Jan. 6, 1880.
4 *Mary Elizabeth,* b. Dec. 21, 1848; d. Aug. 14, 1850.
5 *Frank.* b. Sept. 30, 1850.
6 *Fannie,* b. Sept. 16, 1852.
7 *Mary Owen,* b. July 16, 1854.

8 *Mary Batley,* b. Jan. 28, 1824.
9 *Amasa A.,* b. March 31, 1826; m. Janet Sayles. He d. June 22, 1850.

Child:
1 *Fanny Sayles,* m. Moses Quimby. Resides in Erie, Pa.

10 *Augustus F.,* b. Dec. 28, 1828.
11 *James M.,* b. April 25, 1831; m. Harriet Peckham.

Children:
1 *James Peckham.* b. Oct. 15, 1857.
2 *Jennie M. M.,* b. May 1, 1870.

5 *Anna,* b. Nov. 14, 1785; d. Feb. 24, 1800.
6 *John,* b. July 23, 1786; d. Sept. 18, 1797.
7 *Abagail,* b. May 2, 1796; d. March 29, 1816.

4 *Stephen*, b. ——; m. Lerrah Ross. He d. May 12, 1782.

Children :
1 *Eli*, b. April 13, 1779; d. Feb. 16, 1878; m. Mercy, dau. of Amasa and Abagail Eddy. She b. Jan. 13, 1776; d. Sept. 30, 1810. His second wife was Rhoda Jefferson; d. Feb. 24, 1868.

  Children by first wife :
  1 *Fidelia*, b. Jan. 15, 1800; d. March 1, 1880; m. Warner M. Aldrich.

    Children :
    1 *Julia A.*, b. May 27, 1822; m. John S. Eddy.
    2 *Fenner S.*, b. June 1, 1824; m. Martha Mowry.
    3 *Mary E.*, b. Nov. 20, 1826; m. William McDonald.
    4 *Leonard*, b. May 29, 1829; m. Lavinia Jackson.
    5 *Warner E.*, b. Feb. 22, 1831; m. Emily Eaton.
    6 *Fidelia*, b. July 25, 1834; m. Anthony Jones.
    7 *Stephen*, b. Sept. 8, 1837; m. Mary Clark.
    8 *Susan J.*, b. Dec. 18, 1840.
    9 *Elma*, b. May 4, 1843.

  2 *Stephen*, b. Nov. 5, 1801; m. Harriet Olney.

    Children :
    1 *Phebe*, b. Jan. 30, 1830; m. Henry Smith.
    2 *Job O.*, b. June 20, 1834; d. Feb. 16, 1845.
    3 *Amanda*, b. Nov. 4, 1846; m. Henry Sayles.

  3 *Fenner*, b. July 11, 1803; d. Jan. 14, 1878; m. Celia Taft.

    Children :
    1 *Alleyn O.*   2 *Julia A.*   3 *Eliza J.*
    4 *Jeremiah.*   5 *Mary Ann.*   6 *Mary T.*
    7 *Lavinia.*   8 *Retta C.*

  4 *Julia Ann*, b. June 23, 1805; d. May 29, 1841.
  5 *Eli R.*, b. July 8, 1808; m. Sarah Northrop. Resides in Rockford, Ill.

    Children :
    1 *Elliot*, m. Elizabeth Wigant.

Children :
1 *Estella.*   2 *Charles.*

2 *William.* m. Hannah M. Carmichael.

Children :
1 *Ernest.*   2 *Fred.*   3 *Lulu.*

3 *George E.*, m. Amanda Carmichael.

Children :
1 *Arthur.*   2 *Mabel.*
3 *Alfred.*   4 *Mary.*

Children of Eli Eddy (b. April 13, 1779), by second wife, Rhoda Johnson :

6 *Horace,* b. March 8, 1819; d. Dec. 14, 1864; m., Oct. 26, 1854, Jane M. Woodward, b. July 21, 1834.

Children :
1 *Harriet M.*, b. Aug. 31, 1855; m. J. Dewey, Oct. 22, 1874.
2 *Eli S.*, b. April 3, 1857.
3 *Ida M.*, b. May 1, 1859; m. George J. Andrews, Sept. 19, 1878.
4 *Lucinda E.*, b. April 18, 1861; m. Austin Cooper, May 9, 1879.
5 *Effie S.*, b. April 10, 1864.

7 *William,* b. Feb. 2, 1821; m. Lydia J. Sweet.

Child :
1 *George I.*, b. May 30, 1855.

8 *Labin,* b. April 26, 1822; d. Nov. 7, 1826.
9 *Savalla,* b. July 5, 1825; d. May 13, 1877; m. Lorenzo Ward.

Child :
1 *Eugene.*

10 *Zeruah,* b. Oct. 16, 1827; d. Aug. 20, 1878; m. Henry Keach.

Children :
1 *Emma.*   2 *Henry T.*
3 *Frederick.*   4 *Clarence.*

2 *John* (son of Stephen, who m. Zerrah Pratt).

Child :
1 *John,* m. Marcy Sales.

Children :
1 *John S.*, b. June 16, 1812; m. Julia A. ——, b. May 27, 1822.

Children:

1   *Fidelia*, b. June 2, 1840; m., Mar. 14, 1863, Fenner E. Smith.
2   *Eaton*, b. July 24, 1842.
3   *Marcy*, b. Jan. 26, 1845; m., Aug. 2, 1871, Edward Freeman.

     Child:
     1   *Nellie E.*, b. Feb. 1, 1877.

4   *John*, b. June 26, 1847; m. Narciss Salisbury, June 8, 1873.

     Child:
     1   *Cassius*, b. Nov. 10, 1875.

5   *Warner*, b. July 7, 1849.
6   *Elma*, b. Sept. 22, 1851.
7   *Edward*, b. May 24, 1853.
8   *Julia*, b. Nov. 28, 1856.
9   *Minnie*, b. Aug. 24. 1860.

2   *Celia.*
3   *Otis*, m. Lenia Mattison; resides near Rockford, Ill.

     Children:
     1   *Walter*, resides in California.
     2   *Welcome*, resides in Minnesota.
     3   *Warren*, resides in Rockford, Ill.

4   *Easton O.*, d. young.
5   *Elliott*, d. in Mobile, Ala.
6   *Marcius*, lives in Iowa (1880).

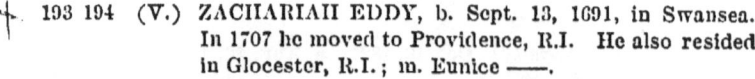

8   ANNE, b. Dec. 17, 1708.
9   SAMUEL, probably d. young.

---

193 194   (V.)   ZACHARIAH EDDY, b. Sept. 13, 1691, in Swansea. In 1707 he moved to Providence, R.I. He also resided in Glocester, R.I.; m. Eunice ——.

     Children:

200 195   1   SAMUEL.
201 196   2   ZACHARIAH, master shipwright.
         3   JOSHUA.
204 197   4   BENJAMIN.
205 198   5   JOSEPH.
206 199   6   WILLIAM, b. July 26, 1751; d. Sept. 4, 1835.
         7   PATIENCE, m. Barnard Eddy of Providence, R.I.
         8   ELIPHALET, m., first, Phebe King, Nov. 10, 1737. Second, Tabitha Freeman.

Child:

1 *Thomas.*

Children:

1 *Perley.*　　　2 *Thomas, Jr.*
3 *Eliphalet,* d.　4 *Tabitha.*
5 *Eliphalet.*
6 *Phebe,* d. Oct., 1860 ; m. ―― Skeels.

Child:

1 *R. M.,* residing (1880) in City of New York.

7 *Esek,* now (1880) living in Vermont.

---

193 200 (VI.) SAMUEL EDDY, m. Deborah Lewis, Sept. 14, 1730.

Children :

1 ABAGAIL. b. Aug. 22, 1734.
2 LEWIS, b. May 28, 1735.
3 SAMUEL, b. June 17, 1736; d. Aug. 1, 1804; m., about 1757, Peggy McDonald, b. Feb. 27, 1739; d. May 24, 1822. They are supposed to have resided in Thompson, Ct.

Children :

1 *Deborah,* b. Jan. 13, 1759; d. Jan. 30, 1769.
2 *Lewis,* b. Jan. 28, 1760; d. June 10, 1766.
3 *Esek,* b. May 27, 1762, in Thompson, Ct.; d. Aug., 1845, in Boston, N.Y.; m. Annie Cutter, b. in R.I., 1761; d. March 4, 1841.

Children :

1 *Samuel,* b. April 29, 1797, in Saratoga Co., N.Y.; m. Eunice Culver (b. in Dutchers Co., N.Y., Sept.. 1799; d. April, 1823). He m., second, Sarah A. Culver. b. April 9, 1810, in Cayuga Co., N.Y. He d. in Barre, N.Y., Feb. 16, 1859.

Children :

1 *Ozias C.,* b. in Henrietta, N.Y.; d. Dec. 16, 1838.

By second wife :

2 *Orange A.,* b. Feb. 20, 1832, in Barre, N.Y.; m. Harriet M. Hendrick (b. in Clarkson, Monroe Co., N.Y., March 24, 1834). He resides in Holly, N.Y.

Children :

1 *Mary Louis,* b. Nov. 3, 1868.
2 *Grace A.,* b. Nov. 20, 1870; d. March 31, 1875.

3 *Eunice C.*, b. Jan. 24, 1834, in Barre, N.Y.;
m. —— Rice. Resides in Eagle Harbor, N.Y.

Child:
1 *Ella.*

4 *Addis Emmett*, b. May 7, 1836, in Barre, N.Y.,
m. ——. Resides in Belmont, Iowa.

Children:
1 *Addis*, b. about 1832.
2 *Clarence*, b. about 1870.

5 *Helen M.*, b. May 5, 1838.
6 *Semantha W.*, b. Jan. 8, 1842; m. —— Haines.
Resides in Hosmer, Ill.

Child:
1 *Mary*, b. about 1864.

2 *Osmer*, b. Oct. 29, 1794; m., first, Hannah Peck,
July 15, 1815; m., second, Phebe Blanchard (b.
Jan. 26, 1808; d. July 25, 1868). He d. in Boston,
N.Y., May 2, 1849.

Children:
1 *Polly Ann*, b. Feb. 8, 1816; m. Reynolds; lives
in Bristol, N.Y.
2 *Sally Ann*, b. Feb. 5, 1818; m. Orrin Groff.
Resides in Disco, Mich.
3 *Lewis*, b. Jan. 6, 1820. Resides in Morris Co.,
Mich.
4 *Eliza*, b. Dec. 14, 1823. Resides in Boston,
N.Y.

Children by second wife:
5 *Samuel*, b. April 20, 1829, in Boston, N.Y.; m.
Harriet Nichols (b. March 20, 1831). Resides
in N. Boston, N.Y.

Children:
1 *Adelle*, b. Aug. 10, 1853.
2 *Hattie*, b. Feb. 25, 1864.

6 *Andrew*, b. Oct. 16, 1830. Resides in Minn.
7 *Osmer*, b. Aug. 21, 1833; d. Sept. 24, 1856.
8 *Amaziah*, b. Feb. 8, 1836; d. June 8, 1865.
9 *Almira*, b. Feb. 14, 1838; m. —— Warren.
10 *John*, b. Oct. 8, 1841.
11 *Nelson*, b. Dec. 20, 1846.

3 *Willard*, d. in Racine, Wis.
4 *Lewis.*

5   *Susan*, m. —— Reynolds in Racine, Wis.
6   *Erastus*, b. Oct., 1806, in Saratoga Co., N.Y.; m. Dorliska Middleditch, b. Aug., 1815.

   Children:
   1   *Esek Milo*, b. Feb. 11, 1833, in Erie Co., N.Y.; m. Charlotte —— about 1860.

      Children:
      1   *Myrtle*, b. about 1864.
      2   *Willard F.*, b. about 1869.
      3   *Sartus*, b. about 1876.

   2   *George W.*, lives in Hamburg, N.Y.
   3   *Ozias C.*
   4   *Huldah.*
   5   *Sarah.*
   6   *Willard*, b. July 30, 1834, in Erie Co., N.Y.; m. F. Gertrude ——, b. June 16, 1864, in Warterloo, Iowa, where he is a physician.

      Child:
      1   *Walter F.*

   7   *William W.*
   8   *James M.*
   9   *Phebe.*
   10 *A daughter.*

4 *Barack*, b. May 27, 1762; d. Aug.. 1845, in Boston, N.Y.; m., 1794, Rebecca Blackmar.

   Children:
   1   *George*, b. 1794; d. 1818.
   2   *Willard*, b. 1796; d. 1877; m. Ruth M. Bisbee in 1820.

      Children:
      1   *George*, b. 1821; living, 1881, at Prov., R.I.
      2   *Willard*, b. 1826.
      3   *Albert*, b. 1828.

5 *John*, b. May 30, 1767; d. April 11, 1820.
6 *Alice*, b. Jan. 1, 1770.
7 *Samuel*, b. March 6, 1772; d. Aug. 5, 1850.
8 *Peggy*, b. Jan. 21, 1774; d. Aug. 3, 1794.
9 *Levina*, b. Feb. 12, 1776; d. June 13, 1850.
10 *Asel*, b. Dec. 5, 1778, at Buck Hill, R.I.; m. Lucy Mower (b. Nov. 4, 1790), June 10, 1816. He d. June 13, 1850. She d. April 19, 1855.

Children:

1 *Charles B.*, b. Oct. 29, 1817; was in Company D., 151st Regiment, U.S.A., in war of 1862; d. in Va., Aug. 7, 1863.
2 *Caleb C.*, d. young.
3 *Marshall M.*, d. young.
4 *Charity C.*, b. March 15, 1829; m. —— Jennings. Resides in Sparta, Mich., 1880.
5 *John Austin*, b. Aug. 2, 1825; m. Cornelia Savage. Resides in Alden, N.Y., has one son, *B. G.*
6 *Laura N.*, b. June 10, 1827; d. 1876.

11 *Patience*, b. July 9, 1781; d. June 1, 1821.
12 *Anna*, b. Aug. 14, 1783; d. March 27, 1794.

4 DEBORAH, b. Feb. 17, 1738.
5 WEALTHY, b. Oct. 7, 1739.
6 PATIENCE, b. April 22, 1741 (m. James Woodmaney).
7 JOHN, b. June 7, 1743.

---

196 201 (VI.) ZACHARIAH EDDY, m. 1763; of Providence, R.I.; shipwright.

Children:

203 202
1 BENJAMIN, b. Feb. 10, 1764.
2 NATHANIEL, b. Oct. 13, 1766.
3 JONATHAN, b. Jan. 19, 1774.
4 ZACHARIAH, b. June 16, 1760.
5 ELIZABETH, b. April 25, 1762.
6 CHESTER, b. Sept. 20, 1771.

---

202 203 (VII.) BENJAMIN EDDY, shipwright; b. Feb. 10, 1764.

Children:

1 ZACHARIAH, b. April 23, 1788; d. Feb. 5, 1795.
2 CHESTER, b. March 19, 1790; d. Sept. 28, 1790.
3 BENJAMIN C., b. July 25, 1791; d. April 20. 1869.
4 JAMES, b. March 17, 1802; d. Feb. 10, 1806.
5 JAMES, b. May 29, 1806; m., Sept. 21, 1848, Mrs. Eliza F. Meriam of Boston, Mass.

Children:

1 *James*, b. June 21, 1849; d. Sept. 20, 1853.
2 *Sarah James*, b. May 9, 1851.
3 *Benjamin*, b. Aug. 23, 1853; d. Dec. 18, 1853.
4 *Amy*, b. Dec. 5, 1854.

NOTE.— *James Eddy*, b. May 29, 1806; was in early life an engraver, and resided for a while in Boston, Mass. He afterwards visited Europe ten times, and was an extensive purchaser and seller of valuable paintings and works of art, by which, and by real estate purchased in New York, he acquired a considerable fortune. He now (1881) resides in Providence, R.I., in a spacious and elegant mansion on Broadway. His grounds are very extensive, and laid out with great artistic skill. His house is a museum of art, and at his own expense he has erected near his residence a beautiful edifice for public worship, it being termed the "Bell Street Chapel." — *At a meeting of the Eddys, Oct. 29, 1880, to commemorate the two hundred and fiftieth anniversary of the landing of John and Samuel Eddy at Plymouth, Mass.*, such meeting being holden in said chapel, Mr. James Eddy welcomed to his house and treated to a bountiful collation the persons present. His two daughters residing with him inherit their father's artistic qualities, and like him are highly esteemed.

6 EUNICE, b. June 27, 1793; d. Aug. 3, 1793.
7 BETSEY, b. July 21, 1794; d. Oct. 19, 1794.
8 SALLY, b. Jan. 1, 1796; d. May 11, 1861.
9 ZACHARIAH, second, b. Feb. 5, 1798; d. ——, 1822.
10 ABAGAIL, b. Feb. 17, 1800; d. Jan. 15, 1880.
11 EUNICE CHESTER, b. April 2, 1804; d. Aug. 1, 1877.
12 ELIZABETH PETTIS, b. Oct. 30, 1809; d. June 25, 1839.

---

197 204 (VI.) BENJAMIN EDDY, Providence, R.I.

Child:
1 ZACHARIAH; in 1840 a boat-builder in Smithfield, R.I.

---

198 205 (VI.) JOSEPH EDDY of Providence, R.I.; d. 1839.

Children:
1 ANNA.   2 RICHARD.   3 JOSEPH.
Four or five daughters.

---

199 206 (VI.) WILLIAM EDDY, b. July 26, 1751, in Providence, R.I.; m., Nov. 11, 1711, Huldah Ide in Rehoboth. She b. June 11, 1754; was dau. of Josiah and Bethia Ide, and d. Aug. 12, 1788. His second wife was Bethia Hayes, b. Oct. 1, 1751. Their marriage took place May 12, 1789, she being dau. of Zebedee and Mary Hayes. William Eddy d. Sept. 4, 1835, and his widow d. Sept. 30, 1837, at Providence, R.I.

Children:
211 207 1 WILLIAM, b. March 24, 1773; d. April, 1855.
283 208 2 JOHN S., b. April 2, 1780; d. 1866.
212 209 3 EZRA, b. 1785; d. 1836.
213 210 4 JOSIAH, b. May 3, 1783; d. Aug., 1785.

5 HULDAH, b. Jan. 15, 1778; d. Oct. 10, 1828; m. Benjamin Batty of Providence, R.I., May 10, 1796, in Providence, R.I.

Children:

1 *Elizabeth*, b. Feb. 14, 1797, in Providence; d. 1829.
2 *George Arnold*, b. Feb. 18, 1799; d. Dec. 15, 1799.
3 *Rebecca A.*, b. July 25, 1800; d. Sept. 5, 1802.
4 *Henry*, b. Nov. 22, 1802; m. Susan T. Smith, b. Feb. 15, 1804, and d. Nov. 17, 1822. His second wife was Susan Tay.

Children:

1 *Abby T.*, b. Oct. 15, 1823; m., July 3, 1842, to John Hagan in Providence, R.I. He b. Aug. 5, 1818, at Paterson, N.J., and d. April 8, 1877, at Providence, R.I.

Children:

1 *Susan B.*, b. March 3, 1843; d. Feb. 10, 1864.
2 *Edward*, b. Sept. 15, 1845; d. Jan. 14, 1869.
3 *Frederick G.*, b. Sept. 6, 1849; m. Susan C. Drown, Dec. 2, 1875.
4 *Imogene A.*, b. Nov. 26, 1852.
5 *John H.*, b. Aug. 26, 1855; m., Aug. 15, 1877, Nellie R. Andrews.
6 *William A.*, b. July 5, 1858.
7 *Henry B.*, b. Feb. 24, 1864.

2 *Mary Elizabeth*, b. Sept. 8, 1825; m. Edmund Arnold Fiske, May 2, 1846, in Providence, R.I. He was son of Samuel and Sarah Fiske, and was b. May 16, 1823, in Johnston, R.I., and d. Oct. 3, 1873.

Children:

1 *Laura Ann*, b. May 2, 1847, in Providence, R.I.
2 *Mary Frances*, b. July 29, 1850, in Providence, R.I.
3 *Esther Elizabeth*, b. Jan. 18, 1852, in Providence, R.I.
4 *George Arnold*, b. Jan. 10, 1854; d. Dec. 10, 1856.
5 *Susan*, b. April 4, 1856; d. Aug. 23, 1857.
6 *Henry*, b. Feb. 8, 1858; d. Feb. 27, 1858.
7 *Edmund Arnold*, b. April 26, 1859; d. Oct. 26, 1859.
8 *Joseph Smith*, b. Nov. 4, 1861.

3 *Esther Ann Smith*, b. Sept. 8, 1825; m., May 11, 1851, to Edward Hooker, b. Dec. 25, 1822, at Farmington, Ct.; son of Edward Hooker of New Haven, Ct.

Children:

1 *Lillie Josephine*, b. Jan. 14, 1854, in Prov., R.I.
2 *Lucy Cowles*, b. May 17, 1856; d. Oct. 7, 1856.
3 *Rosa Belle Townsend*, b. June 9, 1851.
4 *Henry Daggett*, b. April 14, 1859.

4 *Henry Augustus*, b. Dec. 12, 1827; d. Sept. 19, 1839.

5 *Orin F.*, b. Jan. 1, 1830; m. Anna M. Pattee, Sept. 3, 1857.

Child:

1 *Huldah Eddy*, b. Sept. 4, 1859, in Boston, Mass.

6 *William Smith*, b. June 18, 1832; d. Feb. 10, 1835.
7 *Susan Smith*, b. July 31, 1835; d. Oct. 9, 1837.
8 *Joseph Smith*, b. Oct. 19, 1837; d. Jan. 25, 1838.

5 *Benjamin A.*, b. May 8, 1805; d. July 11, 1856; m. Phebe Hart Wilbert (b. Oct. 6, 1812, in Eden, N.Y.), May 7, 1835, at Milton, N.Y.

Children:

1 *George Field*, b. May 26, 1836, in Boston, N.Y.; m., Oct. 8, 1866, Emeline Sophia Dobbins, b. Sept. 20, 1843.

Children:

1 *George D.*, b. June 24, 1867; d. Oct. 6, 1868.
2 *Daisy Alice*, b. April 14, 1869.
3 *Mary Josephine*, b. June 8, 1871.

2 *Julia*, b. Nov. 26, 1837, in Boston, N.Y.
3 *Mary*, b. Oct. 8, 1839, in Springville, N.Y.
4 *William N.*, b. July 23, 1841, in Springville, N.Y.; d. June 19, 1843.
5 *Josephine*, b. Feb. 20, 1846; d. May 19, 1847.
6 *Charles*, b. July 23, 1848, in Lockport, N.Y.
7 *Edward*, b. Oct. 5, 1850, in Lockport, N.Y.
8 *Jennie Maria*, b. April 9, 1854, in Lockport, N.Y.

6 *Charles*, b. June 4, 1809; m. Julia A. Handell, May 17, 1831. She b. Jan. 31, 1810.

Children:

1 *John A.*, b. April 14, 1832; d. Nov. 26, 1833.

2 *Charles D.*, b. Sept. 2, 1834; m., Sept. 29, 1856, to Lucy M. Luther in Providence, R.I.

  Children:
  1 *Julia E.*, b. Oct. 18, 1857, in Providence, R.I.
  2 *Ida II.*, b. Jan. 5, 1860; d. Oct. 11, 1866.
  3 *Charles D.*, b. March 1, 1863.

3 *Elisha P.*, b. July 7, 1836; d., 1858, at sea.
4 *Mary S.*, b. Feb. 2, 1840; m., Feb. 21, 1869, to Josiah T. Smith.

  Children:
  1 *Victor C.*, b. Feb. 21, 1871, in Brooklyn, Cal.
  2 *Earl T.*, b. April 22, 1872, in San Silito, Cal.

5 *Benjamin A.*, b. March 1, 1843.
6 *Lucy M.*, b. Dec. 4, 1845.
7 *Clara E.*, b. Aug. 4, 1850, in Providence, R.I.

7 *Horace*, b. Sept. 4, 1811.
8 *William Eddy*, b. May 23, 1814; m. in 1836 to Marcy R. Burrows, in Walpole, Mass. She b. April 20, 1818, and d. May 17, 1872.

  Child:
  1 *Huldah*, b. Jan. 25, 1838; d. Nov. 3, 1839.

9 *Isaac S.*, b. Nov. 1, 1817.
10 *Owen Arnold*, b. Jan. 7, 1821; d. Dec. 21, 1821.

6 PATIENCE (dau. of William Eddy and Huldah Ida), b. Aug. 6, 1775; d. Aug. 9, 1775.
7 PAMELIA (dau. of William Eddy and Huldah Ida), b. March 22, 1781; d. young.
8 HANNAH (dau. of William Eddy and Huldah Ida), b. Aug. 4, 1788; d. Feb. 25, 1789.

By second wife (Bethiah Hayes) William Eddy had Children:
9 JOANNA PROCTOR, b. March 22, 1790; d. Sept. 12, 1791.
10 JOSIAH IDE, b. March 19, 1792; m. Sophia Peckham, May 24, 1812. She b. in Providence, R.I., Jan. 10, 1795; d. Aug. 11, 1848. He d. Sept. 28, 1837.

  Children:
  1 *Cordelia*, b. Aug. 25, 1812, in Providence, R.I.; d. Aug. 27, 1875; m. William H. West.
  2 *James P.*, b. Oct. 16, 1814; d. Aug. 5, 1850; m. Louise Thorpe.
  3 *Delia Maria*, b. March 27, 1817; d. Dec. 13, 1845, in Providence, R.I.

4 *Josiah*, b. March 26, 1819; d. June 5, 1840.

5 *Leander W.*, b. May 11, 1821; d. July, 1840, at sea.

6 *Sophia E.*, b. June 30, 1823; d. July 6, 1843; m. Walter Collins.

7 *Frances N. C.*, b. Oct. 14, 1825; d. June 13, 1827.

8 *Justin J.*, b. March 9, 1828; m. March 16, 1852, in Providence, R.I., to Matilda Monroe; b. Dec. 3, 1833, in New Bedford, Mass.

Children :
1 *Albert A.*, b. Jan. 11, 1853, in Providence, R.I.
2 *William H. W.*, b. July 26, 1856.
3 *Cordelia W.*, b. Aug. 25, 1858.

9 *Sarah F.*, b. May 21, 1830; d. Sept. 20, 1845, in Providence, R.I.

10 *Caleb W.*, b. Sept. 10, 1832 ; m. Mary E. Holland, June 10, 1855. She b. Dec. 17, 1833, in Providence, R.I.

Children :
1 *Carrie E.*, b. Dec. 30, 1857, in Providence, R.I.
2 *Justin J.*, b. July 20, 1861, in Providence, R.I.

11 *Bethiah H.*, b. March 16, 1835; d. July 20, 1836.

11 MARGARET SNOW, b. Nov. 12, 1794; d. May 6, 1871, in New Haven, Ct.: m. John Ferguson, April 28, 1819, in Providence, who was b. Dec. 9, 1788, in Danse, Scotland, and d. Nov. 11, 1858, in Whately, Mass.

Children :
1 *Mary Hammett*, b. Feb. 25, 1820, in Providence, R.I.; m., Oct. 2, 1838, to Charles D. Stockbridge, in Whately, Mass. Resides in New Haven. He was b. Oct. 2, 1816, and d. April 2, 1872, in Whately.

Children :
1 *Sarah Annis*, b. Oct. 20, 1839 ; d. Jan. 11, 1865.
2 *Charles Henry*, b. May 9, 1841; m., Jan. 4, 1864, at South Fairfield, Mass., Laura Hunton, who d. March 4, 1874, at Whately. He m., second, Eva Malinda ——, Jan. 6, 1876.

Children :
1 *Anna May*, b. Nov. 11, 1864.
2 *Charles David*, b. Feb. 1, 1866.
3 *Sarah Rosette*, b. Nov. 24, 1868.
4 *George Henry*, b. Dec. 13, 1870.
5 *Nellie Mabel*, b. Feb. 29, 1872.

    3 *Margaret Ann*, b. Aug. 13, 1842 ; d. Sept. 24, 1862.

2 *Peter*, b. Dec. 13, 1821; d. Oct. 14, 1822, at East
Attleboro', Mass.

3 *Peter*, b. July 20, 1823; m. Feb. 15, 1852, to Maria
J. Bixby, b. Oct. 24, 1824. He resides in New
Haven, Ct., and is a civil engineer.

    Children :
    1 *James Joseph*, b. Nov. 27, 1853 ; d. Oct. 14, 1854.
    2 *Mary*, b. Dec. 15, 1855.
    3 *John William*, b. Dec. 19, 1857.
    4 *George Robert*, b. June 13, 1859.
    5 *Charles Edward*, b. Dec. 22, 1860.
    6 *Elizabeth*, b. June 18, 1862 ; d. Aug. 18, 1862.
    7 *Arthur Bixby*, b. Jan. 13, 1864.
    8 *Herbert Allen*, b. March 28, 1865; d. Jan. 26, 1869.

4 *William Eddy (Ferguson)*, b. April 1, 1825 ; m.
Elizabeth Sawtelle at New Ipswich, N.H., 1848.

    Child :
    1 *Ella Williemene*, b. March 25, 1854, at Cleveland,
Ohio.

5 *George Reid*, b. March 19, 1829; m. Susan A. Pratt,
Jan. 20, 1864, who was b. June 4, 1833, at Auburn,
Mass. He is a minister, and in 1877 went to Africa
to establish a school.

    Children :
    1 *Margaret Emma*, b. Jan. 14, 1865.
    2 *George Pratt*, b. Dec. 15, 1868.
    3 *Maxwell*, b. April 15, 1870 ; d. Jan. 14, 1876.
    4 *Catharine*, b. Oct. 4, 1872.
    5 *Walter Mills*, b. March, 1876.

6 *Margaret Eddy (Ferguson)*, b. Dec. 9, 1830 ; m.
Herman B. Allen of New Haven, Ct., June 15, 1854.

    Children :
    1 *Mary E.*, b. Oct. 25, 1856, in New Haven, Ct.
    2 *Lella M.*, b. Aug. 9, 1858, in New Haven, Ct.;
d. April 22, 1863.
    3 *James Ferguson*, b. Dec. 23, 1860, in New Haven,
Ct.
    4 *Caroline Graves*, b. March 1, 1865.

7 *James Anthony*, b. Nov. 17, 1832; m., 1856, Claudia
Churchill of New Orleans, La.

Child :

1 *Lulu*, b. Oct. 15, 1857, at New Orleans, La.

8 *Anna Bethia*, b. May 3, 1835; d. Aug. 6, 1840.

9 *Abby Park*, b. April 4, 1837, in Whately, Mass.

---

207 211 (VII.) WILLIAM EDDY, b. March 24, 1773; m., Aug. 31, 1794, Huldah Albro of Foster, R.I. He d. July 22, 1805. She d. Oct. 26, 1841.

Children :

1 EDWARD BURR, b. Dec. 3, 1797; d. Aug. 29, 1798.

2 RICHARD, b. Aug. 20, 1800; d. Nov. 21, 1871; m., May 2, 1822, Martha James, b. Aug. 10, 1803.

Children :

1 *William*, b. Jan. 17, 1823; m. Helena A. Parker, Jan. 18, 1853.

2 *Henry James*, b. March 6, 1824; d. July 2, 1826, in Providence, R.I.

3 *Benjamin James*, b. Nov. 8, 1825: m. Sept. 5, 1849: killed in battle near Richmond, Va., June, 1862.

4 *Richard*, b. June 21, 1828; m., March 10, 1852, to Sarah Stoddard of Hudson, N.Y. She b. Feb. 24, 1831.

Children :

1 *Frederick William*, b. Feb. 24, 1853, in Rome, N.Y.

2 *Martha Maria*, b. Oct. 3, 1856, in Philadelphia, Pa.

3 *Richard Henry*, b. Feb. 26, 1858, in Canton, N.Y.

4 *Benjamin Franklin*, b. March 6, 1860, in Canton, N.Y.

5 *Sarah Mabel*, b. Aug. 6, 1867, in Philadelphia, Pa.

3 ANN ELIZA, b. Jan. 7, 1803; d. 1823.

4 HARRIET, b. April 14, 1805; d. April 28, 1872; m., Aug. 11, 1822, Joseph Davis, b. March 19, 1798; d. Oct. 6, 1876.

Children :

1 *Stephen*, b. Sept. 6, 1823; d. Aug. 4, 1826.

2 *Daughter*, b. Sept. 3, 1825; d. Sept. 4, 1825.

3 *Ann Eliza*, b. Sept. 4, 1826; m. Reuben M. Bowman in 1846, who d. July 25, 1859.

4 *Stephen H.*, b. Feb. 2, 1829; m., July, 1862, at Stockton, Cal., Caroline Steinhilber, b. July 28, 1842.

Children :

1 *Joseph Henry*, b. July 10, 1863.

2 *Clara Belle*, b. Feb. 5, 1865.

    3 *Arthur B.*, b. Nov. 9, 1866.
    4 *Addie Margaret*, b. Jan. 11, 1869.

  5 *Sarah W.*, b. June 21, 1831; m., April 29, 1856, Edward G. Burrows, b. May 14, 1828, in Providence, R.I.

    Children:
    1 *Sarah M.*, b. Feb. 12, 1857, Providence, R.I.
    2 *Edward G.*, b. Sept. 23, 1858, Providence, R.I.
    3 *William Eddy*, b. Aug. 22, 1860, Providence, R.I.
    4 *Anna C.*, b. July 18, 1864, Providence, R.I.
    5 *Charles Davis*, b. Jan. 19, 1867, Providence, R.I.
    6 *Harriet*, b. Sept. 25, 1871; d. March 5, 1872.

  6 *Harriet*, b. June 10, 1834.
  7 *Caroline*, b. Oct. 2, 1836; m., Jan. 1, 1855, John W. Lee of Swansea, Mass.; b. Jan. 10, 1831, son of George Lee.

    Children:
    1 *Joseph Henry*, b. Nov. 28, 1855, in Providence, R.I.
    2 *Harriet Eddy*, b. May 26, 1857; m., Oct. 3, 1877, to Edward McLaughlin.
    3 *Ann Elizabeth*, b. March 15, 1859, in Providence, R.I.; d. Aug. 4, 1860.

  8 *Benjamin*, b. March 5, 1839; m. Louisa F. Thurbur, Jan. 29, 1866.

    Children:
    1 *Benjamin G.*, b. Oct. 22, 1866, in Providence, R.I.
    2 *Arthur II.*, b. May 20, 1868, in Providence, R.I.
    3 *Joseph*, b. July 30, 1870; d. July 11, 1871.
    4 *Albert C.*, b. Dec. 13, 1873.

  9 *Clarissa*, b. Oct. 22, 1848; d. Nov. 12, 1861, in Providence, R.I.

---

209 212 (VII.) EZRA EDDY, b. July 10, 1785; d. July 4, 1836, at Swansea; m. Sally Peckham, dau. of Peter Peckham, Nov. 10, 1804. She was b. Jan. 29, 1788, and d. April 22, 1830, at Providence, R.I. He d. July 4, 1836, at Swansea.

    Children:
  1 MARTHA, b. July 4, 1806; d. Aug. 3, 1807.
  2 CYRUS B., b. July 17, 1808; m. Jan. 7, 1829, at Provi-

dence, Eunice G. Dyer. She was b. Oct. 31, 1803, at Little Compton, R.I., and d. May 8, 1846, at Bristol, R.I. His second wife was Phebe G. Thurston; m. Oct. 28, 1846; b. in New Brunswick, Me., Aug. 23, 1820, and d. July 28, 1876.

Children:

1 *Charles Dyer*, b. Oct. 1, 1829, in Providence, R.I.; m., March 9, 1862, in Bristol, R.I., Sarah M. Bennett; b. April 16, 1842.

    Children:

    1 *Mary Eunice*, b. March 12, 1864, in Bristol, R.I.
    2 *Grace Dyer*, b. Nov. 25, 1868, in Bristol, R.I.
    3 *Sarah Martin*, b. Aug. 22, 1875, in Bristol, R.I.

2 *Sarah Jane*, b. Sept. 6, 1831; d. Dec. 1, 1864.
3 *Alfred L.*, b. April 27, 1834; d. Dec. 9, 1852.
4 *Mary Ann*, b. Oct. 2, 1841; d. Dec. 20, 1860.

By second wife:
5 *Rensselaer O.*, b. March 7, 1848; d. Nov. 10, 1852.
6 *Susan Amelia*, b. Aug. 16, 1849; d. June 21, 1871.
7 *Anne Maria*, b. June 13, 1851, in Bristol, R.I.; m. Henry Paul.

    Children:
    1 *William.*   2 *Nellie.*
    3 *Susan Amelia.*   4 *Annie.*

8 *Emily G.*, b. Aug. 11, 1854; m. June 19, 1872, at Bristol, R.I., William H. Young, b. Aug. 11, 1851, at Orient, L.I.

    Child:
    1 *William E.*, b. Nov. 15, 1876, at Bristol, R.I.

9 *Frank A.*, b. July 25, 1857; d. July 22, 1861.

3 AMELIA P., b. Dec. 1, 1810; m. —— Munroe.

    Children:
    1 *James Nelson.*   2 *Frederick Augustus.*

4 MARIA, b. Jan. 26, 1813; m. Nicholas R. Easton, Jan. 23, 1833, at Providence, R.I.

    Children:
    1 *Rebecca Redwood*, b. July 8, 1834; m. John W. Tillinghast, April 17, 1856, b. Dec. 3, 1831, at Exeter, R.I. She d. Aug. 25, 1858, in Providence, R.I.

        Child:
        1 *John Redwood*, b. July 4, in Providence, R.I.

2 *Amelia M.*, b. Feb. 5, 1836.
3 *Charles W.*, b. Dec. 22, 1840; d. Dec. 11, 1841.
4 *Charles Faybyan*, b. Jan. 12, 1843; m., June 4, 1867, Laura A. Peck, b. Oct. 26, 1849.

    Children:
    1 *Mabel Redwood*, b. Aug. 22, 1869, at Bristol, R.I.
    2 *Charles Reginald*, b. May 12, 1874, at Lincoln, R.I.

5 *Emily Clark*, b. Nov. 11, 1846; m. Albertus Stafford in Smithfield, R.I., Sept. 22, 1868. He b. July 12, 1836.

    Children:
    1 *Albertus*, b. Aug. 31, 1869; d. Sept. 7, 1869.
    2 *Howard*, b. Nov. 27, 1871; d. Feb. 21, 1872.

6 *Frederic W.*, b. Oct. 17, 1852; m., 1876, Agnes F. Barker.
7 *Nicholas Howard*, b. June 8, 1856.

5 HULDAH BATTEY, b. May 29, 1815, in Providence, R.I.; m., Dec. 1, 1833, George O. Bourn, b. July 4, 1809; d. Aug. 17, 1859.

    Children:
    1 *Augustus Osborn*, b. Oct. 1, 1834, in Providence, R.I.; m. Feb. 24, 1863, in Providence. R.I., Elizabeth R. Morrill, b. Feb. 17, 1838. Resides in Bristol, R.I.

        Children:
        1 *Augustus Osborn*, b. May 7, 1865, in Providence, R.I.
        2 *Elizabeth Roberts*, b. Jan. 6, 1874, in Bristol, R.I.
        3 *George Osborn*, b. Jan. 6, 1874.
        4 *Alice M. W.*, b. Aug. 5, 1875.
        5 *Stephen W.*, b. April 15, 1877.

2 *Emma Elliott*, b. Jan. 8, 1839, in Providence, R.I.
3 *Rachael*, b. Jan. 22, 1845, in Providence, R.I.; m., June 28, 1865, in Providence. R.I., William Chapman Downs, b. in Frame, England, April 23, 1825.

    Child:
    1 *Edith Bourn*, b. Feb. 18, 1873, in Providence, R.I.

6 CHARLES WILLIAM, b. Oct. 12, 1817; m. Ann E. Hamlin, Sept. 1, 1838.

    Children:
    1 *Laura Mason.*
    2 *Susan Perry*, b. Jan., 1843.
    3 *Sarah Frances.*

7 MARY WEST, b. Aug. 31. 1821 ; m. John M. Buffington,
March 8, 1843, in Providence, R.I.   He b. in Somerset,
Mass., Feb. 15, 1818.

Children:

1 *Mary Mason*, b. May 14, 1844, in Somerset, Mass.;
m., Jan. 1, 1864, Nathan Everett Grimes, b. March
12, 1839, and d. April 25, 1872. in Oakland, Cal.   She
m., second, Albert G. Garnett, May 25, 1874, in San
Francisco, Cal.   He b. in Woodstock, Canada, Jan.
19, 1844.

Children:

1 *Everett Mason*, b. Oct. 31, 1864, in San Francisco,
Cal.
2 *May Alice*, b. April 18, 1866. in San Francisco.
3 *Emma Bourn*, b. May 9, 1868 ; d. June 11, 1870.
4 *Thadeus Eddy*, b. Jan. 14, 1870.
5 *William Chester*, b. Oct. 21, 1871 ; d. April 6, 1872.

2 *Margaret Bowers*, b. Nov. 5, 1846 ; m. Eugene Cooper.
3 *John Mason*, b. April 20, 1849 ; m., Oct. 26, 1875, in
Nevada, Cal., Hattie Pierre Rolfe, b. Oct. 20, 1856,
in Nevada, Cal.

Child:

1 *Laura May*, b. March 20, 1877, in Nevada, Cal.

4 *William Horace*, b. July 3, 1854. in Stockton, Cal.
5 *Laura James*, b. March 15, 1857.

8 ALBERT CLARK, b. Feb. 26, 1824 ; m., Feb. 18, 1844,
Emily C. Green.

Children:

1 *George Osborn*, b. Nov. 25, 1844, in Philadelphia, Pa.
2 *Henry Clay*, b. May, 1848, in Providence, R.I.; m.,
Dec. 26, 1869, in Brooklyn, N.Y., Mary Eldridge, b.
Oct. 24, 1848.

Children:

1 *George Martin*, b. Sept. 26, 1870, in New York.
2 *Emily Louisa*, b. Nov. 24, 1872.
3 *Mary Elizabeth*, b. July 1, 1875, in New York.

9 AMY ANN, b. Sept. 7, 1827 ; d. Sept. 24, 1827.
10 ANN SARAH, b. Sept. 7, 1827 ; d. Sept. 29, 1827.

210 213 (VII.) JOSIAH EDDY, b. May 3, 1783; d. Aug., 1785, in Providence, R.I.

Children :
1 JAMES.   2 LEANDER. Both b. in Providence, R.I.

187 214 (IV.) JOHN EDDY, b. Oct. 10, 1666; m.. first, Mary; second, Hopestill ——.

Children :
1 CHARLES, b. Nov. 14, 1703; m., May 10, 1768 (probably second wife), Sarah Gray.

Child :
1 *Daniel*, killed by lightning in Boston Harbor, June 27, 1778.

Child :
1 *Daniel*, m. Martha Honeycomb in Salem, Mass.

Children :
1 *William II.*, b. ——; d. 1844.
2 *Daniel Clark*, b. May 21, 1823; a graduate of Harvard University, receiving the honorary degree of A.M.; m., April 9, 1846, Elizabeth Stone, b. April 25, 1827. He for some years has been prominent as a clergyman, both in Boston and Hyde Park, Mass., and now (1881) is pastor of a church in Brooklyn, N.Y.

Children :
1 *George L.*, b. April 21, 1847; d. in 1858.
2 *Lizzie F.*, b. Feb. 17, 1851; d. in 1855.
3 *Anne L.*, b. June 10, 1855.
4 *Charles H.*, b. Jan. 11, 1860.

2 JOSEPH, b. Sept. 16, 1705.

188 215 (IV.) EBENEZER EDDY, b. Feb. 5, 1675; m. Sarah Harding, June 17, 1701. He lived March 3, 1706, in Swansea. Moved to Providence in 1707. He also resided for many years in Middleboro'.

Children :
1 LYDIA, b. March 5, 1703; m. Mr. Bullock of Freetown.
2 EBENEZER, b. Oct. 28, 1706.
3 NATHAN, b. June 19, 1709.
4 PHEBE, b. Dec. 25, 1712.

189 216 (IV.) CALEB EDDY, b. Sept. 21, 1678; m. Bethia Smith, Jan. 11, 1703.

Children:

220 217   1   EDWARD, b. Oct. 7, 1703.

          2   ANN, b. Sept. 8, 1705; d. Sept. 8, 1755; m., Feb. 3, 1725, to John Kinnekat.

          3   ABAGAIL, b. Oct. 11, 1708; m. John Clark, Jr., Oct. 11, 1726.

273 218   4   ELISHA, b. May 2, 1711.

          5   AMEY, b. March 27, 1713; m. John Harden, Dec. 24, 1730.

278 219   6   MICHAEL, b. July 25, 1715.

          7   ELIZABETH, b. Jan. 8, 1717–18.

          8   BETHIA, b. Feb. 21, 1720–21.

---

217 220   (V.)   EDWARD EDDY, b. Oct. 7, 1703; m. Elizabeth Cole.

Children:

          1   ROBE, b. Oct. 28, 1728; m. Cromwell Childs of Warren, R.I.

          2   MARTHA, b. April 20, 1732; m. Giles Little of Swansea.

223 221   3   EDWARD, b. June 9, 1735.

224 222   4   CALEB, b. June 25, 1738; lost at sea, 1770.

---

221 223   (VI.)   EDWARD EDDY, b. June 9, 1735; m. Abigail Child of Warren, R.I.

Children:

          1   CALEB.   2   EDWARD.

          3   ENOS.   4   JOHN.

---

222 224   (VI.)   CALEB EDDY, b. June 25, 1738; drowned, 1770, on a voyage from New York to Warren; m. Sally Cole, March 14, 1765, who was b. Dec. 3, 1746.

Children:

226 225   1   CALEB, b. June 12, 1768.

          2   BETSEY, b. May 14, 1766; d. June 1, 1799; m. Joseph Kelly of Warren, R.I.

            Children:

            1   *Abby.*   2   *Ebenezer.*

          3   BENJAMIN, b. Aug. 7, 1773; m. Abigail Kelly (b. 1776) in Warren, R.I., Oct. 9, 1794. He d. Dec. 15, 1845. She d. May 6, 1865.

Children :

1 *Sarah*, b. April 28, 1795; d. Nov. 11, 1874.
2 *Sylvester*, b. June 19, 1797, in Warren, R.I.; m. Mahala Luther, Oct. 7, 1823. He d. in Warren, Aug. 22, 1842. She d. 1875.

    Children :

    1 *John L.*, b. Jan. 14, 1825; d. May 16, 1846, in Trinidad, Cuba.
    2 *Elizabeth Cantero*, b. Jan. 17, 1827; d. April 10, 1835.
    3 *Charles Cantero*, b. May 27, 1829.
    4 *Abby Kelly*, b. Feb. 26, 1835; m. Caleb S. Carr in 1865; d. 1876.
    5 *George H.*, b. Feb. 26, 1839.

3 *Benjamin*, b. March 18, 1804; lost at sea, Jan., 1846.
4 *Mary Kelley*, b. Jan. 27, 1808.
5 *John Laughton*, b. April 21, 1811, in Warren, R.I.; m., Jan. 16, 1840, Adelaide Louise Frances Montant of Philadelphia, Pa. He was a merchant in Trinidad, Cuba, and d. there Jan. 4, 1858. She d. in the City of New York, Jan. 6, 1865.

    Children :
    1 *Adelaide Josephine*, b. Nov. 13, 1842, in Trinidad, Cuba.
    2 *Anita Mary Louise*, b. June 3, 1844; d. in Havana, Dec. 28, 1879.

---

225 226 (VII.) CALEB EDDY, b. June 12, 1768; m. Abagail Maxwell of Warren, R.I., Dec. 2, 1790.

Children :
1 CALEB, b. May 11, 1799; lost off Chili, April 6, 1823.
2 MONTGOMERY, b. Nov. 10, 1808; d. at Trinidad, Cuba, May 20, 1827.
3 JAMES M., b. Feb. 8, 1811; m. Nancy Smith of Warren, R.I.; b. Feb. 8, 1811; m., second, Eliza D. Kelley.

    Children :
    1 *Annie*, m. Sidney Dean.

        Children :
        1 *Walter S.*   2 *Arthur K.*

2 *Mary S.*

3 *James M.*

4 HENRY W., b. Jan 1, 1813; m. Hannah Batall of Warren, R.I.

Children:
1 *Mary I.*   2 *Annjanette.*   3 *Henry W.*

5 WILLIAM P., b. Sept. 25, 1816; m. Nancy G. Chase of Providence, R.I.

Children:
1 *Edward T. C.*   2 *Joseph T. A.*   3 *Caleb M.*

6 SAMUEL RANDALL, b. Oct. 2, 1818; m. Abbey E. Randall. He d. July 4, 1866.

Children:
1 *Clara F.*, m. William W. Cooper.

7 ABBEY, m. Joseph Adams of Providence; d. May 8, 1875.

8 BETSEY, b. Dec. 11, 1800; m. Joseph Smith of Warren, R.I.

Children:
1 *Hannah*, m. E. H. Swinney of New York.
2 *Ann Frances*, m. C. W. Abbot, U.S.N., and had two children; viz.: *Anne F.* and *Charles W.*

9 REBECCA M., b. March 4, 1804; m. John R. Wheaten of Warren, R.I.

Children:
1 *Annie*, m. Luthur Haven of Chicago; m., second, —— Nichols of Chicago.

Children:
1 *Kittie.*   2 *Alice.*

2 *Abby*, m. B. B. Adams of Providence, R.I.

Children:
1 *Helene.*   2 *Alice.*
3 *Abby.*   4 *Benjamin.*

3 *Rebecca*, m. Homer E. Sargent of Chicago, Ill.

Children:

1 *Frederick.*   2 *John.*
3 *William.*   4 *Homer.*

4 *Catharine.*
5 *Alice.*
6 *John R.*

10 ANNJANETTE, b. Feb. 8, 1807; m. Theo. Andrews of Providence, R.I.

---

190 227 (IV) JOSHUA EDDY, b. Feb. 21, 1680; moved to Glocester, R.I., 1709, where he d. Nov. 13, 1768; m. Hannah Stevens, May 3, 1708; she d. Oct. 22, 1757.

Children:

234 228   1   BENJAMIN, b. March 5, 1709.
235 229   2   JONATHAN, b. Jan. 20, 1712; d. aged 80.
246 230   3   DANIEL, b. Nov. 7. 1713.
          4   HANNAH, b. June 21, 1718; d. young.
          5   NATHANIEL, b. April 4, 1716.
247 231   6   ZACHARIAH, b. July 23, 1720.
          7   THOMAS, b. Aug. 14, 1723.
          8   JAMES, b. June 21, 1725.
          9   PETER, b. Aug. 4, 1727; moved to Clarendon about 1765, with all his family except his son John. He was b. in Swansea, Mass., and m., Dec. 5, 1751, Mary Round.

Children:

1 *John*, b. 1754, in Scituate, R.I.; was a soldier in the Revolutionary War, and his widow had a pension for his services. He m. Sarah Hill at Swansea, and d. in Foster, R.I., Sept., 1823. She d. Dec. 4, 184–.

Children:

1 *Peleg*, b. Feb. 2, 1779; m. Betsey Randall; d. Dec., 1800.

Children:

1 *Ira*, m. Penelope Davis.

Children:

1 *Warren.*   2 *Job.*
3 *Daniel.*   4 *Darius.*

2 *Ellen.* m. Daniel Stone.

Child :
1 *Henry.*

3 *Asa*, m. Lucinda Davis.
4 *Charlotte*, m. Samuel Wilbur.

Children :
1 *Peleg.*   2 *Benjamin.*
3 *Mercy.*   4 *Nancy.*

5 *Betsey*, m. Reuben Whitman.
6 *Lydia*, d. unmarried.
7 *George*, m. Anna Barker.

Child :
1 *Henrietta.*

8 *Orra*, m. Horace Phillips.

Children :
1 *Oscar.*   2 *Edward.*

9 *Peleg*, m. Lucinda Davol.

Child :
1 *Peleg.*

2 *Thomas*, b. May 5, 1781; m. Cynthia Phillips;
d. Sept. 18, 1812.

Child :
1 *Sarah*, m. Andrew Hopkins.

3 *Nathan*, b. March 7, 1783; d. May 18, 1822.
4 *Daniel*, b. March 6, 1785; m. Elizabeth Davis.
He d. Oct. 18, 1827.

Children :
1 *John*, unmarried.
2 *Thomas*, m. ——.

Children :
1 *Daniel.*   2 *George.*

3 *Lucina*, unmarried.
4 *Alice*, m. Waterman Green.
5 *Lerviah*, unmarried.
6 *Mary*, m. ——.
7 *William*, unmarried.

5   *Jarvis*, b. April 10, 1787; d. Jan. 13, 1862; m.
Mary Hill, 1817; b. Sept. 5, 1795; d. Sept. 19,
1826. He m., second, Elizabeth Millet, b. July
5, 1800.

Children by first wife :
1   *John H.*, b. June 1, 1818, in Foster, R.I.; m.,
March 1, 1844, widow Mercy P. Horton (original name Holden); she b. April, 1803. He
(1881) is a merchant in Providence, R.I.

Children :
1   *John H.*, b. Jan. 15, 1845, in Foster, R.I.;
m., Oct. 9, 1866, Isadore F. Barden, b. Oct.
22, 1848.

Children :
1   *Bertha F.*, b. Sept. 26, 1867.
2   *William H.*, b. Aug. 5, 1869.
3   *Elmer A.*, b. Feb. 10, 1872.

2   *Mary E.*, b. Nov. 6, 1848, in Providence, R.I.

6   *Peter*, b. June 15, 1789; m. Doty Studley; d.
Feb. 15, 1844.

Children :
1   *John S.*, m. Mary A. Parkis.

Children :
1   *Anna M.*   2   *Francis.*

2   *Nathan*, m. Alice Stone.

Child :
1   *Albert.*

3   *Polly*, m. Samuel West.
4   *Sarah A.*, m. John G. Chase.
5   *Richard*, m. ——.
6   *James*, m. ——.

7   *Mary*, b. Aug. 13, 1792; m. Ephraim Phillips; d.
Dec. 18, 1811.

Child :
1   *Horace.*

8   *Gardner*, b. Dec. 8, 1795; d. Jan. 18, 1827.
9   *Anna*, b. Dec. 8, 1798; d. 1840; m. Ethan Angell.

Children :
1 *Mary A.*   2 *Emerald L.*
3 *Sarah.*   4 *Nehemiah.*

2 *Mary,* m. William Randall; d. about 1800.
3 *Lcrciah,* m. Peregrine Smith.
4 *James,* b. in Foster or Scituate, R.I.

254 232   10 WILLIAM, b. March 6, 1729.
269 233   11 JOHN, b. Dec. 25, 1730.

---

228 234 (V.)   BENJAMIN, b. March 5, 1709; m. Mary Hill of Freetown, Feb. 14, 1744–5.

Children :
1 MARTHA, b. Dec. 11, 1745; m. Nathaniel Toogood, Dec.
14, 1766.
2 MARY, b. June 22, 1745; m. William Morel, Feb. 18,
1768.
3 ELIZABETH, b. June 17, 1749.
4 HANNAH, b. Aug. 17, 1750; m. Daniel Shearman, March
11, 1773.
5 ISRAEL, b. July 22, 1755.
6 CALEB, b. Sept. 9, 1757.

---

229 235 (V.)   JONATHAN EDDY, b. Jan. 20, 1712; d. March 12,
1791. June 6, 1732, m. Sarah Evans, b. May 2, 1709;
d. Feb. 17, 1770. Settled in Glocester, R.I. He and
wife were Baptists. He was a pious man, called his
family together on the morning of his death, addressed each, and told them he should die at sunset,
which he did.

Children :
1 ABAGAIL, b. March 9, 1733; d. July 6, 1764.
2 LUCRETIA, b. March 30, 1735; m. P. Potter, Nov. 28,
1754.
239 236   3 RICHARD, b. Dec. 11, 1736; d. Oct. 20, 1784.
4 HANNAH, b. Jan. 30, 1739; d. Oct. 19, 1743.
5 JONATHAN, b. June 16, 1741; d. Jan. 29, 1744.
6 SARAH, b. Dec. 29, 1743; m. J. Mathewson, April 15,
1764.
244 237   7 JONATHAN, b. Sept. 8, 1746.
245 238   8 JOHN, b. Oct. 20, 1748.
9 EVANS, b. Aug. 18, 1750; d. March 29, 1757.

236 239 (VI.)   RICHARD EDDY, b. Dec. 11, 1736; d. Oct. 20, 1784,
in Providence, R.I.; m. Martha Comstock, July 10, 1765.
She was b. Feb. 24, 1744; d. Dec. 8, 1802; she was dau.
of Samuel and Anne (Brown) Comstock. He settled
in Johnston, where all his children were born. In
1783 he moved to Providence, R.I., where he died.
He was Steward of the College. His widow m. David
Bucklin, Feb. 5, 1786. She died Dec. 8, 1802.

Children:
242 240   1   MOSES, b. March 26, 1766; m. Hannah Carpenter.
243 241   2   SAMUEL, b. March 31, 1769.
            3   JONATHAN, b. Jan. 21, 1772; d. Aug. 25, 1800; no issue.

---

240 242 (VII.) MOSES EDDY, b. March 26, 1766; d. May 29, 1823;
m. Hannah Carpenter, Oct. 17, 1794, who d. May 14,
1838.

Children:
1   ABAGAIL.
2   ANNA, b. July 5, 1796; m., Oct. 5, 1820, Reuben Torrey.
3   MARIA, b. Oct. 16, 1799.
4   RICHARD EVANS, b. July 19, 1802.
5   MOSES, b. Nov. 16, 1803; d. Aug. 26, 1813.
6   HANNAH, b. April 4, 1807.

---

241 243 (VII.) SAMUEL EDDY, b. March 31, 1769, in Johnston, R.I.;
d. Feb. 3, 1839; m. Elizabeth Bucklin (b. Sept. 20,
1768; d. Oct. 27, 1799), Nov. 11, 1792. His second wife
was Martha Wheaton (b. Oct. 22, 1780; d. Feb. 1,
1808), m. Dec. 2, 1801; she was dau. of James and Ann
(Angel) Wheaton. His third wife was Naomi Ann
Angel (b. March 7, 1788; d. Feb. 13, 1817), m. April
25, 1809. His fourth wife was Sarah Howell, widow
of G. L. Dwight; she was b. Feb. 1, 1781; m., Oct. 7,
1824, Samuel Eddy; d. Feb. 23, 1839.

Children by first wife:
1   MARTHA, b. Sept. 2, 1793.
2   JONATHAN ABBOT, b. June 23, 1795; d. Jan. 1, 1881.
3   ELIZABETH, b. Sept. 1, 1799; d. Nov. 19, 1799.

Children by second wife:
4   JAMES, b. Nov. 2, 1802; d. July 11, 1814.
5   MARY, b. April 16, 1804; m., 1855, William Chase. } Twins.
6   ELIZA, b. April 16, 1804; d. Sept. 19, 1821.

7 SAMUEL, b. Oct. 27, 1805; d. Oct. 18, 1806.
8 THOMAS, b. Jan. 9, 1808; d. July 3, 1808. } Twins.
9 SAMUEL, b. Jan. 9, 1808; d. Feb. 12, 1809. }

Children by third wife:

10 ANNA, b. Dec. 15, 1810; d. April 13, 1813; m. George M. Richmond, Aug. 15, 1831.
11 EMMA, b. May 27, 1812; d. April 12, 1813.
12 REBECCA, b. Jan. 14, 1815; d. March 11, 1815.
13 ZACHARIAH, b. Aug. 14, 1816; d. Jan. 25, 1822.
Fourth wife, no issue.

GEORGE M. RICHMOND, b. Jan., 1808; was the son of Samuel N. Richmond of Dayton, Mass.; was m. to Ann Eddy, Aug. 11, 1831; had children as follows:

1 ELLEN, b. May 15, 1832.
2 GERALD, b. May 29, 1834; d. Feb. 28, 1839.
3 FRANK, b. Dec. 18, 1835.
4 HARVEY, b. Oct. 14, 1837; d. March 1, 1839.
5 WALTER, b. July 27, 1839.

NOTE. — *Martha*, the first daughter of Samuel Eddy, m., Dec. 10, 1814, Oroodates Mauran, son of Joseph Carlo Mauran, late of Barrington, a native of Villa Franca, Italy; a resident in New York, 1840.

Sarah Howell had a son by her first husband, Gamaliel Lyman Dwight.

The above-named Samuel Eddy was a highly respectable, eminent, and literary man. He was educated at Brown University, 1787, and studied law, but did not long practise it. He was Clerk of the Superior Court in 1790-3; was Secretary of State in 1798-1819; was Member of Congress, 1819-25, and in 1827-35 Chief Justice of the Superior Court of Rhode Island. He received the degree of LL.D., made valuable contributions to the collections of the Massachusetts Historical Society, and published a work on Antiquities.

The various public offices to which he was elected or appointed he filled with great credit to himself and satisfaction to the people of his native State.

His first wife was the daughter of Samuel Bucklin and Eliza Carpenter. His second wife was daughter of James Wheaton and Hannah Angel. His third wife was daughter of Elisha Angel and Annie Fenner. His fourth wife was daughter of Daniel Howell and Mary Brown.

237 244 (VI.) JONATHAN EDDY, b. Sept. 8, 1746.

Children:
1 JOHN.

2　THOMAS; lives (1840) in Glocester, R.I., a farmer.
3　RICHARD; lives (1840) in Glocester, R.I., a carpenter.

> NOTE. — *John* was an eminent M.D. in Providence. Went to Havana for his health ; there died of yellow fever.
> *Frederick A. Eddy,* his son, was an M.D. in Boston in 1840. He died in 1847.

238 245　(VI.)　JOHN EDDY, b. Oct. 20, 1748.

Children :
1　AUGUSTUS, b. in Dudley ; lives (1840) in Webster, Mass.
2　RICHARD.
3　HORATIO.
4　JOHN ; lives (1840) in Dudley, Mass., highly respected ; held many offices ; member Legislature several times.

Children :

1 *George M.*	2 *John W.*	3 *Erasmus.*
4 *Pasal P.*	5 *James F.*	6 *William Penn.*
7 *Edward.*	8 *Louisa.*	9 *Perris.*

> NOTE. — *Richard* had four sons at Prattsburg ; one, *Ziba,* is a doctor there (1840). His son *Erasmus,* a tanner in Steuben Co., N.Y. *Horatio* is a farmer in Prattsburg ; has children :
> 　4 *Eaton.*　5 *Stephen.*　*Six Daughters.*

230 246　(V.)　DANIEL EDDY, b. Nov. 7, 1713, in Scituate, R.I. ; d. at Glocester, R.I., March, 1791 (?).

231 247　(V.)　ZACHARIAH EDDY, b. July 23, 1720.

Children :
249 248　1　NEWBURY, b. Jan. 15, 1747.
　　　　　2　DANIEL.　　3　ABNER.　　4　ASAPH.
　　　　　5　MERCY.　　6　RHODA.　　7　ANNA.

248 249　(VI.)　NEWBURY EDDY, b. Jan. 15, 1747; d. about 1814. Removed from Thetford, Vt., to Wethersfield, Vt., where his children were born.

Children :
252 250　1　ALLEN, b. Feb. 22, 1770 ; residence, Mt. Holly, Vt.
　　　　　2　ZACHARIAH, lived and d. in Fulton, N.Y.

Children :
1　*John M.,* b. in Wethersfield, Vt. ; removed to Volney, N.Y. ; m. Nancy A. Wells. He d. at Volney.

Children:

1 *Luther W.*, d. in Troy, N.Y., 1877.

Child:

1 *Titus W.*, resides (1880) in Troy, N.Y.

2 *Louisa*, d. young.
3 *Cortes C.*, b. Feb., 1824; m. Maryette Foster, 1849. Is a farmer, and resides in Mexico, N.Y.

Children:

1 *Samuel W.*, b. 1850.
2 *Olive L.*, b. 1857.
3 *Clara E.*, b. 1866.

4 *George Wells;* lives in Illinois.

2 *Curtis;* remained in Vermont.
3 *Benjamin;* removed to Oswego County, N.Y., and afterwards to Ohio.

3 JOAB; lived and d. in Cavendish, Vt.
253 251 4 ISAAC, b. 1777; lived in Waterport, N.Y.; d. 1847.

---

250 252 (VII.) ALLEN EDDY, b. Feb. 22, 1770; residence, Mt. Holly, Vt.

Children:

1 AMY, b. Aug. 25, 1791; m. March, 1809. } Twins.
2 LUCY, b. Aug. 25, 1791; m. Dec., 1809. }
3 ISAAC, b. June 20, 1795; m., Nov., 1817, to Eunice ——. She b. Feb. 13, 1799; d. Nov. 21, 1877. He d. Sept. 1, 1833.

Children:

1 *Leonora J.*, b. June 26, 1819, in Vermont; living in 1880.
2 *William H.*, b. March 16, 1823, in Vermont.

Children:

1 *Charles*, b. Sept., 1850.
2 *Clinton D. F.*, b. Dec., 1859.

3 *John W.*, b. May 6, 1825, in Vermont. Resides in Mechanicsville, Vt. (1880).

Children:

1 *Emily J.*, b. April 13, 1852.

2 *Marshall W.*, b. July 17, 1859.
3 *Ellen N.*, b. Nov. 27, 1861.

4 *Mary L.*, b. April 4, 1829.
5 *Finette E.*, b. Dec. 24, 1833.

4 MARY, b. July 3, 1797; m. June, 1815.
5 NEWBURY, b. May 28, 1799, in Vt.; d. Jan. 25, 1867, in Rushford, N.Y.; m. Amelia Tarbill, Sept. 20, 1820 (or May, 1821), who d. Dec. 17, 1866. They moved from Mt. Holly, Vt., to Rushford in 1820.

Children :
1 *Sophronia*, b. Jan. 12, 1822; d. June 13, 1854.
2 *George W.*, b. Oct. 18, 1824; d. Oct. 7, 1828.
3 *Sophia*, b. Sept. 6, 1836, in Rushford, N.Y.; m., Sept. 15, 1856, Hiram B. Gilbert. She resides in Rushford, 1880.

Children :
1 *Eddy C.*, b. July 15, 1857.
2 *Frona L.*, b. Feb. 24, 1864.
3 *Nettie M.*, b. May 6, 1866.
4 *Daniel W.*, b. Jan. 1, 1872.

4 *Lucy*, b. April 9, 1839; d. July 3, 1854.

6 ESTHER, b. June 6, 1801; m. Sept., 1816.
7 JOHN C., b. Dec. 2, 1804; m. Dec. 2, 1827; d. 1862.

Children :
1 *John L.*, b. about 1829; m., 1856, Elvira Lewis; is a physician in Olean, N.Y., 1880.

Children :
1 *Willie*, d. young.   2 *Blanch.*
3 *Carrie*, d. young.   4 *Nellie.*
5 *Loren.*

2 *Justina*, b. 1832; m. J. P. Bixby, M.D.; d. 1858.
3 *Marcia*, m. Rev. N. Pierce.

Child :
1 *Bertha.*

4 *Emma*, m. John Howard; have a son and daughter.

8 ELIPHAZ A., b. July 9, 1806; m., 1829, Mary Stockwill (b. at Croyden, N.H., June 6, 1810). He d. July 11, 1872. She d. Jan. 8, 1880. He b. at Thetford, Vt.

Children:

1 *Ann Louisa*, b. March 12, 1835; m. Alexander Thomas, Oct. 15, 1856.
2 *Marcian Wilson*, b. Dec. 8, 1837; d. Jan. 3, 1873.
3 *Mary Frances*, b. July 3, 1839; m. Isaac M. Brown, Jan. 3, 1859. Residence, Terre Haute, Ind.
4 *Harrison Tyler*, b. Jan. 1, 1841; m. Mary C. Magnus, Feb. 4, 1868.
5 *George Allen*, b. Jan. 11, 1844; d. Oct. 29, 1862, from wounds received in Battle of Richmond, Ky., Aug. 30, 1862.
6 *Ellen Viola*, b. July 21, 1848; m. Henry C. Genung, Sept. 29, 1868.
7 *James Monroe*, b. Feb. 18, 1851; d. March 25, 1853.

9 WILSON, b. Feb. 24, 1813; m. Feb. 25, 1838. Is a master mechanic in the B. & A. R. R. Co.'s mills, at Springfield.

Children:

1 *Helen M.*, b. Sept. 18, 1842; m., July 19, 1869, Monroe B. Washburn; d. Feb. 11, 1870, in Brooklyn, L.I.
2 *Horace W.*, b. Aug. 16, 1845; m. Nov. 19, 1870. Resides in Springfield, Mass., 1880.

Child:

1 *Arthur C.*, b. Sept. 23, 1875.

---

251 253 (VII.) ISAAC EDDY, b. Feb. 17, 1777; d. July 25, 1847; m. Lucy Tarbell; she d. March 8, 1828; m., second, Susannah Foster, who d. 1855, aged 55. He b. in Wethersfield, Vt., and moved from there in March, 1826, to Troy, N.Y., and subsequently to Waterford, N.Y. In early life he was an engineer.

Children by first wife:

1 OLIVER TARBELL, b. about 1800; d. in Philadelphia. Pa., about 1873.

Children:

1 *Henry Clay*, resides in Philadelphia, Pa. (1880).
2 *Henrietta*, m. James C. Adams. Resides (1881) in Baltimore, Md., and have two sons and a daughter.
3 *Jennie*, m. —— Wingate. In 1881 is a widow and an Episcopal Sister of Charity in Boston, Mass.

2 SARAH, b. Feb. 24, 1798, in Wethersfield, Vt.; m Samuel Skinner (he b. in Cavendish, Vt., Dec. 6, 1796), March 20, 1817, in Wethersfield. Resides (1880) in Rosendale, Wis.

Children:

1 *Lucy Ann,* b. Dec. 21, 1817; m. J. R. Johnson, Oct. 9, 1837, in Carthage. N.Y.
2 *Mary,* b. Dec. 29, 1818, in Cavendish, Vt.; d. young.
3 *Samuel Eddy,* b. Nov. 15, 1819, in Keene, N.Y.; d. young.
4 *Sarah,* b. Feb. 17, 1821, in Keene, N.Y.; d. young.
5 *Samuel Eddy,* b. Oct. 22, 1822; m. Mary Nash, Aug., 1850, in Utica, N.Y.
6 *Adaline Amanda,* b. March 18, 1829, in Keene, N.Y.
7 *Mary Jane,* b. Dec. 23, 1826; m. William L. Vincent, Dec. 14, 1843, in Carthage.
8 *Leonora Maria,* b. March, 18—.
9 *James Franklin,* b. June 29, 1832; m. Vina Jervis at Evans Mills, N.Y., Sept., 1853.
10 *Sarah Louise,* b. July 5, 1834; m. Albert Richardson, Nov. 25, 1857, in Rosendale, Wis.
11 *Pomelia Frances,* b. Jan. 20, 1841, in Champion, N.Y.

3 TITUS, b. March 1, 1803; d. Feb. 6, 1875; m. Ann Eliza Casalier. Residence (1880), Troy, N.Y.

Children:

1 *Lucy Jane,* b. Jan. 27, 1830; m., Aug. 25, 1858, Rev. Alexander B. Bullions, D.D.

Children:

1 *Jessie,* b. April 29, 1861; d. young.
2 *Alice Blythe,* b. March 2, 1863.
3 *Charlotte Eddy,* b. July 5, 186-.

2 *Charlotte McGill,* b. Dec. 26, 1831; m., Dec. 26, 1854, Stephen Haskell.

Children:

1 *Anna Whipple,* b. April 19, 1856; m., Oct. 9, 1878, David Allen Judson.

Child:

1 *Stephen Haskell,* b. Aug. 26, 1879.

2 *Eliza Eddy,* b. May 12, 1830.

3 *James Albert*, b. Nov. 2, 1833; m. Julia Stebbius, who d. without issue.
4 *Titus Egbert*, b. Nov. 2, 1833; m. —— Seymour. Resides in New York City.

Child:
1 *Maria Seymour*, b. Oct. 14, 1871.

5 *Ann Eliza*, b. Aug. 10, 1839; m., Oct. 18, 1866, to David J. Johnston.

Children:
1 *David Stuart*, b. Feb. 21, 1868.
2 *Albert Eddy*, b. Nov. 7, 1871; d. March 12, 1875.
3 *Harold Eddy*, b. July 24, 1878.

6 *Mary Alice*, b. Nov. 28, 1841; m. Warren T. Kellogg.

Children:
1 *Grace Eddy*, b. Nov. 14, 1866.
2 *Charles Harvey*, b. Sept. 10, 1869; d. May 4, 1871.
3 *Elizabeth Haskell*, b. June 8, 1872.
4 *Titus Eddy*, b. Jan. 8, 1876.

7 *Elizabeth Agnes Stewart*, b. April 17, 1846.
8 *Delia Emma*, b. June 5, 1849; m., Dec. 23, 1873, Charles Nash.

Child:
1 *Charles Howard*, b. June 12, 1877.

NOTE.— *Titus Eddy* had four other children who d. young.

4 BENJAMIN FRANKLIN, b. Dec. 29, 1804, in Wethersfield, Vt. Resides in Wisconsin (1880).
5 LEONORA JANE, b. May 21, 1807, in Wethersfield, Vt.; m. George W. Macardle, Aug. 12, 1830, in Elizabethtown, N.J. She d. Sept. 26, 1856, in Lansingburg, N.Y.

Children:
1 *Franklin Garrison*, b. Jan. 9, 1832, in Newburg, N.Y.; d. Dec. 26, 1853.
2 *George Henry*, b. March 20, 1834, in Newburg, N.Y.; m. Anna W. McKelsey, Jan. 14, 1858, who is a clergyman in Byron, Ill.

Children:
1 *Chandler D.*, b. Oct. 7, 1860; d. Aug., 1863.
2 *George C.*, b. July 12, 1864; d. young.

3 *William Powers*, b. Aug. 31, 1835, in Newburg; m. Sarah L. Tallman, Oct. 11, 1859.

4 *Eustace Whipple*, b. Oct. 7, 1837, in Newark, N.J.; d. young.

5 *Eustace Whipple*, b. Aug. 23, 1839; m. Eliza Burns. Resides in Warren, Ill. (1880).

6 *Lucy Ann Powers*, b. May 8, 1841; m. Augustus Frear; m., second, William O. Niles.

7 *Isaac Eddy*, b. July 12, 1844, in Newark, N.J.; d. young.

8 *Ann Eliza*, b. Nov. 8, 1849, in Lansingburg, N.Y.; d. May 10, 1856.

6 THOMAS JEFFERSON, b. May 17, 1809, at Wethersfield, Vt.; m. Lucy McGuire, Oct. 15, 1833. Resides in Waterford, N.Y.

Children:

1 *Isaac Newton*, b. April 17, 1835; d. Jan. 18, 1854.

2 *Harriet Frances*, b. Oct. 16, 1837; d. Dec. 10, 1869.

3 *Charles Carroll*, b. Aug. 14, 1840; d. young.

4 *Elizabeth Agnes*, b. Sept. 16, 1841; resides in Waterford, N.Y.

5 *Mary Emily*, b. Aug. 17, 1847; m. Dr. Allen G. Peckham, in Waterford, N.Y. Living there 1880.

Child:

1 *Harvey Newman*, b. Oct. 15, 1873; d. Aug. 6, 1879.

6 *Thomas Bliss*, b. Aug. 7, 1844; d. April 21, 1875.

7 GEORGE WASHINGTON, b. March 10, 1811, in Wethersfield, Vt.; m. May, 1833, Mary Polk Wetherbee of Cambridgeport, Mass. She d. May 9, 1836. He m. second, 1838, Delia Emma Ferris of New York City. He is a manufacturer, and a very ingenious man, having procured many patents, especially for wheels for railway carriages. He now resides in Waterford.

Children, all by second wife:

1 *Clarence*, b. Nov. 17, 1839, in Waterford, N.Y., graduated at Yale College, 1861, and at Princeton Theological Seminary in 1864. Is a clergyman; m. Jane Elizabeth Scott of Waterford.

Children:

1 *George Ira*, b. May 23, 1865.

2 *Jessie Eugenia*, b. March 9, 1869.

2 *Adelaide*, b. June 2, 1841, in Waterford; m., May 19, 1863, John L. Hill; resides in Brooklyn, L.I.

Children :
1 *Grace Adelaide*, b. March 1, 1875.
2 *Christine Eddy*, b. Oct. 25, 1877.

3 *Lyman Kinsley*, b. July 13, 1848, at Waterford; m. Agnes Burton of Lansingburg, N.Y., Nov. 17, 1870. She d. June 18, 1874. He is a civil engineer.

Child :
1 *James Van Schoonhoven*, b. Sept. 9, 1871; d. Dec. 15, 1871.

4 *Lilly Jean*, b. Oct. 24, 1853; d. Dec. 27, 1855.
5 *Florence May*, b. June 20, 1856.
6 *George Herbert*, b. Sept. 9, 1860.

8 WALTON MEAD, b. Oct. 13, 1818, in Wethersfield, Vt.; m. Mary C. Rynders, Sept. 9, 1841, in Waterford, N.Y. Second, m. Mary Jane Pendleton, Oct. 15, 1846, in Lansingburg, N.Y. Resides there 1880.

Children by first wife :
1 *James Isaac*, b. Dec. 5, 1842; m., May, 1867, Caroline A. McKelsey. She d. ——.

Children by second wife :
2 *George Walton*, b. Oct. 13, 1847, in Lansingburg, N.Y.; m., June 12, 1873, Helen Alida Farnham of Lansingburg.

Children :
1 *Florence Alida*, b. April 21, 1874.
2 *Chauncy Walton*, b. Aug. 23, 1876.

3 *Henry Pendleton*, b. April 7, 1860; d. March 14, 1861.
4 *Mary Elizabeth*, b. June 24, 1862.
5 *Nellie Grant*, b. June 28, 1869.

By second wife, Isaac Eddy had children :
9 ISAAC FOSTER, b. July 22, 1830; d. Nov. 25, 1854.
10 EVANDA NEWBURY, b. Nov., 1832, at Waterford, N.Y.; d. Feb. 11, 1833.
11 LUCY E., b. March 22, 1834; m. Garrett Fulton; d. Aug. 12, 1859.

12 SUSAN DESDEMONA, b. Feb. 11, 1834; d. Sept. 3, 1849, at Waterford.

13 CASTELLA ESPERANZA, b. June 21, 1841; m. W. F. Sherwin. Resides in Elmira, N.Y. (1880).

Children:
1 *Florence*, b. 1862.
2 *Harry*, b. 1880.

---

232 254 (V.) WILLIAM EDDY, b. March 6, 1729, in Swansea, Mass.; moved to Clarendon, Vt., from Smithfield, R.I.

Children:
260 255 1 OLIVER, b. in Scituate, R.I.
261 256 2 LUTHER, b. in Scituate, R.I.
262 257 3 ASAHEL, b. in Scituate, R.I.
263 258 4 BAYES, or BAZIN, b. in Scituate, R.I.
264 259 5 ALLEN, b. in Scituate, R.I.

---

255 260 (VI.) OLIVER EDDY.

Children:
1 WILLIAM of Salena, N.Y., has one son (*Charles*) and two daughters.
2 IRA of Canada has five sons (*James, Ira, Johnson*).
3 CHARLES of Euclid, Ohio; b. in R.I., in 1800; his sons are *Hazel P., James M., Oliver W., Charles H., Nathaniel W.,* and *Lewis B.,* etc., ten in all.
4 OLIVER of Scipio, N.Y.; shoemaker.

---

256 261 (VI.) LUTHER EDDY; lived in Scituate, R.I.; dead; b. in R.I.; is there in 1840.

Children:
1 WILLIAM; lives in Euclid, Ohio; farmer.
2 HAZAEL; lives in Euclid, Ohio; farmer.
3 GARDINER; lives in Euclid, Ohio; farmer.
4 HALSEY; lives in Euclid, Ohio; farmer.

NOTE. — *Hazael's* sons are:
1 *Andrew.* 2 *Luther.* 3 *Henry.* 4 *George.* 5 *William.*

Halsey's sons are:
1 *Luke.* 2 *Otis.*

257 252 (VI.) ASAHEL EDDY, b. in Scituate, R.I.; moved to Otsego Co., State of New York; d. in Java, N.Y.

Children:

1 BETSEY, b. in Otsego Co., N.Y.; m. Edmund Potter; d. in Java, N.Y.
2 DEBORAH, b. in Otsego Co., N.Y.; m. Winsor Potter.
3 SALLY, b. in Otsego Co., N.Y.; m. Stephen Emery; d. in McHenry Co., Ill.
4 JOHN, b. Dec., 1795, in Otsego Co., N.Y.; m., Dec. 18, 1817, Caroline Ward; b. Jan. 6, 1799.

> Children:
>
> 1 *Alfred*, b. Nov. 2, 1818; m. Feb. 21, 1843.
> 2 *Lydia*, b. May 20, 1820; m., Oct. 7, 1841, Lewis W. Gill, in Java, N.Y. Reside, 1881, in Grand Rapids, Mich.
>
> > Children:
> >
> > 1 *Ophelia*, b. in China (now Arcade), N.Y.; m. —— Chappelle. She d. ——. They lived in Michigan.
> > 2 *Romelia*, b. ——; m. Chappelle.
> > 3 *Edward K.*, resides (1881) in Grand Rapids, Mich.
>
> 3 *Laura*, b. Feb. 1, 1822; m., Feb. 6, 1855, George W. Nichols. They live, 1881, in Java, N.Y.
>
> > Children:
> >
> > 1 *Asahel;* lives in Java, N.Y.
> > 2 *Salla;* lives in Java, N.Y.
>
> 4 *Asahel*, b. Oct. 2, 1823; m., Jan. 1, 1845, Sarah Cook. Reside in Gibbon, Neb., 1880.
>
> > Children:
> >
> > 1 *Spaulding.*
> > 2 *Henry.*
> > 3 *Amanda.*
> > 4 *Belle.*
>
> 5 *Parthina*, b. Sept. 27, 1825; m., Sept. 28, 1847, Joseph P. Dickenson. Live in Milford, Mich., 1880.
>
> > Child:
> >
> > 1 *George L.*
>
> 6 *Edwin*, b. May 30, 1829; m., March 10, 1852, Lorinda Blood. Reside in Arcade, N.Y., 1880.

Children:
1 *Lewis.*
2 *John.*
3 *A son.*
4 *A daughter.*

7 *James*, b. May 30, 1832; m., Feb. 19, 1857, Isabella A. Worsley (b. April 17, 1835). He resides in Aurora, Ill.; has practised law, been a member of the State Senate, and has been prominent in politics. In 1881 is engaged in mining and railway affairs.

Children:
1 *Carrie Lucilla*, b. June 18, 1858.
2 *George Edwin*, b. March 9, 1868.

8 *Caroline*, b. June 13, 1834; m., May 14, 1856, Elliott J. Barber. Live in Java, N.Y. (1881).

Children:
Two daughters.

9 *John*, b. Oct. 7, 1836; m., March 23, 1859, —— Nichols; was killed in the battle of "Fair Oaks," Virginia, July, 1863, he being a soldier in the Union Army.

Child:
1 *Lydia*, residing in Java, N.Y. (1880).

10 *Rachel*, b. Jan. 22, 1840; m., Jan. 6, 1861, Abram Thompson. Reside in Gibbon, Neb. (1880).

Children:
1 *Jessie.*   2 *A son.*

11 *Spaulding*, b. Jan. 5, 1843; d. July 25, 1843.

5 HARRY, m. Annie Whitney; resided in St. Charles, Ill.
6 PHEBE, m. Daniel Smith; resided in Rochester, N.Y.
7 ERMINA, m. Dr. Reuben Lewis, resided in Attica, Iowa.
8 SPAULDING, b. in Otsego Co., N.Y., 1807; m. Mary Stevens. Removed to St. Charles, Ill., 1836.

Children:
1 *Savilla*, b. March 4, 1834, in Java, N.Y.; m. Daniel Cooper in St. Charles, Ill., March 11, 1856.

Children:

1 *Nellie*, b. Feb. 18, 1857, in Fulton, Ill.
2 *Eddy*, b. Aug. 31, 1868, in Omaha, Neb.
3 *Alda*, b. Feb. 28, 1871.

2 *Celestia*, b. Dec. 3, 1835, in Java, N.Y.
3 *Hosmer*, b. Oct. 24, 1839, in St. Charles, Ill.; m. Mary Ladd in Elgin, Ill., Dec. 25, 1866.

Children:

1 *John M.*, b. Oct. 26, 1868, in Plato, Ill.
2 *Frank*, b. Jan. 8, 1870.

4 *John M.*, b. April 29, 1843; m. Alda Van Camp, July 12, 1869; resides in Chicago (1880).
5 *Adella*, b. Sept. 8, 1848; m. James Parton, Sept. 30, 1870; resides in Iowa.
6 *James W.*, b. Nov. 21, 1855; resides in Omaha (1880).

9 AMY, m. Youngs Gregery; resides in Marshall, Mich.
10 AMANDA, m. Daniel Clase; resides in Marshall, Mich.

---

258 20: (VI.) BAYES EDDY, b. in Scituate, R.I. In 1840 residing in Halderman, Upper Canada.

Children:
1 HIRAM.   2 WILLIAM.   3 NELSON.
4 IRA.   5 GEORGE W.

---

259 264 (VI.) ALLEN EDDY, b. in Scituate, R.I.; d. in Canada about 1835.

Children:
1 HARDING, b., 1796, in R.I.; resides in Eddystone, Ont., Canada (1880).

Children:
1 *Elisha.*   2 *Steven.*
3 *Dorcas.*   4 *William.*
5 *Allen.*   6 *Carlton.*
7 *Alfred M.*   8 *Philo.*
9 *Isaac.*   10 *Bayze.*

266 265 2 ALFRED.
3 DORCAS, b. 1799, in R.I.; m. —— Purdy, and d. in Canada.

4 ROBIE, b. 1801; m. Elizabeth Doolittle; d. in Canada.
5 ALLEN, b., 1804, in R.I.; d. in Illinois, 1876.
6 PHILO, b., 1805, in R.I.; lives in Sardinia, N.Y., 1880.

Children:
1 *Dudley D.*
2 *Augustus C.*, b. Aug. 17, 1836; was a soldier in the War of the Rebellion; m. Margaret Clark in Baltimore, Md., April 7, 1863. Resides (1881) in Sardinia, N.Y., and has children.
3 *Volora D.*, was a soldier in the War of the Rebellion; was taken prisoner and confined at Andersonville. Resides (1881) in Minnesota.
4 *Roby.*   5 *Lois.*
6 *Samuel W.*   7 *William.*
8 *Philo.*   9 *Clarissa.*
10 *Dorcas M.*

7 HENRY; resides in Canada in 1850?

————————

265 266 (VII.) ALFRED EDDY, b. 1798 in R.I.; m., Sept. 18, 1817, Charlotte Day, in Canada. She b. Sept. 8, 1800; d. 1879.

Children:
1 ALFRED DAY, b. Sept. 22, 1820; m. Abagail Dickerson; resides at Fremont, Ohio; was a soldier in the Union Army of the War of the Rebellion, 29th Ohio Regiment, and went through a long campaign in the West.

Children:
1 *Louisa.*   2 *Rollin.*
3 *Florence.*   4 *Clara.*

2 ELIZA MAY, b. May 22, 1818; d. 1872; m. John A. Johnson.
3 ROBERT M., b. Aug. 16, 1822; m. Sarah M. Quackenbush; b., Jan. 2, 1822, in Buffalo, N.Y. Resides (1880) in Chicago, Ill.

Children:
1 *Ellen Augusta*, b. March 13, 1846.
2 *Charles Mortimer*, b. Aug. 14, 1847; d. young.
3 *George Day*, b. Aug. 18, 1849. Resides in Chicago, Ill.

Child:
1 *George Albert.*

4 *Albert M.*, b. July 4, 1851. Resides in Chicago, Ill.

Children:
1 *Blanch.*   2 *Charles.*

5 *Francis Rollin*, b. Aug. 16, 1853; d. young.
6 *Willie*, b. May 2, 1855; d. young.
7 *Harriet Madeline*, b. Nov. 28, 1863; resides in Chicago, Ill. (1880).

---

233 267 (V.) JOHN EDDY, b. Dec. 25, 1730; d., aged 92 years 2 months and 28 days. Was buried in Northbridge, Mass., where he resided fifty years.

Children:
1 HULDA, b. May 27, 1756.
270 268   2 THOMAS, b. Jan. 25, 1759; d. Oct. 5, 1786.
3 ASA, b. Dec. 4, 1760; d. young.
4 HANNAH, b. May 29, 1763.
271 269   5 JESSE, b. Nov. 29, 1769.

---

268 270 (VI.) THOMAS EDDY, b. Jan. 25, 1759; d. Oct. 5, 1786.

Child:
1 ASA; living in 1840 in Milford, N.Y.; is a tanner and quite wealthy (1840).

---

269 271 (VI.) JESSE EDDY, b. Nov. 29, 1769. In 1840 was living in Palmyra, N.Y. Until 1826 he resided in Northbridge, Mass.; m., for his first wife, Sarah Congden, and for second, Hannah Shove of Mendon. He d. March, 1855.

Children:
1 JOHN (of Fall River), b., Northbridge, July 18, 1799.
430 272   2 JESSE (of Fall River), b., Northbridge, Feb. 18, 1801.
3 SARAH.   4 MARY.
5 HANNAH.   6 JOANNA.

---

218 273 (V.) ELISHA EDDY, b. May 2, 1711; m. Hannah. She d. Sept. 23, 1765, aged 51.

Children:
275 274   1 JOHN, b. Aug. 23, 1742.

2 BARNARD, b. Dec. 7, 1746.
3 BETHIAH, b. Dec. 28, 1748; m. Job Anthony, Feb. 23, 1790.

---

274 275 (VI.) JOHN EDDY. b. Aug. 23, 1742. He moved from Norton to West Brookfield, Mass., in 1775. A farmer, and was a soldier in the Revolutionary Army (once at least in Halifax). He served seven years; d. Jan., 1819.

Children:
277 276 1 SETH, b. in Norton, July 2, 1765; d. Oct. 16, 1823.
        2 JOHN.   3 ELIJAH.   4 ABIEL.
        All three d. in Brookfield before reaching manhood.

---

276 277 (VII.) SETH EDDY, b. July 2, 1765; d. Oct. 16, 1823; a farmer in Brookfield, Mass.

Children:
1 TITUS, b. in Brookfield, July 12, 1795.

Children:
1 *Elijah*, b. April 23, 1818; shoemaker.
2 *Erastus O.*, b. July 24, 1819; farmer.
3 *John*, b. June 26, 1826.
4 *George*, b. Jan. 7, 1828.
5 *Charles W.*, b. April 6, 1837.

2 ABIEL, b. in Brookfield, July 31, 1808; lives in Ware; has an adopted son, *Dexter Eddy*, who was originally named *James Stebbins*.

---

219 278 (V.) MICHAEL EDDY, b. July 25, 1715.

Children:
        1 ANN, b. Dec. 13, 1741; m. Brooks Mason, Oct. 28, 1758.
281 279 2 HESEKIAH, b. April 2, 1744.
282 280 3 WILLIAM, b. March 9, 1748.
        4 JALE, b. Jan. 20, 1750; d. Nov. 3, 1756.
        5 SYBIL, b. Sept. 19, 1757.
        6 MICHAEL, b. Nov. 1, 1760; m. Phebe Webber, who d., aged 94. Pastor of First Baptist Church, Newport, R.I., from Dec. 12, 1789, to his death.
        7 JALE, b. May 6, 1753; m. William Heath, Nov. 4, 1773.

279 281 (VI.) HESEKIAH EDDY, b. April 2, 1744; m. Lydia Wilbur, April 14, 1768, of Swansea.

Children:
1 BETSEY, b. Sept. 9, 1768.
2 HESEKIAH, b. Sept. 19, 1770.

---

280 282 (VI.) WILLIAM EDDY, b. March 9, 1748; m. Amy Eddy, Sept. 27, 1770.

Children:
1 ANNA, b. Sept. 6, 1772.
2 PHEBE, b. May 20, 1774.
3 SYBIL, b. Jan. 7, 1778.
4 AMY, b. May 28, 1781.
5 WILLIAM, b. July 15, 1784.
6 PATIENCE, b. March 20, 1786.
7 MARY, b. April 7, 1790.
8 HESEKIAH, b. April 12, 1797.

---

208 283 (VII.) JOHN S. EDDY, b. April 2, 1780, in Rehoboth, Mass.; m. Martha Jenckes Tefft (b. Aug. 22, 1782, in Providence, R.I.), May, 1798, in Providence. He m., second, Hannah Glazier, and third, Julia G. Eddy (widow of Barnard Eddy); she d. April. 1865. He d. July 29, 1866, at Providence, R.I. His children were by his first wife.

Children:
1 WILLIAM, b. Jan. 7, 1799, in Providence, R.I.; m. Sarah Briggs of Hyannis, Mass. He d. at Rio Janeiro, Brazil.

    Children:
    1 *Elijah Briggs*, b. 1823; d. 1827.
    2 *Alexander W.*, b. June 2, 1825; m. Almira L. Harrington, April 26, 1846, in Providence, R.I.

        Children:
        1 *Almira Susan*, b. July 3, 1847; d. Aug. 10, 1849.
        2 *Lydia*, b. Dec. 22, 1848; m., 1869, to Henry H. Hatch in Norwich, Ct.
        3 *Charles E.*, b. Aug. 19, 1852; d. March 3, 1856.
        4 *Ellen Frances*, b. July 10, 1854; m., 1872, to J. Watson Belden of Connecticut.
        5 *Martha Augusta*, b. July 23, 1800.

2 MARY ANN, b. Aug. 10, 1801, in Providence, R.I.; m. Edwin Field in Providence. He b. in Pawtucket, R.I., Dec. 29, 1799; d. Aug. 3, 1867. She d. March 7, 1850.

Children:
1 *Mary Ann*, b. Sept. 14, 1821; m. James M. Bradford in Providence, R.I.

Child:
1 *Jessie Field*, b. March 5, 1858, in Providence, R.I.

2 *Edwin*, b. Nov. 22, 1822; m. Ellen Morrison; m., second, a Mexican.
3 *Martha Eddy*, b. Feb. 2, 1824; m., Jan. 21, 1844, in Providence, Henry C. Clark of Providence.

Children:
1 *William Henry*, b. Feb. 20, 1845, in Providence, R.I.
2 *Henry Clinton*, b. Oct. 24, 1857, in Providence, R.I.

4 *Angelina*, b. 1825; d. young.
5 *John S. Eddy*, b. Jan. 4, 1827, in Providence; m. Anna Collis.
6 *Frederick Hampton*, b. Oct. 16, 1827, in Providence, R.I.; m., Oct. 16, 1851, in Newport, R.I., Adelaide C. Elsbree. She was b. Sept. 30, 1831, in Fall River.

Children:
1 *Clara L.*, b. Aug. 23, 1854; d. Jan. 3, 1857.
2 *Carrie E.*, b. July 4, 1861; d. Aug. 23, 1862.
3 *Frederic E.*, b. Jan. 7, 1864, in Providence, R.I.

7 *Charles H.*, b. April 29, 1823; m., April 13, 1851, in Providence, R.I., Jane C. Kent, b. Dec. 1, 1835, in St. Johnsbury, Vt.

Children:
1 *Charles H.*, b. Feb. 15, 1865.
2 *Cora V.*, b. Feb. 3, 1868.

8 *Edna J.*, b. March 23, 1838; m., Sept. 4, 1859, Alfred H. Willard, son of Hezekiah Willard.

Children:
1 *Martha*, b. March 13, 1861, in Providence, R.I.

2 *Alice*, b. Oct. 16, 1864, in Providence, R.I.; d. Dec. 13, 1865.

3 *Harriet E.*, b. Nov. 9, 1866, in Providence, R.I.

4 *Adah C.*, b. Nov. 3, 1871, in Providence, R.I.

9 *George Washington*, b. 1835; d. young.

3 BETSEY SALISBURY, b. July 24, 1803; d. March 27, 1806.

4 CHARLES T., b. June 7, 1805; d. Jan. 18, 1807.

5 JOHN HAMPTON, b. March 4, 1807; d. Aug. 6, 1807.

6 ALBERT, b. March 23, 1808; d. Jan. 28, 1836; m., March 23, 1823, Ruth Green of Scituate, who was b. April 30, 1805; d. Aug. 27, 1832. His second wife, Harriet Pike, m. Dec. 22, 1833, and b. March 6, 1809.

Children:

1 *Albert Montfred*, b. Jan. 10, 1829; d. June 5, 1830.

2 *Pembroke S.*, b. July 27, 1830; m., Nov. 18, 1851, Mary Jane Patterson; b. July 13, 1832, in Manchester, England.

Children:

1 *Charles Albert*, b. July 3, 1853; m. Ella V. Payton, April 14, 1877.

2 *Frank Pettie*, b. July 6, 1858.

7 MARTHA JENCKES, b. Jan. 22, 1810; d. Feb. 4, 1810.

8 DANIEL TEFFT, b. April 14, 1811; d. June 10, 1812.

9 JOHN, b. March 26, 1813.

10 REBECCA, b. March 25, 1815; m. J. G. Pettis, July 1, 1835.

11 DANIEL TEFFT, b. March 2, 1817; m., 1840, Alice P. Whaley of South Kensington, R.I.; b. Oct. 23, 1808.

Children:

1 *Elizabeth S.*, b. Nov. 4, 1841, in Providence, R.I.: m., 1862, to J. H. McGuire.

2 *John S.*, b. Aug. 27, 1843; d. 1864.

3 *William*, b. June 3, 1846; m., Dec. 25, 1871, Mary Bryden, b. July 1, 1850, in Thompson, Ct.

Child:

1 *Alice Jane*, b. Oct. 28, 1872, in Webster, Mass.

4 *Daniel Tefft*, b. March 6, 1849; m., Oct. 4, 1873, Sarah E. Clark.

5 *David M.*, b. June 30, 1853, in Smithfield, R.I.

6 *Mary W.*, b. Aug. 22, 1861.

12 HENRY BABBITT, b. Jan. 7, 1819; m. Jan. 6, 1842, at
North Scituate, R.I., Amanda Randall; b. March 9, 1819.

Children :
1 *Albert*, b. March 23, 1843, in Providence, R.I.
2 *Martha M.*, Oct. 16, 1848, in Providence, R.I.

13 STEPHEN, b. Dec. 12, 1821.
14 AMANDA MALVINA, b. July 13, 1824, at Providence,
R.I.; m., Sept. 22, 1842, Robert Goodwin; b. July 10,
1824. They reside in San Francisco, Cal.

Children:
1 *Edwin Field*, b. Sept. 2, 1843, in Providence, R.I.;
d. Oct. 14, 1853.
2 *Martha*, b. June 6, 1846, in Providence, R.I.; m.
June 6, 1867.
3 *Robert Henry*, b. Nov. 13, 1854.
4 *Amanda Malvina*, b. Sept. 14, 1857.
5 *Carrie Evelyne*, b. April 6, 1860.
6 *James Albert*, b. March 29, 1863.

---

132 284 (V.) ZACHARIAH EDDY, b. about 1700.

Children:
1 ELIPHALET.
286 285 2 ENOCH.
3 THOMAS.

---

285 286 (VI.) ENOCH EDDY, m. Hannah Lippit. He was b. 1721,
and d. Nov., 1783. She d. 1798

Children:
1 LOIS, m. John Howland.
2 ROBA, d. unmarried.
3 ZACHARIAH, m., first, Urena Boun; second, Evans;
third, Lois White.
4 LIPPIT, m. Esther Gurtis.
288 287 5 WILLARD, b. Jan. 26, 1760.
6 HANNAH, m. John Stone.
7 MARY, d. unmarried.
8 JOHN, m. Experience Cooke. Lived in 1820 in Jefferson
Co., N.Y., and afterwards in Ohio.
9 ENOCH, m. Amy King. Lived in Jefferson Co.; d.
about 1850.
10 RENEW, m. James Howland.

Jonathan G Eddy
Brattleboro 78

287 288 (VII.) WILLARD EDDY, b. Jan. 26, 1760. He, at the age of sixteen, enlisted in the Revolutionary Army for three years, after which he shipped in the privateer *Providence*, and made a voyage to France in her. Subsequently was in the privateer *Boston*, and blockaded in Charlestown, S.C., and aided in defending the fort, he being captured there, and afterwards exchanged at Philadelphia. In 1782, m. Dorcas Matthewson, b. Dec. 7, 1762; d. April 5, 1847; she was dau. of Noah Matthewson of Johnstown, R.I. He lived in Gloucester, R.I. In 1795 went to Unadilla, N.Y., and subsequently to Sherburn, N.Y., and from there to Richfield, N.Y., where he d. April 13, 1854.

Children:

291 289   1 MATTHEWSON, b. May 8, 1785; d. 1842.
294 290   2 OTIS, b. Jan. 20, 1787; d. Sept. 5, 1843.
           3 RHODA, b. Aug. 13, 1790; m. Charles Calwell; d. June 19, 1818, at Henrietta, N.Y.

    Children:
    1 *John*, d. in Monroe Co., N.Y.
    2 *Emily*.
    3 *Rhoda;* resides in Skaneateles, N.Y. (1880).

    4 HANNAH, b. June 20, 1792; m. John Hackley, Sept. 8, 1825; d. May 5, 1833.
    5 BETSEY, b. Nov. 7, 1794; m. Joseph Beardsley, Jan. 4, 1818. He d. about 1857 in New York City. Mrs. Beardsley resides (1880) in Ilion, N.Y.

    Children:
    1 *Dorcas Eliza*, b. Feb. 7, 1819; m., Dec. 20, 1843, Stephen H. Lathrop. Resides in Oswego, N.Y. (1880).

        Children:
        1 *Joseph Beardsley*, b. Oct. 17, 1844; m. Mary F. Herrick, Aug. 25, 1869.
        2 *Stephen Alfred*, b. Aug. 14, 1848. Resides in New York City (1880).
        3 *Mary T.*, b. Jan. 20, 1850.
        4 *Jane Elizabeth*, b. Feb. 23, 1852.
        5 *Samuel Holden Parsons*, b. Oct. 29, 1854.
        6 *James William*, b. July 19, 1856; d. young.

    2 *Joseph Warren Beardsley*, b. 1820; d. Aug., 1868; m. Caroline Maxson.

Children :

1 *Amelia Elizabeth*, b. Aug. 3, 1848, in Johnston, Wis.
2 *Arthur Maxson*, b. Sept. 5, 1849; d. young.
3 *Frank Warren*, b. Aug. 17, 1852, in Bradford, Wis.; d. March, 1872.
4 *Clara*, b. April 3, 1854; m. Edmund G. Babbidge. Resides in Prescott, Wis. (1880).

Child :
1 *Jessie Clara*, b. July 26, 1875.

5 *Anna Cora*, b. Aug. 15, 1858, at Prescott, Wis.; d. 1871.

3 *Frances Olivia*, m., Jan. 26, 1846, Erastus Clark. She d. March, 1872; resided in Utica, N.Y.

Children :

1 *Mary Kirkland*, b. Aug., 1848; m. Charles P. Kirkland, Jr.
2 *Arthur Beardsley*, b. Dec., 1854; d. 1864.
3 *Walton*, b. April, 1856. Resides (1880) in New Orleans, La.; m., Dec. 28, 1880, Alice Maud Shaw of Natchez, Miss.
4 *Edward Blayton*, b. Aug., 1860; is (1880) a cadet at West Point Military Academy.

4 *Lydia Louise*, m. Floyd C. Shepard. Resides in Ilion, N.Y. (1880).

Children :

1 *Mary Louise*, b. April, 1848; m. Gilbert W. Warren. Resides in Cleveland, Ohio (1880).

Child :
1 *Jennie Louise*, b. Dec., 1878; d. July, 1879.

2 *Alfred Coats*, b. Feb., 1851; m. Idelia V. Owens.

Child :
1 *Floyd C.*, b. May, 1879.

3 *Fanny Clark*, b. Feb., 1853.
4 *Harry North*, b. Feb., 1855; d. Feb., 1874.
5 *Elizabeth Beardsley*, b. 1857; m. Frederic William Armstrong.

Child:

1   *Alexander Floyd,* b. June, 1879.

6   *Robert Alden,* b. Aug., 1859.
7   *Kate Lyon,* b. Jan., 1862; d. June, 1875.
8   *Floyd Matthewson,* b. Jan., 1864; d. Oct., 1864.
9   *Grace Walton,* b. April, 1865.
10 *Alice Hyde,* b. March, 1867.
11 *Floy Dorcas,* b. May, 1870.

5   *Lewis,* m. Charlotte Judah. He d. Jan., 1858, in New York City.

Child:

1   *Anna R.,* b. July, 1857.

6   *Mary Moore,* m. Edmund Underwood of U.S. Army.

Children:

1   *Edmund Beardsley,* b. March, 1853, at Humboldt Bay, Cal. In the U.S.N. (1880).
2   *James,* b. Nov., 1855, at Richfield, N.Y.; d. young.
3   *Champlin Louis,* b. 1857, at Richfield, N.Y.

7   *Anna Raymond,* m. Alexander Seward. Reside in Utica, N.Y. (1880).

Children:

1   *Frederick Raymond,* b. Feb. 27, 1871.
2   *Elliott Huntington,* b. May 31, 1874.

6   NANCY, b. Sept. 13, 1796; d. June 28, 1822.
7   LYDIA, b. May 28, 1798; m. Calvin Hawley, March 3, 1823; d. May 25, 1825.

---

289 291 (VIII.) MATTHEWSON EDDY, b. May 8, 1785; d. 1842, at Richfield, N.Y. He m. Anna Russell, Dec. 24, 1800; b. Dec. 22, 1788; d. Feb. 10, 1852. His death was on Oct. 24, 1842.

Children:

293 292 1   OTIS, m. Lucy A. Clark. He was b. Aug. 30, 1810.
2   LUCY ANN, b. Dec. 11, 1811; m., Jan. 13, 1841, Russell Catlin, who d. Nov., 1879.
3   RUSSELL, b. March 27, 1814; m. Zerviah Cary; lived in Wisconsin, but d. in California, March 27, 1878.

292 293 (IX.) OTIS EDDY, b. Aug. 30, 1810; m., Jan. 10, 1837, to
Lucy A. Clark at Ithaca, N.Y., who d. Dec. 1, 1879, at
Plymouth, Mich.

Children:

1 JANE, b. Dec. 27, 1839; m. Delos F. Smith, Nov., 1880;
residing at Whitmore Lake, Mich.
2 WILLARD, b. Feb. 27, 1838; killed in battle at Williams-
burg, Va., May 5, 1862.
3 WILLIAM HANNAHS, b. Dec. 25, 1841; killed at Fred-
ericsburg, Va., Dec. 12, 1862.
4 CLARK, b. July 30, 1843; d. Jan. 18, 1865, from wounds
received in battle at Gettysburg. Pa.
5 SARAH ELIZABETH, b. July 8, 1845; m., Nov. 21, 1872,
to Albert Nelson.
6 JAMES OTIS, b. Nov. 28, 1847.
7 ANNA, b. March 31, 1849. Resides at Whitmore Lake,
Mich.
8 JOHN MATTHEWSON, b. June 16, 1851; m. Alpha White,
March 1. 1880.

---

290 294 (VIII.) OTIS EDDY, b. Jan. 20, 1787, in Glocester, R.I.; d.
Sept. 5, 1843, at Sinclairville, N.Y.; m. at Chambers,
N.Y., Oct. 3, 1811, to Harriet Tracy, who was a dau. of
John Tracy. She was b. at Franklin, Ct., May 16,
1792, and d. at Ithaca, N.Y., Sept. 3, 1877. Otis Eddy
built an aqueduct of the Erie Canal; also a cotton
factory in 1825 at Ithaca. He was a manufacturer of
cotton goods up to his decease.

Children:

297 295   1 WILLARD TRACY, b. Sept. 13, 1812.
300 296   2 LOTHROP STORRS, b. July 1, 1814; d. Nov. 9, 1851.
301 297   3 WILLIAM MATHEWSON, b. Aug. 10, 1818; d. March 9,
1854.
302 298   4 JAMES, b. Oct. 23, 1821.
5 FAYETTE, b. Oct. 18, 1816; d. Oct., 1817.
6 HARRIET EMILY, b. Oct. 5, 1826; d. Dec. 16, 1826.

---

295 299 (IX.) WILLARD TRACY EDDY, b. Sept. 13, 1812; m.
Susan Williams, June 17, 1816; she b. July, 1819; d.
at Bayonne, N.J., Jan. 3, 1879. Resided in Ithaca,
N.Y., but in 1880 at Brooklyn, L.I.

Children:

1 HARRIET EMILY, b. Sept. 30, 1838.

2 SUSAN MARIA, b. Oct. 20, 1846; m. Aug. 20, 1868, to William J. Savage. Resides in Brooklyn, L.I.

Children:
1 *Walter Tracy*, b. July 29, 1869.
2 *Otis Eddy*, b. Aug. 16, 1871; d. Aug., 1872.
3 *William T.*, b. Nov. 5, 1873.
4 *Mabel S.*, b. Aug. 25, 1879.

3 WILLARD TRACY, b. June 20, 1849; m., Sept. 16, 1869, Hattie Louisa Savage. He resides in Bayonne, N.J., and is a land-surveyor.

Children:
1 *Louise Estelle*, b. March 16, 1871.
2 *Willard Tracy*, b. Nov. 12, 1872.
3 *Harold Savage*, b. March 26, 1876.
4 *Herbert Griffin*, b. Sept. 1, 1878.

4 ALICE, b. June 17, 1859.

---

296 300 (IX.) LOTHROP STORRS, b. July 1, 1814; d. Nov. 9, 1851; m. Adaline E. Hargin, June, 1857. Residence, New York City, where he was a Master in Chancery. Went to California in 1850, and in 1852, on his return d., and was buried at Acapulco, Mexico.

Children:
1 ADELINE HARGIN, b. Sept., 1838; d. Nov. 29, 1838.
2 FRANCES LETELIA, d. 1841, aged 16 months.
3 LOTHROP STORRS, b. Sept. 1, 1814, in New York City. In 1880 resides in New York, and is a stenographer.

---

297 301 (IX.) WILLIAM MATTHEWSON EDDY, b. Aug. 10, 1818; m. Hannah Anthony, May 8, 1844, in Rhode Island; afterward, for second wife, he m. Harriet Ecker. Resided in New York City; but went to California in 1849, and surveyed and laid out San Francisco City; d. in San Francisco, March 9, 1854. Was in 1852 Surveyor-General of the State. He d. in 1854. His widow subsequently m. Mr. Hawks, who has since died. She in 1880 is in San Francisco.

Child:
1 CHARLES ECKER, b. Jan. 6, 1853; d. June 16, 1867.

298 302 (IX.)   JAMES EDDY, b. Oct. 23, 1821; m. Maria Judd, May 6, 1844. Residence, Ithaca, N.Y. She was dau. of Reuben Judd of Ithaca; was for some years with the Maine Telegraph Co., and afterwards was General Superintendent of the American Telegraph Co. He d. Aug. 23, 1858. His widow is now (1880) Mrs. A. H. Phillips of Brooklyn, L.I.

Children :

1   OTIS JUDD, b. June 30, 1846; m., Oct. 10, 1877, Gertrude I. Phillips.
2   CHARLES, b. Feb. 28, 1850, in Bangor, Me. In 1881, is a physician in Brooklyn, N.Y.; m., June 25, 1875, Anna Edner of that city. For some years past has interested himself in " Eddy Genealogy," and collected valuable information relating thereto, which he has recently published. The compiler of this work acknowledges his great indebtedness to Dr. Charles Eddy for much herein relating to the recent generations of Eddys.

Children :

1   *James William,* b. July 2, 1876, in Brooklyn, N.Y.
2   *Lillian Edner,* b. July 11, 1878, in Brooklyn, N.Y.

NOTE.—James A. Reid, in his recent book entitled "The Telegraph in America," mentions James Eddy with great respect and esteem.

___

133 303 (V.)   CALEB EDDY went to Berkshire and joined the Shakers.

Children :

1   ABIAH, d., aged about 90.
305 304   2   CALEB, b. Jan. 21, 1742; d. at Norton, aged 80.
3   POLLY, d. at Norton, aged 80.
4   ABIATHAN, a member of Harvard Shakers, aged 80.
5   ELIJAH, d. very old at Norton; had large family.
6   JOHN, drowned in a pond near his father's house at Norton.
7   EZRA, was very old at his decease.
8   ELEAZER, d. at 22 years of age of small pox.

___

304 305 (VI.)   CALEB EDDY, b. Jan. 21, 1742; m. Cloe, who was b. Oct. 14, 1743; date of marriage, May 26, 1765.

Children:

1 CALEB, b. March 5, 1766; d. Nov. 20, 1857; a Shaker.
2 NAOME, b. June 12, 1768; d. at 22 years of age; a Shaker.

307 306 3 AMOS, b. May 28, 1770; d. at Frankfort, N.Y.

4 CLOE, b. Feb. 21, 1773; d. at 21, at Pittsfield; Shaker.
5 JOHN, b. March 12, 1775; d. at Sheldon, near Buffalo, N.Y.
6 ELEAZER (or perhaps LEVI), b. Feb. 17, 1777; in 1852 was living in Maine.
7 ELEAZER, b. March 1, 1779; d. June 30, 1863; m. Deborah Moore; she b. Abril 15, 1784, and d. Feb. 14, 1857. Resided in Maine.

  Children:

  1 *Hiram M.*, b. March 8, 1807; d. Nov. 25, 1878.
  2 *Randall F.*, b. June 16, 1808; m. ~~Fanny W.~~ Boies, *Frances Neal* Jan. ~~7, 1842.~~ Resides in Maine, 1880. *nm Eddy. d. June 1884. 17. 1832 — d. Nov. 26. 1884.*
    Children:
    1 *Amanda M.*, b. Oct. 30, ~~1842~~ *1832*
    2 *Helen M.*, b. Dec. 11, 1844.
    3 *Frank L.*, b. Jan. 8, 1851.

  3 *Elbridge Gerry*, b. April 4, 1811; d. June 24, 1835.
  4 *Mary P.*, b. Jan. 22, 1814; d. April 1, 1866.
  5 *Wheelock R.*, b. April 1, 1816. Resides (1880) in Skowhegan, Me.
  6 *Decatur R.*, b. Aug. 20, 1822.
  7 *Nancy R.*, b. June 30, 1826; d. Aug. 10, 1847.
  8 *Franklin S.*, b. July 23, 1828; d. May 2, 1875.

8 MARGARET, b. April 1, 1781.

---

306 307 (VII.) AMOS EDDY, b. May 28, 1770; d. at Frankfort, N.Y., Dec., 1840; m. Rebecca.

  Children:
  None, but adopted four.

  NOTE. — There appeared in the " Utica Observer," in 1852, a statement by William H. H. Parkhurst, M.D., of Frankfort, N.Y., as follows: " On Friday, the 7th inst., a *post mortem* examination was held by Dr. Parkhurst on the body of the widow of Amos Eddy, in the town of Frankfort, Herkimer County, aged 77 years, and to the astonishment of all present, a full-grown fœtus was found, which she carried for the term of forty-six years. It was encased in a sort of bony or cartilaginous structure, except one leg and foot, and one elbow, which were almost entirely ossified.

The facts and circumstances of the case will be published at full
length as soon as Dr. Parkhurst finds leisure to put together the
history that he kept for the last twelve years, as well as of her
life before and after marriage, which took place fifty-two years
ago."

The above statement was confirmed by a letter of Dr. Parkhurst's, dated May 24, 1852, to Caleb Eddy, Esq., 4 Exeter Place,
Boston. — R. H. E.

---

135 308 (V.)   ELEAZER EDDY; no authentic account of him.

---

128 309 (IV.) ELEAZER EDDY, b. Oct. 16, 1681; d. in Norton, 1739;
m., first wife, Elizabeth Randel, March 27, 1701; second
wife, Elizabeth Cobb of Taunton, Feb. 6, 1723.

Children:
1 JOHN.
2 CALEB, m. Judith ——, and resided in Norton, Mass.

Children :
1 *Rachael*, b. June 23, 1728; d. 1729.
2 *Abiel*, b. April 5, 1740.
3 *Caleb*, b. Jan. 25, 1742.
4 *Beniah*, b. Dec. 28, 1744.
5 *Abiather*, b. June 16, 1746.
6 *Mary*, b. Sept. 10, 1748.
7 *John*, b. Jan. 25, 1751.
8 *Elijah*, b. Aug. 2, 1752, in Norton, Mass; m. Wealthy
——. She was b. in Taunton, 1751. He d. April
25, 1836. She d. 1835.

Children :
1 *William*, b. June 2, 1778; d. 1856; m. Salley ——,
b. Jan. 30, 1875; d. March, 1879.

Children :
1 *Sally*, b. Oct. 31, 1812; m. —— Jennings.
2 *Rhoda*, b. June 23, 1814; m. —— Whitman.
3 *Hannah*, b. June 14, 1816; m. —— Blake.
4 *William*, b. July 14, 1818; d. 1862.
5 *Cynthia*, b. Sept. 11, 1820; m. —— Luther.
6 *Wealthy*, b. Sept. 17, 1822; m. —— Lothrop.
7 *Elizabeth*, b. Oct. 13, 1825; m. —— Reed.

2 *Darius*, b. Aug. 20, 1779.
3 *Rhoda*, b. Sept. 26, 1781.

4 *Elijah*, b. March 10, 1785; d. 1805; m. Lucy ——, b. 1787; living 1880.

Children:

1 *Wealthy.*
2 *Rhoda.*
3 *Hodges.*
4 *Clarissy.*
5 *Eliza.*

5 *Wealthy*, b. Sept. 29, 1787.
6 *Lyman*, b. Nov. 11, 1792, in Norton, Mass.; d. May 21, 1784, in Providence, R.I. His wife, Lucinda ——, was b. in Taunton, Feb. 23, 1808, and d. April 26, 1837.

Children:

1 *Lyman Harvey*, b. Dec. 19, 1827, in Norton, Mass. He m. Margaret M ——; b. March 19, 1825, in Jefferson, Me. Residing in Providence, R.I.

Children:

1 *Charles Harvey*, b. June 11, 1852, in Providence; m. Caroline G. ——.
2 *Ella May*, b. March 30, 1855; d. Feb. 23, 1858.
3 *Ida May*, b. March 22, 1860.

2 *Lucinda M.*, b. April 9, 1829; d. Oct. 20, 1843.

3 ELEAZER.
4 JOSHUA.
5 OBEDIAH, m. Lois Hicks of Taunton, Mass.

Children:

1 *Ephraim*, b. Nov. 17, 1744.
2 *James*, b. Jan. 12, 1746.
3 *Obediah*, b. March 10, 1751.

311 310 6 JONATHAN, b. 1726.
7 OLIVER.
8 ELIZABETH, m. Penney.
9 HANNAH, m. Robert Miller of Rehoboth, March 7, 1726.
10 CHARITY, m. Baker.

310 311 (V.) JONATHAN EDDY, b. 1726-7 (d. Aug., 1804); m. Mary (b. Oct. 16, 1729), dau. of Dr. William Ware, May 4, 1749, by Geo. Leonard, Esq. His wife d. in 1814. In 1755 he was an officer in Col. Winslow's Regiment at Nova Scotia. In 1758 he enlisted a company for the war in Canada, under commission of the Governer of Massachusetts. In 1759 he raised another company in Marshfield, Mass., for Col. Fry's regiment, in which he served as Captain from April 2, 1759, to Sept. 30, 1760. After his discharge, in 1760, he remained at Norton (calling himself of Cumberland, N.S., in a deed), having emigrated with his family about that time. On the breaking out of the Revolutionary War he fled to the United States, leaving his family behind; and March 27, 1776, he was at Gen. Washington's headquarters at Cambridge, Mass. (See Washington's letter to Congress dated March 27, 1776.) For the exploits and services rendered by Col. Jonathan Eddy, see a memoir of him by Joseph W. Parker, Esq., of Burlington, Me., 1877. In Aug., 1784, Col. Eddy, with his family, removed to Township No. 10 in Maine, which in compliment to him was afterwards named *Eddington*.

Children:

316 312	1	JONATHAN, b. Jan. 28, 1750.
317 313	2	WILLIAM, b. Aug. 16, 1752.
326 314	3	IBROOK, b. Jan. 9, 1754.
327 315	4	ELIAS, b. Nov 30, 1757.

---

312 316 (VI.) JONATHAN EDDY, b. Jan. 28, 1750, in Mansfield; m. Rebecca Hicks. He was cast away in the Bay of Fundy about 1808. In 1848 his wife was living in Sackville, N.B. Children, none.

---

313 317 (VI.) WILLIAM EDDY, b. Aug. 16, 1752, in Mansfield; m. Olive Morse, whose second husband was Hesekiah King. William Eddy was killed by a shot in May, 1778, from a British man-of-war. In 1848, she was living at the age of 96 in Nova Scotia, with her son, George King.

Children:

| 320 318 | 1 | JOSEPH, b. Oct., 1766; m. Elizabeth Rowe. |

325 319   2   WILLIAM, b. July, 1775; m. Rachael Knapp.

           3   MARY, b. ——, 1778; m. George Lawrence of Sackville, N.B., where she was born.

Children:

1 *Nathan*, m., and d. a few years ago. Had a son and two daughters, one of whom m. Robert Bell.
2 *Rebecca*, m. —— Boomer; d. leaving children.
3 *George*, m. Bina Barnes; d. leaving many descendants.
4 *Laban*, m. twice; d. leaving a son by second wife.
5 *William;* living (1880); has three children.
6 *Olive M.*, d. young.
7 *Joseph.*
8 *Mary.*

     4   LAWRENCE.

> NOTE.— *William Eddy* (VI.) was a Lieutenant in the Continental army, Sept. 27, 1777. Resolved that a flag of truce be granted to bring from Nova Scotia the families of William Eddy and others.

---

318 320   (VII.) JOSEPH EDDY, b. in Sackville, N.B., Oct., 1766; m. Elizabeth Rowe, Dec. 26, 1800, in Eddington, Me. He d. at Corinth, Me., May 9, 1850; she also d. at Corinth, Me.

Children:

323 321   1   THOMAS F. (m. —— Campbell); b. Sept. 13, 1805.
324 322   2   ELISHA (m. Loney Pullen); b. Nov. 4, 1807.
           3   GEORGE W., b. Feb. 2, 1812, in Eddington, Me. His wife was from Exeter, Me. They reside in Corinth, Me.

Children:

1 *George W.*, m. his cousin Elizabeth, dau. of Timothy Eddy. Reside in Corinth, Me.

Children:
1 *Ada M.*
2 *Frank L.*

2 *Georgianna*, m. William Bean. Reside in Corinth.

Children:
1 *William Leslie.*

  2　*Fred.*
  3　*Cora.*
  4　*Forest.*
  5　*Winfield.*

3　*Eleanor*, m. George Preble of Corinth.　They reside
in Charlestown, Me.; have two sons.

4　*Gustavus C.,*
5　*Gustin,* }Twins.　Reside in Corinth, Me.

CAROLINE, b. Aug. 27, 1801; m. James Adams of
Exeter, Me.; b. Jan. 15, 1794. Resides (1880) in
Dayton, Me., where she d. a few years ago.

Children:
1　*Caroline*, b. in Exeter, Me.; m. Frank Freeland of
Sutton, Mass. Reside there; have children.
2　*Joseph E.*, m. in St. Albans, Me. Resides (1880)
in Charlestown, Me.; has children.
3　*Aurilla*, m. ——. Resides in Massachusetts.
4　*Eliza*, m. Allen Marden of Bangor, Me. Both are
dead.

    Children:
  1　*Addie.*　　2　*Frank.*　　3　*Jennie.*

5　*Emily*, m. ——; lives in Massachusetts; has children.
6　*Mary Esther*, m. Charles Toothaker of Dayton, Me.

5　ELIZABETH, b. in Eddington, Me., Dec. 1, 1809; m.
Josiah Bailey (he d.). She lives (1880) in Corinth, Me.

Children:
1　*Olive*, m. Alonzo Batcheldor (he d. in Corinth).　She
m., second, Alden Comins. Resides in Corinth.
2　*Richard*, m. Abbie Allen of Levant, Me. Resides in
Corinth.

    Children:
  1　*Walter.*　　　　2　*Mary.*

3　*Clara*, lives in Corinth.

6　OLIVE M., b. in Eddington, Dec. 12, 1813; m. George
S. Hodson, Feb. 28, 1842, by whom she had two chil-
dren. He d. 1849. She m., second, John C. Sweet of
Corinth, in 1852, by whom she had two daughters.
She d. May 23, 1880.

Children:

1 *Charles Henry*, b. Nov. 12, 1846; m. Eunice Clark; d. ——.
2 *Sylvina*, b. Nov. 1, 1847; d. young.
3 *Marzenah*, b. Nov. 29, 1862.
4 *Martha E.*, d. Dec. 2, 1862.

MARY, b. in Corinth, Me., April 17, 1818; d. April 22, 1877; m. Jotham Jenkins.

Children:

1 *Janette*, d. young.
2 *Joseph E.*, m. —— Day; resides in Clifton, Me.
3 *George Bartlett*.
4 *Jotham Wills*.
5 *Thomas J.*
6 *Martha*, d. July, 1879.
7 *Harriet*.

8 SARAH, b. Jan. 15, 1816.
9 WILLIAM C., b. in Corinth, July 27, 1820; m. Margaret Nutter of New Brunswick. He d. Nov. 26, 1877, in Bangor. She lives in Corinth, 1880.

Children:

1 *Susan*, m. —— Phillips of Bangor
2 *Elizabeth;* resides in Corinth.
3 *Robert*.
4 *William*.
5 *George*.
6 *Nellie Maud*.

10 TIMOTHY C., b. in Corinth, Me., Aug. 12, 1822; m. Lydia Junkins of Corinth; reside there, 1880.

Children:

1 *Elizabeth*, m. George W. Eddy; have two children.
2 *Eliza*, m. George Gray, March 12, 1873.
3 *Rhoda*, m. Howard Spratt of Corinth; have two sons.
4 *Anna*.
5 *Edwin E.*
6 *William*, b. March 29, 1861.

11 JOSEPH, b. Nov. 11, 1824, in Corinth, Me.; m. Angeline Foster of Amherst, Me. Reside in Clifton, Me.

Children:

1 *George.*   2 *A son.*

12 BENJAMIN, b. Dec. 8, 1826; d. 1831.

---

321 323 (VIII.) THOMAS F. EDDY, b. in Eddington, Me., Sept. 13, 1805; m. Rachael Campbell of Corinth, Me. (she d. Nov. 6, 1876). He lives (1880) in Corinth.

Children:

1 CHARLOTTE, m. Frank Knowlton of Eddington; he d. leaving two sons, *Oscar* (who m. Anna Day of Holden, Me.) and *Eddie*. She m., second, James Nichols of Eddington, and resides there, 1880.

2 FREDERICK H., m. Nellie M. Bissell of Milford, Me., have a son and daughter (*Blanche*), and reside (1880) in Corinth, Me.

---

322 324 (VIII.) ELISHA EDDY, b. Nov. 4, 1807, in Eddington, Me.; m. Elona Pullen of Exeter, Me. He d. in Corinth a few years ago. She (1880) resides in Dexter, Me.

Children:

1 BENJAMIN, b. 1834; m. Eliza Watson; have children. Reside in Corinth, Me.

2 ALMIRA, m. John Larry. Reside in Dexter, Me.; have children.

3 ANGELINE, b. 1836; m. Cyrus ——. Both dead, leaving two daughters.

Twins. { 4 ELIJAH, b. 1838; m. Sarah Knowlton of Eddington. Reside in Corinth; have three sons.
5 ELISHA, b. 1838; m. Elizabeth Palmer. Reside in Wisconsin; have children.

6 EMELINE, m. Charles Bodge; she d.; left two sons and one daughter, who reside in Brewer, Me.

7 HENRIETTA, m. Charles Chase; she d., leaving two sons and one daughter.

8 HARRIET, m. ——; lives in Dexter, Me.

9 HELEN, m. ——; lives in Dexter, Me.

---

319 325 (VII.) WILLIAM EDDY, b. in Sackville, N.S. (now N.B.), July 1, 1775; d. in Corinth, Me., Jan. 22, 1852; m. in Eddington, Rachael P. Knapp, Nov. 17, 1796. She b. in Mansfield, Mass., May 22, 1779, and d. in Corinth, July 11, 1869, aged 90 years.

Children:

1 JONATHAN MAYNARD, b. Oct. 22, 1797, in Eddington, Me.; m. Eliza Morrill of Corinth, Me., April 3, 1825 (she b. Jan. 30, 1798, and d. Aug. 5, 1876).

Children:

1 *Henry M.*, b. Aug. 16, 1826, in Corinth, Me.; m. Adelia G. Gammon, Sept. 29, 1853.
2 *Lucia Ann*, b. Aug. 16, 1832; m. Dr. E. A. Thompson of Dover, Me., May 13, 1858.
3 *John Nelson*, b. Aug. 26, 1837; m. Emily G. Huestis, Nov. 19, 1868. Resides in Chicago, Ill. (1880).

2 OLIVE M., b. Aug. 15, 1799; m. Samuel K. Campbell, May 10, 1820; d. Dec. 24, 1851.

Children:

1 *Emeline*, b. Dec. 27, 1820; d. 1827.
2 *Benjamin F.*, b. Aug. 22, 1822; m. Clara R. Bryant, Feb. 7, 1847. He m., second, Mrs. Relief Reed. They reside in Corinth, Me. (1880).

Children:

1 *John*, d. young.
2 *Ellen*, m. Charles Bagley of Corinth, Me.

Child:

1 *A son.*

3 *Olive F.*, b. Dec. 8, 1855, in Corinth, Me.
4 *Clara A.*, b. Dec. 12, 1857, in Exeter.
5 *Hattie B.*, b. Nov. 27, 1860, in Exeter; d. Feb. 22, 1861.
6 *Frank M.*, b. June 19, 1864.
7 *Charles K.*, b. June 19, 1866.

Child by second wife:

8 *Walter*, b. in Corinth, Me., Sept. 14, 1878.

3 *John Wesley*, d. Oct., 1846.
4 *Willard E.*; resides on Pacific Coast.
5 *Mary Elizabeth*, d. Dec., 1837.
6 *Charles M.*; lives in Indiana.
7 *Maria Louise*, d. young.

3 WILLARD, b. May 24, 1801; m. Elmira Goodwin of St. Albans, April 9, 1828. He d. June 10, 1866, in Corinth.

Children:

1 *Olive Jane*, b. March 4, 1839; m. Virgil Brown, Jan. 1849.
2 *Sophronia*, b. March 21, 1834; m. Rev. Porter M. Vinton, Aug. 16, 1861.

4 ROXANNA, b. Aug. 16, 1803, in Eddington, Me.; m. John Campbell of Corinth, Me., Feb. 10, 1831.

Child:

1 *Martin*, b. June, 1837; m. Sarah J. Daniels, May, 1860.

5 SYLVESTER, b. Oct. 21, 1805, in Eddington, Me.; m. Almira Goodwin of St. Albans, Jan. 6, 1836 (she d. Dec. 11, 1869); he m., second, Mrs. Mehitable Williams, Dec. 17, 1871 (she b. in Ossipee, N.H., Sept. 13, 1828). They reside (1880) in Corinth, Me.

Children:

1 *Frances A.*, b. March 3, 1838; m. George V. Blackman, Sept., 1859.
2 *Hannibal H.*, b. July 5, 1840; m. Mary Burnham, May 4, 1870.
3 *Holman J.*, b. Sept. 19, 1847; m. Eliza Devens, April 29, 1876.
4 *Hiram E.*, b. March 21, 1850.

6 TEMPERANCE B., b. Feb. 9, 1815; m. Hon. Noah Barker, Dec. 29, 1839; who was b. in Exeter, Me., Nov. 14, 1807.

Children:

1 *Georgia*, b. June 1, 1841, in Exeter, Me.; m. Mary E. Latham, Sept. 2, 1868.
2 *Charles V.*, b. Sept. 22, 1848; m. Lizzie E. Folsom, Dec. 1, 1872. She d. July, 1875.
3 *William E.*, b. April 18, 1852; resides in Corinth.
4 *Nellie Arethusa*, b. July 22, 1858.

7 MARIA L., b. July 27, 1818, in Corinth, Me.; m. Thomas J. Haines of Levant, May 22, 1853 (he b. in Portsmouth, N.H., Nov. 25, 1816). Resides in Corinth.

Children:

1 *William T.*, b. Aug. 2, 1855.
2 *Fred A.*, b. Sept. 12, 1859; d. Dec. 6, 1863.
3 *Frank E.*, b. Sept. 12, 1861.

8 CHARLES K., b. Dec. 29, 1820, in Corinth, Me.; m.
Albina Dunning of Charlestown, July 31, 1853.

Children:
1 *Walter Stanley*, b. June 17, 1855, in Corinth.
2 *Arthur Dunning*, b. July 27, 1861, in Ottawa, Can.
3 *Charles K.*, b. Aug., 1867, in Saginaw, Mich.
4 *Lila*, b. 1870, in Saginaw. Resides (1880) in East
Saginaw.

---

314 326 (VI.) IBROOK EDDY, b. in Mansfield, Mass., Jan. 9, 1754;
m. Lona Pratt, b. May 6, 1760. He went to Nova
Scotia with his father in 1764, and was one of the
refugees from that Province during the Revolutionary
War, for which he received a grant of land in Eddington, Me. He was Deputy Sheriff in Bristol Co., Mass.,
and resided in Mansfield until about 1758, when he went
to Eddington, Me. First wife d. about 1802. He m.,
second, Celia Wilde. He d. Jan., 1834, and his second
wife d. May 23, 1842. All his children were by his
first wife.

Children:
1 JONATHAN, b. Jan. 31, 1780, in Mansfield, Mass.; d.
young.
2 EXPERIENCE, b. June 5, 1782; d.
3 WARE, b. May 3, 1784, in Mansfield, Mass.; m., first,
Nancy Clapp (she b. in Walpole, Mass., May 3, 1784;
d. March 23, 1829). He m., second, Olive Foster, April
11, 1830 (she b. in Winthrop, Me., 1800). He d. Nov.
20, 1852.

Children:
1 *Jonathan*, b. Aug. 1, 1811, in Eddington, Me.; m.
Caroline Bailey at Milford, March 5, 1839; she b. in
Milford, July 9, 1819. Removed to Bangor, Me.,
1847. He was a Colonel; d. Aug. 24, 1865.

Children:
1 *Laura M.*, b. Aug. 12, 1840; m. Edward E.
Parker, Oct. 19, 1864; had two children.
2 *Sarah Bailey*, b. Aug. 3, 1842; d. Feb. 25, 1862.
3 *Caroline M.*, b. Oct. 11, 1844; m. Charles M.
Hamblen, June 22, 1865; had two children.
4 *Frederick A.*, b. Aug. 23, 1846.

5 *John Franklin*, b. March 23, 1848; m. Lottie Whittemore of Rome, N.Y. Resides in Bay City, Mich.

6 *Charles F.*, b. March 21, 1852; m. Elizabeth Glenn of Buckport, 1874; have two children.

7 *Newell Avery*, b. May 20, 1856; in Yale College (1878).

2 *Lucy Clapp*, b. Aug. 3, 1813; m. Horace Blackman, Nov. 23, 1835.

3 *Celia Wilde*, b. Sept., 1817; m., Jan. 23, 1840, Edwin Eddy (b. Jan. 8, 1817); children all b. in Bradley, Me. Removed to Saginaw, Mich., Dec., 1863.

Children:

1 *George C.*, b. Jan. 24, 1841; d. Feb. 20, 1843.

2 *Nancy M.*, b. Aug. 14, 1842; m. Temple E. Dorr, Feb. 8, 1866.

Children:

1 *Earth E.*, b. April 17, 1870.

2 *Cora M.*, b. May 29, 1874.

3 *Florence C.*, b. May 30, 1876.

3 *Ellen A.*, b. Nov. 3, 1843; m. Augustus Clark, Jan. 28, 1874.

Children:

1 *A daughter*, b. April 27, 1846; d. May 24, 1846.

4 *Selwyn*, b. March 25, 1847; m. Cornelia C. Hall, Sept. 21, 1867.

Children:

1 *Clara F.*, b. Feb. 14, 1873.

2 *Ella M.*, b. April 8, 1875.

5 *Charles A.*, b. March 15, 1849; m. Harriet L. Lane, Dec. 26, 1871.

Children:

1 *Lottie C.*, b. March 4, 1873.

2 *Flora E.*, b. Nov. 18, 1874.

6 *Lucy E.*, b. April 14, 1851; d. June 23, 1870.

4 *Lona Pratt*, b. July 15, 1815; d. July 23, 1818.

5 *Darius W.*, b. Aug. 17, 1819; m. Eliza Blackman of Bradley, Me., March 5, 1849. She d. March 5, 1854.

He m., second, Elizabeth C. Tapley in Oldtown, Me., Feb. 13, 1855 (she b. in Brookville, Sept. 7, 1833). Removed from Milford to Bangor, 1870.

Children:

1 *Eliza B.*, b. Dec. 2, 1855, in Milford, Me.
2 *Etta M.*, b. Jan. 27, 1860, in Milford, Me.
3 *Edwin II.*, b. Nov. 8, 1863, in Milford, Me.
4 *Walter D.*, b. Jan. 6, 1870, in Bangor, Me.

6 *Mercy Wilde*, b. June 28, 1821; d. July 4, 1821.
7 *Lona Pratt*, b. Aug. 31, 1822; d. March 17, 1824.
8 *Nancy Clapp*, b. Dec. 22, 1824; m. Newall Avery, Jan. 3, 1843. He b. in Jefferson, Me., Oct. 12, 1817, and d. March 13, 1877, in Detroit, Mich. Engaged for several years in the lumber trade. She lives (1880) in Detroit.

Children:

1 *Edward O.*, b. Oct. 23, 1845, in Bradley, Me.; m. Flora Huntington of Port Huron, Mich., 1867.

Child:
1 *Ruth*, b. Nov., 1872.

2 *Darius N.*, b. Jan. 10, 1847; m. Elizabeth Dole, June 24, 1873.
3 *Leonard C.*, b. Oct. 18, 1848; d. 1853.
4 *Clara A.*, b. Jan. 12, 1850.
5 *Nancy M.*, b. May 18, 1851; m. Henry Skinner of Detroit, Oct. 18, 1879.
6 *George E.*, b. April 18, 1853; m. Fannie Tarble of Detroit, Mich., May 8, 1878.

Child:
1 *Bessie F.*, b. March 20, 1879.

7 *John II.*, b. July 29, 1854, in Bradley, Me., m. Ella Smith, Jan. 8, 1880, in Detroit.
8 *Horace W.*, b. April 12, 1857; m. Lulu West of Madison, Wis., April 12, 1880.
9 *Nellie J.*, b. April 29, 1850, in Port Huron, Mich.
10 *An infant*, b. ——; d. 1862.
11 *Arthur Ware*, b. 1863; d. 1864.
12 *Kittie M.*, b. 1866; d. 1867.
13 *Henry E.*, b. in Detroit, Mich., Dec. 3, 1867.

9 *Eliza Holland*, b. Feb. 27, 1827; m. Sewall Avery,
   May 3, 1849, in Bradley, Me. He b. in Jefferson,
   Me., Feb. 2, 1824. They reside, 1880, in East Sagi-
   naw, Mich.

   Children:
   1 *Waldo A.*, b. March 14, 1850, in Bradley, Me.;
      m. Nellie C. Lee, at Saginaw, Feb. 18, 1871.

      Children:
      1 *Sewall Lee*, b. Nov. 4, 1873, in Saginaw.
      2 *Arla S.*, b. May 11, 1875, in Saginaw.

   2 *Ara L.*, b. March 16, 1853, in Bradley, Me.; m.
      Herbert C. Sanborn, Oct. 30, 1873, at Saginaw.

      Child:
      1 *Herbert W.*

   3 *Idella E.*, b. Nov. 16, 1854, at Bradley, Me.
   4 *Lulie E.*, b. Oct. 19, 1859, at Bradley, Me.

10 *Cyrus*, b. Nov. 8, 1830.
11 *Ware*, b. April 6, 1834.
12 *Marion*, b. Sept. 4, 1838; m. Ezra Richardson, Dec.
    1, 1865; d. 1867.
13 *Lavinia*, b. Sept. 2, 1842; m. Henry Foster, Nov.
    20, 1862.

4 NANCY, b. Aug. 8, 1786, in Eddington, Me.; m. Daniel
   Collins.
5 RACHEL, b. Feb. 22, 1788, in Eddington, Me.; m.
   Moses Collins.
6 ELEAZER, b. Oct. 10, 1789, in Eddington, Me.; m. Sylvia
   Campbell, March 20, 1814. She b. Nov. 14, 1790; d.
   April 30, 1860. He d. March 13, 1826.

   Children:
   1 *Timothy*, b. Feb. 12, 1815.
   2 *Edwin*, b. Jan. 18, 1817, in Eddington, Me.; m. Celia
      W. Eddy, dau. of Ware Eddy. See for their children,
      Ante " 3 Celia Wilde; b. Sept. 1817; m., Jan. 23,
      1840, Edwin Eddy."
   3 *Angelina*, b. Aug., 1818, in Eddington, Me.; m.
      Charles G. Richardson; b. in Jay, Me., Feb. 14,
      1813. She d. in Burlington, Me., April 22, 1869.

Children:
1 *George A.*, b. Oct. 1, 1837; d. July 14, 1856.
2 *James M.*, b. March 12, 1839; d. April 11, 1839.
3 *Charles R.*, b. Dec. 31, 1840; m., and lives in Bradley, Me.
4 *Charlotte E.*, b. July 6, 1844: d. Aug. 22, 1850.
5 *Francetta S.*, b. June 23, 1847; d. Aug. 15, 1852.
6 *Edwin M.*, b. April 11, 1849; d. Aug. 22, 1850.
7 *Frank W.*, b. June 15, 1851.
8 *Adda M.*, b. April 1, 1853; m. Eben Files of Gorham, Me.

4 *Eleazer P.*, b. May 24, 1821; d. Oct. 7, 1834.
5 *Henry C.*, b. May 24, 1821; d. Aug. 2, 1866.
6 *Sabara*, b. Aug. 29, 1823; m. W. E. Hanson.
7 *Ware*, b. Aug. 3, 1835; m. Mary E. Doten.

7 ABAGAIL, b. Sept. 29, 1791, in Eddington, Me.; m. Moses Knapp.
8 MARY, b. Nov. 26, 1793, in Eddington, Me.; m. Jesse Corniss.
9 SYLVIA, b. Aug. 12, 1796, in Eddington, Me.; m. Beniah Clapp.
10 EXPERIENCE, b. April 19, 1800, in Eddington, Me.; m. George Crane.

---

315 327 (VI.) ELIAS EDDY, b. Nov. 30, 1757, in Mansfield; m. Mary Fales. Lived, and d. in Eddington, Me., about 1808. Soldier in Revolutionary War.

Children:
1 OLIVER, m. Widow Hathorn; d. at Buffalo, 1813, from a wound received in United States service in Canada.

Children:
1 *Curtis.*   2 *Charles.*

2 WILLIAM; went to New York about 1816.
3 EDWARD, d. 1817.
4 LAVINA, m. N. Hinkley.
5 ELIZABETH, m. Rev. E. Bedel.
6 EXPERIENCE, m. Wright Stockwell.
7 MARY, m. Rev. A. Bedel.

191 328 (IV.) OBEDIAH EDDY, b. Sept. 2, 1683; m. Abagail Devotion, Dec. 9, 1709. Lived in Swansea.

Children:
333 329   1 CONSTANT, b. Sept. 7, 1710.
336 330   2 ICHABID, b. June 1, 1713.
           3 OLIVE or ALICE, b. Feb. 24, 1715.
           4 MARY, b. Nov. 10, 1716; m. George Cornel of Dartmouth, May 16, 1737.
           5 ABAGAIL, b. Oct. 14, 1721.
           6 HANNAH, b. Jan. 23, 1723; m., March 20, 1742, Elkanah Pierce of Middleboro'.
337 331   7 JOB, b. July 23, 1726.
338 332   8 AZARIAH, b. June 16, 1742; lived in Dighton until 1780, when he moved to Leicester, Mass.; d. 1820.

---

329 333 (V.) CONSTANT EDDY, b. Sept. 7, 1710; m. Mary Winslow, Dec. 16, 1733; b. April 26, 1716; d. Sept. 7, 1784. He d. Nov. 16, 1784.

Children:
335 334   1 DEVOTION, b. Sept. 8, 1734; d. June 9, 1813.
           2 SILVA, b. Feb. 27, 1736; m. Jacob Avery of Groton, June 4, 1753; had eleven children.
           3 JEMIMA, b. Oct. 13, 1737; m. John Slade, April 10, 1755; had five children.
           4 ABIGAIL, b. Nov. 19, 1739; m. Edw. Thurbur, Aug. 26, 1762.
           5 TISDALL, b. Jan. 16, 1743.

              Children:
              1 *Sebble*, m. Watson.
              2 *Hannah*, m. William Fellows.
              3 *Avery*.
              4 *Nancy*, m. Haner.
              5 *Humphrey*.

           6 RUTH, b. July 11, 1765; m. Simeon Button.
           7 ELIZABETH, b. Oct. 25, 1745; m. Ebenezer Winslow, Feb. 27, 1766; had eleven children.
           8 OBEDIAH, b. March 21, 1742; m. Lois Palmer, June 15, 1769; she d. June 2, 1770.

              Children:
              1 *Lois*, b. May 18, 1770; m. Mr. Williams.
              2 *Jonathan*.

Children:

1 *Prudence.*   2 *Sally.*   3 *John.*

4 *Henry.*   5 *Eliza.*   6 *Lydia.*

9 MARY, b. Dec. 16, 1750; m. Cyrus Spicer.

---

331 335 (VI.) DEVOTION EDDY, b. Sept. 8, 1734; d. June 9, 1813, at Partition, N.Y. He m. Mary Sherman, and owned privateers in the Revolutionary War. She d., aged 95.

Children:

1 GILBERT, b. Jan. 23, 1761; m. Prudence Avery. He was captured on his father's privateer, and imprisoned at Halifax, N.S., a year. Was at the battles of Saratoga and Bennington; was a General of Division in 1812 in New York State; was Presidential Elector. Lived in Rome Co., N.Y., and d. in 1846.

Children:

1 *Russell*, b. April 23, 1787, in Pittstown, N.Y. He was a paymaster in the army in 1812; m. Ruth Ann Wells of Berkshire Co., Mass., 1815. In 1835 he removed to Crown Point, Ind. His wife d. Sept. 1, 1859. He m., second, Abby M. Kimball of Newark, N.J., who now resides there. He d. July 2, 1871.

Children:

1 *Eliza*, m. Rev. Mr. Townsend, and had one child, *Juliet*, m. Jacob Winfield of Washington, D.C.

2 *Ruth Ann*, m. D. R. Pettibone.

3 *Russell Avery.*

2 *Eliza*, m. Jacob P. Deforest; d. in Missouri.

3 *Sibyl*, m. Nathaniel Bausalt; resides in Troy, N.Y., 1880.

4 *Tisdale.*

5 *Mary.*

2 TISDALE, b. 1762; m. Elizabeth Button. He d., 1828, at Pittstown, N.Y.

Children:

1 *Ira B.*, b. 1807, at Pittstown, N.Y.; resides (1880) in Chicago, Ill.

2 *Elizabeth*, b. 1808; m. Elisha S. Benton of Albany, N.Y.

3 *Henry T.*, b. 1811; d. 1845; of Troy, N.Y.

4 *Devotion C.*, b. 1812, in Pittstown, N.Y.; m. Isabella Campbell of Schenectady, N.Y. Graduated at Union College, 1834. Is an attorney-at-law. Resides in Chicago, Ill.

Children:

1 *Mary B.*, b. 1844, in Chicago; m. Dr. H. R. Stout.
2 *Isabella*, b. 1847; m. Frank C. Bishop; resides in Salon, Ohio.
3 *Devotion C.*, b. 1849; d. 1873.
4 *Clementine*, b. 1858.
5 *Antoinette*, b. 1862.

5 *Mary Sherman*, b. 1815; d. 1840; m. Samuel P. Hand of Albany, N.Y.

Children:

1 *Tisdale Aaron*. b. 1838; is a lawyer.
2 *Samuel Burton*, b. 1840; d. 1860.

6 *Jacob Follett*, b. 1817; d., 1838, at Chicago. Ill.
7 *Ruth Ann*, m. Samuel P. Hand.

Children:

1 *Henry F.*, —— in Dixon, Ill. (1879).
2 *Bayard E.*, —— in Chicago, Ill.

3 SHERMAN, b. 1765, in Rhode Island; m. Abby Thurbur; d. without issue at Pittstown, N.Y.

4 ELIZABETH, b. March 16, 1767; m. Thomas Williams of Albany, N.Y.; d., 1868, at Pittstown, N.Y.

NOTE. — From "Rhode Island Mercury," March 21, 1867: "An interesting meeting was held at Pottstown, N.Y., on Saturday last, which brought together some two hundred of the descendants of the Rhode Island Eddys to honor the one hundredth birthday of Elizabeth Williams, dau. of the late Devotion Eddy, who moved to this State in 1781. Mrs. Williams is still in perfect health, and has a very retentive memory. She was eleven years of age when the siege of Newport took place, and the British troops made their devastating march, destroying all the shipping at New Haven, and burning Fairfield, Norwalk, and Greenwich. She was in Connecticut with her father when Arnold burned New London in 1781, and herself witnessed the conflagration while sitting on her father's ox-cart."

5 JOHN, b. 1772; d. at Brunswick, N.Y.

Children:

1 *Luthur.*   2 *Mary.*
3 *Ambrose.*   4 *Betsey Sherman.*

6 LUTHUR, b. 1776; m. —— Wells of Williamstown, N.Y.; d. at Brunswick, N.Y., 1845.

Child:
1 *John*, resides in Brunswick, N.Y., 1880.

7 ROBERT, b. 1769; m. Rachel Avery; d. in Missouri.

Children:

1 *Lucy.*	2 *Sherman.*
3 *Avery.*	4 *Sabra.*
5 *John.*	6 *Ambrose.*
7 *Hannah.*	

8 RUSSELL; no children; b. 1774.

---

330 336 (V.) ICHABOD EDDY, b. June 1, 1713; d. 1798, in Westport; m. Sarah.

Children:
1 BETSEY, b. Sept. 1, 1737.
2 HANNAH, b. Aug. 23, 1749.
3 HENRY, b. Nov. 8, 1741; d. at Easton, N.Y.
4 DAVID, b. Dec. 17, 1743; d. at Tiveton; lived in Norton.

Children:
1 *Keziah*, b. Nov. 28, 1764; m. Mr. Green of Calais, Vt.
2 *Jonathan*, Aug. 20, 1766; d. March 11, 1827, at Montpelier, Vt.

Children:
1 *Lauriston;* lived (1841) in Boston.
2 *James M.;* lived (1841) in Boston.
Three daughters, dead.

3 *Daniel*, b. Aug. 11, 1786; lived in Sterling, Mass., in 1841; living in Jamaica, Vt.

Child:
1 *Daniel* of Jamaica, Vt.

---

331 337 (V.) JOB EDDY, b. July 23, 1726; m. Patience ——.

Children:
1 ANN.

2 PRESERVED, b. July, 1748; d. in Somerset, 1838; m. Lydia Davis, Jan., 1771.

Children:
1 *Preserved C.*, b. in Somerset.

    Children:
    1 *Julia Ann.*   2 *Eliza.*   3 *Adaline.*

2 *Wing E.*, b. Nov. 1, 1781; d. March 13, 1832; m. Phebe Price; b. Jan. 13, 1776; d. Dec. 16, 1853.

    Children:
    1 *David P.*, b. April 3, 1808; d. April 2, 1875; m. Mary Sherman, b. June 14, 1800.

        Children:
        1 *Ira W.*, b. July 11, 1830, (1879) in Providence, R.I.
        2 *Sarah A.*, b. Oct. 7, 1831; m. —— Baker; resides in Rehoboth, Mass.
        3 *Robert S.*, b. Oct. 24, 1833; lives in Swansea, Mass.
        4 *Seth W.*, b. Jan. 22, 1836; lives in Swansea, Mass.
        5 *Cornelius S.*, b. Dec. 25, 1838; d. ——.
        6 *Charles H.*, b. April 5, 1842; d. Oct. 18, 1863.
        7 *Edwin B.*, b. Sept. 15, 1844; lives in Swansea.
        8 *Elizabeth*, b. Oct. 29, 1846; lives in Providence, R.I.
        9 *David P.*, b. Sept. 8, 1849; lives in Providence, R.I.
       10 *Mary E.*, b. Aug. 27, 1853; m. Jesse Chase.

    2 *Jarvis W.*, b. July 6, 1810; m. Nancy Horton.

        Children:
        1 *Phebe Ann*, m. Obediah Chase; lives in Fall River, Mass.
        2 *Sarah D.*, m. —— Hathaway; lives in Fall River, Mass.

    3 *Charles B.*, b. Feb. 22, 1813; m. Lydia H. Reed; resides in Fall River.

        Children:
        1 *Lydia E.*, b. Dec. 23, 1845; d. Sept. 18, 1869.
        2 *Charles B.*, b. Feb. 15, 1849; lives in Fall River.

4 *Phebe,* d. young.
5 *Henry C.,* b. Nov. 29, 1817; m. Elizabeth Buffington; m., second, widow Maria Buffington. He d. Jan. 14, 1815.
6 *Eliza Ann,* b. March 29, 1822, in Swansea, Mass.; m. Edwin Brightman, July 5, 1841. Resides in Fall River, Mass.

    Children:
    1 *Henry E.,* b. Aug. 27, 1849.
    2 *Abbott W.,* b. Sept. 10, 1856.

3 *Daniel.*

    Children:
    1 *Elkanah P.*   2 *Eliza.*
    3 *Henrietta.*   4 *Horatio Nelson.*
    5 *William P.*   6 *Daniel B.*
    7 *Zenoni W.*

4 *David B.,* b. Jan. 1, 1797; d. May 26, 1868; m. Harriet Baker, who resides (1880) in Swansea, Mass.

    Child:
    1 *Hiram B.,* b. Jan. 22, 1829, in Swansea, Mass.

5 *Lois.*
6 *Patience.*
7 *Eunice.*
8 *Lydia.*
9 *Mary.*
10 *Hannah.*

3 HOPESTILL, b. Dec. 17, 1749.
4 PATIENCE, b. Jan. 8, 1752.
5 JOB, b. Dec. 23, 1753.
6 JAMES, b. Dec. 30, 1755 (Private in Ashley's Company, Vose's Regiment, Revolutionary War).
7 ZACHARIAH, b. April 29, 1758.
8 ELIZABETH, b. March 22, 1760.
9 JOHN, b. May 28, 1763.
10 RICHARD, b. Sept. 8, 1765.
11 JOSHUA, b. April 7, 1767.

    Children:
    1 *Job.*   2 *Joseph.*
    3 *Preserved.*   4 *James.*

332 338 (V.) AZARIAH EDDY, b. June 16, 1742. Lived in Dighton until 1780; moved to Leicester, Mass.; d. Aug. 14, 1820; farmer.

Children:

1 JONATHAN, b. April 14, 1774; d. July 12, 1843, at Hooseck.

   Children:

   1 *Azariah*, in Sandusky, Ohio, 1840.
   2 *Nathaniel Bishop*, in Sandusky, Ohio, 1840.
   3 *Jonathan*, in Troy, N.Y., 1840.
   4 *John*, in Hooseck, 1840.

2 HENRY, b. June 12, 1776; in 1841, a preacher in Stoughton, Mass.

3 SETH, b. July 18, 1780; resided (1840) in Stillwater, N.Y.

   Child:

   1 *Samuel;* resides (1840) in Schagticoke Point, N.Y.

4 *Azariah*, b. Oct. 7, 1776; d. without issue.

---

123 339 (III.) CALEB EDDY, b. in Plymouth, Mass., 1643; d. March 23, 1713. His wife's name was Elizabeth. He lived in Somerset and Swansea; was buried on land belonging, in 1840, to the family of Elder Michael Eddy of Newport, R.I. In 1661 Caleb Eddy was a resident in John Brown's family of Rehoboth, and he and his brother Zachariah received from Brown a deed of 100 acres of land in Narragansett. He was a deacon of the church in Swansea, and was one of the persons named in the confirmating grant of Governor Bradford, and associate in 1689, having been a freeman in 1681. At the death of his father certain lands in Middleboro' were deeded to him, June 7, 1659. He applied for lands which the Court gave him leave to look out. He was among the first settlers in Swansea. Was there in 1667, and signed the articles of agreement between Willet and the church in 1669. He was in 1671 in the third rank of the people. In 1681 was propounded as a freeman at Plymouth, and admitted June 1 of the next year. In the division of the lands between the brothers, in 1706, he took half the lands belonging to his father on the west side of the Namasket River. He was a man of great consideration. He d. in Swansea, in that part of the town afterward called Somerset.

Children:

343 340   1   CALEB, b. May 29, 1672; d. in Boston, 1747.

429 341   2   SAMUEL, b. July 15, 1675; d. March 27, 1744.

        3   ZACHARIAH, b. Jan. 23, 1682; d. Feb. 26, 1682.

430 342   4   BENJAMIN, b. ——.

        5   ELIZABETH, b. ——.

        6   HANNAH (probably m. Thomas Cole, June 22, 1710).

        7   HOPESTILL.

        8   MARY, who m. Barnabus Chase of Swansea, Oct. 6, 1745.

---

340 343   (IV.)   CALEB, b. May 29, 1672; m. Hannah Brown, Sept. 11, 1711; d. 1747. Admitted to communion, Old South Church, July 1, 1711, by Rev. Benjamin Wadsworth. For her second husband, his wife m., Nov. 13, 1749, Eben Clapp of Dorchester; she d. Nov., 1750 (probably she was the second wife of Caleb Eddy, for in the Boston Registry Office is a record that, " Sarah, wife of Caleb Eddy, d. May 15, 1711 "), and is believed to have been a dau. of Joseph Brown of Rehoboth. He lived with her about six months, and d. at the age of 71 years. Caleb Eddy was a shipwright and merchant in Boston in 1708. He received a deed of gift from his father (acknowledged in Boston, May 18, 1709) of the latter's share of lands, divided and undivided, in the 16 purchase, and in Assawampset Neck, both of which he sold for £12, in 1712, to J. Thompson of Middleboro', Mass. Jan. 31, 1808. he bought of John Alline a piece of land at south part of Boston. This was Eddy's shipyard, which in 1842 was Tileston's Wharf. On Sept. 16, 1712, he sold this land to Richard Gridley. On Jan. 30, 1730, Mr. Eddy with John Clough bought, for £100, of His Excellency Jonathan Belcher, land bounded partly on a highway leading into Orange Street. He hired for £9 per annum, of Samuel Phillips, the shipyard of Capt. B. Gillam on the lower end of Battery-march Street, Boston. March 2, 1730, Gov. Belcher's wife conveyed to Caleb Eddy and others a piece of land on which the Hollis Street Church was subsequently erected. The church was built by said Caleb and others. He was a very influential man in it, and chose pew No. 4, which was appraised at £52. After his decease, his estate was appraised at about £2430. Among the subjects of the Inventory was a "Negro woman" named Luce, valued at £100. Also a "Silver

Tankard," which went to his son Caleb, and in 1880 is in possession of Robert Henry Eddy of Boston, Mass., it being marked "Caleb and Martha Eddy, 1747." It has on it, beautifully engraved, armorial bearings.

Children :

1   SAMUEL, b. April 5, 1716; m. Mary Grover, Dec. 21, 1738; also, Joanna Savage, July 29, 1756; also, Lucy Clark, March 8, 1764.

2   HANNAH, b. Nov. 9, 1718; m. John Simpson, Feb. 7, 1761.

345 344   3   CALEB, b. March 30, 1721; d. in Boston, 1752.

————————

344 345   (V.)   CALEB EDDY, b. March 30, 1721; m. to Martha Marks of Boston by Rev. Mathew Byles, Sept. 11, 1740. Entered into covenant without coming into communion, May 31, 1741; d. Nov. 3, 1752. She m., second, Jan. 17, 1760, John Youngman, and d. in Nov., 1777, aged 49 years. He (Caleb Eddy) was the author of the following lines : —

> "Long have I sought that wish of all,
>   True happiness to find, —
> That some would health, some pleasure call,
>   And some a virtuous mind;
> Sufficient wealth to keep away
>   Of want, that doleful scene,
> And joy enough to gild the day
>   And make life's cares serene;
> Virtue enough to ask my heart,
>   Art thou secure within?
> Hast thou performed that honest part,
>   Hast thou no private sin?
> Now these, and these alone possessed,
>   Will raise a noble joy !
> Will constitute a happiness,
>   That nothing can destroy ! "

Children :

1   HANNAH, b. May 29, 1741; baptized May 31, 1741; d. Jan. 1, 1827; m. Robert Gardner, Dec. 5, 1762, and afterwards Robert Currie of Providence, R.I. By her first husband she had two children: *Robert* and *Hannah.* The latter was born in Boston, Dec. 1, 1765, and was the wife of Judge Benjamin Whitman of Boston. Robert Gardner m. Sally Dench, and had children: *Robert, Sally, John, George,* and *Fanny.* In her youth Hannah Eddy was a beautiful woman. After the death of her husband she became a teacher, and during the siege of

Boston, was so employed. She was an admirer of the eccentric Dr. Byles, of whom she could relate many anecdotes. She was a very intelligent person, one of uncommon industry and perseverance. Her wit and anecdotes were pungent and interesting, always marked by good sense and modesty. The Holy Bible she had almost committed to memory. She became one of the Rev. John Murray's church, was free from all bigotry and censoriousness, and was affectionate and liberal-hearted to excess.

347 346 2 BENJAMIN, b. Feb. 19, 1743; d. Aug. 11, 1817.

3 MARTHA, baptized April 28, 1745, entered communion at Mathew Byles's church, July 7, 1765; d. at Boston, 1799; m. Matthew Grice, Oct. 28, 1765.

Children:
1 *Elizabeth*, b. April 30, 1775; m. Philip Amidon, Esq., of Boston.

Children:
1 *Philip*, m. a dau. of Hon. Jonathan Russell of Milton, Mass.; issue, one son, *Phillip Russell Amidon*.
2 *Eliza*, m. John Liscom.
3 *Angeline*, m. Rev. Mr. Howe.
4 *Melania*, m. Rev. Mr. Parker.
5 *Sylvia*, m. Parker.

2 *Martha*, b. Aug. 18, 1762; m. Balch.
3 *Hannah*, b. July 31, 1738; m. French.
4 *Mathew*.
5 *Caleb Eddy*.
6 *Susan*.

---

346 347 (VI.) BENJAMIN EDDY, b. in Boston, Feb. 19, 1743; m. Martha Bronsden, Nov. 10, 1763; d. at West Cambridge, Mass., Aug. 11, 1817. His wife was b. in Boston, Nov. 11, 1742, and d. in West Cambridge, Dec. 28, 1830. "He was an honest man, a good husband, an affectionate and indulgent father, possessing the qualities of a true Christian. His wife was a treasure to him, devoted to him and her children. She was a woman of great energy and perseverance, and was beloved by all who knew her. During the siege of Boston she was driven out by the British, and, with a few dollars, sought shelter with her five children in Needham,

where she remained until joined by her husband; who,
after having his ship captured by the English, was
thrown into prison at Halifax, N.S., and with several
others escaped, and travelled on foot by land to Needham. At nineteen years of age he commenced a sea-
faring life, and shortly arose to the command of a vessel
in the West India trade. In 1776 he, with his family,
removed to Shrewsbury, Mass., and when there kept
a store, and was a large land-holder. After conclusion
of the war, he became interested in and commanded
packets in the London trade. In 1804 he purchased an
estate in Waltham, Mass., which a short time before
his death he sold, and removed to West Cambridge.
He, with his wife, was buried in the graveyard there,
and in the tomb of his son-in-law, William Cotting."

Children:

1　MARTHA, b. in Boston, July 24, 1764; baptized Aug. 5,
1764; d. at Rochester, N.Y., Dec. 7, 1846. She m. Dr.
Z. Jennings of Cherry Valley, N.Y., Nov. 20, 1799.

　　Children:
　1　*Harriet;* living in Salem, 1881.
　2　*Eunice Eddy,* b. March 17, 1803, in Fitzwilliam,
　　　N.H.; m. in West Cambridge, Mass., April 11, 1823,
　　　to John C. Stevens; b. in Boston, Dec. 20, 1798.
　　　They (1881) reside in Rochester, N.Y.

　　　Children:
　　1　*Benjamin Eddy,* b. Jan. 4, 1820; d. April 18, 1870,
　　　　in New York; m., Nov. 1, 1850, Caroline Camp-
　　　　bell, b. Aug. 7, 1832.

　　　　Children:
　　　1　*Lucy Della,* b. July 2, 1831; d. Aug. 20, 1852.
　　　2　*Harriet Eddy,* b. March 27, 1853; m. Lawrence
　　　　　Pomroy.
　　　3　*John Caldwell,* b. Sept. 30, 1856; d. March
　　　　　16, 1860.
　　　4　*Sarah C.,* b. Feb. 17, 1860; d. March 8, 1876.

　　2　*Eunice C.,* b. in Boston, Mass., Sept. 10, 1826;
　　　m., May 9, 1850, Levant L. Mason of Buffalo,
　　　N.Y.; b. Dec. 25, 1826.

　　　Children:
　　1　*John C. Stevens,* b. in Jamestown, N.Y., Oct.
　　　　5, 1850.

2 *Eunice C.*, b. July 30, 1855; m., Oct. 23, 1877, at Jamestown, N.Y., Henry S. Penfield of Chicago, Ill.

3 *Eunice*, b. at Jamestown, April 27, 1861.

3 *Lucy O.*, b. in Rochester, N.Y., Jan. 17, 1827; m., May 11, 1852, to James Dow of Jamestown, N.Y.

Children :

1 *Eunice Eddy*, b. and d. Nov. 4, 1855.
2 *Levant Mason*, b. March 4, 1858; d. March 6, 1858.
3 *James*, b. ——; d. Feb. 15, 1859.
4 *James Albert*, b. Aug. 17, 1859; d. Feb. 18, 1860.

4 *Harriet Martha*, b. in Gates, N.Y., June 7, 1829; d. April 9, 1832.

5 *Sarah Caroline*, b. in Rochester, N.Y., Aug. 28, 1842; m., Oct. 23, 1872, at Jamestown. N.Y., Joseph Twyman; b. Oct. 8, 1842, at Ramsgate, England.

Children :

1 *Lucy Rosetta*, b. at Chicago. Ill., Jan. 21, 1874.
2 *Levant Mason*, b. June 27, 1876, at Jamestown, N.Y.; d. Aug. 1, 1876.
3 *Vernon Montefiore*, b. June 27, 1877, at Chicago, Ill.
4 *Josephine Nathalie*, b. April 19, 1880, at Chicago, Ill.

2 MARY, b. July 22, 1766; d. April 25, 1800; m., Sept. 24. 1786, to Dr. Eliakim Morse (b. Feb. 14, 1759; d. Jan. 7, 1858), by whom she had three children, *John*, *Benjamin E.*, and *Ebenezer*. John, b. Feb. 12, 1789; d. May 7, 1817; m. Frances H. Torrey of Boston. and by her had three sons; viz.: *John T.*, b. March 27, 1813; *Samuel T.*, b. May 19, 1816; and *Benjamin E.*, b. Feb. 22, 1814; all of whom are now (1881) residing in Boston. She, Mrs. Mary Morse, had the reputation of being one of the most beautiful women in Boston. Benjamin Eddy Morse, b. Sept. 11, 1787; d. May 22, 1814. Ebenezer Morse, b. July 11, 1790; d. May 3, 1791.

John Torrey Morse, b. March 27, 1813; m. Lucy Cabot Jackson, and had issue: 1 *John T., Jr.* 2 *Charles J.* 3 *E. Rollins.*

John T., Jr., m. Fanny Hovey, and has issue: 1 *Cabot.* 2 *Torrey.*

Samuel Torrey Morse, b. May 19, 1816; m. Harriet J. Lee, and has issue: 1 *Francis R.* 2 *Henry L.* 3 *Mary L.*

E. Rollins Morse, m. Mary, dau. of Admiral Steedman.

3 HANNAH, b. July 11, 1768; baptized July 17, 1768; d. at Chicopee, Mass., March 31, 1837. She m. Luke Bemis of Watertown, Mass.

Children:

1 *Robert Eddy*, b. June 4, 1798; m. Martha G. Wheatland of Salem; b. May 29, 1807; d. Dec. 26, 1872.

  Children:

  1 *Robert Wheatland*, b. July 30, 1826 (resides in Chicopee, Mass., 1881); m. Nov. 26, 1852, Rachel Z. Smith, b. Aug., 1827.

    Children:

    1 *Anna Goodhue*, b. at Chicopee, Jan. 28, 1855.
    2 *Benjamin Wheatland*, b. at Chicopee, Dec. 3, 1857.
    3 *Mary Catharine*, b. at Chicopee, Feb. 5, 1861.
    4 *Caroline Rachel*, b. at Chicopee, Jan. 20, 1865.
    5 *Robert Eddy*, b. at Chicopee, Oct. 30, 1870.
    6 *Edward Smith*, b. at Chicopee, July 20, 1873.

2 *Caroline Eddy*, b. June 12, 1830, at Salem.
3 *Hannah Eddy*, b. Nov. 17, 1832; d. Jan. 23, 1835.
4 *Hannah Eddy*, b. Sept. 15, 1836; d. Oct. 15, 1837.
5 *Mary Wheatland*, b. Aug. 6, 1838; m., Jan. 30, 1879, Henry Martin Whitney. Resides in Lawrence, Mass.
6 *Sarah Davis*, b. April 3, 1844; m. Jerome H. Fiske. Resides (1881) in Malden, Mass.
7 *Martha Goodhue*, b. June 10, 1844; m. James G. Smith of Chicopee, Mass., and resided in Holyoke, Mass. He was accidentally killed in Chicopee by a railway train.

  Children:
  1 *Robert.*
  2 *James.*

2   *Mary Eddy*, b. July 4, 1801; m. Benjamin Wheatland of Salem, Mass., April 9, 1827, who d. at Salem, Dec. 28, 1854, aged 53 years. She d. June 23, 1864.

Children:
1   *Martha Goodhue*, b. at Newmarket, N.H., March 12, 1828.
2   *Elizabeth Bemis*, b. at Newmarket, N.H., April 9, 1831; d. March 5, 1839.

3   *Luke*, b. March 6, 1800; d. Aug. 19, 1803.
4   *Luke*, b. April 7, 1806; living in 1881 in Westchester, Pa.; m., April 7, 1831, Elizabeth, dau. of Hawkes Lincoln of Boston, Mass. She b. Aug. 3, 1807, and d. at Cabotville, Mass., Feb. 13, 1841. He m., second, Oct. 9, 1845, Maria, b. April 1, 1821, dau. of William Stubbs of Litchfield, England; d. ——. He m., third, Dec. 15, 1857, Lucy Ann, dau. of Nathan and Hannah (Jewett) Thayer of Hollis, N.H. She b. March 13, 1824.

Children by first wife:
1   *Mary Howe*, b. Nov. 28, 1832; d. Dec. 1, 1832.
2   *Martha Wheatland*, b. June 4, 1834; d. ——.
3   *Mary Elizabeth*, b. May 19, 1837; d. Feb. 6, 1842.
4   *Henry Luke*, b. June 10, 1839; d. Oct. 11, 1840.
5   *Hannah*, b. Feb. 3, 1841; d. Sept. 5, 1841.

Children by second wife:
6   *Maria Elizabeth*, b. July 21, 1846; m., Feb. 10, 1874, at Westchester, Pa., Gillies Dallett, Jr., son of Gillies and Josephine (Martin) Dallett of Philadelphia, Pa., and with her husband was drowned from the brig Roanoke, March 22, 1877, on her passage from Philadelphia toward Laguira.

Children:
1   *Josephine*, b. Dec. 1, 1874; d. Dec. 3, 1876.
2   *Elizabeth Bemis*, b. Jan. 29, 1876; d. July 15, 1876.

7   *Benjamin Eddy*, b. March 10, 1848; d. April 14, 1848.
8   *James Scott*, b. Sept. 29, 1850; d. Oct. 22, 1851.
9   *Clara Frances*, b. June 23, 1852; m., Jan. 24, 1878, Barton Darlington Evans, son of Henry S. and Jane (Darlington) Evans.

Children:

1　*Elizabeth Bemis*, b. at Westchester, Feb. 7, 1879. Resides (1881) in Westchester, Pa.

Children by third wife:

10　*Frederic Angier*, b. Nov. 3, 1858; d. July 24, 1859.
11　*Arthur Webster*, b. Nov. 18, 1862.

4　SARAH, b. Aug. 11, 1770; d. Sept. 11, 1778.
5　CHARLOTTE, b. March 16, 1773; d. March 21, 1773.
6　ROBERT RAND, b. March 18, 1774; d. Sept. 13, 1778.
7　EUNICE, b. Oct. 11, 1776; d. July 17, 1796.
8　SARAH, b. May 17, 1779; d. Nov. 29, 1848. She m., Jan. 21, 1810, William Cotting, Esq., of West Cambridge, and was the mother of Dr. Benjamin Eddy Cotting of Roxbury, an eminent physician, now (1881) living, and late President of the Massachusetts Medical Society, Curator of the Lowell Institute, etc.

Children:

1　*Benjamin Eddy*, b. Oct. 22, 1810; d. Oct. 23, 1810.
2　*Benjamin Eddy*, b. Nov. 2, 1812; m. Catharine Sayers, who d. 1881.
3　*Martha Eddy*, b. April 2, 1814; m. Miles T. Gardener. She d. at Rochester, N.Y.
4　*Mary Caroline*, b. July 22, 1816.
5　*Sarah Maria Wellington*, m. Dr. Holmes of Lexington, Mass.
6　*William;* dead.

9　ROBERT RAND, b. Aug. 25, 1781; d. June 20, 1796.
349 348　10　CALEB, b. May 27, 1784; d. Feb. 22, 1859.

---

348 349 (VII.) CALEB EDDY of Boston, Mass.; b. in Shrewsbury, Mass., May 27, 1784; d. at Chicopee, Mass., Feb. 22, 1859. Sept. 30, 1810, he married Caroline Gay, daughter of Timothy Gay, deceased, — a highly successful and wealthy merchant of Boston. He (Caleb) and his wife are buried in Mount Auburn Cemetery, Cambridge, Mass., in lot No. 362, Narcissus Path. She was b. April 4, 1792, and d. at Chicopee, Mass., May 28, 1862, and was descended from John Gay, who came to this country in 1630, and settled in Watertown, Mass. Her mother was Jane Henry, daughter of Robert Henry and Jane McQuesten of Boston, Mass. One of their daughters was the mother of the

Caleb Eddy

late Commodore David Porter, U.S.N., father of the present Admiral of the Navy, David D. Porter. She was also mother of the late Captain John Porter, U.S.N., the father of Major-General Fitz John Porter, now (1881) residing at Morristown, N.J. Timothy Gay, Esq. (father of Caroline, wife of Caleb Eddy), was b. Feb. 27, 1763; m. Oct. 13, 1791, and d. July 28, 1799. He was son of Timothy (b. July 30, 1730; m. Amity Holmes, Sept. 17, 1756); son of Timothy (b. Dec. 29, 1703; m. in Stoughton, Mass., Feb. 10, 1727, Azubah Thorp, who d. Dec. 9, 1773. He d. March 29, 1793); son of Timothy (b. Sept. 15, 1674; m. Patience ——. He d. May 26, 1719); son of Samuel (b. March 10, 1639; m., Nov. 23, 1661, Mary, dau. of Edward Bridge of Roxbury, Mass. He d. April 15, 1718; his wife d. April 13, 1718); son of John the Pilgrim, who d. March 4, 1688.

Children:

352 350	1	ROBERT HENRY, b. Sept. 27, 1812.	
	2	MARY CAROLINE, b. Aug. 3, 1817; d. May 23, 1829.	
	3	BENJAMIN, b. May 25, 1820; d. Nov. 9, 1822.	
	4	THOMAS MELVILLE, b. July 16, 1822; d. Sept. 1, 1822.	
353 351	5	BENJAMIN, b. Jan. 26, 1829; now (1881) living.	
	6	ALBERT MELVILLE, b. June 30, 1832; d. about 1860.	

NOTE. — *Caleb Eddy* resided in Boston from the time he was fourteen years of age until he removed to Chicopee, about 1856. He was a merchant for seventeen years, of the firm of Bemis & Eddy. Was Alderman of the City for two years. In 1825 he was appointed agent of the Middlesex and Merrimac River Canals, and continued in that capacity until Jan. 15, 1846. He conducted the affairs of the corporation with eminent success, having built nearly all the works anew, and converted a non-paying into a highly profitable concern. He was a gentleman of sound judgment, and enjoyed the confidence and esteem of the community. He gave great attention to the genealogy of the Eddys, and wrote a large folio volume on the subject, after an extensive correspondence with persons of the name. His son, the writer of this work, is greatly indebted to his father for what he has herein produced. While living, Mr. Caleb Eddy stated to the writer that for his genealogical researches he was amply repaid by having through such been able to return to his relations a person lost in childhood. Mr. Eddy one afternoon, while travelling in the State of New York, took a walk, and being somewhat fatigued, and meeting a man who was hewing a stick of timber, sat down on it, and entered into conversation with the person. After a while the man asked Mr. Eddy his name, and on Mr. Eddy replying, said, "Why, my name is Eddy!" Mr. Caleb Eddy on inquiring as to the origin of the man, was informed that he had reason to believe that he came from Canada in his childhood, but who his parents were he did not know, or whether he had any relations living. After further questioning the individual, Mr. Eddy obtained a clue to the mystery, and subsequently wrote to the man informing him from whence he sprung, and that he then had brothers and sisters living, and where they were, — thus restoring him to them. — R. H. E.

---

350 352 (VIII.) ROBERT HENRY EDDY, b. in Boston, Sept. 27, 1812, where he has resided up to the present time; m., Dec. 24, 1851, Annie Goddard Pickering, dau. of John Knight Pickering, Esq., of Portsmouth, N.H.

NOTE. — The compiler of this "Genealogy" was educated in Boston. At an early age studied architecture with the late Asher Benjamin, Architect. Afterwards studied civil and military engineering with the late Col. Loammi Baldwin of Charlestown, Mass. Was engaged at the building of the dry dock, Charlestown Navy Yard; also on the Middlesex and Merrimack River Canals. At the age of twenty-one, was chosen Civil Engineer to the East Boston Company, and surveyed and laid out East Boston; built wharves, bridges, roads, and various other improvements there. Was afterwards appointed Engineer of the Concord Railroad, though owing to absence did not conduct that work. For several subsequent years he was extensively professionally engaged in making surveys, etc., in New England and New York for public internal improvements. Was employed by the City of Boston to make surveys of lakes in the vicinity for the introduction of water; the result being that he reported on Spot and Mystic Ponds as good sources of supply. Subsequently he abandoned engineering and became a Solicitor of Patents, being the first to establish the business in this country. Up to 1880 he has been a very extensive practitioner, and, in all probability, has procured for inventors more patents than any other person. In 1838 he visited Europe for examination of the public works there, such as docks, canals, bridges, railways, water-works, etc.; was with the late Elie de Beaumont at the meeting of the French Institute, when Arago, the President, announced the discovery of the daguerreotype, — being the only American present. Some three years ago was elected " Fellow of the Royal Historical Society of Great Britain."

---

351 353 (VIII.) BENJAMIN EDDY, b. Jan. 26, 1829; residing (1880) at Groton, Mass.; m. Nellie M., dau. of George Weld of Jamaica Plains, Mass.

Children :

1　CHARLES BENJAMIN, m. Lucy Corey of Groton.
2　MINNIE CAROLINE.
3　NELLIE ISABELLA.

124 354 (III.) OBEDIAH EDDY, b. 1645; d. 1722. His wife's name was Bennet.

Children:

1 JOHN, b. March 22, 1669; lived in Taunton, Mass.
2 HASADIAH, b. April 10, 1672; m. Samuel Sampson.
-358 355 3 SAMUEL, b. 1675; d. 1752.
403 356 4 JABEZ.
412 357 5 BENJAMIN.
6 JOEL, m. Sarah Harris, 1708; had one dau., Sarah.
7 MERCY, m. S. Sampson. They resided in Middleboro', Mass.

Children:

1 *Obediah*, m. Mary Soule.
2 *Gershom*, m. Bethia Clark.
3 *Ichabod*, m. Mercy Savory.
4 *Esther*, m. Abraham Borden, 1726; removed to Stafford, Ct.
5 *Mary*, m. Isaac Fuller.

8 ELIZABETH, m. David Delano.

Children:

1 *Lemuel.*   2 *Betty.*
3 *Abigail.*   4 *David*, b. March 17, 1745.

9 MARY, m. Dr. Isaac Fuller.

Children:

1 *Reliance.*   2 *Isaac.*
3 *Elizabeth.*   4 *Samuel.*
5 *Micah.*   6 *Jabez.*
7 *Mary.*

NOTE. — *Obediah Eddy*, admitted freeman June 9, 1683; was constable 1679, 1681, 1683, and 1689. In 1692 he was grand-juryman from Middleboro'. In 1682 he was a surveyor, and in 1690 a selectman. Lived in Middleboro' in 1674.

---

353 358 (IV.) SAMUEL EDDY, b. in Middleboro', 1675; d. 1752; m. Malatiah Pratt, b. Dec. 11, 1676; d. March, 1769.

Children:

361 359 1 SAMUEL, b. 1696; d. Nov. 3, 1726.
376 360 2 ZACHARIAH, b. 1701; d. 1767.
3 MALATIAH, m., March 23, 1730, to Samuel Tinkham.

4 BENNET, m. William Reading, Feb. 7, 1738.
5 FEAR, m. George Williamson, Nov. 7, 1738.

> NOTE. — *Samuel Eddy* resided in Middleboro'. He was a man of uncommon strength and robust constitution, his frame being very large. Tradition has preserved remarkable proofs of his physical powers.

---

359 361 (V.) SAMUEL EDDY, b. 1710; d. Nov. 3, 1746; m. Lydia Alden, dau. of John and Hannah (White) Alden, and a descendant of John Alden the Pilgrim.

Children:
361 362 1 NATHAN, b. Sept. 8, 1733.
         2 JOSHUA, b. March 6, 1734; d. young.
         3 SUSANNAH, b. Nov. 22, 1736; spinster.
         4 MARY, b. May 9, 1740; d. young.
375 363 5 SAMUEL, b. Jan. 23, 1742.—
         6 SETH, b. Feb. 11, 1744; d. young.

> NOTE. — He was a public officer, and an eminent man in the church, by which he was long remembered for his superior prudence and sense.

---

362 364 (VI.) NATHAN EDDY, b. Sept. 8, 1733; m. Eunice Sampson of Middleboro', Nov. 17, 1757. He was b. in Plymouth County, and about 1785 moved to Sherburne, Vt. He d. in Pittsfield, Vt.

Children:
370 365 1 EPHRAIM, b. Dec. 21, 1759; d. about 1800.
         2 LYDIA, b. Sept. 16, 1769.
         3 HANNAH, b. Feb. 1, 1766.
371 366 4 NATHANIEL, b. July 6, 1768; d. at Galliopolis.
372 367 5 NATHAN, b. April 21, 1771.
373 368 6 ISAAC, b. June 24, 1774; d. June 26, 1833.
374 369 7 ZACHARIAH, b. Nov. 17, 1778.

---

365 370 (VII.) EPHRAIM EDDY, b. Dec. 21, 1729; m. Mary Safford, and d. about 1800 in Woodstock, Vt. He was a Captain in the Revolutionary War. Had one son (Safford) and two daughters. The son settled in Montpelier, Vt., was a merchant, and highly respected; d. young, without issue.

366 371 (VII.) NATHANIEL EDDY, b. July 6, 1768; d. at Galliopolis, Ohio. He had no sons; had a daughter who m. Johnson.

---

367 372 (VII.) NATHAN EDDY, b. April 21, 1771; m. Rebecca Safford, at Woodstock, Vt., Oct. 28, 1794, and lived in Louisville, Kentucky; d. about 1843.

Child:

1 IRA, b. March 31, 1796. In 1840, he lived in Edinburg, Ohio.

Children:

1 *Loretta*, b. Sept. 20, 1820.
2 *Sarah*, b. Jan. 10, 1823.
3 *Cynthia*, b. Oct. 4, 1824.
4 *Safford* and *Bridgden*, b. April 10, 1826.
5 *Eliza*, b. June 4, 1825.
6 *Ezra Booth*, b. Dec. 14, 1829.
7 *Rachael*, b. Feb. 5, 1837.
8 *Susan M. B.*, b. June 20, 1838; d. Feb. 8, 1840.

NOTE.—*Nathan Eddy* served in the war of 1812-15; afterwards was a schoolmaster and a student of divinity. Subsequently he became a Methodist Preacher, and was such for twenty years, up to 1840.

---

368 373 (VII.) ISAAC EDDY, b. Jan. 24, 1774; d. June 26, 1833, at Pittsfield, Vt.

Children:

1 ELIZABETH, b. June 5, 1797; m. James Cary.
2 EUNICE, b. Dec. 29, 1799; m. Alvah Brown.
3 ISAAC, b. Oct. 22, 1801; was a Methodist clergyman, but afterwards joined the Congregational Church. He first settled in Geneva, N.Y., and afterwards in Jamestown, N.Y.; was an able minister. He had two children, *Myron* and *Corydon*.
4 WILLIAM M. CARY, b. Sept. 16, 1803; lived (1840) in Jamestown, N.Y.
5 NATHANIEL, b. Nov. 29, 1805; lived (1840) in Jamestown, N.Y., had two children, *Ephraim* and *Halbert*.
6 ELMINA, b. Aug. 10, 1807; m. Scott.
7 SAFFORD, b. April 15, 1810; living in Jamestown, N.Y., 1840.

8 HIRAM, b. May 17, 1813, in Warren, Pa., in 1840; but in
1881 a distinguished clergyman in Jersey City, N.J.

Children:
1 *Kezia.*   2 *Elizabeth.*
3 *Keziah II.*   4 *Hiram M. G.*
5 *Mary R.*   6 *Katharine.*
7 *Sarah II. A.*   8 *William A.*

9 ZACHARIAH, b. Dec. 19, 1815; an eminent clergyman of
Detroit, Mich.; was Orator of Eddy Festival; m.,
first, Susan Gray, Nov., 1835. She d. March, 1847.
m., second, Malvina R. Cochran, April, 1845.

Children by first wife:
1 *Henry Martin,* b. Oct., 1836; d. Feb. 15, 1865; unmarried.
2 *Haven D.,* b. Oct., 1838; d. Aug. 2, 1873; m. Elizabeth Burke, who d. 1872, childless.
3 *Harriet E.,* b. June, 1842.
4 *Arthur,* b. July, 1846; d. Oct., 1846.

Children by second wife:
5 *Edith M.,* b. Feb., 1849; m. Albert Lyons, M.D.

Child:
1 *Edith Lucia.*

6 *Frank,* b. July, 1851; m. Florence Taylor.

Child:
1 *Katharine.*

7 *Mary D.,* b. Jan., 1854; m. Leonard A. Treat; reside
(1881) at Brookline, Mass.

Children:
1 *Alice.*   2 *Ethel.*   3 *Donald.*

8 *Milly Hayward,* b. May, 1855; d. 1856.
9 *Alice Maud,* b. Nov., 1857.
10 *Charles William,* b. June, 1859.
11 *Fanny Fosten,* b. July, 1861.

---

369 374 (VII.) ZACHARIAH EDDY, b. in Plymouth, Mass., Nov. 18,
1778; living in Warren, Pa., in 1844, and d. there in
1872, aged 93 years and eight months; m. Rose Stewart,
May 17, 1804. She b. Feb. 6, 1786, and d. Aug 6, 1857.

Children:

1 ISAAC, b. April 6, 1805; m. Olive Gates.

    Children:
    1 *Henry.*
    2 *Zachariah.*
    3 *Hiram,* m. Mary Schofield.

        Child:
        1 *Mary.*

    4 *Sarah,* m. William Scott; live (1881) in Warren, Pa.

        Child:
        1 *Frank.*

2 CATHARINE, b. Nov. 2, 1806; m. W. T. Parker.

    Children:
    1 *Catharine.*
    2 *Harriet.*
    3 *Fletcher.*

3 NATHAN, b. May 14, 1810.
4 EUNICE, b. April 28, 1812; m. T. Struthers of Warren, Pa.

    Children:
    1 *Anna,* m. George Wetmore.

        Child:
        1 *Thomas.*

    2 *Thomas.*

5 JAMES HOOD, b. Nov. 11, 1814; m. Hannah Hook. In 1880, president of the First National Bank of Warren.

    Children:
    1 *Belle.*
    2 *Henrietta,* m. James Roy.
    3 *Irvine H.*
    4 *James B.*
    5 *Francis Dudley.*
    6 *Rosa.*

6 ZACHARIAH, b. March 15, 1818; m. Theodosia Turner.

Children:
1 *Mary*, m. Frank Barnheart.

   Child:
   1 *Harry*.

2 *Eliza*, m. Patrick Falconer.

   Children:
   1 *Henry*.
   2 *Frank*.
   3 *Rosa*.

7 HANNAH, m. Erastus Barnes.

   Children:
   1 *Rosa*, m. W. H. Andrews, she d. 1879.

      Children:
      1 *William*.
      2 *Belle*.
      3 *Frank*.

   2 *Letitia*, m. George Horton.

      Children:
      1 *Byron*.
      2 *Hattie*.

   3 *Timothy*, m. Ada Houghton.

      Children:
      1 *Hiram*.
      2 *Percy*.

   4 *Catharine*.

8 ELIZA, b. Jan. 20, 1820; m. Erastus Barnes.

   Children:
   1 *Rosa*, m. Frank Blair.

      Children:
      1 *Eddy*.
      2 *Ernest*.

   2 *Timothy*.
   3 *Letitia*.
   4 *Catharine*.

9 ROSANNA, b. Aug. 29, 1826.

363 375 (VI.) SAMUEL EDDY of Marion, N.Y., b. Jan. 23, 1742; d. about 1822; m. —— Clark of Plymouth, Mass.; was an Orderly Sergeant in Revolutionary Army, and was a learned and religious man.

Children:

1 DAVID, b. March 3, 1774, in Middleboro', Mass.; m. Deborah Shaw, May 25, 1806, who d. in 1847. He d. at Eddy Ridge, N.Y., June 9, 1840.

    Children:

    1 *Morton*, b. 1807; d. at Adrian, Mich., 1880.
    2 *Hiram Lawrence*, b. Feb., 1811, at Eddy Ridge, N.Y.; m. Hetty Peterson, 1810. He (1880) is a physician in Geneva, N.Y.

        Children:

        1 *Lawrence Peterson*, b. Nov. 2, 1843, at Canago, N.Y.; m. Mary B. Graves, Nov. 17, 1874. He (1880) is a lawyer at Grand Rapids, Mich.

            Child:

            1 *George Beauclerc*, b. Feb. 27, 1878.

        2 *Herbert Morton*, b. Nov. 27, 1845; is a physician in Geneva, N.Y.

    3 *Alfred*, b. March 1, 1815, in Williamson, N.Y.; m. Catharine H. Wilcox. Is a clergyman at Niles, Mich., 1810.

        Children:

        1 *Alfred D.*, b. June 3, 1846; m. Carrie H. Silvey. Resides in Chicago, Ill., 1880; is a lawyer.

            Child:

            1 *Alfred Hugh*, b. Aug. 18, 1874; d. April 13, 1875.

        2 *Cora;* resides in Niles, Mich., 1880.

    4 *George.*

2 SAMUEL, b. 1762; lived in 1840 in Coleraine, Mass.
3 WILLIAM, d. in Marion, N.Y., 1824.
4 SETH.

    Children:
    1 *Samuel*, b. 1806.

2 *Alden*, b. 1808.
3 *Hiram*, b. 1810.
4 *John S.*, b. 1813.
5 *Norman P.*, b. 1816.
6 *David M.*, b. 1815.
7 *William*, b. 1826.

5 LYDIA.
6 SUSANNAH.
7 REBECCA.
8 MARTHA.

360 376 (V.) ZACHARIAH EDDY, b. 1701; d. 1777; m. Mercy Morton; dau. of Eben Morton, Nov. 18, 1737. She d. Aug. 25, 1802, aged 80. He lived in Middleboro', Mass., in the homestead of his father. Was active in the Revolutionary War.

Children:
1 JOHN EDDY, b. Jan. 14, 1738; d. 1761; was in service in 1761 in the French War, and died near Lake George. He was a resident of Middleboro', a mathematician, and a publisher of almanacs, the last one being dated Sept., 1759. He married Hannah Pomroy, May 29, 1760. Issue, *Sally*, b. April 15, 1761; m. Josiah Washburn of Randolph, Mass.; and d. about 1832.
2 MARY, b. May 9, 1740; d. Oct. 15, 1796; m. Moses Standish of Plympton, Mass.

Children:
1 *Josiah.* 2 *Jonathan.* 3 *Joshua.*

3 HANNAH, b. April 19, 1749; d. Dec. 22, 1752.
4 NATHANIEL, b. Feb. 13, 1744; d. Dec. 23, 1752.
5 EBENEZER, b. April 24, 1742; d. Dec. 22, 1752.
381 377 6 JOSHUA, b. May 5, 1748; d. 1833.
7 ZACHARIAH, b. March 16, 1752; d. June 9, 1777.
396 378 8 SETH, b. May 30, 1754.
401 379 9 THOMAS, b. March 28, 1756.
402 380 10 SAMUEL, b. April 29, 1760.
11 LUCY, b. March 25, 1758; m. Dr. J. Fuller of Middleboro'.

Children:
1 *Zachariah.* 2 *Thomas.*
3 *Jabez.* 4 *Seth.*
5 *Betsey.*

12 MERCY, b. April 2, 1746; m. Elisha Freeman of Middleboro', Feb. 26, 1778. He b. April 15, 1745. She d. Aug. 19, 1838.

Children:

1 *Josiah*, m. Virtue Morton, 1806.

Children:

1 *Morton*, b. Oct. 29, 1807; m. Louisa Jennings, 1836.

Child.

1 *Maria*, b. April 27, 1737, at Middleboro', Mass.

2 *Harrison*, b. Feb. 3, 1810.
3 *Louisa*, b. March 20, 1812; m. Josiah T. Cornish, Jan. 9, 1834.
4 *Elisha*, b. Sept. 26, 1814.
5 *Samuel*, b. April 9, 1816; m. Anne B. Pinkham, 1838.
6 *Benjamin*, b. Feb. 3, 1818; m. Nancy F. Fuller, 1846.
7 *Virtue M.*, b. Oct. 8, 1819; m. Prince Penniman of Abington, Mass., 1842.
8 *Mercy Eddy*, b. May 14, 1821; m. John Bryant, 1845.
9 *Jane*, b. Oct. 7, 1823; m. Oliver T. Tinkenham, 1846.
10 *Lydia*, b. April 25, 1826.

2 *Hannah*, b. 1783; d. unmarried, Sept. 22, 1842.
3 *Morton*.
4 *John*, b. 1787.

---

277 381 (VI.) JOSHUA EDDY, b. May 5, 1748, in Middleboro', Mass. m. Lydia Paddock, b. 1756. He d. May 1, 1833. She d. Feb. 13, 1838.

Children:

389 382   1 JOSHUA, b. Feb. 3, 1779; d. Nov. 12, 1863.
390 383   2 ZACHARIAH, b. Dec. 6, 1780; d. Feb. 14, 1860.
391 384   3 EBENEZER, b. March 12, 1783; d. Dec. 22, 1829.
292 385   4 NATHANIEL, b. Sept. 5, 1785; d. March 29, 1869.
          5 LYDIA, b. July 23, 1787; d. Feb. 13, 1842; m. Barzillia Crane of Berkeley, Mass.

Children:

1 *Charlotte*, d. young.

2 *Nancy*, d. young.
3 *Susan*, m. Samuel Breck; had four children.
4 *Elisha*, d. ——.
5 *Charlotte Maria*.
6 *Joshua Eddy*, m. Lucy A. Reed.

Children:
1 *Joshua Eddy*.
2 *Morton*.
3 *Charles*.
4 *Annie*.
5 *Henry*.
6 *Edward*.

7 *Irene F.*, m. Thomas G. Nichols of Freetown.
8 *Lydia E.*, d. young.

393 386   6 WILLIAM S., b. Dec. 19, 1789; d. Dec. 22, 1876.
          7 JANE, b. June 6, 1792; m. Asahil Hathaway.

Child:
1 *Priscilla D.*, b. 1817; m. Quincy A. Keith, b. 1816.

Children:
1 *William H.*, b. 1842; d. young.
2 *James*, b. 1843; d. 1879.
3 *Caroline A.*, b. 1845; m. Rev. Mr. Grear of Providence, R.I.
4 *Jane E.*, b. 1847; m. Charles Crane.

          8 MORTON, b. May 7, 1795; d. Oct. 3, 1796.
394 387   9 MORTON, b. Oct. 3, 1797.
395 388 10 JOHN MILTON, b. Feb. 18, 1800; d. 1862, in Cal.

NOTE. — *Joshua Eddy* entered the army in 1775 in Capt. Benson's Company, Col. Cotton's Regiment. He was at Roxbury, Mass., during the siege of Boston and battle of Breed's Hill. In 1776 he was a Lieutenant in Col. Marshall's Regiment, and went to Castle Island. He was in the retreat from Ticonderoga. He was at Saratoga at the surrender of Burgoyne. Thence he went to New Jersey, and into winter quarters with Gen. Washington. He left the army on furlough Dec. 24. On April 10, 1778, he was m. to Lydia Paddock of Middleboro', who was b. July 22, 1756. The next May he returned to the army, and was at the battle of Monmouth. After he left the army he was extensively engaged in business of various kinds. He was Deacon of the Church, Oct. 10, 1805, which office he held many years. He d. May 1, 1833. He was a gentleman of uncommon energy and ability, and enjoyed the respect and esteem of his fellow-citizens.

382 389 (VII.) JOSHUA EDDY, b. Feb. 3, 1779, in Middleboro'; d. Nov. 12, 1863; m. Lydia Morton, who was b. Sept. 11, 1779; d. July 21, 1855.

Children:

1 THALIA, b. Sept. 23, 1805, in Middleboro', Mass.; m., Dec. 25, 1832. to Thomas Weston, b. Feb. 27, 1804, in Middleboro'.

Children:

1 *Thomas*, b. June 14, 1834, in Middleboro'; m., Oct. 16, 1867, Nellie S. Childs, b. May 21, 1843, in Milledgeville, Georgia.

Children:

1 *Grace*, b. May 15, 1870, in Springfield, Mass.
2 *Abby Childs*, b. July 21, 1873, in Newton, Mass.
3 *Thomas*, b. Aug. 12, 1875, in Newton, Mass.

2 *Mary*, b. April 30, 1836, in Middleboro'; m., Sept. 15, 1864, to Jesse T. Higgins, born Oct. 20, 1833, in Wellfleet, Mass.

Child:

1 *Thomas Weston*, b. Aug. 27, 1865, in Wellfleet.

3 *Thalia*. b. May 2, 1841, in Middleboro'; m., Dec. 13, 1864, to Sprague S. Stetson, b. Feb. 12, 1841, in New Bedford, Mass.

Children:

1 *George Ward*, b. Feb. 27, 1866, at Lakeville, Mass.
2 *Jennie*, b. Sept. 10, 1870, at Lakeville, Mass.

2 JANE ELLEN, b. Oct. 18, 1807, in Middleboro'; m., Dec. 12, 1841, to Timothy Cobb, b. Sept. 12, 1806, in Carver, Mass.; he died Sept. 11, 1857.

Children:

1 *Jane Elizabeth*, b. Nov. 17, 1842, in Carver; m., Feb. 3, 1870, to Marcus M. Shaw, b. Oct. 21, 1842, in Carver.

Children:

1 *Agnes Morton*, b. Nov. 7, 1870, in Carver.
2 *Stillman*, b. April 15, 1872, in Plymouth.
3 *Ellen Eddy*, b. April 1, 1874, in Woburn.
4 *Lizzie Cobb*, b. June 30, 1877; d. Nov. 3, 1877.
5 *Marcus Morton*, b. March 12, 1879; d. March 20, 1879.

2 *Timothy Edwin*, b. April 15, 1844; d. Oct. 15, 1844.
3 *Annie*, b. Aug. 5, 1845.

4   *Richard Eddy*, b. Nov. 13, 1846, in Carver; m., Nov. 13, 1872, to Lucy H. Pickens, b. Feb. 25, 1852, in Middleboro'.

5   *Sarah Barrows*, b. Aug. 10, 1848, in Carver; m., Dec. 9, 1868, to Earl T. Smith, b. Feb. 19, 1843, in Middleboro'.

    Children:

    1 *Fred. S.*, b. Sept. 4, 1872, in Brockton.

    2 *Richard E.*, b. May 24, 1875; d. March 25, 1880.

    3 *Helen*, b. Jan. 12, 1878, in Middleboro'.

6   *Isabella*, b. Jan. 6, 1850, in Carver; d. Feb. 2, 1851.

3 CHARLES EDWARDS, b. Sept. 17, 1809, in Middleboro'; m., June 23, 1847, Elizabeth Eddy Simmons, b. Sept. 13, 1825, in Providence, R.I. He lives in Westboro', 1881.

    Children:

    1 *Charles Edwards*, b. Nov. 12, 1848, at Providence, R.I.; m., May 19, 1874, Ella L. Rand, b. in Boston, Mass., Jan. 2, 1850. They reside in Newton, Mass. He is deacon of the Eliot Church there, and is in business in Boston (1881).

        Children:

        1 *Mabel Rand*, b. April 29, 1875, at Newton, Mass.

        2 *Caroline Simmons*, b. March 4, 1877, at Newton, Mass.

        3 *Edith Elizabeth*, b. Aug. 7, 1879, at Newton, Mass.

    2 *George Simmons*, b. March 11, 1854; m., May 11, 1876, to Emma S. Billings, b. May 11, 1854; resides in Westboro', Mass.

        Child:

        1 *Margie Kinsley*, b. Nov. 15, 1878.

    3 *Walter Morton*, b. Sept. 26, 1856, in Providence. Resides in Westboro', Mass. (1881).

    4 *Ella Morton*, b. Nov. 19, 1850, in Providence, R.I.

    5 *Louise*, b. Dec. 28, 1861, in Providence, R.I.

    6 *Elizabeth Kinsley*, b. Oct. 28, 1864, in Westboro', Mass.

4 LYDIA MORTON, b. Aug. 1, 1813, in Middleboro'; m., Dec. 2, 1876, Andrew Barrows Cobb, b. Feb. 5, 1812, at Carver. He d. March 3, 1878.

    Children:

    1 *Henry Eddy*, b. June 21, 1839, in Hartford, Conn.; m., May 11, 1864, Harriet M. Cooley, b. Feb. 24, 1842, in Norwich, Conn.

Children :

1 *Morton Eddy*, b. Dec. 5, 1865, at Newton, Mass.
2 *Lucy Ely*, b. April 29, 1870, at Newton, Mass.
3 *Kate Brewster*, b. Dec. 28, 1871, at Newton, Mass.
4 *Helen Minerva*. b. Oct. 3, 1873, at Newton, Mass.

2 *Kate Morton*, b. May 25, 1842, in Bridgewater, Mass.; m., May 30, 1865, Theodore Nickerson, b. March 28, 1842, in South Boston.

Children :

1 *Marion Eddy*, b. July 29, 1866, in New York.
2 *Ernest*, b. Jan. 19, 1870, in Newton.
3 *Ella Winnifred*, b. April 5, 1874, in Newton.
4 *Margaret Morton*, b. Dec. 9, 1876, in Newton.
5 *Thomas*, b. Sept. 15, 1878, in Newton.

3 *Andrew Barrows*, b. Nov. 2, 1852, at Newton, Mass.; m., Aug. 15, 1878, Ellen M. Converse, b. Feb. 23, 1855, at Boston.

Child :

1 *Andrew Edmond*, b. Nov. 17, 1879, at Calcutta, India.

5 ELIZA, b. Sept. 18, 1817, in Middleboro', Mass.
6 SUSAN MORTON, b. Sept. 27, 1819, in Middleboro', Mass.
7 JOSHUA MORTON, b. Feb. 16, 1824, in Middleboro'; m. Elira T. Carpenter, b. June 10, 1826, in Providence, R.I. They reside upon the homestead in Eddyville.

Children :

1 *Florence*, b. May 4, 1855.
2 *Mary Morton*, b. May 24, 1861.

383 390 (VII.) ZECHARIAH EDDY, b. in Middleboro', Mass., Dec. 6, 1780; d. Feb. 14, 1860; m., Sept. 1, 1803, Sally Edson of Bridgewater; b. Nov. 12, 1781; d. Sept. 7, 1850. He was a highly-eminent lawyer, a religious man, a kind parent, and an excellent counsellor and friend.

Children :

1 ALEXANDER II., b. July 15, 1804; d. Sept. 19, 1805.
2 ANN JULIET, b. June 9, 1806; m., Nov. 28, 1829, Samuel Barrett; b. July 10, 1801; d. April 27, 1877; a graduate of Harvard University, and an eminent teacher in the Public Schools of Boston for thirty-nine years.

Children :

1 *Anne Maria*, b. Sept. 26, 1830; d. Nov. 24, 1834.
2 *Caroline Juliet*, b. May 18, 1832; m. Samuel Breck, 1857, a graduate of West Point Military Academy. He is (1881) Assistant Adjutant General, U.S.A.

Child:

1   *Samuel Breck, Jr.*, b. Aug. 8, 1862.

8 *Samuel Eddy*, b. May 16, 1834; m. Alice D. Brush of Cleveland, Ohio, May 20, 1868. Resides in Chicago.

Children:
1   *Robert LeMoyne*, b. May 28, 1871.
2   *Adela*, b. Nov. 7, 1873.
3   *Juliet*, b. March 2, 1875.
4   *Wisner*, b. July 19, 1877; d. Oct. 17, 1879.
5   *Alice*, b. Dec. 30, 1878.

4 *Marion*, b. March 16, 1836.
5 *William Henry*, b. July 9, 1839; d. Jan. 24, 1840.
6 *Addison*, b. May 15, 1841; m. Marion Harrison of Washington, D.C., 1866. He is Captain in the Quartermaster's Department, U.S. Army.

Children:
1   *Horace S.*, b. Jan. 3, 1871.
2   *Harold Eddy*, b. Nov. 27, 1873.
3   *Addison*, b. Oct. 5, 1875.
4   *Marion Ravenel*, b. March 19, 1878.
5   *Ernest H.*, b. March 4, 1881.

7 *Martha Gardner*, b. April 4, 1844; m., 1864, Henry A. Thorndike of Boston; d. Sept. 25, 1867.
8 *Adelaide Gerrish*, b. April 4, 1850; m., 1872, William Miller of Winchester, Va.

Child:
1   *Arthur Barrett*, b. Aug. 11, 1874.

3 CHARLES EDWARD, b. May 22, 1808; d. in two months.
4 LUCIA MARIA, b. Sept. 7, 1809; d. Jan. 26, 1811.
5 SARAH AMELIA, b. Oct. 12, 1811; d. Aug., 1838; m. Samuel Breck of Taunton.

Children:
1   *Samuel*, b. Feb. 25, 1834; m. Caroline J. Barrett, 1857.
2   *Sarah Amelia*, b. April 14, 1836.
3   *Charlotte Elizabeth*, b. Aug., 1838; d. young.

6 WILLIAM HENRY, b. Jan. 10, 1813; d. March, 1839; a graduate of Brown University.
7 SAMUEL, b. Jan. 9, 1816; d. Jan. 3, 1837; lawyer; a graduate of Brown University.
8 CHARLOTTE ELIZABETH, b. April 20, 1819; m., Sept. 7, 1846, Rev. Francis G. Pratt, b. Jan. 30, 1821. He graduated at Amherst College in 1840, and is a clergyman at East Middleboro'.

Children:

1 *Zechariah Eddy*, b. May 13. 1848; d. young.
2 *Francis Greenleaf*, b. Aug. 8, 1850.
3 *George Winthrop*, b. Feb. 22, 1855.
4 *A daughter*, d. young.

9 JANE CAROLINE. b. Jan. 22, 1822; d. Dec. 27, 1835.
10 ZECHARIAH, b. Nov. 2, 1826; d. young.

384 391   EBENEZER EDDY, b. in Middleboro', March 12, 1783; d. Dec. 22, 1829; m., Feb. 18, 1807, Betsey Stetson, b. Oct. 26, 1785; d. Jan. 18, 1864.

Children:

1 LUCIUS JUNIUS. b. Feb. 21, 1808; d. Feb. 4, 1865; m., April 29, 1834, Louisa M. Pratt of Middleboro', b. Feb. 7, 1812; d. April 11, 1876. Resided in Fall River.

Children:

1 *Caleb F.*, b. July 20, 1836, in Amherst, Mass.; m. Georgianna Winslow, Nov. 29, 1860, at Fall River. Resides (1881) in West Newton, Mass.

Children:

1 *George W.*, b. May 12, 1862.
2 *Louisa M.*, b. Dec. 20, 1863.
3 *Lillian*, b. Dec. 17, 1865.
4 *Clinton L.*. b. May 9, 1868.
5 *Frederick W.*, b. Dec. 27, 1869.
6 *Frank S.*, b. Sept. 27, 1871.
7 *Bertha*, b. Feb. 23, 1876.
8 *Bessie*, b. Feb. 23, 1876.
9 *Clifford*, b. Nov. 25, 1877.
10 *Marion*, b. Sept. 29, 1879.

2 *Sarah E.*. b. in Rockaway, N.J., Jan. 12, 1838; m., Dec. 13, 1865, George Parsons of Kennebunk, Me. Resides in New York City, 1881.

Children:

1 *Henry*. b. Nov. 1, 1866.
2 *May Eddy*, b. May 18. 1868.
3 *Joseph*, b. Sept. 17, 1869.
4 *Charlotte*, b. April 21, 1871.
5 *William Usher*, b. Oct. 24, 1873.
6 *Mary Abby*, b. May 31, 1878.
7 *Louisa*, b. Jan. 17, 1880.

3 *John J.*, b. in Rockaway. N.J., May 2, 1840; m., Oct. 17, 1867, Katharine Cleaveland of Cleveland, O.

Cashier Maverick National Bank, Boston.   Residence at West Newton, Mass.

4   *George S.*, b. Jan. 23, 1843.   Graduated at Harvard Medical School.   Physician at Fall River.   m., first, Emeline A. Jones, Nov. 7, 1870; she died Dec. 19, 1876, leaving one child, *George S.*, Jr., b. Aug. 9, 1873; m., second, Mary E. Thompson of Woonsocket, R.I., Aug. 6, 1879.   One son b. May 13, 1880.

2   CALEB STETSON, b. Feb. 14, 1811; d. Jan. 18, 1831.
3   BETSEY MARIA, b. Aug. 21, 1813; m. Amasa Thompson, Jan. 15, 1835.

Children:
1   *Maria P.*, b. Nov., 1835; m. Sylvanus Fuller.
2   Two children d. young.

4   MARTHA WASHINGTON, b. July 10, 1815; m., May 31, 1848, Henry Weston.   He d. June 10, 1863; one child, d. young.
5   EBENEZER MILTON, b. May 30, 1819.
6   ALBERT, b. April 12, 1823; d. Jan., 1865; m., 1854, Lucia Maria Ellis.

Children:
1   *Maria F.*, b. March 24, 1856.
2   *Louise D.*, b. June 1, 1860.

7   ERASTUS, b. Nov. 18, 1827; d. July 24, 1828.
8   FAYETTE, b. March, 1825; d. young.

---

385 392 (VII). NATHANIEL EDDY, b. Sept. 5, 1785; d. March 30, 1869; m., Sept. 27, 1811, Nancy Andros of Plainfield, Ct., and for his second wife, May 22, 1814, Abby, sister of Nancy.   His third, March 12, 1851, was Mrs. Melinda B. Reed.

Children by second wife:
1   NATHANIEL ANDROS, b. May 6, 1815; m. Abby H. Adams of Boston.   Resides in Indianapolis, Ind.

Children:
1   *Nathaniel*, d. young.
2   *George Adams.*
3   *Florence*, d. young.
4   *Marion*, m. Charles Moore.

Child:
1   *Emma Gardner.*

2 FRANCIS FRINK, b. April 6, 1817; m. Clara A. Hagan.

Children:

1 *Mary Jane.*   2 *Clara.*
3 *George.*   4 *Frances.*

3 ANNE ELIZABETH, b. April 6, 1817; m., Sept. 27, 1843, William Pratt, b. Sept. 10, 1816.

Children:

1 *Anne Elizabeth*, b. Nov. 4, 1845; d. March 1, 1862.
2 *Alice Maud*, b. July 25, 1849; d. March 29, 1862.
3 *Nathaniel Waterman*, b. Jan. 31, 1852; resides in Brooklyn, L.I.; m., June 16, 1880, Carrie V. Deudney of Roudout, N.Y.; one child, *Auguste Goubert*, b. March 31, 1881.

4 JOHN, b. Sept. 12, 1819; in 1881 an eminent lawyer in Providence. R.I. President at the Eddy Festival, Oct. 29, 1880, in commemoration of the landing of John and Samuel at Plymouth, Oct. 29, 1630.

Graduated from Brown University in 1840. Studied law with his uncle, the late Hon. Zechariah Eddy of Middleboro', Mass.; m., Nov. 28, 1848, Juliet H. Bonney, dau. of George Bonney, Esq., of Rochester, Mass. She d. March 31, 1850. Their daughter, *Juliet B.*, b. Dec. 5, 1849: m. E. P. Haskell, Esq., of New Bedford, Mass. She d. April 10, 1879, leaving two children: *Alice Haskell*, b. Jan. 15, 1875, and *Ernest.* b. Sept. 24, 1876. For his second wife John Eddy m., Oct. 10, 1855. Caroline M. Updike, dau. of Hon. Wilkins Updike of South Kingston, R.I.

Children by second wife:

1 *Alfred Updike*, b. Jan. 6, 1857.
2 *Mary Andros*, b. Aug. 20, 1859.
3 *Isabel*, b. July 14, 1862.
4 *Walter Updike*, b. Oct. 11, 1865.

5 ABBY ANDROS, b. July 19, 1822; m., 1844, George E. Adams of Boston.

6 MARY JANE, b. June 10, 1827, in Middleboro'; m. Charles F. Thayer (son of George W. and Catharine F. Thayer). He was b. in Boston, Nov. 24, 1825.

Children:

1 *Charles Eddy*, b. March 24, 1854; d. March 10, 1872.
2 *Francis Andros*, b. Aug. 12, 1856.
3 *Henry James*, b. Aug. 9, 1858
4 *Grace*, b. Sept. 14, 1860.

5 *Winthrop*, b. Nov. 22, 1862.
6 *Arthur Emerson*, b. July 28, 1870.
7 *Rodney*, b. March 27, 1873.
8 *Hulburt*, b. March 5, 1867; d. Dec. 13, 1867.

386 393 (VII.) WILLIAM S. EDDY, b. Dec. 19, 1789; d. Dec. 22, 1875; m. Lucy Cady of Plainfield, Ct.

Children :

1 WILLIAM CADY, b. May 12, 1821; m., May, 1847. Adeline Hamilton Osgood, dau. Rev. Israel Putnam, D.D.

Children:
1 *Anna Cady*, b. May 17, 1848.
2 *Warburton Osgood*, b. April 12, 1852; m. Elvira Elizabeth Cushman.

Child:
1 *William Osgood*, b. March 18, 1881.

3 *William Hamilton*, b. June 23, 1855.
4 *Mariquita Putnam*, b. Jan. 23, 1857; d. Aug. 2, 1881.

2 GEORGE SHAW, b. Oct. 5, 1824; d. young.
3 LUCY ANN, d. young.
4 EDWIN AUGUSTUS, d. young.
5 LUCY ANN, b. July, 1826; m., Oct. 13, 1852, Dr. George King of Rochester, Mass.; had ten children; eight d. young.

Children:
1 *Jennie Maria*, b. Nov. 9, 1855; m. John P. Farmer of Franklin, Mass., June 19, 1878.

Child:
1 *Harry Lyndon*, b. Oct. 23, 1879.

2 *Frances Eddy*, b. Sept. 20, 1862.

6 SUSAN MARIA. b. Jan., 1830; m. Lewis Thomas.
7 FRANCES AUGUSTA, b. May 21, 1835; m. Rodney Parker.

387 394 (VII.) MORTON EDDY, b. Oct. 3, 1799. In 1881 residing in Fall River, Mass. Was deacon in Bridgewater. Is a gentleman highly esteemed. Has been m. three times; viz.: first, Irene F. Lazel, d. 1847; second, Mary C. Whitman, d. 1874; third, Elizabeth A. Cleveland.

388 395 (VII.) JOHN MILTON EDDY. b. Feb. 21, 1800; d. May 16, 1861, in California; m. Olive Saunders, Aug. 13, 1828. Resided in 1840 in Rockaway, N.J.

Children:

1 ELIZA BYRAM, b. July 24, 1830; m., Dec. 23, 1852. first, Jacob Atkinson, a lawyer of Boston; m., second, 1861, C. E. P. Wood.

    Children by first husband:
    1 *John Milton Eddy*, b. Nov. 25, 1853.
    2 *Lizzie Eddy*, b. Dec. 20, 1854.
    3 *Jacob*, d. 1857.

    Children by second husband:
    1 *Mary.*   2 *Charles Nelson.*
    3 *William.*   4 *Seabury.*
    5 *Benjamin.*

2 ANN JULIET. b. June 29, 1836; m., May 26, 1859, Henry M. Phillips of Boston: he d. Dec. 26, 1876.

    Children:
    1 *Edward Payson*, b. Jan. 29, 1861.
    2 *Henry Morton.* b. Aug. 27, 1870.

3 MORTON, b. 1832; d. young.
4 MORTON, b. Jan. 30, 1834; d. 1871.
5 JANE CAROLINE, b. Jun. 14, 1841; d. Sept. 13, 1857.
6 IRENE, d. young.

---

378 396 (VI.) SETH EDDY, b. May 30, 1754; served in the Revolutionary War: m. Jerusha Barden, who d. Nov. 29, 1835, aged 76.

    Children:
399 397   1 JOHN. b. July 22, 1780.
      2 MARY. b. Feb. 22, 1782; d. April 2, 1784.
      3 THOMAS. b. Aug. 14, 1784; d. Nov. 25, 1785.
400 398   4 SETH. b. April 5, 1786; d. 1808.
      5 SALLY. b. March 15, 1788; m. Arthur Cobb, d. in active service in War of 1812: also, in 1816, Caleb Lapham of Pembroke.

    Children by first husband:
    1 *Joseph,* b. July 12, 1810; m. Royilla Ford of Pembroke.
    2 *Sarah Eddy*, b. July 28, 1812; m. Wm. C. Pettee of Foxboro'.

Children:

1 *Ellen Frances*, m. Wallace Corthell of Hingham.
2 *Sarah Augusta.*

6 APOLLOS, b. Oct. 10, 1792; removed to Buffalo, N.Y.
7 JOSEPH, b. Aug. 11, 1790; d. July 20, 1792.
8 LUCY, b. Dec. 6, 1794; d. March 2, 1852; m. Lemuel Cole, 1817.

Children:

1 *Lucia M.*, b. May 13, 1818; m. James G. Nichols, Oct., 1836. Resides in East Middleboro'.

Children:
1 *Susan.*   2 *Darius.*   3 *Sarah.*

2 *Charles*, b. Oct. 3, 1820; m. Maria Willard, 1842; also Annie Fuller, 1879. Lives in West Newton.
3 *Susan E.*, b. June 1, 1822; d. 1852.
4 *Lemuel*, b. Jan. 19, 1824; m. Mary A. Patten. Lives at Boston Highlands.
5 *Jane E.*, b. May 19, 1827; m. E. Ames, also George W. Bowker. Lives in South Boston.
6 *Harriet G.*, b. Jan. 30, 1830; d. Aug. 6, 1844.

9 EZRA HOLMES, m. Nancy Churchill; no children.

----

397 399 (VII.) JOHN EDDY, b. July 22, 1780; m. Abiah Sturtevant, May 25, 1806; d. Feb. 10, 1816, in Plymouth, Mass. She b. Nov. 22, 1780; d. June 20, 1869, in Plymouth.

Children:

1 FANNY, b. Aug. 11, 1804; m. R. Davie of Plymouth; he died 1832.
2 SALLY STURTEVANT, b. March 15, 1806; m. Coomer Weston.

Children:
1 *Hannah Coomer*, m. William H. Nelson of Plymouth.
2 *Laura Ann*, m. Edward Harlow of Plymouth.
3 *Harriet D.*, m. Albert Thayer of Hingham, Mass.
4 *Sarah*, m. Everett F. Sherman of Plymouth.
5 *Edmund*, m. Florence A. Wood of Plymouth.

3 JOHN, b. Dec. 20, 1807; m. Betsey Ann Dunham of Plymouth. Lives in Plymouth (1881).

Children:
1 *Ann Elizabeth*, b. Dec. 17, 1832; d. July 24, 1836.
2 *George*, b. Oct. 28, 1835; d. April 19, 1839.

3 *Curtis*, b. May 13, 1838; m. Martha Ann Ryder. Served for three years in the War of the Rebellion in the 29th Regiment Massachusetts Volunteers. Resides (1881) in West Bridgewater, Mass.

4 *John*, b. Feb. 25, 1841. Resides in Boston.

4 DARIUS, b. Sept. 15, 1809; m. Jan. 25, 1835, to Lydia Otis Hersey of Hingham. In 1881 Darius Eddy is living in Dorchester (Boston), Mass., and for many years has been largely engaged in the manufacture of refrigerators.

Children:

3 *Darius F.*, b. May 6, 1837, in Boston, Mass. Was a Lieutenant in Company D, 42d Massachusetts Regiment, in the War of the Rebellion; m., Nov. 2, 1865, Jerusha Talbot, b. in Plymouth, Mass., and dau. of Samuel Talbot. Resides in Boston (1881).

Child:

1 *Helen F.*, b. Aug. 17, 1872, in Boston.

2 *Lydia A.*, b. 1839 in Boston; d. young.

3 *Lydia H.*, b. Sept. 13, 1841, in Boston.

4 *Otis*, b. Oct. 15, 1843; m., April 29, 1869, Mary Willard. Resides in Boston (1881).

5 *Lewis*, b. July 9, 1846; m., Oct. 6, 1870, Mary P. Talbot. Was in the War of the Rebellion, having enlisted at the age of sixteen as a drummer-boy in Company D, 42d Mass. Regiment.

Children:

1 *Robert Talbot*, b. July 20, 1871, in Boston.

2 *Mary Lewis*, b. Jan. 4, 1874, in Boston.

6 *Isaac H.*, b. in Boston, Jan. 10, 1849; m., Sept. 14, 1875, Rebecca Hathaway of Plymouth, Mass.

7 *George*. b. March 15, 1852, in Hingham, Mass.; m. Helen D. Tilden, Nov. 10, 1875. Resides in Boston (1881).

8 *John Lodge*, b. Jan. 19, 1858, in Boston.

5 MERCY MORTON, b. July 15, 1811; m. H. H. Robbins of Plymouth, who resides (1881) in Plymouth, Mass.

Children:

1 *Charles Henry*. m. Mary Buffington (dau. of the Hon. James Buffington). Resides in Fall River.

2 *Margaret;* resides in Plymouth, Mass.

3 *Augusta;* resides in Plymouth, Mass.
4 *Jane,* d. young.
5 *Fanny,* d. young.
6 *John,* d. young.

6 ELIZA, b. March 6, 1818; m. B. Churchill of Plymouth, where he resides (1880).

   Children:
   1 *Elizabeth E.,* m. Lathrop T. Kimball.   Resides in Buffalo, N.Y.
   2 *Emma Frances,* m. Henry L. Larned of Buffalo, N.Y.
   3 *Mary Louise,* m. Charles Cobb.
   4 *Robert Roberts,* d. young.
   5 *Annie Lathrop.*
   6 *Frances Marion,* d. young.
   7 *Barnabus Lathrop,* d. 1851.
   8 *Robert Bruce.*   Resides in Plymouth.

7 LEWIS EDDY, b. Nov. 3, 1815; m. Sarah W. Hersey. She d. in Boston, Oct., 1868; he resides in Plymouth, Mass.

   Child:
   1 *Frank Lewis,* b. March 24, 1854. Resides in Boston.

8 FANNY, b. Aug. 11, 1804; m. Capt. Robert Davie.

------

398 400 (VII.) SETH EDDY, b. April 5, 1786; d. 1818; m. Sophia Holmes of Plymouth, Mass., who afterwards m. John Morehead.

   Children:
   1 HENRY HOLMES, m. Abigail Richmond.

      Children:
      1 *James T.,* m. Mary A. Whall.
      2 *Harriet F.,* m. Herman Robbins.
      3 *Seth W.,* m. Frank M. Campbell.
      4 *Henry F.*

   2 HARRIET, m. Barnes of Wrentham, Mass.

------

379 401 (VI.) THOMAS EDDY, b. March 28, 1756; m. Betsey Putnam of Stonington, Mass.; lived in Woodstock and Burlington, Vt.; d. Sept. 21, 1842. Was a soldier in the Revolutionary War; fought in Canada, and at the battles of Saratoga and Monmouth.

Children:

1 THOMAS, b. June 17, 1785.
2 WILLIAM P., b. May 17, 1787; lived in 1846 in Waterbury, Vt.

Children:

1 *Henry B.*, b. Nov. 9, 1815.
2 *George*, b. Aug. 31, 1817.
3 *Lucia*, b. ——, 1822.
4 *Nathaniel*, b. Sept. 7, 1820.
5 *Lucretia*, b. June 13, 1824.
6 *Cornelius*, b. Oct. 29, 1825.
7 *Mary*, b. March 13, 1827.
8 *Ann E.*, b. July 3, 1828.
9 *Jane*, b. Oct. 25, 1830.
10 *William*, b. March 30, 1832.
11 *Harvey*, b. Sept. 14, 1833.
12 *Edward*, b. April 18, 1837.

3 BETSEY.
4 ANOTHER DAUGHTER.

---

380 402 (VI.) SAMUEL EDDY, b. April 29, 1760 (or perhaps March 6 or 16, 1786); m. Sally Paddock; d. in Greenbush, N.Y., 1812-15. He was in the Revolutionary War and the War of 1812-15. He moved to Woodstock, Vt. After his death his family moved to Sing Sing, N.Y.

Children:

1 SYLVANUS.   2 SAMUEL.
3 SALLY.   4 MARTIN.
5 THOMAS.   6 MYRON.
7 MERCY.   8 LEVINA.

---

356 403 (IV.) JABEZ EDDY, m. Mary, also Patience Pratt, — the last marriage being Oct. 16, 1729; lived in Carver, Mass.

Children:

405 404   1 JABEZ, b. April 14, 1700.
         2 MARY, b. Jan. 24, 1701-2; m. Giles Pitchard, Nov. 19, 1730.
         3 LYDIA, b. Feb. 3, 1703; m. Theophilus Crocker, Nov. 19, 1730.
         4 BEULAH, b. June 6, 1707; m. Nathaniel Fisher, Sept. 26, 1728.

5 MOSES, b. Aug. 24, 1709. Had two wives, but no children.

6 HASADIAH, b. March 6, 1711; m. Shubel Lewis.

———

404 405 (V.) JABEZ EDDY, b. April 14, 1700; m. Thankful ——.

Children:

1 EBENEZER, b. Nov. 3. 1730; d. Nov. 15, 1730.

2 SUSANNAH, b. Dec. 15, 1731; d. Dec. 23, 1731.

3 MARY, b. Dec. 23, 1732; m. Eleazer Lewis, Nov. 27, 1755.

407 406   4 JOHN, b. Nov. 26, 1733.

5 MARGARET, b. Aug. 11, 1735.

6 JABEZ, b. April 5, 1744; m., Jan. 21, 1768, to Mehitable Burrows. Served in Revolutionary War.

———

406 407 (VI.) JOHN EDDY, b. Nov. 26, 1733; m. Ruth Hayford, b. Dec. 6, 1757; d. about 1790. His second wife was Joanna. She d. in 1840, aged 100 years, one month. Served in Revolutionary War; lived in New Salem, Mass.

Children:

409 408   1 MOSES, b. Nov. 17, 1762; lived in 1840, in Deerfield, Mass.

2 JACOB, d. in Troy, N.Y.

3 SOLOMON, m. Mary Vose of Boston, Feb. 15, 1803.

Child:

1 *John.*

Children:

1 *Edward.*

2 *Clinton.* b. in Troy, N.Y.

4 PRISCILLA.

5 LYDIA, d. 1840; m. Samuel Moulton.

———

408 409 (VII.) MOSES EDDY, b. Nov. 17, 1762; m. Elizabeth Alverson. Resided (1840) in Shutesbury.

Children:

411 410   1 JOHN, b. Sept. 17, 1787; d. Feb. 6, 1784.

2 MOSES, b. Feb. 19, 1792; d. Aug. 22, 1797.

    3 Hosea, b. Nov. 13, 1797; d. July 27, 1803.
    4 David, b. April 11, 1802; d. Aug. 4, 1803.
    5 Eliza, b. Nov. 23, 1807; m. Caleb James.
    6 Seth, b. July 30, 1811; d. Oct. 17, 1840.

---

410 411 (VIII.) JOHN EDDY, b. Sept. 17, 1787; d. Feb. 6, 1834; m. Nancy Lochlen, 1808.

    Children:
    1 Albert G., b. Jan. 13, 1809; m. Sophia Colton, Sept. 13, 1832.

        Children:
        1 *Ruth S.*, b. June 19, 1833.
        2 *Ann H.*, b. May 30, 1835; d.
        3 *Elizabeth J.*, b. May 18, 1836.
        4 *Martha S.*, b. July 28, 1838.
        5 *Moses*, b. Sept. 12, 1840.

    2 Mary Ann, b. April 7, 1811; m. Elisha Wood.
    3 David A., b. Feb. 5, 1814; m. Betsey Wood, Nov. 26, 1837, and had *John*, b. Jan. 10, 1840.
    4 Elizabeth M., b. Oct. 24, 1815; d. June 17, 1837.
    5 Sarah T., b. Dec. 3, 1817.
    6 Moses, b. Feb. 14, 1822.

---

357 412 (IV.) BENJAMIN EDDY, b. 1673; d. previous to Nov. 5, 1744; lived in Middleboro', Mass.; m. Abagail Hathaway.

    Children:
418 413   1 Joel, b. Aug. 27, 1717.
425 414   2 Caleb, b. Jan. 31, 1718.
           3 Jonathan, b. March 6, 1720; d. after 1744.
426 415   4 Obediah, b. Feb. 28, 1722.
           5 Abagail, b. March 13, 1725; m. Benjamin Hathaway of Bridgewater, 1743.
           6 Betsey, b. Aug. 6, 1727; m. John Leach of Halifax.
427 416   7 Benjamin, b. Jan. 19, 1729–30.
           8 John, b. April 16, 1732.
428 417   9 Barnabas.

---

413 418 (V.) JOEL EDDY, b. Aug. 27, 1717; m., March 1, 1741, Rachael Vose of West Bridgewater.

    Children:
           1 Hannah; baptized in Bridgewater, 1743.
422 419   2 Jonathan.

423 420　　3　LEVI; lived in Woodstock, Ct.
424 421　　4　BENJAMIN, b. 1755; d. 1813.
　　　　　　5　OTHNIEL, d. ——, Hudson River; left no family.
　　　　　　6　SUBMIT.
　　　　　　7　RACHAEL.
　　　　　　8　OLIVE.

> NOTE. — *Joel Eddy* lived in Bridgewater several years. In 1743 moved to Halifax. Afterwards went to Woodstock, Ct.

---

419 422 (VI.)　JONATHAN EDDY resided in Stratford, Vt.; d. in Revolutionary Army.

Children :
1　RESOLVED; was never married.
2　OTHNIEL, b. May 8, 1773, at Woodstock, Ct.; m. Alice McKinsly, b. Aug. 17, 1774; lived (1840) in Orwell, Ohio.

Children :
1　*Moore*, b. Jan. 15, 1795, at Stafford, Ct.
2　*Polly*, b. June 22, 1798, at Stafford, Ct.
3　*Rubie*, b. April 11, 1800, at Stafford, Ct.
4　*Clarissa*, b. Aug. 9, 1802, at Stafford, Ct.
5　*Hiram*, b. May 3, 1805, at Stafford, Ct.
6　*Emily*, b. June 26, 1807, at Stafford, Ct.
7　*John Randolph*, b. ——, 1809, at Randolph, Ct.
8　*Almira*, b. July 19, 1813, at Stafford, Ct.

---

420 423 (VI.)　LEVI EDDY, lived in Woodstock, Ct.; d. during the War of 1812–15.

Child :
1　CHARLES.

---

421 424 (VI.)　BENJAMIN EDDY, b. 1755; d. 1813; m. Alice Abbot; d. 1827, aged 63. He was b. in Woodstock, Ct., and d. in Rockingham, Vt.

Children :
1　JUSTIN, b. 1787; resided in Westport, N.Y; m. —— Walker.

Children :
1　*James W.*　　2　*Charles H.*
3　*Lewis S.*　　4　*Eliza.*

2 JOHN, d. in Rockingham. Vt., in 1850, aged 60.
3 RENSALIER, d. 1827, aged 32.

Children:
1 *L. Schuyler.*   2 *John R.*

4 CHESTER, d. 1828, aged 31.
5 CHARLES; living (1850) Chester, Vt.; m. Lucy Bellows.

Children:
1 *Alice.*   2 *George Chester.*
3 *L. Maria.*   4 *William F.*
5 *Charles Benjamin,* b. July 27, 1829; m. Sarah M. Spaulding of Cavendish, Vt., in 1850. He lived in Rockingham and Chester, Vt., until 1849, from which time, to 1857, he was a teacher in Hunterdon and Warren Counties, N.J. Since 1858 he has been in the profession of law, and is a practising attorney of distinguished eminence and ability, his residence being at Bellows Falls, Vt. From 1870 to 1872 he represented Windham County in the State Senate, and now (1880) is senior member of the law firm of C. P. and C. F. Eddy, his son being the junior partner.
6 *Levi,* d. young.   7 *Amy.*
8 *O'ice.*   9 *Polly.*
10 *Hannah.*

---

414 425 (V.)   CALEB EDDY, b. Jan. 31, 1718; lived with his brother Joel, and went with him to New Jersey in 1749.

---

415 426 (V.)   OBEDIAH EDDY, b. Feb. 28, 1722; m. Sarah Lawrence of Bridgewater, Oct. 31, 1788; d. 1789, aged 67. Was in Revolutionary War.

Children:
1 MARY, b. Nov. 7, 1751; m. T. Owen, Sept. 20, 1772.
2 DESIRE, b. Oct. 8, 1754; d. 1830.
3 AZOR, b. Aug. 25, 1759; d. 1833; m. Hannah Fuller, had a son *Martin;* b. March 18, 1792.

Children:
1 *Martin L.,* b. April 23, 1814.
2 *Edmund,* b. May 28, 1816.
3 *Emeline.*   4 *Eunice.*
5 *Elvira.*   6 *George.*
7 *Charles.*   8 *Lorenzo.*

416 427 (V.) BENJAMIN EDDY, b. Jan. 19, 1729–30.

    Children:
    1 WILLIAM.   2 BENJAMIN.   3 JOEL.

---

417 428 (V.) BARNABAS; lived in Guilford, Vt.

    Child:
    1 BARNABAS.

---

341 429 (IV.) SAMUEL EDDY, b. July 15, 1675; d. March 27, 1744; m. Sarah Easterbrooks, April 10, 1707. Lived at Swansea.

    Children:
    1 CALEB, b. March 2, 1707; m. Mehitable Luther, June 18, 1730.

        Children:
        1 *Caleb*, b. Dec. 31, 1730.
        2 *Elkanah*, b. Jan. 31, 1732.
        3 *Samuel*, b. Nov. 8, 1736.
        4 *Mehitable*, b. May 23, 1739.

    2 ELIZABETH, b. March 26, 1711; m. David Hill, Feb. 24, 1733.
    3 SARAH, b. Dec. 8, 1713; m. Daniel Carpenter, Nov. 5, 1730.
    4 HANNAH, b. March 14, 1716.

---

342 430 (IV.) BENJAMIN EDDY, m. Mary Hallowell of Boston, Aug. 11, 1712. He d. previous to 1730. She m. David Law, May 25, 1736.

    Children:
    1 MARY, b. Oct. 22, 1713; m. John Sheppard, May 24, 1736.
    2 BENJAMIN, b. March 15, 1721; d. in Jamaica, W.I.
    3 NATHANIEL, b. Aug. 22, 1723; m. Mary Obbins, May 4, 1746.
    4 JOSEPH, b. Oct. 24, 1727.

---

272 431 (VII.) JESSE EDDY (of Fall River, Mass.), b. in Northbridge, Mass., Feb. 18, 1801; m. Sarah Paine at Plainfield, Ct., Feb. 22, 1824. He d. in Fall River, Mass., Nov. 15, 1873.

Thomas L Eddy

Children:

1 GEORGE P., b. Dec. 3, 1824; d. Dec. 12, 1832.
2 THOMAS F., b. Sept. 13, 1827; m. Marianna Coggeshall, Nov. 23, 1854.

    Child:

    1 *Thomas J.*, b. Dec. 25, 1855.

3 JAMES C., b. Aug. 1, 1829; m. Julia M. Fish, Dec. 4, 1867.

    Children:

    1 *Jesse*, b. Sept. 21, 1868.
    2 *Henry H.*, b. Jan. 19, 1872.

4 JOSEPHINE, b. April 5, 1834; d. Aug. 8, 1835.
5 ANNA A., b. April 22, 1837; m. Peter J. Gage of Hamilton, Can., Sept. 18, 1866.

    Children:

    1 *Jesse.*   2 *John.*   3 *Clarence.*

APPENDIX.

The following persons bearing the name of *Eddy* have been educated at Colleges of New England and New York : —

HARVARD UNIVERSITY.

1765. JOHN (A.B.).
1840. FREDERICK A. (M.D.).
1855. DANIEL CLARK (Honorary A.M.).
1866. GEORGE STETSON (M.D.).
1875. FORREST G. (A.B.).
1876. ARTHUR S. (A.B.).

YALE COLLEGE.

1832. HENRY.   1870. WILLARD.
1861. CLARENCE.   1879. NEWELL A.
1867. HENRY T.

BROWN UNIVERSITY.

1787. HON. SAMUEL, LL.D.   1831. WILLIAM HENRY.
1799. ZACHARIAH.   1834. SAMUEL.
1805. STEPHEN W.   1840. JOHN.
1815. JOHN M.   1853. ZACHARIAH.
1822. RICHARD EVANS.   1879. ALFRED N.

COLUMBIA COLLEGE, N.Y.

1811. CASPAR WISTAR.   1871. CHARLES.
1819. JAMES.   1873. E. BERTLY.
1862. WILLIAM.   1873. R. P. EDDY.
1870. HERBERT MARTIN.

WILLIAMS COLLEGE, MASS.

1814. CHAUNCEY.   1853. LEVEUS.
1845. WILLIAM WOODBRIDGE.

UNION COLLEGE, SCHENECTADY, N.Y.

1817.	ANSEL DOANE, A.M., D.D.	1844.	ANSEL D. (D.D.).
1821.	CHAUNCEY, A.B., D.D.	1854.	ALBERT CULLEN.
1831.	HENRY TISDALE.	1860.	DAVID ROWE.
1834.	DEVOTION CARNOT, M.D.	1862.	GEORGE PATTERSON, JR.
1840.	SHERMAN, A.M., M.D.	1863.	J. WESLEY (A.M.).
1840.	E—— (A.M.).		

Sept. 3, 1877, Daniel Eddy of Saratoga Springs, N.Y., writes that his grandfather's name was John, who he believes came from Dutchess Co., N.Y., and was one of the first settlers of Saratoga, and died there. He had two sons: *John W.* and *Daniel D.* That John W. is residing near Saratoga, and had three sons: *John M., Daniel A.,* and *James S.* That Daniel D. went to Michigan about 1867. He had four sons: *Daniel, John, Charles,* and *Hiram.* That Daniel had two sons: *Daniel* and *John.*

FROM "CURTIS'S HISTORY OF STATEN ISLAND."

EDDY.

The present representatives of this family are Cornelius C. of Stapleton and his son James of Huguenot in Westfield. The former is a son of William, who was killed by his horse running away in January, 1828; the latter is a son of John, also deceased; William, John, and Andrew, who are still living near Woodrow Church, Westfield, were brothers, and sons of William, the first of the name who came here from New Jersey during the War of the Revolution with the intention of remaining but a short time, but either the refusal of a pass, or protracted delay in furnishing it, detained him on the Island until, finally, having probably formed some attachment, he relinquished the idea of returning, and settled permanently.

"ANDREWS' HISTORY OF NEW BRITAIN, CT."

270   ASENATH BASS, to church Nov. 16, 1794; dau. of Mercy North; baptized Aug. 2, 1778; m., Nov. 29, 1798, Charles Eddy, son of Charles and Hannah (Kelsey); his wife b. March 26, 1773; he lived in the house on West Main Street, owned (Nov., 1866) by Mrs Tolles, which was built by Elijah Dickinson. Mr. Eddy was a stout, tall, and athletic man; he d. Sept. 21, 1826, aged 53; when she m., second, Jan. 1, 1830, James Fortune of Wethersfield; she d. April 8, 1852, aged 74, and he d. Aug. 8, 1855; she was a devout woman.

Children :

1 REBECCA BASS, b. Oct. 3, 1799; baptized Nov. 17, 1799; m., June 28, 1825, Albert Norton of Kensington.
2 EMELINE, b. Feb. 22, 1802; baptized April 25, 1802; m., Oct. 12, Ralph S. Cornwell; m., second, ——.
3 WILLIAM HARLOW, b. Feb. 4, 1805; baptized May 9, 1805; m., Sept. 23, 1827, Mary Dobson of John.
4 LEVI, b. June 9, 1809; baptized Aug. 20, 1819; d. Oct. 3, 1828, aged 19.
5 CAROLINE, b. Aug. 30, 1811; baptized Oct. 27, 1811; m. James H. Webb.
6 SAMUEL HENRY, b. July 15, 1815; baptized Oct. 15, 1815; d. May 7, 1828, aged 13.

---

449 NANCY, wife of Thomas Eddy, to church Oct. 4, 1818, by letter from the church at Farmington; dau. of Phineas Hamblin of Farmington, and his wife Rhoda (Andrus), b. Aug. 3, 1789; baptized Aug. 6, 1795, at Farmington, by Rev. Mr. Marsh of Wethersfield, and to church there Oct., 1813. He was son of Charles, Sen., and Hannah (Kelsey) his wife; m. Abi Lewis, Nov. 5, 1802, dau. of Adonijah Lewis and Mary. She d. May 6, 1814, when he m., second, Sept. 18, 1814, as above. She d. Sept., 1852, at Lama, Penn., and my informant says, with very clear views of her future good estate. He d. May 28, 1830, aged 52.

Children :

1 PHILIP, b. March 5, 1804; m., May 7, 1828, Sarah Pitkin of East Hartford; he d. 1863.
2 HENRY, b. Oct. 1, 1805.
3 JULIA, b. June, 1807.
4 ABI LEWIS, b. Sept. 1, 1811; m., Oct. 6, 1831, Charles Parker of Meriden. She was baptized Nov. 1, 1818, in New Britain, on her stepmother's account.

Children by second wife :

5 THOMAS HAMBLIN, b. April 2, 1815; baptized Nov. 1, 1818; m., Sept. 29, 1833, Sarah M. Moses of Canton, Ct.
6 WALTER BARTHOLOMEW, b. May, 1818; baptized Nov. 1, 1818; m. Mary A. Judson, 1837.
7 DOLLY JONES, b. July, 1822; baptized Nov. 3, 1822; m., Jan. 2, 1836, Charles Blakeslee.
8 BENJAMIN FRANKLIN, b. Sept. 17, 1826; m., Nov. 4, 1849, Emeline L. Curtiss, dau. of Polly, wife of Shubel Curtiss.
9 JEREMIAH A., b. ——; d. in Southington.
10 ANTHONY, b. 1829; d. March 14, 1830, aged 9 months.

451 WILLIAM EDDY, to church Aug. 5. 1821; son of Charles and his wife Hannah (Kelsey); b. Oct. 20, 1781; m., Dec. 13, 1808, Mary Butler of Farmington, dau. of Richard of Hartford, and his wife, Prudence (Parks), b. Sept. 21, 1778. They lived near the foot of "Osgood Hill." He d. Jan. 25, 1829, aged 46; when she m., second, Oct. 1, 1835, Theodore Riley. She d. Sept. 26, 1844, aged 66.

Children:

1 CATHARINE GRIDLEY, b. Oct. 25. 1809; baptized Sept. 9, 1821; m., Feb. 4, 1827, Silas Wright.
2 WILLIAM BUTLER, b. Nov. 15, 1810; baptized Sept. 9, 1821; d. Sept. 10, 1823, aged 10.
3 CHARLOTTE, b. May 25, 1812; baptized Sept. 9, 1821; m., May 9, 1836, George Hills of Plainville.
4 MARY, b. March 8. 1814; baptized Sept. 9, 1821; m. William E. Clark of Windsor, May, 1840.
5 GEORGE WASHINGTON, b. Feb. 22, 1817; baptized Sept. 9, 1821; m. Maria Merrill of New Hartford.
6 SYLVESTER, b. 1818; baptized Sept. 9, 1821; d. Oct. 6, 1828, aged 10.
7 CHARLES BUTLER, b. July 2, 1823; baptized Sept. 21, 1823; d. Nov. 27, 1843, aged 20.

---

462 JOSEPH EDDY, to church Aug. 5, 1821; son of Charles, Sen., and his wife Hannah (Kelsey); b. Feb. 27, 1786; was both farmer and mechanic; could turn his hand usefully and cheerfully to several employments; had an active mind, with great force of character, but uncultivated. He m., May 13, 1807, Salome Pennfield; he built near his father's, on the road to "Job's Corner." He d. June 14, 1836, aged 50.

Children:

1 HORACE, b. April 25, 1808; baptized June 26, 1808; m., Sept. 22, 1829, Roxy Ann Wright.
2 LORENZO, b. Oct. 30, 1810; baptized Jan. 27, 1811; m., Nov. 4, 1832, Nancy Judd.
3 INFANT, b. ———; d. Feb. 27, 1813.
4 NORMAN PENNFIELD, b. Feb. 7, 1813; baptized Aug. 1, 1813; m., March 25, 1834, Maria M. White.
5 LUCY ANN, b. Nov. 15, 1816; baptized April 13, 1817; m. Isaac Bird of Hartford, an Englishman; she d. April 27, 1838, aged 21.
6 MARTHA, b. Nov. 6, 1819; baptized May 14, 1820; m., Oct. 16, 1839, Daniel B. Fowler of Meriden.
7 EUNICE, b. July 15. 1822; baptized Oct. 6, 1822; d. March 8, 1837, aged 15.

582 HENRY EDDY, to church Aug. 6, 1826; baptized same time; b. Oct. 1, 1805, to Thomas and his wife Abi (Lewis); graduated at Yale, 1832; studied theology at Andover and New Haven; settled in the ministry at Granville, Mass.; dismissed, and studied medicine; m., Jan. 1835, Cornelia Wood of Clinton, Ct., dau. of Rev. Luke Wood; she d. 1841, when he m., second, Sarah H. Torrey of North Bridgewater, Mass., where he resided in 1861, engaged in inventions and patent improvements. He was dismissed and recommended to Yale College Church, May 31, 1829. He was aided in acquiring his education, and was in the ministry about fifteen years.

Child by first wife:
1 CORNELIUS, b. July 13, 1839.

Children by second wife:
2 HENRY T., b June 9, 1844.
3 WILLIARD, b. Aug. 29, 1845.
4 SARAH H., b. July 8, 1848.

Joshua Eddy

THE EDDY FAMILY AS RELATED TO MIDDLEBORO'.

WE give a brief sketch of the Eddy family as related to Middleboro' : —

(1) Samuel Eddy, the Pilgrim, who was the head of this branch of the family, as indeed of a large majority of all who bear the name of Eddy in this country, lived in Plymouth till old age. His name appears on the Old Colony Records many times, and in connection with various transactions, until the year 1662. In 1685 his name is in a deed in which he is designated " of Plymouth, residing in Swansea," and he finally died in the latter place in 1688, aged 80 years.

While the posterity of Samuel is very numerous, that of his brother John, who removed from Plymouth in 1632 and with others settled in Watertown, is comparatively few.

Samuel left four sons, John, Zechariah, Caleb, and Obadiah, and one daughter, Hannah. John, the eldest, settled in Taunton, and subsequently removed to the Vineyard. Among his descendants are the late Rev. Chauncey Eddy, D.D., and Rev. Ansel D. Eddy, D.D., widely known as eminent preachers of the Gospel. Caleb and Zechariah settled in Swansea, where they had been sent in their boyhood to be apprenticed, and died there, leaving large families. Many of their descendants now live in Swansea, Providence, Fall River, and Boston.

Obadiah, the youngest son of Samuel, settled in Middleboro', which had been purchased of the Indians in 1661 for £70, and incorporated in 1669 ; every transaction in relation thereto being fully confirmed by the court at Plymouth.

At the outbreak of the Indian war in 1675, all the settlers, comprising sixteen families, fled to Plymouth, and their houses were burned by the Indians. Thus ended this first attempt at settlement.

After Philip's War, which lasted from 1675 to 1679, the original settlers, of whom Obadiah Eddy was one, "without baiting one jot of heart or hope," returned to Middleboro', rebuilt their habitations which had been destroyed, and once more laid the foundations of their social, civil, and religious life. Brave men! whose courage no danger intimidated; whose unyielding purpose no adversity could thwart. We honor your names! We dwell with affectionate reverence on your memories!

After the death of the Pilgrim Samuel there seems to have been no one of the name of Eddy left in Plymouth. The original family is broken up, and its sons are already established in Middleboro', Swansea, and Taunton. And these places now in their turn become historic ground, and the centres of a new growth from which the lines of descent go forth in ever-widening circles, till to-day they touch the Pacific slope.

(2) Obadiah, the son of Samuel, was a large landholder in Middleboro', having succeeded to his father's share of "the 26 mens purchase," and having bought out the rights of his brothers Zechariah and Caleb.

He became the father of four sons and three daughters, the eldest being born 1669. The spot is still pointed out where his first house stood, that was burnt by the Indians. Near by its site he built his second house.

Says one who passed away in 1860, in his 80th year, and whose written testimony lies before us: "In 1795 I was acquainted with Dea. Barnabas Thompson, then 93 years old, who well knew this man Obadiah Eddy. He lived in that part of Middleboro', now Halifax, near Winetuxet River, and he pointed out the spot where his house stood. It was hard by two apple-trees in the field back of Nathan Fuller's house, where an old cellar can now be seen." That cellar is still seen and those old apple-trees still stand, faithful witnesses of bygone generations. Within the memory of those who are dwelling on the place the hearth-stone of the old house was taken from the cellar, and is now a part of the foundation-walls of another house built there more than fifty years ago. How do these patriarchal lives span the wide intervals and bring us near our origin, and enable us to solve many dark historic problems which otherwise were too difficult.

Obadiah died in 1722, aged 77 years, having divided his estate among his seven children, all of whom, with perhaps one exception, had settled near him in the patriarchal style.

(3) Samuel, the son of Obadiah, the son of Samuel the Pilgrim, owned and occupied that part of his father's estate which includes chiefly, and is now known as, Eddyville. His house stood by the great pear-trees, long a landmark, and famous in all the region for their size and fruit. It stood on a gentle knoll with a spring at its foot, the soil being fertile and easy of tillage, and well watered; while the whole region for miles around abounds in springs, rivulets, and larger bodies of water. In such highly-favored localities did the Pilgrims, like the early fathers of mankind, pitch their tents.

Samuel married Meletiah Pratt, Feb. 3, 1702. She was the daughter of Jonathan Pratt of Plymouth, son of Joshua the Pilgrim, who came over in the third ship, Anne, in 1623. And thus early were allied these two sturdy Pilgrim stocks. She was born in the fort, during Philip's War, Dec. 11, 1676, and late in life was wont to say that "she could remember when the Indians were ten to one of the whites." Her parents dying when she was young, she was brought up in the family of Ebenezer Tinkham, who was chosen deacon at the organization of the First Church in 1694. Hence she and Samuel — who was born one year earlier, 1675 — were play-mates, and no doubt lovers from their youth.

It is said of Meletiah that she was very religious, and when her children were sick she knelt down and prayed with them. Being of slender constitution, she told her doctor that she should not live long, but he told her that she would outlive her husband, who was more robust, and she did. He died in 1752, aged 77, and she died in 1769, aged 93 years.

Several autographs of Samuel are affixed to old deeds, and a part of his will with his signature, dated 1752, is preserved, in which his wife and his son Zechariah are appointed his executors.

Samuel and his wife Meletiah joined the church in Middleboro' in 1715, and in the same year their children were baptized. These, in the order of their births, were Samuel, Zechariah, Meletiah, Bennet, and Fear.

When his house was burnt, by some unexplained casualty, he built another, a few rods further south, in the year 1721, as is well ascertained. We give a view of this house, which will be of special interest to all who are in the line of Samuel, son of Obadiah. It is the oldest house existing in this line of ancestry, and is to-day in good preservation, cheerful and homelike, and exhibits few marks of its great age. It belongs to Caleb F. Eddy of West Newton, a lineal descendant of Samuel, who with his family of ten children occupies it during the summer holidays; a quiet retreat from business and study.

(4) Zechariah, son of Samuel, son of Obadiah, son of Samuel the Pilgrim, received from his father the homestead and all the lands adjoining, being a part of " the 26 mens purchase." The deed is a deed of gift, dated in 1742, ten years before that father's death, and is " in consideration of the love and good affection I have and do bare unto my son Zechariah," — the right of use and occupation, however, being reserved to the parents during their natural life.

The elder son, Samuel Jr., would have legitimately succeeded to the homestead. He bore the father's name and inherited much of his spirit and character. But he had already been established many years in his own house near by, now known as the Clark Place, while the younger son, later married, tarried at home with the parents. This Samuel, we may add, was a man of much note in the church and parish, and fulfilled many important services for each. He died in 1746 at the early age of 36 years, much honored and lamented. His two sons, Nathan and Samuel, many years later removed from Middleboro'. Nathan went to Vermont and there died, leaving many children, from whom are descended Rev. Zachary Eddy, D.D., and Rev. Hiram Eddy, D.D. Samuel removed to Coleraine in this State, and when his house was burnt he went thence to Western New York, where he died, leaving many descendants, some of whom settled in Ohio, Pennsylvania, and other States. Nathan died in 1813, aged 80 years, and Samuel in 1821, aged 79 years. They were both men of unusual intelligence and force of character.

There lies before us a letter of Samuel, dated Williamson, N.Y., 1819, written in his 77th year to his cousin Captain Joshua Eddy of Middleboro', which in point of language and sentiment, not to add penmanship, does credit to the head and heart of this venerable man.

"I have heard nothing from you," he says, "nor from any of my friends in Middleboro' for a long time. I know not who are living nor who are gone into the eternal world; nor do I know whether my sister is living or not. I am in my 77th year, a feeble old man, full of the infirmities of old age, and for several years past have been looking out for the grim messenger." Then referring to the matters of business which were the immediate object of his writing, and in a style so clear, exact, and logical as indicates none of "the infirmities of old age," he concludes by saying: "I should be very glad of an interview with you and to recognize the dangers, the difficulties, and the privations that we have endured together at Saratoga, at White

Marsh, at Valley Forge, and at Monmouth, which appear now like a dream. I shall soon quit this transitory world, this world of sin and sorrow. I hope for a better world; and I wish we may meet in that happy world. I add only my sincere love and friendship, my love to my sister and to all my relations and friends that are living." — That sister, Susanna, had died two years before, in 1817, aged 81 years.

Zechariah, now the only surviving son of Samuel, son of Obadiah, lived and died in the house mentioned built by his father. He was the father of twelve children, eight sons and four daughters. He was born in 1712, and died of small-pox in 1777. His widow died in 1802. After her death the house built by Samuel and bequeathed to Zechariah was moved across the street to its present situation, and the house, office, and stable which are given in the view here presented were built. How well Zechariah bore up the family name may be judged by the following record which is left of him: —

"His general character was that of a mild, sedate, and discreet man, well informed for that day. He was of slender habits but industrious, and called by the town and parish to many public services. He was a warm Whig, and four or five of his sons were in the Revolutionary army, two of whom died in the service. He had several interviews with Judge Oliver, who was a Tory, and who endeavored to terrify him with the power of England, but without success."

His eldest son John was a mathematician and an astronomer. When a youth he would repair to the attic and spend the live-long day absorbed in his favorite pursuits, and deaf to every call. At the age of twenty years he published an almanac for 1759, and also one for 1760. The latter lies before us, a well-executed work of good type and paper, and very like in its general features to the "Old Farmer's Almanac." The title-page is gone. In the preface the author says, "These calculations, I believe and do not doubt, my readers will find to agree very near the truth. Some may condemn what is here wrote, perhaps, for nonsense and folly; but I shall have this for my consolation, that the world is a scene of folly, and strange if an almanack maker may not have his part therein."

With this spice of wit, John Eddy gave his second almanac to the world, "Middleboro', Sept., 1759." It was printed in this village, and from the first press established in this town, if not the first in this county. Prof. West of Providence said of this almanac that "it was the best that was made at that time." This youthful student of nature's laws, this serene and ardent lover of the stars, so enthusiastic and so untiring in his devotion, disappointed the bright hopes of his early promise. He died prematurely at Crown Point, in the old French War, at the age of 24 years, leaving a wife and one daughter. Three other sons of Zechariah, viz., Zechariah, Thomas, and Samuel, removed to Vermont, from whom many of the name of Eddy are descended in that State. But we pass in our review to the next generation.

(5) Joshua, the fifth son of Zechariah, and of the fifth generation from Samuel the Pilgrim, built his house hard by the paternal roof, and with the homestead and lands of his father Zechariah possessed much of his Pilgrim spirit and blood. He enlisted in the army of the Revolution, and, raising a company of eighty men in the vicinity of his home, marched to the Hudson to resist the progress of Burgoyne. He served during four campaigns, from 1775 to 1778 inclusive, and was at the siege of Boston and the battles of Saratoga and Monmouth, and in all the operations in New Jersey in the year 1778.

On his return from the war he settled down to the quiet pursuits of his farm, to iron manufacturing, and to trading, employing many men, and at one time building a schooner on Taunton River, near Woodward's Bridge, which he launched and floated down to the bay.

He was noted for his business tact, enterprise, and activity, and in all his dealings was a man of singular integrity and uprightness. To the bold, stern, and fearless qualities of his nature he allied the most tender and affectionate sympathies. He was kind, warm-hearted, and generous, while just, authoritative, and requiring. Tall and robust and of sound discretion, others bowed to his opinion and treated him with deferential awe. The most humble, consistent, and unaffected piety diffused itself throughout his whole life. Preëminently was he a man of prayer and strict in every observance of religious duty. Long after his sons were grown to manhood and settled around him in their own families, he enjoined upon them to come in and gather about the old family altar on the Sabbath ; and one evening every week he conducted religious exercises in his house, which his sons regarded a duty and a privilege to attend. Nothing surely was ever more beautiful and impressive than those free, social, religious gatherings of one family, of different members and ages and of one faith, — "the church that was in his house." The memory and the influence of those meetings abide, although the aged patriarch who was their life and inspiration has slept in his grave for nearly half a century. He died in 1833, aged 85 years.

The wife of Joshua was Lydia Paddock, who on her mother's side was a lineal descendant of Elder Faunce and Governor Bradford, and was worthy of her lineage. She was intelligent, pious, and discreet, and to her chiefly was committed the training of their numerous children, a duty which she fulfilled with marked and exemplary care. A large circle of living grandchildren remember with grateful pride the many excellent virtues of this godly pair. We give in these pages pictures of Joshua Eddy and wife. They are copies of portraits painted more than fifty years ago by an eminent artist of this town in their advanced age, and not fitly representing them as they were in the freshness and vigor of their powers, "before the eye was dimmed and the natural force abated."

LYDIA EDDY

Still they are excellent likenesses, and of priceless value as the oldest family portraits and of the earliest remembered couple in this line.

(6) We pass to the next generation, and the final one of which we propose to write. The children of Joshua, the sixth generation from Samuel the Pilgrim, were eight sons and two daughters. One son died in infancy. Among the nine surviving children, Joshua the father, while living, divided the most of his estate, after the ancestral example, giving to each a fair start in life. Five of these sons settled almost within the shadow of the old homestead. They reared large families and passed away in a ripe age.

Joshua, the first-born of Joshua and a noble exponent of that father, built his house next door to his father's, and was widely known and respected during his long and useful life. He gave most diligent care to his business, was exact and correct in all his dealings, of sound discretion, firm in principle, decided in action, constant in religious duty, and fulfilled every public and private trust with honor and fidelity. Calm, collected, and scrupulous, there was much in his example to excite admiration and respect. Of fine visage and of commanding presence, it is a matter of deep regret that his prejudices never yielded to the solicitation of his friends, and that no portrait of him is preserved. He died in 1863, aged 85 years, leaving two sons and five daughters.

Zechariah, second son of Joshua, possessed unusual natural gifts and was liberally educated. He was the most distinguished citizen of Middleboro'. He had perhaps no superior at the bar in legal attainments. To his most extensive knowledge of books, to the finest and most cultivated taste, were united the most genial disposition and the highest conversational powers, which rendered his society exceedingly attractive. He was universally honored and loved for his purity, sincerity, and benevolence; for his single and ingenuous aim; for his humble, disinterested, and Christian spirit; for his consistent, exemplary, and well-nigh perfect life. He lived and died in the house which he built on the foundations of his grandfather Zechariah and his great-grandfather Samuel before him; but his name rests on the more imperishable basis of justice, truth, and benignity. He died in 1860, in the 80th year of his age, leaving two daughters, — five sons and three daughters having deceased.

Ebenezer, the third son of Joshua, was not in his general characteristics unlike his elder brothers. He built his house a half-mile remote on a spot naturally picturesque and beautiful, and in connection with his farm was engaged in iron smelting and casting. He was of athletic frame, of industrious habit and enterprising, of good abilities and character, but died early, aged 46 years, leaving three sons and two daughters.

Nathaniel, the fourth son of Joshua, inherited the physical and mental lineaments of his father more than either of his brothers. Like him he was very devout and strict in religious observances, very simple and unostentatious in manner, firm, judicious, and commanding, of dignified bearing, and always won the confidence and respect of those with whom he was associated. Of clear and decided views, and ardently attached to the faith and order of the fathers, he was sincere, warmhearted, and charitable. He twice declined the office of deacon to which he was elected. Like his brothers he had no ambitious aim, but his counsel was highly valued in the church and parish, and his influence widely felt and commended. Of grand physical proportions, of strong and capacious mind, he achieved much worldly success, and for forty years was associated with his brother William in the manufacture of ironware and shovels, the transactions in relation to which often took him from home. He died in 1869, in the 84th year of his age, leaving two sons and three daughters, one son having previously died.

Nath. Eddy

William S., the fifth son of Joshua, in connection with his uncommon business talent, was distinguished for his strong personal attachments, his warm social feelings, his tender domestic ties, his kind, loving heart. His home, from which he rarely went, was his life's centre and thought, and he spared neither expense nor pains to render it attractive in its surroundings and pleasant to the eye. His hospitality was unbounded; he was generous to a fault. Living in the bosom of his family, courting the companionship of his friends, he was peculiarly dear to them all. He built his house near Mount Carmel, on a gentle rise of ground sloping down to the pond, and overlooking the stream on which were his shovel works, then of wide note for their size and extent of business. He was a man of great benevolence and magnanimity, and all his affairs were most carefully, conscientiously, and honorably managed. He died in 1874, aged 86 years, leaving one son and three daughters, other children having died in early life.

John Milton, the seventh and the youngest son of Joshua, was conspicuous among his brothers for his height, being six feet and four inches. He was of manly form, of large and brilliant eye, of animated and cheerful countenance, of strong social tendencies, and of the most tender sensibilities, highly intelligent and capable, of stirring activity, of uncompromising principle, and generous in every impulse. He removed to California in the year 1850, and died in 1862, aged 62 years, leaving children in that State.

Morton, the sixth son of Joshua, and the last of his generation, still lives, in his 84th year, of unimpaired mental and physical vigor, and honored and respected of all who know him.

Of the daughters of Joshua, son of Zechariah, Lydia married Barzillia Crane and died in 1842, aged 55 years, leaving a large family of sons and daughters. Jane married Asahel Hatheway, and died in 1853, aged 62 years, with one surviving daughter. They were intelligent and refined, modest and retiring, and to their natural gracefulness and beauty added the most lovely Christian spirit.

This sixth generation from Samuel, more than any that preceded, has given its name and character to Eddyville. The family seems to have reached its culmination, its highest point of advancement, in the children of Joshua, rendering it quite unique and exceptional among even our best New England families. These seven sons were all men of mark, remarkable in physique, and combined great strength and worth of character — noble sons of a noble sire. They were tall and erect (no one less than six feet), of massive frame and well proportioned, intelligent, circumspect, and of princely bearing. The purest virtues adorned their lives. The community in which they lived felt the elevating influence of their example, turned to them with admiring regard, and marked their superiority. Five of their estates joined, a part of the "26 mens purchase," now in the family more than two hundred years. They dwelt together in closest fraternal sympathy, mutually helpful in every good work, kind, considerate, and condescending to all, loving and loved. They dignified human nature, exhibiting its highest forms of development, and presented ever the power of a holy, simple, and sublime faith. Is it not unusual, is it not a rare sight to see men of such type, of such stalwart growth of principle and character, born under one roof, children of one parent, occupying the seats of two centuries, governed by the same lofty aim, and living and dying in the same joyful experiences and hopes?

This is *Eddyville*, rightly named, loved and honored for the fathers' sakes. Its intellectual, social, and manly growths have given it a name and an interest beyond any merely natural features of beauty. But there is a charm in its fields and forests, in its springs and rivulets and overhanging skies. Nature seems here to smile with unwonted loveliness. Memories of childhood and youth here cluster thick and precious.

While much is changed as generations have come and gone, the grand lives which have here been lived and the noble characters here wrought out abide in their undying presence, in their effaceless impress. Nature indeed has not changed. The rocks and hills and meadows keep their primeval form and beauty. The same sun that looked into the windows and warmed the furrows and lighted the steps of the venerable dead fulfils the same offices to-day ; and sun and sky and field and habitation bring us into close and constant communion with their spirits :

> " The dead are like the stars by day,
>   Withdrawn from mortal eye, —
> But not extinct, — they hold their way
>   In glory through the sky."

To revert to the more important characteristics of the family whose history we have noted, we say that in all its generations it has exhibited a striking uniformity and likeness of character, true to its antecedents, loyal to its birthright. In exceptional cases individuals have risen above the general household level and attained special eminence in learning and rank. But the family as such has been marked by its manly forms ; its innate vitality and long life ; its numerous offspring ; its unalienated inheritances ; its worldly industry, enterprise, and thrift ; its strong social and domestic ties ; its good sense, intelligence, and generosity ; its sobriety, decorum, and uprightness ; its patriotic spirit, and its devotion to religious principle. And what we say of this particular branch we doubt not may be said with truth of other branches that bear the Eddy name.

ZECHARIAH EDDY.

Our sketch of the Middleboro' branch of the Eddy Family would be incomplete without a further notice of its most eminent son, Zechariah Eddy, who by his natural gifts and acquirements contributed so much to the honor and fair name of Eddyville and its associated families. We speak of him in the conviction that, in the whole ancestral line, there is no one who has attained greater distinction for learning and high moral and Christian worth.

The second son of Joshua, he was born in 1780, and graduated from Brown University in 1799, with the second honors of his class. Having pursued the study of the law, he established himself in its practice in the retired spot of his childhood, and by his talents, diligence, and culture rose to the first rank in his profession. Of studious habits and of capacious memory, he mastered many branches of knowledge, and was equally at home in law, literature, theology, and civil government. Men of various professions and in various departments of study were drawn to him and sought his assistance, coöperation, and advice. Clients and lawyers came from near and far, and with assurance submitted their most intricate cases to his profound legal discrimination. Being a personal friend of Mr. Webster, he was at times associated with him in the most difficult suits, the great pleader relying upon him for the outline of the argument and the points of the law.

In a letter to his son in college, in 1833, he says, " I have just returned from Plymouth, seventy-one cases on the docket." This evinces the extent to which litigation was carried fifty years ago. The Massachusetts Reports contain about three hundred cases which he argued, and which were carrried up to the Supreme Bench on questions of law. What then were the number of his cases in the lower courts during a practice of forty years? It is well known that, by his judicious advice and conciliatory spirit, by his knowledge of men and his extraordinary influence over them, he kept more cases out of court than he carried into it. He was a peacemaker. He stood like a tower of strength between contending parties, calm, dignified, sagacious; holding the troubled elements of human passion in his firm and skilful grasp, and winning the approbation and support of friend and foe. There was no one who did not admit his superior wisdom, feel the savor of his influence, and confide in his stainless honor and truthfulness. These qualities made him great and were the ground of his peculiar favor and success.

His office became for a long time a school for young students in the law, and many resorted to it from the city and the country. Sometimes, with much pleasantry, it was called a theological school. For some of those young men became ministers, and some who entered as ministers went away lawyers. He gave his most hearty support to each profession.

His knowledge of the Scriptures was accurate and profound, and there were few passages, however intricate, which he had not studied, and in regard to which he could not give a consistent interpretation. Being intimate with sacred history, well read in the writings of the fathers, and in modern works of theology, he was often an authority in each. Eminent divines came to him, and with the most evident satisfaction listened to his religious conversation and doctrinal views. Many of these views, on practical and controverted subjects, were contributed to the religious press. Imbibing with the first breath the Pilgrim spirit, grateful for his origin and deeply conversant with the principles and order of the congregational polity,

familiar with the rules and precedents of the churches from
the beginning, no one was better fitted to expound those
principles and define the rights of both pastors and people.
Hence he was designated the " ecclesiastical lawyer," and by
his written opinions and by his frequent appearance before
councils he did an immense and praiseworthy service for the
denomination to which he belonged.

But always and in everything he was humble, simple,
unostentatious, open to conviction, unconscious of self, and
guileless. He was averse to formalism, conceit, and religious
cant, opposed to bigotry, and insisted upon the supremacy of
conscience. Catholic in every feeling, open in fellowship,
liberal toward all who differed from him, and large-hearted, he
encouraged universal peace, charity, and good will. His very
look was love. He seemed a personal friend to every man.
Every neighbor sought him in trouble, his best and most con-
scientious adviser. His whole pathway was strown with the
sweetest charities, and a moral grandeur and impressive dignity
pervaded his person. His home was peculiarly one of social
and domestic attraction, overflowing with the freest hospi-
talities — himself the central object of every heart. Endowed
with the finest sensibilities and the rarest tastes, intensely
tender and sympathetic, he loved much and enjoyed much
in the dearest relations of life, and he also suffered much.
He rarely went from home save at the call of duty, and
he returned as soon as the burden was lifted, with a light
heart and beaming countenance.

His fondness for little children was remarkable. No one
could win their confidence and gain their ear and draw their
person so well as he. He would turn to them from his books.
There were lessons of higher wisdom and nicer beauties and
adaptations in a child's mind than he found in his encyclopæ-
dias. With what sweet delight would he hear their childish
prattle, watch every artless way, nurture their tender, delicate,

and struggling thought, study their preferences and individual bent, mark their daily progress, and tell their triumphs. In the house of strangers and by the wayside, with ineffable dignity he would recognize and approach them, greet them with a smile, ask their names, extend the open hand, and tell some pleasing incident. And the oldest as well as the youngest would be drawn and captivated by his words. In all his treatment, discipline, and teaching of children he entirely reversed the Puritanic methods and rules.

But his own home was made desolate beyond the common lot of men. The pet lamb of the flock, the youngest idol of his heart, was taken, after a lingering sickness, in the fourteenth year of her age. The next year a son died, gifted beyond his years, a ready writer, and about to enter on his professional career. The father had gone with him to the West Indies in the delusive hope that a change of climate would repair his shattered health. He left him among foreigners, buried in the lone isle, and returned bowed under his great grief and desolate. The next year another son, now more than ever the solace and staff of his heart, having already achieved success in the practice of the law, passed away under the paternal roof. And then the same year died another daughter, leaving three motherless children. Thus were removed one by one, in rapid succession, his earthly treasures, till of a family of ten children only two survived to soothe his heart and bless his later years. And yet in all these overwhelming sorrows he exhibited such a spirit of resignation and peace, such quiet and patient suffering, such tender and abiding trust, such sweet and thoughtful submission, as are most remarkable and rare to see. His religious hope in all its sincerity and genuineness shone forth in peculiar splendor out of the depths of his unutterable bereavements.

> "The soul that's filled with virtue's light
> Shines brightest in affliction's night,
> And sees in darkness beams of hope."

Says one who from early life knew Zechariah Eddy intimately, and observed him in every public and private relation : I never shall forget his image nor the impression he made upon me. His life and character at this distance and separation rise before me as intrinsically the greatest, truest, and best I have ever known. He was free from artifice ; separate from everything low, grovelling, and selfish ; frank in every feeling and uttterance ; pure in every motive, and upright and ingenuous in every action. He seemed endowed most truly with everything that ennobles and exalts humanity, while he was devoid of everything corrupt and debasing. His life was great, — not in its adventure, not in its startling achievements or sudden surprises of genius, for he shunned public gaze ; he sought retirement and the society of his friends, and had no love of worldly strife, ambition, and applause, — but it was great in its capabilities, its inherent excellencies ; its self-control and unperturbed spirit ; its uniform and well-balanced powers ; its correct intuitive and logical judgments ; its acquired treasures of knowledge ; its intimate acquaintance with books, men, and public affairs ; its loyalty to truth ; its fidelity to principle and duty ; its warm and unalterable attachments ; its clear and comprehensive perceptions ; its patient endurance in adversity ; its refined social fitnesses ; its sublime and trustful faith. These things made him great, gave him an unequalled preëminence. So that, judged by the highest standards, and placed in the best circles of the learned, the great, and the good, he would scarcely find his peer. I am aware that my language will seem extravagant to some, — more like eulogy and the passionate admiration of friendship, — but it will not seem so to those who knew him, for he was as much superior to mere praise and encomium as he was far from ever seeking it. He was in all respects grand, complete, and gifted beyond the poor forms of words to express.

Who that ever saw will forget his majestic form ; his fine

Roman head; his deep-set, mild, and expressive eyes; his thoughtful, penetrating look; his broad, over-hanging, and intellectual brow; his sweet, persuasive voice; his beautiful, beaming smile; his whole countenance irradiated with the sunlight of a higher sphere, transfigured by the glory of his great soul dwelling within. Such a life, such a character, such a man, excites our deepest reverence, demands our most grateful love.

THE FIRST PARISH CHURCH IN MIDDLEBORO'.

THE Eddy Family in its religious life is a scion of the Church of England. Its earliest ancestor hitherto traceable is the Rev. William Eddye, Vicar of the Church in Cranbrook from 1589 to 1616, — a useful, able, and godly pastor, and to this day held in pleasing and deserved remembrance by the people of that ancient church.

Of his family of twelve children, his two sons, John and Samuel, and a daughter, Abigail, came to this country in 1630, landing at Plymouth. They are the honored ancestors of the large family of Eddy in this country. They bore with them the paternal spirit and character, and were zealous for the principles of religious liberty and the word and worship of God. Their numerous descendants to this day have been characterized by the same spirit.

We have given a view of the grand old church in Cranbrook, where William Eddye fulfilled his ministry of twenty-seven years and where his children were baptized. We also give a view of the First Church in Middleboro', which claims some historic interest, with whose existence and growth the Middleboro' branch of the family has been closely identified from the beginning.

CRANBROOK and MIDDLEBORO' sustain the relation of parent and child, — Cranbrook the mother of us all; Middleboro', a daughter born a century later, now the mother of a large offspring, scattered far and near over the land, and filling many important offices and relations in Church and State, as lawyers, judges, physicians, ministers, artisans, and artists. It is a family of which one may not be ashamed, of whose record we may be justly proud.

There are many families of the Eddy name still in active membership with this church. There are many others who have gone forth from it, and are now connected with other churches, who turn back ever to this with the warmest filial love as their first religious birth-place and home.

The edifice, of which we give a view, is the fourth which has stood near the same foundations. The first was comparatively a rude affair, and was built soon after King Philip's War, about the year 1680. Each edifice in succession has been more of a praise than its predecessor, till the present structure was erected in 1828. It was built largely by the encouragement and coöperation of the sixth generation from Samuel the Pilgrim, and when in the prime of its intellectual strength and temporal prosperity. It was very much of an undertaking for a country parish separated from the wealth, population, and enterprise of larger communities. The cost of construction, however, was easily met, and was far less at that time than it would be now. When built it was considered the finest church edifice in Plymouth County, and is even now remarkable for its architectural beauty. Its grand, stately proportions, its fine Ionic façade, impress every beholder, while there is an inspiration within its walls rarely met. Its beautiful mahogany pulpit and its rich silk damask curtain, which are models of their kind, give a very pleasing and solemn effect.

Whitfield preached in the former church. Dr. Lyman Beecher preached the dedication sermon of this. He was wont to say that there was no such Sabbath congregation out of Boston composed of so many noble and educated men.

Five of the Eddy families occupied pews on the broad aisle, and many other families of no less marked physiognomy, character, and bearing filled the surrounding seats, and gave the assembly and worship their peculiar aspect. This church, where the fathers worshipped, whose prayers ascended from its altar, whose walls were reared by their bounty and consecrated by their faith, may well be held in lasting veneration by their children.

www.ingramcontent.com/pod-product-compliance
Lightning Source LLC
Chambersburg PA
CBHW060518030726
47498CB00004B/989